What Kills Good Men

~ a novel ~

DAVID HOOD

Vagrant
PRESS

Vagrant Press
(an imprint of Nimbus Publishing Limtited)
3731 Mackintosh St, Halifax, NS B3K 5A5
(902) 455-4286 nimbus.ca

This is a work of fiction. Names, characters, incidents, and places, including organizations and institutions, either are the product of the author's imagination or are used fictitiously.

Printed and bound in Canada
NB1207

Library and Archives Canada Cataloguing in Publication
    Hood, David, 1960-, author
    What kills good men / David Hood.
    Issued in print and electronic formats.
    ISBN 978-1-77108-350-8 (paperback).—ISBN 978-1-77108-351-5 (html)

I. Title.

PS8615.O5114W43 2015   C813'.6   C2015-904322-0
                                    C2015-904323-9

Canada Council   Conseil des arts
for the Arts   du Canada

Nimbus Publishing acknowledges the financial support for its publishing activities from the Government of Canada through the Canada Book Fund (CBF) and the Canada Council for the Arts, and from the Province of Nova Scotia. We are pleased to work in partnership with the Province of Nova Scotia to develop and promote our creative industries for the benefit of all Nova Scotians.

For Josie Hood

Saturday 21 October 1899

The face was sickly white and puffed up like bread dough. One eye was missing, something had eaten it. A piece of seaweed caught in the teeth waved like a kite tail. Ellen Reardon took another swig as she peered down from the end of Mitchell's Wharf. The night sky was overcast, no moon or stars. Shards of city light mirrored in all directions off the harbour chop. She could see well enough. He was dead all right. Ellen looked around for someone to tell. In the distance there were more than the usual hoots and hollers of a Saturday night. The Boers had declared war in South Africa. When Britain turned to the commonwealth, Sir Wilfred Laurier eventually agreed to help. Canada would send a thousand men, one hundred and twenty-five of them would come from Nova Scotia. They would leave Halifax in a few days to join others at Moncton, then Quebec. The *Sardinian* would take a month to reach Cape Town. Some of the Bluenosers would need that long to sober up.

Ellen tried to tune out the background. There might have been footsteps on the other side of the warehouse. There was still no one to be seen. Another swig, much bigger this time, burned all the way down to her stomach. Ellen listened again, holding her breath to keep from gagging. Now the night seemed quiet except for the sound of the harbour lapping against the pilings below. Ellen was alone on the end of the wharf. Well, almost.

Another look convinced her he really was there, that her mind wasn't playing tricks. He was caught at the hips in the X of two support beams. Ellen knew a thing or two about sailors, not so much about tides. It seemed to be going out. Without anything to keep it afloat, the body would eventually be caught up in the cross members under the wharf, left hanging there along with driftwood and lengths of rope and other bits of harbour flotsam. Better to walk away now, unseen and uninvolved. He wouldn't know the difference. With most of a bottle, it wouldn't be hard to find a friend, sneak in someplace and drink themselves to sleep. In the morning all would be forgotten. She took another drink. It was easier now. On the other hand, maybe less company would be better.

She sat down, boots dangling over the water. There were no holes in her Salvation Army coat, but the buttons were missing. She held it closed with one hand and drank with the other. "So you wanna hear a funny story?" she asked the space between her feet. The one eye stared off to the right at something it couldn't see. "Sure ya do. Last week Tommy Berrigan was coming out of an alley down on Hollis Street. Maybe you know Tommy?" Ellen took another swallow, gave her conversation partner a chance to offer anything he had on the subject of Thomas Berrigan Jr. His puffy white face bobbed gently in the black water. He didn't say whether or not he knew Mr. Berrigan. "Well, anyhow," Ellen continued, "quick as anything Tommy stops and picks up a chunk a hard snow and heaves it for all he's worth. Catches Jimmy Reagan right in the back of the head. Well, quick as you can spit, Tommy's back down the alley laughing his fool head off. Guess he figured Hannah would stay on his heels. Did I mention Hannah was with him? Well, she was." Before Ellen could continue, there was a screech from a rusty hinge followed by a loud thwack as a flimsy door banged shut somewhere behind her. She went quiet, waited for footsteps or voices. If she had to, she would cause a scene, keep the attention on herself so no one would look under the wharf. She took a short sip and tucked the bottle inside her coat. After a minute or so of listening to the water and her own heartbeat, she continued, trying to remember to keep her voice low.

"So there's Reagan, flopping around in the street like a hooked fish, cursing and holding his arm. Being hit like that, out of the blue, startled him. He went down pretty hard. Hannah shoulda beat it like Tommy done but she just stood up on the sidewalk, outta the ruts and horseshit, and roared. Reagan didn't find it so funny. He's a policeman, case you didn't know." Ellen pulled her shoulders up, held still for a moment, then let out a loud belch. A little rum bile came with it and she leaned forward and spat over the end of the wharf. "Didn't get ya, did I? Sorry 'bout that. Now where was I? Reagan…Yeah, he knew Hannah couldn't throw that hard, not on her best day. But she wouldn't say who was with her. So instead of drunkenness, Reagan hung an assault charge on her. Next day I was there for her in the gallery. I know what it's like to be in police court by yourself. Well, the judge give Hannah thirty days. Said he didn't like sendin' women up, but he wouldn't stand for no violence against an officer of the court. Said he was tired of the inshurrigible… incred…wait, I'll get it, incorrigible, that's it, said he was tired of the incorrigible element of the city giving Halifax a bad name. It wasn't fair what they done, but Hannah knew better than to give the judge any back talk. I been to Rockhead once or twice, ain't so bad. And one a Hannah's cousins is a guard. Her time went quick and when she come out Tommy had a bottle to say he was sorry."

At that point in her story Ellen remembered she had a bottle of her own. She took another taste and then leaned over a little farther. "Now here's the best part," she said. "If Reagan had let Hannah off with a warning like he shoulda done and carried on around the corner onto Upper Water Street, he mighta nabbed whoever it was climbed out a back window of Ronnan Frederick's warehouse. They took enough rope and pitch to start a navy. But he didn't and next day Ronnan wanted to know from the police chief what his men was doing while some ship resupplied itself at his expense. Later the chief asked Reagan the same question. Told him an extra month on night duty might sharpen his vision. Serves Jimmy Reagan right and I hope his elbow is still sore." Ellen spit into the harbour, then took another hit off the bottle.

The tide was going out. Under the wharf it was beginning to look like the crucifixion, feet together, arms outstretched. There were voices again, bouncing around in the darkness and the rigging of the ships nearby. Still, no one came within sight. She hadn't had to do much, hike her dress up and bend over a little. Even though he was quick, Ellen had gotten a chill waiting for the sailor to finish and give her the bottle she had set as a price. Drinking and talking had warmed her up. Then

a sudden gust of wind off the water made her shiver. She took one last
pull from the bottle, then fished the cork out of a pocket and shoved it in
tight. The large hawser lying in a coil on the opposite corner of the wharf
would likely do for a night or two. It was awkward work, what with no
buttons and half a quart in. Still she managed to bury the bottle in the
rope. Looking down again from the end of the wharf, she was still steady
on her feet, but she swayed a little from the waist. She could see he would
soon be completely out of the water, hung up in the timbers supporting
the wharf, arched backward a little, arms hanging down, as if he were
prey in the jaws of some larger animal. "Ok, mister," Ellen whispered,
"you won't have to stay there much longer." She turned and began to
make her way down Mitchell's Wharf and across Lower Water Street.
Her line began to weave a little as she got farther on. You could see from
Mitchell's Wharf straight up Prince Street to Saint Paul's Church. From
there a hard right led directly to the police station at City Hall. Ellen took
a more complicated route, weaving through back alleys, squatting for a
moment in one of them.

Detective Culligan Baxter was in his office trying to put together
the watch schedule for the coming week. It was not his job,
though it used to be. Now it belonged to Sergeant Graham Meagher.
Trouble was, Meagher had been down for three days with a nasty flu.
The chief asked Baxter. He could have asked someone else, though why
bother. They both knew Baxter wouldn't say no. So at eight o'clock on a
Saturday night instead of relaxing at home or taking his wife for a meal
at one of the better hotels in town, he was working, or trying to. "Jesus,
Mary, and Joseph!" Baxter yelled. "What is all the racket about?" He
had put down his pencil and gotten up from his desk. He was standing
in the doorway of his office looking across a half dozen empty desks
toward the front counter.

Baxter knew the history of the city. Nearly half the original settlers
died in the first winter. Injuns got a few more. The survivors hung on.
They built Saint Paul's Church and the Grand Parade in front of it and
a town began to huddle round. The Crown kept up a flow of money.

Some New Englanders joined in. Eventually a fortress was raised atop the hill to the west. If the Mi'kmaq and the French figured this rough crowd would soon wear itself out and shove off, they were wrong.

The Halifax Citadel had been built to wreak the havoc of artillery fire on would-be invaders. It rose up over the nine streets that ran north-south across the face of the steep slope that ran down from the fortress to the harbour below. So far no one had bothered to invade the town except the soldiers of the garrison. The town clock that stood just below the Citadel told them and everyone else when it was time to go home.

Catholicism was eventually allowed in Halifax. The spire of Saint Mary's Basilica now guided Catholics to worship on a site not far behind Saint Paul's. Farther on, in the most southern reaches of the city, the well-heeled had created a haven of good manners and wider streets. City Hall used to be down by the water. Now it sat opposite Saint Paul's on the north end of the Grand Parade. The Anglican pulpit kept a close eye on its new neighbour. Beyond City Hall, as far north as possible, Rockhead Prison faced into the wind that came off the harbour basin. The city commons lay in the flats behind the fort, the open ground between north and south, rich and poor, Catholic and Protestant.

The area between the Citadel and the Grand Parade became known as the upper streets. For the first hundred years, this was no place for decent people. Soldiers who found local women rented rooms in the cheap boarding houses. So did many of the sailors that washed in and out with the tides. All the popular vices were kept in plain view. The business of sin flourished in the upper streets. Naturally there were casualties; drunks face down in the mud or snow. Children nobody wanted abandoned, or worse. Lives lived rough, some ended at their own hand.

After a while a wind of resistance began to blow against these hard facts of life. First more liquor laws, then a police force, schools, and charities of all sorts working to catch the fallen and prevent others from going down. Of course it had been and still was an uphill fight and not just due to the lay of the land. People were prone to weakness. The likes of Ellen Reardon made no bones about it. Others kept that side of themselves hidden. The upper streets and the city that had grown up around them were contested terrain. Baxter had devoted his life and career to the side of decency. But it was late and he wanted to be getting home.

The night sergeant, a patrolman, and the woman they were arguing with all went quiet and looked in his direction. "Oh Lord, not tonight, Ellen, I really don't have time," Baxter muttered to himself.

"Detective Baxter," the sergeant said in surprise, looking up at the wall clock. Finny Mackay couldn't keep the irreverence out of his voice. "Sorry to have disturbed you, didn't know you were burning the midnight oil. I'll wrap this nonsense up quietly."

Ellen objected loudly. "Only nonsense in all this is you, Mackay, too fuckin' fat and lazy to do your job."

Baxter had known Ellen from his early days as a night patrolman when she was new to the city and working at Taylor's Boot and Shoe Factory. Her smile was perfect then, white as the flesh of a Cortland apple. Now it was yellowed and missing a piece. Baxter shook his head at Mackay then looked at Ellen and put a forefinger to his lips. He carefully closed the door to his office and walked slowly toward the counter. The walls of the station were nearly ten years old now, the plaster cracked and yellowed in places. Flattering portraits of the eternal Victoria and the dearly departed John A. refused to take notice.

Watching him approach kept Ellen and Mackay off each other for a few seconds. In the reprieve, the chief inspector focused on the night patrolman who had not said a word since Baxter had come out of his office. He could see now that it was Kenny Squire, brand new, not a mark on him. Word round the station said he was no more jumpy than was to be expected. Some thought he was pretty smart, at least smart enough not to talk when he should be listening.

Baxter came up to the heavy walnut counter that divided the inner offices of the station from its small reception area. In his sock feet he stood six feet three inches tall. He placed his large hands on the counter's freshly polished surface as delicately as a doctor examining a child. He noticed the bandage round his left index finger had gotten dirty. He'd change it when he got home. Before the spell could break and Mackay and Ellen started in again Baxter asked, "Mr. Squire, did you arrest Miss Reardon?"

Kenny Squire was surprised the chief inspector had any idea who he was, and more surprised that he knew the woman who had approached him on Barrington Street, drunk and demanding he take her in. "No, sir. She…"

The heat had sped up Ellen's circulation, but the rush it gave her was not so strong that she was about to let some beginner policeman speak for her. "He didn't have no reason to arrest me. I got nothin' to do with that dead man in the harbour."

Baxter looked at Ellen now, the ratty dress, the wild hair. At least the coat was clean, even if it didn't have any buttons. "Miss Reardon, have you by any chance had a drink or two this evening?"

Ellen tucked in her chin and rolled her eyes up at Baxter. "Do you want to hear what I have to tell you or not?"

Baxter looked up at the clock; it was twenty to nine. After working all day and a quiet supper with Jane there had been a promise to return within an hour. It had already been two. For twenty-two years she had put up with his mistress. Go home, he thought, let Mackay listen to Ellen, let him finish the schedule too. Put the job second, be a husband first. It was a familiar lecture. When he finished chastising himself, Baxter said, "I swear to God, Ellen, if this is just some ploy to get out of the cold, I'll see you in Rockhead for six months. Or better still I won't."

"There is a dead man caught up in the timbers under Mitchell's Wharf. I seen it. I could have kept my mouth shut, let the tide do its work, see whoever put him there get away with it. I'm just trying to do my civic duty. You got no call to be makin' me out a liar." Ellen had to hold on to the counter with one hand to keep from swaying. The free hand waved and pointed throughout her speech with all the righteous indignation of a Roman senator.

Unmoved, Baxter looked back and said, "Assuming there is a body, how do you know someone put it there? How do you know this man didn't jump?"

"There is no body, Detective," Mackay said. "She's just drunk and looking for a place to sleep it off. I'll put her out." Mackay took a step. Baxter's hand raised in a stop sign kept him behind the counter.

With a thumb on her nose, Ellen waved her fingers at Mackay and then quickly moved out from under the weight of Baxter's challenge. "That's your job, you're the detective, not me," she said.

Baxter looked from Ellen to Squire, who responded with a slight shrug of his shoulders. Through a sigh that was more for his wife than himself, Baxter said, "Mr. Mackay, place Miss Reardon in a cell and give her a blanket."

"Surely you're not buying any of this, Detective?" Mackay whined.

Ignoring the sergeant and turning back to Ellen, Baxter said, "If there is nothing but water under that wharf, I will make you very sorry."

"Don't you threaten me," Ellen said with equal resolve.

Mackay came round the counter and took Ellen by an elbow. She quickly pulled free, but kept silent as she followed the sergeant past the counter to a door.

"Mr. Squire, as soon as I get my coat and a lantern, you and I are taking a walk down to Mitchell's Wharf."

———•———

There had always been colder places than Halifax, but come October Halifax always had plenty of bite in its night air. The breeze had been light when Ellen left the waterfront. Now it had really picked up. Baxter and Squire walked quickly with their chins to their chests, collars up and hands deep in their coat pockets as they crossed the Grand Parade. Behind them the sandstone walls and seventy-foot granite clock tower of City Hall watched with dispassionate interest, indifferent to the weather. The building wasn't just home to the police station. It also housed the police court where Baxter would drag Ellen before a judge if this was just some story she'd made up. Neither man spoke in the few minutes it took to hurry down Prince and across Lower Water Street. They were almost to the wharf when Squire asked, "What do you think we'll find, Detective?"

They were behind a small storehouse, out of the wind for a moment. Baxter held up the march. He pulled the lantern out of his coat. He passed it to Squire then began digging for some matches. He spoke as he went through one pocket then another. "This city is full of drunks and people with no self-respect who refuse to work," he said with a flat unsympathetic tone. "Ellen Reardon is the worst female reprobate in the city. She's been arrested more times than I can count. She knows we won't take a statement from her if she is drunk. There likely is a body under Mitchell's Wharf, the last remains of some poor sod tired of working or tired of seeing his children hungry because he isn't. His last act will be one of charity, giving our Miss Reardon a bed for a night or two while we sort matters out. Maybe it will help him with Saint Peter."

"And if she is lying?"

"Then, Mr. Squire, I will see to it that a few of Miss Reardon's cronies are sent to Rockhead for thirty days and I'll let them know she laid information against them with the stipendiary magistrate. They will make up eventually, they always do, but not before making Ellen miserable for a few weeks."

Baxter kept searching as he spoke, looking directly at Squire. He was waiting to see if this new officer would question such methods.

Squire pulled off a glove and opened the top buttons of his uniform greatcoat. Then a bare hand, iridescent and floating in the darkness like a ghost, passed a box of matches. "Here, Detective, strike one of these." Squire moved closer to make more shelter from the wind and pulled up the glass chimney of the lantern. It took three tries. Then the two men came out from behind the building a little closer together, moving forward in a ten-foot circle of flickering yellow light.

Kenny Squire was just twenty years old. He had grown up in the town of Pictou a hundred miles northeast of Halifax. His father had had no interest in seeing his only son follow him into a makeshift life of farming, logging, and working the mines of Pictou County. He'd sent his son to school. It was a bittersweet gamble that had paid off. Kenny took to book learning. By the time he graduated from the Pictou Academy he was desperate to get out of the classroom and the town he grew up in. As soon as he could, he headed to the nearest city in search of breathing space and an opportunity. He had read *A Study in Scarlet* by Sir Arthur Conan Doyle and enjoyed it. There was no desire to be Sherlock Holmes, but he needed a purpose and the city needed policemen. What he needed just now was a sense of direction. They were in a passageway between two long warehouses. The wall of another building stood at the end of it. "Which way is Mitchell's Wharf, Detective?" Squire asked, the nervousness still evident in his voice through the howl of the wind.

Baxter had not forgotten his way around the waterfront. He had gone to sea as a young man. He had made a dozen or so voyages. Then he had come ashore for good, and had gone where his temperance was more appreciated. After only seven years on the force he was promoted to sergeant and lead investigator. Five years later he was given the title special investigator, which meant most of the important cases came to him. In his fifteenth year he was made chief inspector. He preferred Detective Baxter. When the final promotion came at last and the reins were his, then he would be chief. "The building in front of us belongs to Mitchell and Sons. We go around it to the right. The wharf runs straight out behind."

The tide was close to its lowest point. There was at least ten feet between the underside of the wharf and the water, which was angry now, whipped up by the gusts. It crashed and foamed and whirled about, louder in the closed spaces under the wharf between the thick supporting columns. Ships tied up at wharfs on either side rose and fell, their hulls grinding against rope fenders. Sails had been taken in and tied down. Loose corners flapped and cracked in the wind. Every wooden surface along the entire waterfront seemed to be heaving and creaking in the wind. "Can you see anything?" Baxter yelled over the noise. He was standing on the starboard side of the wharf, one arm fully extended, the lantern swaying at the end of it, now struggling to produce even a weak sputtering light.

Ten feet farther out, Squire had gotten down on his hands and knees. Holding onto a bollard, he was leaning over as far as he dared, looking into the dark forest under the wharf. "All I can make out is wooden beams. I don't see a body, Detective, but in these conditions, who can be sure?"

"Ellen Reardon was sure, Mr. Squire. Let's move on to the end." Baxter dropped the lantern to his side and strode past Squire, who was struggling to get back to his feet. The young policeman had been out in the cold now for nearly three hours. The few minutes in the station had not thawed the stiffness that had crept into his joints. Baxter thought of offering him a hand then decided against it. You need to dress warm for night patrol, a greatcoat alone isn't enough, he thought, recalling what he'd learned the hard way from his early days on the force. And you need to get inside for a few minutes at least once an hour. Check in with folks at the hospital or the poorhouse or the fire hall. Good politics keeps the chill from setting in too deep. Let him suffer, he thought. It will teach him. Or rheumatism will finish him before he starts.

Mitchell's Wharf was thirty feet wide and ran more than a hundred feet into the harbour. Standing at the end in a high wind, with the water a good drop below, Baxter could imagine what it felt like to be a ship's captain at the end of the plank, a mutineer's sword at his back. Farther down the harbour the dark hump of Georges Island loomed up out of the water like the back of some horrible sea monster. Baxter shuddered against the wind and the frights of imagination brought on by the cold and perhaps the guilt of being at work instead of home next to his wife. At least if Ellen was just having them on, Jane might still be awake when he got back.

The sound of cold boots trying not to trip over themselves on the wooden planks said Squire had finally gotten back on his pins. With his back still turned and bent over as he struggled to see anything, Baxter pointed to the opposite side and said, "Have a look from over there, Mr. Squire." Then he went back to thinking about his wife as he strained his eyes against the swirling void under the wharf. Jane's mother had a birthday a week away. Baxter had never cared for the woman. When her husband died a year ago, she told her daughter she would rather stay in her own home. Baxter had argued against it, pointed out all the reasons she would be better off with them. She wasn't fooled, neither was Jane. One agreed with him, honest in that sentiment, the other pretended to be grateful while declining. Baxter was angry with himself for not saying what they all knew. There was enough money in the family. Any help or looking after could be provided for. Of course, all that had really been required of him was an honest show of affection. It was late, but he would make the effort. He would quietly pick up something nice without Jane's help. On the morning of, he would bring the carriage round to the front door and ask Jane if she was ready to go, as if visiting her mother on her birthday really was a given.

As though it had been following his thoughts and agreed with them, the wind that had been making life so miserable showed a change of heart. It began to ease into something that did not blow through the soul, something that allowed the freshness of the salt air to be appreciated. The clouds did not suddenly disappear, but they did permit the face of a three-quarter moon to begin showing itself in fleeting glimpses. The sky flashed with what looked like heat lighting, flashes that found their way under the wharf.

Squire knew what he was looking for, and the walk to the waterfront had allowed him time to prepare, time to reassure himself of his sturdiness. Maybe he thought he was ready and his body betrayed him. Or perhaps he became so focused on the search, he lost whatever edge he may have honed. Whatever the case, when a flash of moonlight seared him with the horrible image of the bloated waxen face, his stomach reacted with a violent spasm and his supper splashed into the harbour. When the heaving stopped, Squire managed to say in a voice that needed the remaining wind to carry it on, "Detective, you better come have a look at this."

By the time Baxter had walked over from the opposite corner, Squire had turned away from the front of the dock and was wiping his mouth on the sleeve of his greatcoat. Without looking at Baxter he simply pointed and said, "Miss Reardon was telling the truth, Detective."

Baxter held up the lantern and studied the young policeman for a moment, then nodded. "Any idea who it is?" he asked.

Squire simply shook his head, taking deep breaths and trying to let them out slowly while he told himself this was part of the job and he had better get used to it.

Baxter got down on his hands and knees, and leaned over the edge, holding the lantern out as far as he could. He thought himself to be a moral man. There were moments of anger; he could be jealous and sometimes rash. However, his life could bear scrutiny, he had no darkness to hide, no terrible secrets. The same could be said for the man hung up in the crossing timbers, staring back through an empty socket and the blindness of a doll's eye. Yet that life, a life that measured up, a life he had respected and at times envied, a life that deserved to be much longer and to end gently was now done and dead and being tossed about in the backwash under a wharf. Baxter was struck immediately by a sense of loss, a loss that would be shared by many in the city, from its leaders to its lowest followers. A loss that would be felt most particularly by his wife, a loss he would have to bring to her, a loss she would want him to explain.

Then a strange relief came over him as a sense of urgency began to push his feelings of loss aside. He was the city's best investigator. It was up to him to find out for the family and the people of Halifax what had happened. And if there was blame to be assigned, and most likely there was, it must be assigned swiftly, completely, and with the full weight of the law. He spoke now, his voice full of force and mission. "Mr. Squire, listen to me very carefully. I don't want to wait for the morgue to open. Go to 71 Hollis Street. Tell Doctor Trenaman he needs to open his office, a body is on the way. Then go back to the station. Tell Sergeant Mackay I need a half dozen men here immediately. And tell him no one, and that includes him, is to go near Ellen Reardon or say a word to her. Do you understand?"

Squire didn't really have to listen all that closely. Even with only a few months on the force he knew a medical exam was required. And of course Baxter needed help to get an investigation started and he would want to be the first person to question the only witness in the case so far. What had Squire's attention was the change that had come over Baxter. The man had snapped to full alert, and a little anxiousness seemed to have crept into his demeanour. Clearly the dead man under Mitchell's Wharf was someone important. This would be Baxter's case, it should be. Still, he was the one who had found the body, and he wanted to know who it was, wanted some way to gauge the significance of the moment and what might come next. "Who's down there, Detective?" he asked.

Baxter wasn't angry that Squire seemed to have ignored his instructions for the sake of morbid curiosity. He wanted to keep the victim's identity quiet as long as possible, until he knew more and had time to decide what he wanted to do. The realization that Squire failed to recognize the victim, that he would not have to trust Squire to keep his mouth shut while Mackay demanded details, eased his mind. "Did you hear what I said, Mr. Squire?" Baxter asked, stepping away as he spoke. He didn't go so far as to point in the direction Squire was to go, as one might for a child. Instead he let the distance he created between them say clearly that he was done talking. Squire paused for another moment. He seemed about to say something, then just pressed his lips together in a thin flat line and let out a short huff through his nose. He turned on a heel and started off down the wharf.

Baxter listened to Squire's hard, quick steps fading down the wood planks. Already he was looking over the side of the wharf, hoping to see a small tender or a barge. He checked the other side then went back to the front of the wharf. An hour, maybe two, before the water would be high enough to make the work easier. Too long. A pilot ladder and some rope would have to do. Baxter looked around again. The hawser in the opposite corner was too heavy. No ladder anywhere in sight. He reached inside his coat and felt around for his watch chain. It was going on ten thirty. There would be no getting home before the wee hours of the morning, perhaps not even then. He felt some consolation in knowing Jane's sleep would not be worried as it had been in his patrolman days. She would assume he had fallen asleep at his desk, which happened sometimes when he worked late. It would be another half hour at least before Squire returned with whoever he and Mackay had been able to corral. Baxter returned his watch to its vest pocket. He had better see to some rope and a ladder. The Queen's Wharf was to the right. At the end and a short ways down the waterfront were military stores and a sentry box.

The wind continued to blow, but without the meanness it had showed earlier. The sky was clearer now and the light of the moon almost steady. He stood still for a moment on the end of the wharf watching and listening. The creaking and heaving, the sound of straining wood, was gone. The wind and water were playing gently now. A meringue of small waves lapped against the wharves and hauls and swagger of the Halifax waterfront. If there was a warning in the calm, Baxter never heard it. He did hear sailors talking to one another as they checked lines and fenders. He could not find them in the darkness. There was shadowy movement and hollering through the dim circles of gaslight along the streets that rose sharply from the harbour going west toward the Citadel. There were always a few soldiers AWOL from the garrison on a Saturday night. Men enlisting to fight the Boers were on a last run. The regular drunks needed no excuse. The army had beefed up their shore patrols. The police had had extra men on nights for a week, which reminded him he still had the schedule to finish. Meagher had better be in tomorrow. One of his knees cracked in protest against the dampness. Was he getting too old? He started walking, a bit stiff at first.

Movement helped him focus and for the first time he began to think past the shocking fact that a popular city alderman was dead. People were going to demand to know what had happened. What did he know about this man that might help him find the answers? His stride was smoother as he turned right at the end of the wharf.

Baxter knew that Victor had grown up in the upper streets, in a time when they were even rougher. Wilfred Mosher had been a mason, a fortunate thing for Victor. Wilfred had had work when many fathers didn't. The family was poor, but not so poor that Wilfred's children could not go to school. Wilfred insisted his two sons go as far as the sixth grade, no matter how long it took them. Victor was the youngest by nearly two years. That did not stop him from being the first to meet his father's request. He was smarter than his older brother Carmine, smart enough to get on with things rather than play hooky. He had continued to make good choices, learning his father's trade and saving his money. Just after he'd turned twenty-one, Victor had bought a rundown place on Grafton Street just a few doors down from where he'd grown up. He'd worked on it day and night. Everyone had assumed he would move in, begin looking for a wife. They were wrong to assume. Victor put the place up for rent and looked for tenants who could pay. Not long after that came a second place, and then an office with his name on the door and a real estate and construction business. Soon enough there was a Mrs. Victor Mosher, a woman supportive of ambition. Victor had a labourer's hands, was able to drive a spike home with just three swings of a hammer, but he preferred to settle things with words, to offer the benefit of the doubt. He ran for alderman at the age of thirty and won; that was fifteen years ago. His seat in City Council was uncontested in the last two elections.

He was the sort of upright self-made man Halifax wanted more of. So how had Victor Mosher wound up dead under a wharf?

By the time he had gotten to the sentry box, Baxter was repeating the question aloud to himself. The hut was tall and narrow with a squat pitch roof on top. No door, just a ledge off the back wall for a seat. He could hear the sentry snoring from ten yards away. Baxter fell asleep at his desk sometimes, but never when he was officially on duty. He kicked the side of the box. The sentry woke with a yelp as if Baxter had kicked him. His rifle clattered onto the cobblestones in front of the box. There was some cursing, then boot scuffs on a dirty wood floor followed by a thud. "Oh Christ...Who's there...?" The sentry stepped out, holding his head with one hand, reaching for his rifle with the other.

"Good work, Private. Her Majesty's wharf is secure." A gaslight stood over one side of the sentry box. Baxter spoke from the shadow on the opposite side. "Private, I need you to find me a pilot ladder and some lengths of rope."

As soon as the private heard Baxter's voice, determined that Baxter wasn't British, his body relaxed for just a second, then he moved the rifle from his side, held it in both hands across his chest. He spoke with an accent that was hard and common and very British. "Yeah...and who might you be, gov'nor?"

"My name is Culligan Baxter. Chief Inspector Culligan Baxter of the city police force. Inside your sentry box there are a number of keys on the wall. One of them is for that storehouse over there. Get it please and follow me." Baxter spoke slowly and with exaggerated clarity as if he were instructing a small boy or a dog. The soldier hesitated. Half awake in the amber of gaslight, he stared dumbly at Baxter as if he were a spectre from a lingering dream. "Hurry, man, there is no time to hum and haw." Baxter kept his voice steady, but added an edge to it and pointed as he spoke. Slowly the private peeled off his spot, unstuck by the force of Baxter's will.

"What did you say you needed?" he asked as he pulled back the door and stuffed the padlock and key into his coat pocket. Baxter lifted his lantern to take a survey of the stores and only then realized it had gone out. He began patting himself in search of the matches he was sure he had taken from Squire.

"First I need to get this lantern lit…where did I put those matches… do you have any?"

"Don't smoke, sir. But I think there are some in the sentry box." Baxter refused to give up and continued digging from pocket to pocket, following the private all the same. Moving about, feeling around the small hut, the private was fully awake now and curious. "So, gov'nor, what's this all about then?" he called over his shoulder.

"Did you find those matches?"

"Aye, here they are," the private said, turning and holding them out to Baxter along with a look that repeated his question and said he was owed an answer for his trouble.

Baxter pulled up the chimney and turned up the wick just a hair. He stepped closer. The look on the young soldier's face didn't change. He just followed along, taking a match from the box and striking it. It went out before a hand could be cupped around it. Standing at the back of the sentry box, with the big policeman filling the door, the private worked a second time, now in complete darkness. There was a dry, scratchy fumbling, then a scrape and a snap as a match head burst into flame. Baxter's long thin nose and close-set dark eyes looked serene and terrifying in the glow. The hand holding the match began to tremor slightly, but it found the wick. "What's your name, Private?" Baxter asked, his voice soft, almost gentle.

"Marsh, sir. Arthur Marsh."

"Well, Mr. Marsh, what I can tell you is this." Baxter dropped the chimney. He kept the lantern next to his face, lighting it out of the darkness like a prophecy. "The less you know about this the better off you'll be, believe me." The young private considered for a moment, guided perhaps by infantry logic that said knowledge makes you a good target. He nodded, willing now to see Baxter on his way with what he needed, no more questions asked.

——— · ———

Kenny Squire had left the wharf muttering and shaking his head, embarrassed and angry. To make matters worse he was tired from the wind and cold and from the effort of heaving his supper into the harbour. He had rebuked himself, there was no need for Baxter to do it. And no need to withhold the identity of the victim. What did Baxter think he was going to do, run through the streets shouting the news at the top of his lungs? The chief inspector was an arse.

It took the city's medical examiner nearly five minutes to come to the door. He was a fidgety sparrow of a man, his hands were never still. "Well, who is it?" he wanted to know. Squire told him he would rather not say anything more than that the matter was of great importance and needed to be attended to immediately. "Well, has there been foul play?" the doctor went on, untying and retying the belt on his dressing gown and trying to smooth a thinning head of wiry grey hair that was every bit as manic as the doctor. Squire did the best he could to appease and calm, saying he did not feel at liberty to discuss whether or not there had been an arrest or if the doctor would be called to testify, what the good doctor needed to focus on for now was getting ready to examine a body that he could expect very soon. Yes, Squire did know it was nearly eleven o'clock. Yes, it was likely to be a long night.

Squire left the doctor standing in the front hall of his home with a worried look on his face. When news of the body was delivered at the police station a few minutes later, Mackay could not hide his surprise. "So Ellen Reardon told the truth. Might be the first time," he sneered. From what Squire had seen of Mackay, he did his job well enough to keep it and he was loyal, if only to his paycheque. He wasn't concerned with honour or in pursuit of some ideal. Squire did not dislike him, but he had decided Mackay was not to be taken too seriously. And maybe he was not to be trusted. When Squire gave him Baxter's instructions that no one, including him, was to go near Ellen Reardon, Mackay snorted, "He needn't worry, I've got more important things to do." So far as the men Baxter wanted, a couple of patrolmen were due to check in. Mackay would hold them at the station. Meanwhile Squire had better get round to the homes of some off-duty officers. Mackay wrote some addresses on a scrap of paper. Squire stared at the hen scratch for a long moment. Mackay snatched the paper back from him and read aloud. Then Squire headed off.

—•—

He had managed to keep his ears from falling off by holding his hands over them. That had not stopped the cold from creeping under his collar. It had settled into his shoulders. His feet were numb. When Baxter finally heard the sound of boots and low voices he was relieved and rejuvenated. He checked his watch, twenty to twelve. Thinking Squire would be back in half an hour had obviously been wishful thinking. He tried to stomp some feeling into his feet as he moved off the wharf to greet the men as they came around the corner of Mitchell and Sons. "All right, gentlemen, let's have you in a line along the building." He pointed behind them. "Stand easy, but mind what I say, I've no time to be repeating myself."

"Thought we were here for a body, Detective, not a parade," one of the older officers said as he pulled up.

"Yeah, Detective," another officer chimed in, emboldened by the first. "Bit late for drill practice, don't you think?" Despite the backtalk the men moved into a line as instructed. Baxter paused long enough to let them know he'd heard what they said and didn't want to hear anything more.

"All right, gentlemen, a man is dead and we need to know what happened. What we don't need is to be giving anything away or sparking rumours or gossip that will only get in our way. O'Brien and Morrow you two go south along the waterfront, talk to anyone you see. Board every ship, talk to a boatswain or an officer of the watch, someone in charge. Ask did anyone see anything suspicious tonight or yesterday, anybody see a fight or an argument, anything out of the ordinary. Sweeney and Thompson, you two go north, same drill." Baxter stood still and close to the line of men as he spoke. He kept his voice low and looked directly into one pair of eyes then the next, transmitting seriousness, waiting for nods that said he was getting through. "Chalmers, I want you to go to the city's livery stables and get a team hooked up to a dray or buckboard and drive it back here."

"Do you want the rest of us to come back here when we're finished?" Thompson asked.

"No, wait for me at the station when you're done," Baxter replied.

"Who's dead, Detective?" O'Brien asked. "Way you're carrying on, must be somebody important."

They all looked at Baxter and waited. He bowed his head for a moment then said, "Gentlemen, this business with the Boers and mustering our men to fight will give us some cover. It will not last long. The city will take this hard. There will be all sorts of talk and gossip that's going to be hard on the family. I don't want that to start any sooner than it has to, so for now the fewer people that know, the better. Focus on doing your best to help find the answers everyone will be looking for...Thank you, gentlemen." A couple of the men bowed their own heads for a moment. Others scuffed their feet and looked toward the end of the wharf. Eventually the line broke up and the men moved off.

Baxter stood his ground, looking each man off without saying a word. Squire remained in place, still without a job to do. The look on his face said he expected to be detailed off for some particularly inane task far removed from any sort of responsibility or demand for intelligence. When the last of the other five officers had moved around the corner of Mitchell and Sons, Baxter looked at Squire and said, "I've hooked a pilot ladder over the end of the wharf. Let's get you down there, get some ropes around Mr. Mosher so we can pull him up."

Squire was double stunned. First by the fact of Baxter's sudden trust, and second by the identity of the victim. Squire had been in the city less than a year. They had never met, but Squire had heard the name. "You mean Victor Mosher, the alderman?" he asked just to be sure.

"You understand now the need for care," Baxter said over his shoulder as he led them on to the end of the wharf. "Ok, Mr. Squire, down you go."

———•———

The fidgeting and the manic movements were gone, replaced by a slow steadiness that seemed impossible. Surely the man woken up two hours earlier was a misfit twin mistaken for the medical examiner. The crisp smooth white coat circled slowly around the examination table, pausing, lifting his glasses, making a note, then putting the lenses carefully back in place and moving on. Baxter moved at the same pace in the opposite direction, hands behind his back, shoved into his pants pockets, then behind his back again. Occasionally one or the other of them cleared his throat or made a long "Hmmmm" in response to something they noticed or a question they were chewing on, one not ready to ask aloud. Watching them made Squire a bit dizzy. And he was being suffocated by his greatcoat. Still, he couldn't move from the corner. He seemed mesmerized by the choreography, as if he were watching a company of Russian ballet dancers or an entourage of French courtiers. Not that he had ever attended such fancy soirées. Squire came from ordinary stock, which provided him the freedom to imagine that naked corpses stewed in harbour water were common centrepieces at elegant affairs.

"Mr. Squire… Mr. Squire!" The voice startled him into blinking and turning his head like a barn owl caught in a flash of light. "Mr. Squire, before you faint away and we have to lay you out on a table, please get that coat off and when you have done so, come here and give me a hand." There was a small wooden chair beside him which he hadn't noticed. It stood in the dutiful quiet service of a third-generation valet, Baxter's coat draped across the arms. Squire laid his coat over top with a nod of gratitude then moved around the table to stand by the detective.

Baxter was bent over peering at a wound about two inches long that ran on an angle following the bottom of the ribcage on the left side of the body. The opening was not very wide and slightly rounded top and bottom, like the little red mouth of some toothless sucking animal. "What does that look like to you, Mr. Squire?" Baxter asked, not taking his eyes off the body, or expecting Squire to draw anything other than the obvious conclusion.

"Looks to me like a knife wound, Detective."

"Yes it does… Do you suppose Mr. Mosher stabbed himself and then jumped into the harbour?"

"Would he do that? He was very successful, wasn't he?" Squire asked in return, rising out of the crouch he had assumed to look more closely at the lifeless face of Victor Mosher, a face that grew increasingly ashen and desperate the longer he stared at it. He looked at Baxter, still studying the wound. Was the question facetious? Was there a smirk on Baxter's face? Squire turned away.

The examining room they were working in had been built in the basement to keep the doctor's live patients separate from his dead ones, and to make sure his very squeamish wife could not accidentally walk in on an autopsy. She never came downstairs. Victor had arrived wrapped in a canvas tarp. It had taken all four of them to gently manage him off the buckboard and in through a back door. Officer Chalmers was sent back outside before the body was uncovered. Not really knowing what to do with himself, and still a little overwhelmed, Squire had busied himself with folding the tarp while Baxter and the doctor set about removing Victor's clothes. In the midst of that operation, Baxter had sent Squire off with the tarp and instructions for Chalmers. "Tell him to return everything then head home. And remind him to keep his mouth shut." Squire hadn't bothered asking the detective who he thought Chalmers might be talking to in the middle of the night. Better just to do as he was told and keep his own mouth shut. When he came back, the body was naked except for a small towel. If it was true and the spirit lingered, Victor would thank Baxter for that small kindness when they saw one another again. Victor's clothes had been laid out on a second table. Squire had never known anyone who dressed so well. Of course Victor had not committed suicide.

Baxter was paying no attention to Squire, but continued to stare into the knife wound as if he were waiting for it to speak. Then something did occur to him and he nodded toward the second table. "Mr. Squire, do you remember seeing any holes in Victor's jacket or shirt?" he asked.

Squire turned toward the detective, glad to be called away from Victor's face and the warren of self-pity. "I don't remember seeing any at the wharf. Mind you it was dark and I really wasn't looking. Then you and the doctor undressed him, remember? I was outside for most of it." The doctor looked up briefly from the study he had taken up of the hole that had once been Victor's left eye, nodded to confirm Squire's account, then went back to his business.

"Right, well, have a look now, will you," Baxter said as he moved round to stand beside the doctor and watch him take notes.

Undershirt, shirt, vest, suit coat, and overcoat had been laid one on top of the next. Except for their soggy stench they were in perfect order, new perhaps. Working from one side, each layer was folded back and looked over, then the next and the next. Squire replaced each item carefully then peeled through the layers from the other side. "No holes, Detective. In fact, not so much as a pulled thread."

"What about the blood?" The doctor had finished with the hole in Victor's head. He was holding up a hand that was the colour of fog except for the fingernails, which had gone midnight black with hints of purple. The intense scrutiny, the sense of foreboding, and the stench of death made the air thick and heavy. There were no windows to let it out. A dark sense of humour might have tried to lighten things by waving the hand and putting some words in the mouth of the dead. If the idea occurred to the doctor, he kept it well hidden. With the lifeless hand still in front of his face, the doctor repeated himself. "What about the blood, the blood stains on the clothes, do you find anything interesting or strange about them?" The doctor went back to his study of the hand, as if he already knew the answer to his question and had asked it simply to keep the policemen busy while he got on with matters unresolved. Baxter, curious to learn what the doctor might have seen that he did not, stepped around to stand beside Squire as the young officer once again went through the layers of Victor Mosher's clothing.

The harbour had washed away most of the blood, but the front of the white undershirt was almost completely covered by a stain that was now more pink than red. Victor's dress shirt had the same colour stain, only it was much smaller. The suit was made of wool, a light brown herringbone with threads of orange running through it on the vertical and light blue on the horizontal. The stain on the left side of the vest was the diameter of a grapefruit. The suit jacket was well made, fully canvassed and lined with silk. The stain that had made its way through to the front was light and not much larger than a silver dollar. A skilled laundryman might be able to get it out. The heavy black overcoat didn't seem to have a mark on it.

"What do you make of it, Detective?" Squire asked, watching the stain grow smaller then disappear as Baxter replaced the layers of clothing one over top of the other as Victor had worn them. Baxter said nothing, just let out another long "Hmmmmm."

"What indeed?" the doctor said, which didn't help Squire at all and caused him to throw an aggravated look at the white coat that was now back to him as the doctor moved round to Victor's other hand.

Meanwhile Baxter was examining the contents of Victor's pockets, which he had set out next to a pair of black leather brogues at the end of the table below the wet clothes. Gold pocket watch, silver money clip holding thirty-six dollars in bank notes, an ivory-coloured cotton hand-kerchief, a fountain pen (which Baxter knew had come from Victor's father), the soggy remnants of two cigars, a ring of eight keys, one dime, one nickel, and three pennies. Baxter pushed the items around on the table. He wasn't really looking at them, he had already memorized what was there. Lifting his head from the small cache, Baxter wore a look that was tired and sad and hoping against unspeakable things seen in the mind's eye. After a stuttering sigh he asked, "Mr. Squire, does it seem to you that Mr. Mosher fell prey to a robbery?"

Squire looked at the clothes and then at the gold watch and the silver money clip and the fold of bills it was still holding on to. "Not unless Mr. Mosher was robbed of something more valuable than what's here, Detective."

"Other than his life, you mean…don't answer that. I know what you meant, Mr. Squire, and I agree with you." Looking at him as he spoke, Baxter said, "Doctor Trenaman." A tone of command had returned to his voice. "Inventory Mr. Mosher's effects for evidence, in the usual manner. I'll be back later this morning for your full report before I speak to his wife."

"I can't possibly have it written up before noon, Chief Inspector," the doctor replied without looking up from whatever note he was making.

"That will be fine, Doctor, you can tell me how it will read when I see you at nine."

This time with his pen lifted and peering at Baxter over his glasses, the doctor said, "I assume you will not be telling Mrs. Mosher that it doesn't seem as though her husband died with his boots on, or much else."

Baxter didn't miss the hint of a smile as the doctor went back to his scribbling. No matter how this case played out there would be tittering, eye rolling, and rampant gossip. Some would add their own twists no matter how straight and true the story was told, others would simply make something up if an official version didn't come out in the papers. Few, if any, wagging tongues could claim the moral high ground, or could even see it from where they lived. Baxter had been a policeman far too long to be surprised by pettiness and indiscretion, but he still found them disappointing. He truly hoped Victor had not been involved in anything sordid, the loss of the man was shame enough. Those who snickered and chortled had no shame as far as Baxter was concerned. Lapsing morality was no laughing matter, it was dangerous and sad. What's wrong with people? he wondered. All of this was on the tip of his tongue. All he bothered to say, in a voice as flat as scripture, was, "That is a safe assumption, Doctor." As he turned for the door he said, "Get our coats, Mr. Squire. Time to wake up the closest thing we have to a witness and see what she can tell us."

———•———

"Ellen...Miss Reardon...ELLEN!" Baxter's face grew redder as his voice rose. The little room jumped. Ellen remained dead to the world. The two policemen were standing outside a jail cell in the basement of the police station. Many older buildings still used gaslights. In a modern place like this, electric bulbs did the job. They gave off a low beehive buzz along with their sharper white light.

"She's really out of it, Detective." Squire was simply thinking out loud, he wasn't trying to wind Baxter up by being intentionally inane. But when Baxter turned his head to look at Squire, he was more electric than the bulbs hanging from the ceiling. If Squire had tossed a saucy remark or smirked, Baxter looked like he might have gone for his throat, or worse, simply sent him home and let him have nothing more to do with the case. The young policeman wisely said nothing as he held up the key Sergeant Mackay had given him. Standing at the end of the narrow cot Squire yelled Ellen's name one more time. Nothing. When the end of the cot fell back down its springs bucked and Ellen nearly landed on the floor.

"Jesus Christ...what's the matter with you..." Ellen pushed herself back up on the cot, then got herself into a sitting position, her feet on the floor, her hands either side, clutching the thin mattress in case the cot took her for another ride.

"Miss Reardon, if you would like to finish the night here instead of a horse stall or under a tree, you will tell me what you know and in the process you will keep a civil tongue in your head...Are you listening to me, Ellen?" As he spoke, Baxter stepped back from the cell door until his back found the plaster wall on the opposite side of the hallway. Squire watched the retreat with a quizzical look. The detective stood in place stone-faced and silent. Ellen ignored them both. After a moment Ellen leaned hard to one side, drew a deep breath she seemed to hold on to for balance, let go a long, slow, rolling, thunderous fart, then groaned in sweet relief. There was a basin of water on a small table beside the cot. She leaned back the other way and pulled it closer. The spindly table legs stuttered across the cement floor, the water vibrated. It didn't spill. Ellen dunked her hands then held them up like an open prayer book. She laid her face into them and began massaging the sleep out of her eyes. After a moment or two she looked at Squire over the grubby ends of her fingers and said in a ripsaw voice, "Hey, Bright Eyes, they tell you where the WC is yet? I gotta take a piss."

Squire was busy fanning the air, his features twisted up in disgust. Behind him there was a hint of a smirk on Baxter's stone face. "Straight down at the end of the hall," Squire said, backing out of the cell, now breathing through his mouth.

Ellen used her hands as a comb then tied her hair back with a length of string she may have found somewhere in the thick mane. She stood up straight as a pin. The bodice of her dress was soiled, its hemline muddy and torn. But she brushed at herself carefully, pulled at the ends of her long sleeves and then walked smartly out of the cell and on toward the end of the hall. She paused at the door to the WC. "What time is it, Detective?" she asked through a yawn.

"Just tend to your business please, Miss Reardon, so we can tend to ours."

"You can be really hateful, do you know that? I pity your wife. How is she, by the way?" Ellen waited for a moment as if she really wanted to know or expected Baxter to answer. Then she yawned again and slipped through the door, closing it gently.

Baxter swallowed a ball of anger. He was not angry with Ellen as much as he was angry with himself. The mention of his wife reminded him he was not at home where he should be. He reached for his watch. It was almost two in the morning. He sighed again. Down the hall a few chairs were lined up. He nodded toward them and said, "Mr. Squire, fetch us a couple of those while we wait for our delicate flower to bloom. We might as well have seats for the show." Squire set two chairs in the cell facing the cot. Baxter motioned him to sit. Meanwhile, the detective remained standing in the hall. He managed to hold on for a half a minute more before saying, in a voice certain to be heard on the other side of the narrow door, "You are testing my patience, Miss Reardon." There was a bang, perhaps from the toe of a shoe, followed by a muffled flurry of words that didn't sound kind. Another half minute of silence passed, then there was the sound of falling water and the door opened. Ellen walked back up the hall, not slowly. Not too quickly either. She stared at Baxter the whole way, inviting him to say something that would give her an excuse to make him wait a little longer. The detective looked straight ahead through the bars at the empty cot. He waited silently until Ellen was seated in his view, then he stepped into the cell. Rather than sit in the empty chair he stood behind it laying his hands on its top rail. "Miss Reardon, let's start with you running into Officer Squire. Where was that?"

"I don't know…on Barrington Street maybe… near the corner of Prince Street." Squire, who was watching Ellen from the second chair, with his back straight and his hands folded, looked briefly at the detective and nodded his head. "I didn't hear him ask you anything," Ellen snapped. Squire opened his mouth about to say something, like he was only agreeing with her or trying to help get the story straight. Baxter went on before Squire could speak and Ellen could go off on a tangent.

"Do you remember what time that was?"

"Nighttime," she said, the look on her face playful now. Ellen hadn't been dillydallying in the loo. She had scrubbed her face and hands and done the best she could with her long dark hair. The emerald green eyes could still flash. She shrugged her shoulders then looked at Squire, who had no intentions of saying a word this time. "Ok, sonny," Ellen said, kicking Squire's boot lightly, "go ahead, tell him."

Squire looked at Baxter, but waited. The detective nodded, slightly impatient. Squire cleared his throat and said, "It was eight thirty." He looked and sounded like he was in a witness box.

"Eight thirty." Baxter shifted his weight from one leg to the other, but remained standing. "Now tell me, what were you doing in the hours before then?"

Ellen hadn't finished playing. "Oh, well, let me see. It was early evening, drinks at the Carleton Hotel. Just me and a few of my closest friends, the archbishop, the mayor...oh and your boss, the police chief. By the way, Detective, he's a bit worried about you, thinks you're putting on too much weight, not as sharp as you used to be." Turning to Squire she gave him another pat on the boot and half a wink. "I'm afraid the chief has no idea who you are." Ellen leaned back a little, letting her arms take her weight. Looking up at Baxter, really enjoying herself now, she went on. "So from the Carleton it was dinner at the Halifax Club. Women are only allowed in the Club after five, did you know that, Detective?...After dinner the archbishop and the mayor were off. Not the chief, he and I...well..."

Baxter interrupted by picking up his chair and tapping the back legs on the hard floor. "Yes, Ellen, we have established you were drinking. And I assume the archbishop, mayor, and chief of police were some of the most common toss pots. Let me guess. Annie Higgenbottom, Hannah McDonald, and Thomas Berrigan. What gathering of disreputables would be complete without Thomas? So which one had the bottle?"

The play was over. Her face was hard leather. Ellen sat forward again. Baxter met her loathing with his own. Don't look at me like I have insulted your honour, he thought. You have no honour. Look at you, a drunk and worse, with no one to blame except yourself. He was surprised she didn't spit. They bristled at one another until finally Ellen looked away. The soles of her ladies' brogans, courtesy of some Catholic charity, were nearly worn through. In a voice almost low enough that Baxter couldn't hear, she said, "You're a heartless prick."

Baxter leaned forward over the back of the chair. "I'm sorry, what was that?" he asked in a voice that sounded so genuine Squire thought he truly hadn't heard what Ellen had said.

"I said...I was drinking alone."

"Were you really...or are you just trying to keep some of your friends from being involved in this?" Baxter kept leaning forward over the chair. But Ellen refused to look at him now.

"No one was with me. Well, no one alive anyway."

"So no one was with you, you're sure?"

"You heard me, I said I was alone." Ellen looked straight at Squire as she spoke, as if he were asking the questions now. The young policeman shifted in his chair, glancing at Ellen. Paying greater attention to the floor.

"All right, you were alone. So tell me now, where did the bottle come from?" Baxter moved over behind Squire into Ellen's line of sight.

"I bought it," Ellen said quickly, now looking out between the bars at the blank wall across the narrow hallway. Ellen was the only guest so far. The other cells were empty, no snoring or yelling to be set free. As Ellen withered under Baxter's glare and Squire continued to work on his invisibility, an out-of-season moth tortured itself against the bare bulb overhead.

Baxter raised his arms in mock celebration, his hands nearly touching the low ceiling, further worrying the moth. "Oh, I didn't hear. You're back to work. Well, congratulations. You've finally patched things up with Taylor's, have you? Or maybe your friend the mayor has found you a desk somewhere."

Ellen looked frantically about, her hands fixed like talons, desperate for something to hurl at her tormentor. She let out a shriek in frustration, then looked Baxter in the eye and hissed, "It's none of your business if I'm working or not, or where I get money or a bottle or anything else, you rotten bastard."

Undaunted by her outburst, ever certain of his authority, Baxter replied, "The truth is my business, Miss Reardon, and you will watch your tongue. You got that bottle from someone, and I want to know who and what they may have seen or have to do with Victor Mosher winding up dead under Mitchell's Wharf."

"Is that who it was, I didn't recognize him. He was a decent sort. He had a heart, unlike some people I know." Ellen's feelings about Mosher seemed honest, despite the contempt she was still showing for Baxter.

"The bottle."

"I got it from a sailor."

Baxter was starting to pace the line behind the chairs, arms folded across his chest. "This town is full of sailors. I need a name, Ellen."

"I didn't get it." Ellen followed Baxter with her eyes.

"What did he look like?"

"Like he was looking for something."

"And you gave it to him."

"Yes I did, Detective. I gave it to him fast and hard with my arse out and my hands against a wall. Nothin' nervous or shy about it, no holy union, just business. What do you think about that, Detective?" Squire had bowed his head, unable to get out of sight, and had taken up further study of the floor under the cot. Ellen reached over and put a hand on his knee and kept it there. When Squire looked up, blushing and squirming, Ellen cooed at him in a throaty voice. "Ohhh look, Detective, this young man can't stop thinking about it...can you?" Squire leaped out of the chair as if it were on fire, bumping into the little table with the spindly legs. The water in the basin sluiced back and forth, much of it landing on the floor.

"Leave him alone, Ellen," Baxter chided, looking Squire over as the young officer flattened himself against the back wall of the cell. He was a green country lad, no doubt. At the same time he wasn't getting in the way, and he was at least some help in getting her to talk. Baxter turned his attention back to Ellen, who was still eyeing Squire, her face turned to hide the gap in her smile. "So the sailor gave you a bottle for your trouble and left?"

Ellen dropped the smile and looked back out into the hall. "That's right."

"And then?" Baxter had stopped pacing and was back behind his chair, hands in his pants pockets.

"And then I sat on the end of the wharf and had a few drinks. And that's when I saw Victor. Course I didn't know it was him at the time."

"And you have no idea how he got there?"

Ellen turned to look Baxter in the eye. "None," she said in a tone that suggested she really wanted to help.

"This sailor, was he on the wharf before he and you...met, shall we say?"

"I don't know. I was walking south on Lower Water Street, he was headed north. He showed me the bottle he had under his coat. We found a quiet spot." She crossed her arms in front of her body and drew into herself as she rubbed her shoulders.

"And you saw no one else?

"No."

"You heard nothing suspicious?" Ellen just shook her head, shivering and rubbing. "So why not just walk away, why run to the nearest policeman?"

Ellen looked up at Squire, who was still part of the wall. She shrugged again and gave him a brief closed-lip smile. "I was cold," she said, and then bowed her head.

Baxter looked down at Ellen, who had taken the blanket from the cot and wrapped it around her shoulders. He wanted her to be able to tell him something useful. It might have been good for her. He wasn't feeling sorry for her, he just hated seeing people go to waste. He looked at Squire, who took a minute to realize the detective was waiting for his opinion. "I don't think she can help, Detective. Maybe the officers you sent out along the waterfront have turned up something."

Baxter walked out of the cell, carrying both chairs. Before starting down the hall he looked at Ellen and said, "I'll send someone down with another blanket." From halfway down the hall he called back, "Mr. Squire, lock the door. I'll see you in my office in ten minutes."

———•———

B axter went out a side door onto Argyle Street. The wind had died completely. The sky was high and clear and twinkling with stars. In the stillness, with a dusting of light frost and a hint of wood smoke in the air, it seemed impossible that anything bad could ever happen here. Baxter knew better. The temperature had come up a degree or two, but his breath still hung in the air. He stood with his back close to the building, breathing deeply. An insomniac looking out the window might have taken him for a night watchman stopping for a smoke. He had tried smoking cigars when he was younger. A pipe too. He had never understood the attraction.

The back side of City Hall followed the steep slope down Duke Street. It wasn't until he noticed the awkwardness of striding downhill that

Baxter realized he had gone for a walk. He wasn't thinking about Ellen or the examination of the body or what to do next. He was thinking about his daughter, Grace. She was an only child and a bit spoiled, he had to admit. Her mother was too easy with her. She was eighteen, bright and determined, spurred on by older "modern" women and their talk of equality and rights. As if the city didn't have problems enough.

He had turned right at the opposite corner of the building onto Barrington Street. He followed the wall along the east side of the Grand Parade until he came to its main entrance. He passed through and stopped just inside. Saint Paul's stood to his left in sober silence, waiting on eternity. Its heavy wood frame and walls sealed with a century of whitewash. Fifty years ago these Anglicans would have spurned him for being a papist. Times had changed, at least outwardly. There were Catholics in the provincial government and every other mayor was a Catholic by gentleman's agreement. The current mayor was a Catholic. Baxter made the sign of the cross, something he seldom did even in church. He took a furtive glance around the square. The walk had done as much good as it was going to to wake him up. He went back inside.

The place was normally quiet in the wee hours of the morning. Not the wee hours of this particular morning. As Baxter came through the doors off a main hallway into the police station, he thought for a second he was in the wrong place. Mackay was in his shirt sleeves leaning across the counter toward a line of officers sitting along the wall. All of them were smiling and guffawing and nudging one another. The man on the far end had found something so funny he was bent over stomping the floor, gasping for air, with his face beet red. A low-hanging cloud of cigar smoke, a few drinks and bar towels, and the scene had all the makings of an upper street tavern. Baxter stood quietly looking from man to man as he unbuttoned his coat. Throats were cleared, uniforms were straightened, and apologies muttered. When Baxter had finished with the last button he turned to Mackay and said, "Have the men ready, I'll be back in a moment." He shook his head and then marched off to his office, his coat over one arm.

He found Squire in his office, laid out in a chair, dead to the world. Baxter hung up his coat. He reached out to give Squire a shake, then held up. It was three in the morning after an eventful night, which wasn't over yet. Staying awake for a month at a time took practice. Maybe a few winks would make him more useful. The detective watched the young officer a moment longer, a little envious. His body gently rose and fell, his face peaceful as a child's. The racket in the outer office had not prevented him in the least. As a young policeman, Baxter had to fight to get to sleep and he was wide awake again at the drop of a pin. Only when he was lying next to his wife was he a sound sleeper. Which reminded him: he had to pick up something for Jane's mother.

The men were all buttoned up, their uniform helmets in a straight line like tuned bells in a frame. No one spoke. Mackay had come round the counter and taken up a spot in front of them. A low railing from the end of the front counter to the far wall divided the visitors' area from the common office space. As Baxter reached out to push the swinging door, he said, "Ok, Mackay, I'll take it from here." At the same time he noticed a blanket on a shelf below the countertop. He wondered where Ellen had gotten the one she had. "And since you're not so busy now, perhaps you can deliver that blanket like I asked." Baxter raised his eyebrows as he spoke, and gave Mackay a sidelong glance that none of the other officers failed to notice. The scolding ruffled Mackay's feathers. He stood defiantly still, his chest puffed up. However, when the chief inspector turned to face him Mackay avoided looking him in the eye. "And Mr. Mackay, Miss Reardon doesn't need any grief with her blanket." Mackay held on just a second longer, then collected the blanket and stomped off muttering incoherently something about the dreams of Sleeping Beauty.

The men braced themselves as Baxter's full attention came upon them. "O'Brien and Morrow, let's start with you."

O'Brien looked at Morrow and got nothing except a shrug in response, so he turned back to Baxter and started with a shrug of his own. "Not much to tell, Detective. We did just as you asked. We walked south down along the waterfront from Mitchell's Wharf all the way to the foot of Salter Street."

"We boarded every ship, no one had anything to tell," Morrow broke in, glancing at O'Brien as he continued. "We walked back along Lower

Water Street. We ran into a couple of old soakers wandering home from the bars."

"But they were badly mauled. No help at all," O'Brien said, retaking the lead. "From Mitchell's Wharf back to the station, we didn't see a soul. It's gone real quiet out there, Detective."

Baxter sighed. "You didn't happen to run into a shore patrol, did you?"

As O'Brien and Morrow were shaking their heads, Sweeney raised a hand and said, "We did, Detective, at the end of Buckingham Street where we came up from the docks. The lieutenant said he and his men had been making rounds since ten o'clock. Said they broke up a fight and dragged a drunken private back to the barracks. That was all, though, nothing unusual."

Baxter nodded. Looking up and down the line, he said, "So no one you spoke to saw anyone throw anything in the harbour large enough to be a body?" Heads were shaken, a couple of emphatic no's spoken to back them up. "And no one saw anyone along the docks with a cart or a dray that didn't seem to have an obvious reason for being there?" Again the men looked back at the detective with apologetic faces and shakes of their heads. "And no one noticed any unusual boat traffic in the harbour?" Once again no one had any news that might aid the investigation, or give the detective something to cling to. By this time Baxter had wandered to the far end of the counter area, as if he were distancing himself from what he didn't want to hear. He was leaning against the wall, his arms crossed over his chest. The expression on his face was as grey and cheerless as the portrait of the Queen that hung on the wall over his head. He was staring at his shoes, unable to think of any further questions or directions. He was tired and his head hurt.

"Detective, if you had told us who the dead man was, we could have asked people if they had seen him or had any information about him. Maybe then our efforts would not have been such a waste of time." It was O'Brien who spoke, just as his friend Mackay was returning from the basement. Baxter didn't think the timing was an accident. Mackay had heard the question and quickly got the gist of things from all the long faces. The look on his own said he agreed with O'Brien.

If they were a group of twelve-year-olds and Baxter their leader, there could only be one response to such a challenge, if Baxter wanted to keep his place, that is. He would have to fight O'Brien. Childish, perhaps, and maybe not a completely bad idea. They were about the same age, a long way from twelve. O'Brien drank and ate too much and never took any exercise. Baxter had discipline and about a foot in height along with his pent-up frustration. Men like O'Brien and Mackay had been under his skin for years. They were only a little less shiftless and crooked than the people they arrested. Baxter pushed himself off the wall and took three quick strides toward O'Brien, looking straight through him as he charged. There were sudden inhales, wide eyes, and some backward steps. Still looking holes in O'Brien's head, Baxter slowed his stride and came to an easy halt at the railing gate. Just before pushing it open he said in a voice as calming as warm milk, "Well, Mr. O'Brien, I'm sure things will be better when you're chief inspector. For now we'll do things my way." Halfway back to his office, Baxter called over his shoulder, "Mr. Mackay, see to it that the men get back on their proper patrols."

When Baxter returned to his office he quickly closed the door on the whispering behind him. Squire was standing in the corner, barely visible beyond the square of dusky light coming through the glass in the office door.

"Been up long?" Baxter asked as he fell into the chair behind his desk.

"I thought you were really going for O'Brien," Squire said as he sat back down, facing the desk.

Baxter spoke as he fumbled with the switch under the shade of his desk lamp. "Mr. Squire, a man in my position has to show restraint." That was true and Squire nodded, though he didn't look convinced or beyond the notion that O'Brien could benefit from a good thumping. Even if it didn't do anything for O'Brien, it was sure to be good for general morale.

"Besides," the inspector continued, looking as if he were recalling a moment in particular, "Paddy O'Brien likes to play dead. But he and Mackay are the same, strong as oxen, and mean when provoked."

"I'll keep that in mind."

"I assume you heard the men came back empty-handed." Squire nodded. "So what does that mean, Mr. Squire?" Baxter was leaning back in his chair, hands behind his head.

Squire shifted his weight. "We have a big waterfront."

"Which includes the Dartmouth side and the basin."

"The body could have been thrown in from anywhere...and who knows when." Squire's expression said he was asking as much as telling.

"Maybe Victor Mosher found some quiet place along the water and took his own life. That seems unlikely to me, he was too strong willed, too much of an optimist. Somebody killed him. And they didn't do it out in the open." As Baxter spoke, it seemed to him that Squire was reviewing what he had seen in the basement of the doctor's house. A body with a knife wound. Clothes with no knife holes in them. Money, watch, nothing missing. This was not a typical robbery or crime of passion. O'Brien and Mackay were wrong. Asking after Victor tonight could have done nothing more than alert the killer that the body had been found. Or so it seemed according to the expression on Squire's face. Baxter continued to stare. Or maybe it was just his own thoughts and an effort to reassure himself that Baxter saw in the young policeman's face.

Whatever it was that Squire was thinking, the question he asked was a good one. "So, Detective, who would want to kill Victor Mosher?"

Baxter leaned forward in his chair and brought both hands down firmly on the top of his desk. The desk lamp flickered and made a faint fizzing sound. "That is precisely the question you are going to start with."

"Me?" Squire asked, as if Baxter, who was now pointing a finger directly at him, could possibly mean someone else. Baxter ignored Squire's nerves and went on to explain. Squire was to go home and get some sleep. Then first thing in the morning, as if it weren't already, Squire was to begin digging into the life of Victor Mosher.

"The councilmen's offices are upstairs," Baxter said, pointing at the ceiling. "No one knows yet, so things will still be calm."

"How am I supposed to get into his office?"

"Don't be ridiculous, you're a policeman." Baxter let him ponder the authority of a young patrolman. Not for long, only a moment. "One of these will likely let you in." He tossed Squire the ring of keys he had taken from Victor's effects. Squire stared at them as if they were the first keys he had ever seen. Up to now he had been more of a watchman. Patrolling the streets at night, checking doors, posing a deterrent. He had broken up a few fights. Taken part in a tavern raid, under one or other of the liquor laws. This was the first time he had been called on to think, to look for evidence. Would he recognize it if he saw it? Baxter had anticipated the question. "Go through his desk, everything in his office. Track down his office girl. Find out what he was working on. There will be an appointment book, let's see who he was meeting with. Take anything that looks important. Start following Victor's travels over the past few weeks. When you're done upstairs, go to his business office on Albemarle Street, do the same there."

Baxter stood up and stretched, then went for his coat on the stand by the door. Squire stayed glued to his chair. The weight of new and greater responsibility was daunting, not exulting like he had imagined. Squire twisted to face the detective, who was wriggling his shoulders into his coat and holding up a scarf he seemed surprised to see. Before he could open his mouth to ask for a quick review, Baxter had further instructions. "And when you're done with Victor's offices, close them up, nobody in or out by order of the chief inspector of the Halifax Police Department."

"How am I supposed to…"

"Put up signs, use nails, chains, do what you have to, but nobody goes in after you, understand?"

Squire had managed to put the keys in a pocket and pull himself to his feet. Baxter was buttoned up. He had decided against the scarf. It was back on the coat stand. The office door was open. "Detective?"

"What is it, Mr. Squire?"

"Why me, Detective? Why not someone with more experience?"

Baxter stepped into the doorway then turned back to face the young policeman. "Young man like you, eager to make a name for himself, you'll work hard, do what you're told, and if something goes wrong you'll be easy to blame." Baxter waited, enjoyed watching Squire beam like a first grader with a gold star, then deflate from disillusionment. Despite his efforts to recover, to convince himself his leg was being pulled, Squire had the look of a withered birthday balloon. He studied Baxter's face.

It was stone, then it softened just a little. "The case started with you when Ellen found you on the street. I'm offering you the chance to see it through. Now if you don't want..."

"No...I want to see it through, and thank you, Detective." Unable to think of any other way to look less vulnerable and more like he was up to the task, Squire thrust out his right hand and waited for the detective to take it.

Baxter took it without hesitation in a preacher's reassuring grip. He looked Squire in the eye then turned and walked away. After a few strides he called back over his shoulder, "Switch off the desk lamp, Mr. Squire, and close my office door before you go."

———•———

In the predawn light seeping through the crack in the curtains, Jane looked serene, high above and untouched by the grubby machinations of inhumanity. Baxter watched her sleep as he hung his suit clothes on the valet stand and slipped his pyjamas off the hanger in the wardrobe. Lying beside her he could feel the tension leaving his body. The ugliness and sadness of murder, the unanswered questions that would soon become ringing cries for justice, and the endless frustration that went with the job of trying to push people out of their own way. His wife rolled over, and in a voice only half awake asked if he wanted her to get him up at the usual time. He drifted off with the comfort that comes from complete trust and a sincere desire to be a better husband.

$\mathcal{S}unday$

According to the *Farmers' Almanac*, the city was a month into the fall. But this morning the air felt warmer than usual. Kenny Squire left the police station around 6 A.M. Sunday morning. It would be more than another hour before the sun rose. And yet there was already enough light that he had to look directly at the street lights to notice they were still burning. Squire lived in a boarding house on Albemarle Street. The Dillon family owned it, along with a couple of other houses they rented out. They also stabled horses, and sold liquor and groceries. The Dillons didn't put up with any nonsense and looked after their places pretty well, which was why Squire stayed with them. That, and the fact that the police department didn't pay him enough to afford a home in the south or west end neighbourhoods. He lived alongside factory girls, teachers, and domestics who came from small towns just like his. Many of them found stevedores, carpenters, coopers, and labourers of all sorts, or soldiers or sailors, and they became wives and mothers to the mob of children who also belonged to the upper streets. All the necessities of life were close at hand—schools, churches, shops, firefighters, and undertakers. And when the workday was done, or there was no work to be found, the upper streets had plenty of gambling, liquor, and dollymops, which attracted customers from all over the city, as well as those just passing through. The upper streets made some and ruined others. Mostly the place just got along; its people were tough, seldom dangerous.

Squire tiptoed up the stairs with his boots in one hand and his key in the other. The first room at the end of the hall belonged to Billy Two

People. His real name was William Paul. He was from the Shubenacadie Reservation about fifty miles north of the city. He worked at the Aberdeen Hotel. You wouldn't find an Indian waiting tables there or at any other decent hotel in town, so Billy kept his hair short and passed for white.

Most of the time Billy lived quietly. He worked, sent money home, and kept to himself. Once in a while, though, he would take a drink. He drank whisky, cheap whisky, and he drank for effect. He was loud by the third drink. A couple more and he was impossible to ignore. After a certain point there was no predicting what he might do. He could buy you a drink, then look at you as if you'd stolen his wife. Some drinking buddies gave him the nickname Billy Two People, which stuck. It sounded Indian, but that was an accident. Few people knew William's secret and he wanted to keep it that way. It was only by chance one night that the closet door had been open to reveal the fine beadwork jacket inside. Squire had helped William to bed, closing the closet and then the door to his room. He paused there now. Billy snored, louder when he drank. No sound came through the door this morning. Billy might be on the early shift. Or passed out under a table in some dive.

Josie Blanchard was in the next room. She had recently lost her husband, Raymond. He had wavy hair and straight teeth, and Josie said she couldn't help believing in him. Raymond was shot dead coming out of the Boston patent office. The man who did it said Raymond had stolen his idea for a new dentist drill. Sometimes Josie would admit that deep down she had always known Raymond was a hustler. But in the same breath she'd say that no man every treated her so well. Squire couldn't imagine saying no to her. For now she was singing and dancing in the taverns. Squire couldn't tell if she was looking for another Raymond or just trying to find a way to tell her family she was no longer in Boston and that things hadn't worked out like she planned. There was a light under Josie's door. Sometimes he heard whispering or tears when he passed. He listened for a moment. There was a dull thud as if something had been dropped or bumped into. There was no telling which room it came from.

Squire slipped past Josie's door and opened his own as carefully as he could. Before going inside he looked over to see if Betty's door was open. She left it open sometimes after getting up in the night. Betty was a widow too. She would never say just how old she was. If Squire had to guess he would say she might be twice as old as Josie. Her husband had been a bosun's mate. One night high winds had broken a yardarm on the forward mast. John had helped some other men cut it free and heave it overboard into the rough seas. Weeks later Betty heard a knock at her front door. The captain said no one knew what happened for sure, John had just disappeared. Betty said she wished the captain had made something up so she could feel that he was gone. Billy remembered her once saying that she still saw her husband's face sometimes on men about the right age and then she found it hard to get to sleep. Her door was shut tight. No signs of John.

Squire pulled the thin curtains closed for what little difference it made and lay down. Before he could decide whether or not to take his clothes off and get under the covers he was fast asleep.

———·—

The peel of the bells was confusing. Mostly because Squire had forgotten it was Sunday. In the shock of realizing that Victor Mosher had been murdered and trying to formulate a course for the investigation, they had not thought about what day it was. Yesterday seemed like last week. He was trying to remember all the things Baxter had told him to do. He should have written out a list. It was pointless. He needed to take a piss and get some coffee.

Josie and Betty were at the kitchen table. Betty was dressed for church. Josie looked more like Squire, like she had just gotten up.

"Those clothes still look good, honey. They have another day in them no question." Josie looked Squire up and down as she spoke, but there was a friendly smirk behind the sarcasm. She sipped her coffee and waited to see what would come back from her ping.

"You tear a page out of Billy's book?" Betty asked. The look on her face was one of concern, not mischief.

"Good morning, ladies," Squire said, still trying to rub the sleep out of his face and swallow the taste of the baking soda he'd used on his teeth. "Speaking of Billy, did he say he was going out drinking?"

"Don't change the subject, sweetie. Tell us what you were up to that kept you out till nearly six in the morning." Squire continued massaging his face, now trying to decide what Josie was up to. She wasn't a natural gossip. He didn't suspect her of fishing for juicy stories to spread. More likely she too was concerned, not that Squire may have gone overboard whooping it up. He was young and in her opinion didn't whoop it up enough. The fact that he was a policeman often seemed to escape her mind or she simply didn't see the contradiction. A number of men on the force agreed with her. Detective Baxter of course believed a policeman should never be out of uniform.

"Were you working?" Betty asked, either trying to give him an easy way out of Josie's question or protecting herself from hearing tales of the wild and reckless side of life.

"Didn't you say you were off early last night?" Josie remained hopeful, for Squire's sake, not her own. He had managed to pour himself a cup of coffee from the pot on the stove. It was still too hot for anything more than timid sips. He would stay with it. It didn't seem to have been there too long and wouldn't taste like muddy water when it was finally cool enough to drink.

"I saw a light under your door when I came in. Maybe it's you that has a story to tell." Josie just smiled and pretended to be concerned with her hair, which was falling out of a loose braid. Squire couldn't tell if there was something interesting to tell or if she was just creating an illusion for his amusement or her own.

"Well, you're safe, that is all that matters," Betty declared as she got up and put her cup and plate in the sink. "I'm off to church. Don't suppose either of you would care to join me? There is still time if you hurry."

"You dress warm. This mild weather can't last. We're likely to see snow soon." Josie pulled her housecoat tighter around her neck and looked toward Squire, then tilted her head toward the stove.

"Enjoy the service," Squire said as he bent over the wood bin. Betty smiled through their rejection and hurried off for her coat and Bible. Squire sat back down at the table, feeling a little awkward now without Betty as a buffer. He tried not to look directly at Josie and was glad he really did have to get going once he got enough coffee in. A large part of him wanted to blurt out what he knew. And not just for the thrill of having Josie's full attention. Organizing the details into a coherent story would help him make sense of it all and give him the confidence he needed to follow Baxter's instructions. He almost had himself convinced that going over what had happened with someone was good police work.

"You really are in a fuddle," Josie said watching him struggle with his thoughts. She wasn't prying, just observing. She didn't have to fish, men were quick to tell her things.

"What's the best way to keep a secret?" Squire asked, still not quite ready to go.

"Just like that."

"Sorry?"

She made him wait while she leaned her elbows on the table and took her cup gently in her fingertips. "Keep asking questions," she spoke between sips. "It makes people think they know more than you. That *they* have the secrets and you don't."

"What time is it?"

She smiled. "So that's your trouble, you have a secret."

"No," he lied, which he knew was another key to keeping secrets. "I have to get to work."

———•———

Jane had let him sleep as long as she dared. She woke her husband at eight. She knew it was pointless to leave him any longer. He'd just be in a rush and feel more tired than ever. She left him to get cleaned up and dressed while she went back downstairs. Their five-bedroom house was much more than they needed. After Grace it hadn't been long before Jane was pregnant again. It had lasted five months instead of nine. The midwife was very sorry. She did the tidying up. They stopped trying after the third miscarriage. The doctors had been wrong. There would be no more children. Grace had no brothers or sisters. She had four times the toys and clothes she needed. A wall was removed. Grace's room doubled in size and the house took on less empty space. Four narrow windows looked out from Grace's new second-story kingdom. Downstairs keeping house Jane sometimes heard her daughter moving past them acting out the scenes of a little girl's imagination. Outside above the rooftops the cross of Saint Mary's stayed with them both like the eyes of the *Mona Lisa*. Eventually the downstairs bedrooms became Jane's sewing room and a laboratory of sorts where her husband practised powers of healing on outcasts rescued from dust bins—broken clocks, three-legged chairs, rusted bicycles.

Jane finished making breakfast in the large kitchen at the back of the house. Outside the face of the sun was a pale yolk in the morning haze. Inside the two large windows, the brilliant white walls and the bright yellow oilcloth with its purple daisies absorbed every speck of light. Even after dark the room was full of sunshine. The warmth from the large Findlay with its cast iron cooktop and enamelled oven door carried the smells of food and dried up the dampness. For Jane the kitchen had always been safe from the ghosts of the unborn.

Baxter kissed his wife on the cheek and took a seat in the back corner. From the window he could look out over their backyard, modestly re-fined with its stockade fence, limestone baluster bird bath, and octagon gazebo compete with cupola and turned spindle railing. The grass was slowly going brown with fall and there were no more robins to be seen. Warm scented evenings with a newspaper and some lemonade were still fresh in his memory, though. It was a fortifying thought.

Jane looked her husband over as she set down a plate of eggs on toasted bread with bacon. He wasn't wearing his Sunday best. "You're not coming to Mass, I see."

"I'm sorry." Baxter didn't miss the annoyance and disappointment in his wife's voice and hoped the apology he offered in response sounded genuine. He really was sorry.

"When did you come in? You said you'd only be an hour. Did you fall asleep again?" she asked as she came back to the table with a plate for herself and a pot of tea. She sat down and filled her cup.

Baxter stared out the window as he ate, studying the gazebo. Its light blue with white trim matched the house. Was it five or six years ago they'd had it built? Grace used to sneak into his wardrobe for clothes to play dress-up. The gazebo was her summer castle. How old was she then? The workmen had carried the lumber in from the street. He could see the company name on the side of the wagon, Mosher Masonry, Building and Real Estate. "Victor Mosher is dead," he said through a mouthful of poached egg, still staring at the backyard castle.

"That's horrible." Like many people who would hear the news in the days to come, Jane felt closer to the man than she really was. Once or twice a year the Moshers hosted functions that included the senior men on the force. Such things could be miserable, but Jane had always felt comfortable in the Mosher home. Ranks and titles were checked at the door, along with coats and hats. "Catherine will be devastated. Thank God her boys are older. She will need them now." Jane's eyebrows lowered and she leaned forward a little, forcing her husband to meet her gaze as she poured him some tea. "What happened, did his heart let go? He was such a hard worker. You should take a lesson."

Baxter shrugged off her warning and bathed in the steam rising from the cascade of Earl Grey as it filled his cup. "We don't know what happened yet. I'm going to see the medical examiner after breakfast, and then I'll break the news to Catherine. Did Grace leave early? The choir meets beforehand to go over the hymns, do they not?"

Jane's hands were long and slender and china smooth and moved with precision. When she set the teapot down hard enough to make the lid clink and scrape against its rim, it wasn't an accident. She shook her head. "Grace is your daughter, but she's still young. She hasn't learned how to go days on end without sleep. She was up late reading a brick of a book on human anatomy she got from who knows where. She showed me some of the pictures. Positively ghastly." Jane shivered her shoulders as she cut through the white of an egg with the edge of her fork.

"Any pictures of young doctors in that book?" Baxter glanced sideways at the backyard as he blew on his tea, picturing the aisle from the house to the gazebo, the families seated either side. He could hear the low murmuring of anticipation, feel Grace squeezing his arm, the lump in his throat.

"She says she didn't gain a secondary education to keep house." Jane slowly stirred more sugar into her tea.

He blinked. Still the scene lingered. "Did I miss something?" He sounded incredulous because he was. "We sent her to school precisely so she could have a good home and family."

"I don't think she wants to wait." Jane continued to play with her spoon. She followed her husband's gaze, trying to see whatever it was he was staring at in the backyard.

"Well then, she should be going to socials, doing some charity work maybe…not burying herself in medical books." He had finished his eggs and was pouring more tea.

"No, Cully, she doesn't want to wait for a man to come home."

"Oh, is that so? Well…" He wanted to say more, a lot more. This just wasn't the time. His jaws worked a strip of bacon as if it were rawhide.

Jane wasn't quite done. "Cully, don't underestimate our daughter. I married you because I loved you and I believed in you and I've stood behind you all these years. It wasn't always easy and Grace knows that even if you don't." There was no anger in her expression or voice, only the certainty of stone.

"What do I know?" Grace was pulling her hair up into a bun to get it out of her eyes, which were red and tired-looking. She had her mother's face and her father's shoulders, and height from both sides of the family.

"Good morning, Miss Baxter." Had he placed undue emphasis on the "Miss"? He didn't think so. He was sure his wife felt differently when she cast a sharp look his way.

"Good morning, Mother. Were you telling Father about my anatomy book? I'm learning that to cure an illness you have to hunt for clues. He would have made a good doctor, don't you think?" She nodded towards her father as she let out a heaving yawn, and reached for the ceiling from the tips of her toes with her arms stretched as long as she could make them.

"I could save more lives by closing all the taverns. Will you be attending Mass with your mother?" He didn't mean to sound cross with Grace. He was sorry to be missing Mass, he enjoyed the ritual. Hearing the word doctor reminded him of the day ahead and that he had better get going.

Jane had gotten up from the table and moved behind her daughter. She put her arms around Grace and spoke gently into her ear. "Your father has to work."

"What's wrong?" The question was directed to both of them. Now it was Baxter's face that was hard set as he looked warily at his wife before turning back to the window over the last of his tea.

"Victor Mosher is dead," Jane announced, letting go of her daughter and returning to the table. Had she misread his signal or ignored it?

"Was he murdered? Could I read the medical examiner's report?"

"Absolutely not," Baxter said, in soft denial of his daughter's enthusiasm for the clinical, which had momentarily overcome her more sympathetic nature. He touched his wife's hand as he got up from the table. What was done was done. As he passed his daughter he gave her a peck on the cheek before saying, "And please, not a word of this at church. The family doesn't even know yet." He paused just long enough for Grace to look him in the eye and know it was an order, then he hurried off.

———•———

The sky was low and drab. The air was heavy with mist and dead still, which made it feel warmer than it really was. Baxter stopped at the corner of Sackville and Brunswick. In front of him, Sackville Street ran downhill, through the heart of the upper streets, and their mix of leaning wood frames and sturdy new brick, all the way to the harbour. There wasn't a soul in sight. He looked left. From his side of Brunswick Street, the slope of Citadel Hill rose up to the granite walls of the city's fortress. It looked back in grave silence, adding an eeriness to the morning. Along the east side of Brunswick he could see people moving past the Salvation Army, and farther down, out front of the fire engine house. They walked slowly with open coats, their voices lost in the mist. Before he crossed Brunswick he bent down and picked up a small stick. He tapped it against his thigh as he continued down Sackville Street, tapping in time with his right foot like a regimental sergeant major on parade. He focused on the rhythm, on the facts of the case thus far, and tried to stop thinking about his wife and daughter. Left…tap—Victor Mosher was dead, stabbed wearing his birthday suit, so it seemed. Left…tap—somebody put his clothes back on and threw him in the harbour. Left…tap—Ellen Reardon found Victor and got a bed for her trouble before the tide could drag him out to sea. So far there were no other witnesses, no obvious motive, and he had no idea who might have done it or where it had happened. An open and shut case if there ever was one, he said to himself.

Baxter passed Argyle, then crossed Barrington Street and stopped at the corner. He looked to his left toward the Grand Parade. He was glad to be too far away. He might see himself coming down the front steps. He hadn't had enough sleep. Squire had better be inside going through Victor's office. He rubbed his eyes and walked on, still keeping time with the stick. Ellen was likely still sound asleep. She wouldn't remember it, but she had met Victor at least once before, if met was the right word. It had happened a few years ago in front of Victor's construction business. Baxter couldn't remember if he had heard the story from Victor, or someone else.

Victor had learned masonry and building from his father. When the time came, he began teaching his sons. Victor and his oldest boy, Michael, were gathering tools for a job. Michael had come out first. Ellen was passed out drunk on the doorstep. There was a puddle of vomit not far from her head. Her dress was hiked up around her waist. She had wet herself. Not sure what to do, the boy had yelled for his father.

By then Victor had already been in politics long enough to know half the people in the city. Everyone knew Ellen. Victor had had his own way of seeing things, that was true. As the story went, he had spoken to Ellen as if she were upright and proper as a pin. "Ah, good morning, Ellen, bit of a rough night?" She had farted in her sleep. Victor had sent his son on ahead with money and instructions for Thomas Marshal, a local restaurant owner, to feed Ellen if she showed up. If there was any trouble, they would be working close by.

Victor had pulled Ellen's dress down and folded one of her arms into a headrest. She had groaned a bit. Her eyes had remained closed. He had found an egg-sized rock and set it at the tip of Ellen's nose. He had put a note under it: "Breakfast at Marshal's, paid in full." Victor's heart had been in the right place. At the same time, Baxter could see Ellen trading the note and having some hair of the dog for breakfast.

Baxter turned left off Sackville onto Hollis Street. The history of Europe hung in tapestries from castle walls; the history of the upper streets was preserved in stories like the one he had just recalled. Over the next few days such stories would be the trump cards of every conversation. All of them ending with the same question: who would kill a man like Victor Mosher? Baxter had arrived at the doctor's front door. He tossed his stick into the street and knocked.

"Good morning, Doctor."

"Right on time, Chief Inspector, please come in. Can I offer you anything?" The doctor was wearing the same clothes. The white coat still looked fresh, but the doctor was a bit rumpled. His hair had broken free of its pomade and become a whisk broom. His glasses were smudged and hanging low and crooked.

"I've had breakfast, thank you," he replied as he followed the doctor down the front hall. "With enough tea to make it seem like I had more sleep, at least for now. Will your final report say anything more than what we knew last night?"

As he came off the last step into the downstairs examination room and looked round the doctor, Baxter could see Victor was still lying on the table. The blood-spotted sheet that now covered him suggested Victor had been opened and closed while Baxter was away. He had no urge to lift a corner and make sure. The doctor picked up a sheaf of papers from the second table and began looking through them as he spoke. Baxter listened and tried not to notice the smell that had come to him now that his other senses were a little less overwhelmed by his power of sight.

"Victor was a little heavy, but otherwise he was fit and strong. None of his major organs showed any signs of disease. He had no deformities or missing limbs." The doctor glanced up to be sure he was being followed, then continued. "There was a recent injury to his right wrist. No bones were broken. He was only forty-five years old. As far as I can tell Mr. Mosher was in good health."

Baxter took off his coat and hung it over one arm. "Except for the hole in his side." His voice was matter of fact more than sarcastic.

Still the doctor raised his eyebrows as he peered over his spectacles. "Yes, Inspector, he was stabbed. Probably with a very sharp knife, it was not a jagged wound." He took a moment to shuffle his papers, his lips moving in silence as he struggled with his own handwriting. Baxter noticed the doctor's hands were shaking a little. There was still some dried blood under his fingernails. "His liver was cut. There was some internal bleeding. Judging by the condition of the body, by that I mean the presence of rigor mortis, I would say Victor died sometime Friday night or Saturday morning."

"After someone stabbed him." Baxter had begun to pace the length of Victor's table. The smell followed him.

"I agree with you there, Inspector. Victor died after he was stabbed. But I don't think he died *because* he was stabbed." The doctor remained in one spot on his side of Victor. He didn't seem bothered by the air in the room.

"What…that doesn't make any sense. You said he was stabbed in the liver, he had internal bleeding." Baxter stopped pacing and waited, expecting the doctor to correct himself.

"Internal bleeding, yes. The kind of massive internal bleeding that would cause death almost immediately, no."

"So how did he die then?" Baxter shot back as he turned on a heel and resumed pacing.

"Well, it's difficult to say, Inspector. I am a man of science. Only God knows for sure what happened."

"I'm sure he does. I am also sure God can speak through you. So use the intelligence he gave you and tell me what you think happened." Now the doctor was pacing.

"This is only speculation you understand."

"Doctor, please."

"I think being stabbed threw Victor into shock and unconsciousness. He lost a lot of blood. His pulse would have been almost undetectable, his breathing very shallow. He would have appeared to be dead."

"So whoever stabbed him left him for dead and then he bled to death and then the body was thrown in the harbour."

"Almost."

"Almost? What do you mean almost?" Both men had come to a halt directly across from one another, either side of Victor's chest.

"I think Victor was still breathing when he was thrown in the harbour. I don't think Victor bled to death, I think he drowned." Baxter looked down at the stained white contours that could only be a body. The wild bulging eyes, the final opening of the mouth were too easy to imagine. He was glad the features of Victor's face were made smooth and serene by the sheet. Baxter let out a sigh of sorrow and relief.

"Can you prove that?"

"Beyond any doubt, no." The doctor shook his head, perhaps clearing his own imagination as much as answering the question.

"I thought you were a man of science." Baxter wasn't sure what he wanted from the doctor, conclusive evidence or room to believe that Victor's last moments had been less horrific. He started to pace again. Now it wasn't the smell that followed him. It was the image of Victor's face under water.

"And I thought you were a policeman. Look, something picked out one of Victor's eyes. If he had been in the water a long time he would have been eaten up far worse than that. His body was also in rigor mortis, which again suggests he was not dead or in the water too long. Yet there were tiny bits of algae and seaweed deep in his lungs. That would happen eventually, but not immediately unless…"

"Unless he breathed them in." Baxter saw Victor's mouth opening. He turned quickly as if he could move away from the image in his head.

"Yes. There were also signs of pulmonary oedema. Did Victor have a doctor?"

"I don't know." Baxter wasn't sure what a pulmonary oedema was either. He had heard the term before, unfortunately the meaning hadn't stuck.

"If he did, you can check to see if he had any trouble with his heart or lungs. His body shows no signs of chronic illness. So how does a healthy man suffer from pulmonary oedema? Most likely by drowning." The doctor had laid his papers down. His arms were at his sides, fingertips just reaching the bottom of his coat pockets. He could have been a wax figure except for the eyes. He followed Baxter with his eyes.

"What about the knife wound?" Could that cause pulmonary oedema? Baxter wondered.

"The knife did no damage to Victor's lungs. Still, without medical treatment, the injury would have been fatal. He may have died even if he had been taken to hospital. But we'll never know."

"Because someone threw him in the harbour instead, where it appears he drowned before he could finish bleeding to death." Victor had been a good negotiator, Baxter thought to himself as he put his coat back on. In the end it didn't matter, only a miracle could have saved him.

"It's your job to draw conclusions, Chief Inspector. And by the way, the knife struck a rib. The hand of the killer may have slid forward and been cut. The guilty party may be wearing a bandage just like that one." The doctor kept his hands still and pointed with a nod of his head.

Baxter looked down at his left hand and the dressing around the base of its index finger. The knuckle was still brown from the iodine. He quickly put it in a coat pocket. "Get your report over to my office as soon as it's ready."

"You're welcome, Chief Inspector," the doctor called up the stairs. He didn't get an answer.

———•———

B axter checked his watch as he left the doctor's house. Twenty minutes to ten. He was glad to be out in the fresh air. He took a whiff of his coat sleeve and nearly gagged. Victor's home was at 102 Hollis Street, a minute away in the middle of the next block. Future editions of the Halifax directory would list that address under Catherine Mosher, widow of Victor. It was bad enough he had to be the one to tell Catherine she was now alone. He couldn't do it with the stink of her husband's corpse on his clothes. He headed south in the opposite direction.

Earlier in his career he had often been the bearer of bad news. Usually it had to do with husbands or sons being in jail for drunkenness or causing a disturbance. In his second year on the force a man went missing. They found him on the outskirts of the city, near Point Pleasant Battery. Baxter had imagined a scene with long waning shadows, a low sun in the west blinking through the treetops. He watched the man gasp for breath against the dusk and claustrophobia of the narrow upper streets. Tumbledown buildings grey from ash and coal smoke coming at him sidelong down the hill in an avalanche of futility and rage. Had he felt freedom growing within his heart and stride, having decided to leave the shabbiness and small ways of Halifax behind? Most men made their escape aboard ship or on a train. A few took the rope. Baxter had often wondered how long that man had stood on the rock below the tree, looking out over the water to the horizon, to a future he could not see. Baxter had been sent to tell the wife. He had made small talk, more for his benefit than hers. After a few minutes she let him off the hook and asked where they found her husband's body. She said he had always been a coward. Over the years there were other suicides, only one or two murders. In those moments he found himself unable to sit close, gently hold hands and speak in comforting tones, to be with the living and not the dead. He would have made a lousy priest.

There were church bells in the air, and fancy bonnets and top hats and children with clean faces moving along the sidewalk. Baxter nodded to a few men he recognized, suddenly conscious of his bare head. At the corner of Morris he turned toward the harbour, away from the beaten path. If there were any freshening breezes to be had, they would be found along the docks and warehouses of the waterfront. He stepped off the sidewalk and into the street. Every few steps he collected another small stone. He had not intended to end up on Mitchell's Wharf. He had zigzagged his way through a series of buildings, grateful for the smells of salt, tar, and seaweed.

The church bells had given way to seagulls. He was surprised when he realized where he was. He looked in all directions, a killer returning to the scene of the crime. He smiled at the irony. Well, what difference did it make where he bided his time, rehearsed his lines, and waited for the smells of the doctor's basement to leave his clothes? He walked to the end of the wharf, but he avoided looking down to where Victor's body had been found. He didn't need any more images in his head. He looked off toward George's Island and the mouth of the harbour. His hands were fidgety so he hid them in his coat pockets. He played with the stones, a few in each hand. They were too small to be headstones. Milestones maybe? As he turned them over, feeling their smoothness and sharp edges, the stones began to feel like moments of a life. What had Victor's moments been? Getting married? Having children? Getting into office? Or were there other things more important to him, hidden things, passionate things, ruinous things, things that might now help explain? How many stones did it take to mark a full life, a life remembered? He thought of all the headstones in the old burying ground, and the cemetery at Camp Hill; some large, some small, some ornate, some plain. What would they look like if they were built of milestones? Whose marker would be larger then? He placed all the stones in one hand, then covered them with the other. He shook them gently. He imagined if he could do it long enough the stones would break up, become small and more musical like the beans in a maraca. Victor's bones would eventually break up in the ground. What music would they play? What songs would be sung of him? How would Baxter's own life be remembered?

He opened his hands. He selected a stone and threw it as far as he could. It blinked in and out of view through the mist, eventually coming to the end of its arc and plopping into the still, flat water, its travels continuing below. He chose another stone and threw it after the first. Then a third and a fourth. Birthdays, graduations, anniversaries, mountains climbed, lions tamed, prizes won, plop, plop, plop. He stood for a moment after the ripples of the last stone had run out, staring at the water that showed no signs of having ever been disturbed. Overhead a gull squawked. The church bells started calling out again from the streets behind him. He took another whiff of his sleeve. It was time.

"Good morning, Catherine." Baxter was standing at the front door, hands behind his back, a forced smile on his face. He had practically run back from the wharf. It was a struggle to speak. He wasn't sure if he was a little winded or just at a loss for words. His face was flushed, he hoped the colour would help hide the pallor of bad news until he could make himself ready to deliver it.

"Mr. Baxter. I'm surprised to see you here on a Sunday morning. Not that it isn't a pleasure, please come in."

"Thank you." Baxter had been here a few times before. He often felt awkward at social occasions. Somehow he always ended up in a circle of High Anglicans unable to see how close they were to being Catholic. They would shudder at the horrors of Popery, pretending they didn't know he wasn't one of them. It was worse when the Chief was in attendance. Guests sidled up to him to trade stories and laugh. They shied away from Baxter as if they feared arrest or the menace of an evil twin. He felt worst for Jane who often got left out in the cold for standing by him. Though never here. Catherine took the starch out of a dressy affair. She could put anyone at ease, even a chief inspector and his wife. Baxter followed Catherine out of the foyer and into the front parlour. He could recall how it felt to be here. He was less able to remember what it actually looked like. There were so many things in the room it was hard to know where to look, yet the place was spotless. Dust was chased and persecuted worse than the Catholics from Northern Ireland where Catherine came from. The wallpaper was an elegant light green with small white and pink roses, though much of it was hidden behind ornate frames; family portraits, landscapes, and scenes from European cities. He could imagine her here in the first hour of every day, tea cup in hand, chatting with old friends from cities far away. Looking down from the walls he realized there were far more books than pictures. The two large oak cases were full to the faces of their glass doors. More were piled in corners and on tables here and there. They seemed to be reproducing themselves, slowly colonizing the house. He caught glimpses of authors and titles, Locke, Chaucer, *A Tale of Two Cities*. He remembered Catherine mentioning a beautifully bound first edition of *Grimm's Fairy Tales*. Victor had given it to Catherine not long after they were married.

An archway led out of the parlour into another room which led to a large drawing room at the back of the house. It was really more of an office. More pictures and books, a fossilized mammoth's tooth, and the skull of some rare beast. There were dried flowers and stuffed birds and animals looking very much alive, watching from the tall grass, waiting for the slow and careless to make easy meals of themselves. A working model steam engine served as a centrepiece for a marble-topped buffet table. At a gathering one New Year's Eve he had watched Victor ignite the boiler and blow the whistle to ring in the new year.

He had heard Catherine describe her home. She seemed to see it as a working man's Monticello, though she would never suggest comparisons to that home in Virginia or the man who owned it. She was equally careful to avoid saying what anything cost. When she hosted meetings for the variety of clubs and associations she belonged to or one of her husband's political gatherings she would tell the story behind this or that. What she paid for it remained a secret. Her home was a museum without being stuffy. It didn't say, "Mind your hands." It seemed to be in motion like a sawmill or a washing machine. Baxter had always left with a vague feeling of accomplishment, even though he had done nothing more than sit and have tea.

"I suppose you are here to see Victor. I'm afraid he isn't back yet. He's down in Windsor visiting with his brother. I expect him back this afternoon." Catherine was not a very tall woman. The busy room with its high ceilings made her seem even smaller, like a delicate figurine that belonged on a mantelpiece. Baxter swallowed hard.

"I see. When did he leave?"

"Oh he left on Friday after he cleared his desk. To tell you the truth he ducked out a bit early before anyone could catch him with something last minute."

"You mean his council office…not his business office?" He was beginning to feel hot and wanted to take off his coat. He wanted to and he didn't.

"That's right." Catherine wasn't young anymore, but her round face was still smooth and smiled easily. Baxter was a few years older, with a more drawn-out face that was much harder for the wear. He knew this day would show on him. He could almost feel the lines deepening.

"I suppose he came home to pack a few things before he left."

"Well, no…when Victor's leaving like that in the middle of the day he takes a bag with him in the morning."

"I see. He hires a coach?" Baxter shifted his weight slowly from one foot to the other.

"Yes." Catherine was used to hosting and to answering questions. She continued on at ease, her voice as light and welcoming as a hotel clerk.

"So what time did he leave on Friday morning?" He didn't like what he was doing, the weakness behind it. He also knew that by the time he was able to get where he was going, Catherine would be in pieces. Better to get what he could before he broke her with the bad news.

"He went in a little early, around seven thirty, I believe, just so he didn't feel quite so guilty. You know Victor." She raised her arms in mock hopelessness and love for her husband.

"And you have not heard from him, he didn't send a telegram to let you know he arrived at…I'm sorry I can't remember his brother's name." Maybe the colour had finally faded from his face and his own sorrow was showing. Maybe her curiosity had finally gotten the better of her stately manners.

"Carmine…No, no telegrams from anyone. Mr. Baxter, is something the matter?" She smiled after the question but the ease had gone out of it.

"Catherine, I have something to tell you." He heard his voice betray him, felt his face give way.

"What's wrong?"

"Are your children at home?"

"Why?….Yes, the boys are here. Mary has run off to Sunday school." Now Catherine's voice cracked. Her eyes blinked trying to stay clear.

"Catherine…Maybe you should get the boys."

"Is it Victor?"

"The boys?"

"Just tell me what's going on." Baxter pointed to a short sofa in the next room. Catherine hurried to it and sat waiting for him. She held her face up like a hopeful sunflower, but she couldn't keep from wringing her hands, and one eye had overflowed. She wiped it quickly.

He couldn't bring himself to sit. "I am very sorry to have to tell you this, Catherine…Victor is dead."

As Squire came along Argyle Street toward City Hall, the congregation of Saint Paul's was gathering out front. The well-to-do of the city had come out of hibernation. They had come up from the grand homes where manicured lawns held hands and ran down to the shoreline along the northwest arm of the harbour. As comfortable as those places were, a mild day in late October was not to be missed. The crowd was large and growing. A few more covered carriages with their well-dressed drivers were waiting in line along Barrington Street as the last of the early arrivals passed back through the only gate into the Grand Parade. The young policeman trudged up the steps of City Hall with his head down and hands deep in the pockets of his greatcoat as if it were a much colder day. Behind him the first carriage in the line made its way inside. The curtain was pulled back for a moment by the ornate silver handle of a walking stick. Likely the passenger was looking for friends among the circles of faces chatting about the coming wedding season, and which shipping lines provided the best service during passage to Europe.

Squire had never been upstairs. He took the corridor to the left and had to double back. The bolt moved smoothly and came to rest with a heavy click. Victor's office had recently been redone. He was greeted by the oily smell of fresh paint and varnish. The desk was large, made of oak, he guessed. It matched the chair and the wainscoting, tight grain with a light finish to enhance the natural colour of the wood. There was more hardwood on the floor, a bit darker with a large, rich-looking rug. It was all drawn together nicely by the cream coloured walls. There should have been some well-placed pictures and mementos to fill the air with personality and stories. There should have been an order, a purposeful neatness, maintained by the workings of a logical professional mind and a cleaning lady's weekly dusting. Order could have provided some comfort against the disturbing images following Squire from the wharf and the doctor's basement, given him some strength in the face of a murder case he was somehow in the middle of with no experience and too little sleep. Instead there was chaos. The desk was covered in open books, single pages from various papers with items circled, folders, notes on scraps of paper. Half cups of tea sat on top of things at precarious angles. Underneath the paint smell, he was now getting a whiff of stale cigar from the stumps in a large brown glass ashtray, partially covered by a shoebox filled with jars of preserves. A half-eaten sandwich was drying up beside that. The floor was strewn with more boxes, shoes kicked off in different directions. A bag of tools sat in one corner, some work clothes draped over a small chair beside it. A large map of the city was rolled out like a second rug, held at the corners by a brick, a work boot that didn't seem to have a mate, a well-used copy of the Halifax directory, and a pack of playing cards.

Squire stood just inside the door, halted as if he had been slapped. His mouth had gone dry and he was vaguely aware that his breathing had become rapid. Kenny was the youngest and a surprise, a pleasant one, finally a son. By the time he was ten, his two sisters were married and gone. His father was a kind man. He loved his son and Kenny trailed behind his father, his puppy tail wagging a blur. Then one day things began to change. It was funny at first. His father would set dishes in the wrong cupboard, or forget where he'd put things, or need to be reminded it was time to change his shirt. Next he became bothered. Why is that dog barking? Does the sun have to be so bright? Why are you staring at me?

Kenny always helped with the firewood. At twelve he was strong enough to take a turn with the axe, split halves into quarters. He thrilled with the feeling of power it gave him. With one swing he was a fearless knight in battle chopping down the enemies of the realm. With the next he was a brave pioneer conquering the forest. They had not cut wood for a few days. Kenny was up in his room when he heard the crack of the first log. He ran through the kitchen door out into the yard. It was mid-morning and the sun was hot. Horseflies buzzed in circles. The corn was getting tall. You could just see the roof of a neighbour's house above the tassels, shimmering in the heat. His father had taken off his shirt and tied it about his head. The axe kept coming round with train wheel speed, as if his father were in a contest or a fight for his life, crack, crack, crack. By the time the pieces of one stick hit the ground, he had the next one set up. When Kenny asked his father if he was all right, he said he was fine, but he sounded like a dog straining against a rope. Then Kenny noticed the dark spot on his father's chest. It was cow manure. That's why there were so many flies. When his father caught him staring he said the smell was helping. "With what?" the boy asked. Squire remembered being bewildered at that point. He also remembered he was not yet afraid of his father.

His father stopped. He held the axe handle in both hands across his chest. The sweat was beginning to streak the manure. He was breathing hard. As he struggled for air he said the smell of the manure was helping to clear his head. His father was lean from a life of hard work. As he squeezed the handle of the axe the muscles in his arms and shoulders pulled like piano strings. His father looked up suddenly as if someone had called his name. Kenny thought maybe his mother was coming up behind. He turned to see. No one was there.

When his father told him to hold the log that was standing on the block, perfectly still all by itself, Kenny felt his bladder let go just a little. He reminded himself that he loved his father. He moved over and reached out gingerly to steady the log with one shaky finger. His father said the log could not be trusted, he needed to hold it down with both hands on top. Kenny pulled away at the last second. He stood still with his head down, shaking. His father put up another log and told Kenny to hold it still. His father's voice was calm and reassuring, as if the axe he was holding was really a tablespoon of castor oil. For the first time in his life Kenny disobeyed. When his father started screaming, Kenny went into mild shock and his bladder let go completely. Now his mother did come.

Things got worse after that. His father stopped bathing. His hair grew wild and matted. Sometimes he would shave away a part of his beard and for a day or two at least there was one clean spot on his body. Somehow through his mania he continued to run the farm. He stopped coming in the house unless he was hungry. Kenny tried to help, he collected eggs, cleaned troughs, tended crops, and mended fences. He stayed clear of the wood pile. The barn mirrored the mind and health of his father. Once it had been a tidy factory. Squire remembered standing in the doorway the day after his father was taken away. The barn looked like a doll house that had been shaken by an angry child. But it was his mind his father had lost, not his temper. His eyes rolled wildly as they dragged him away to look for it. Sometimes in school he would hear the word whispered behind him. Of course no one in his family could bring themselves to say asylum, they preferred hospital.

Squire had come out of the corner and moved to the centre of the room. But he was still seeing the chaos of the barn, wondering where to begin, when Victor's office girl stepped through the doorway. She let out a small scream when she saw him and the sound broke his trance.

"I'm sorry." His voice was thick. He cleared the barn dust from his throat. "I didn't mean to frighten you."

The girl was about his age, and looked vaguely familiar. She was short, with medium-length dark hair in a neat bun. Her face was round and plump like the rest of her, and the fullness of her body, its curves, its ripeness, were inviting, even from under her coat. The small mouth and full lips imagined a perfect kiss on a baby's forehead. Most likely she lived in the upper streets. Surely they had passed in the neighbourhood or in the halls of the building they both worked in. "When I saw the door open I thought Mr. Mosher had come back early. He's not here is he?"

"No."

"Well that's a relief. I don't mean it like that. I like Mr. Mosher very much. It's that I promised to have something done for first thing Monday. Then when he left early on Friday, I did too. He didn't say I couldn't. I promised to meet some friends after work. I thought it would be nice not to have to rush, pamper myself a little. I didn't think there would be anyone here this morning. What are you doing here?"

He didn't know if he should tell her. At the same time he didn't see how he could avoid it. He came forward a step. He reached for her arm, thinking to steady her for the blow. She tilted back just a little so he let his hand fall back to his side. He took a breath to steady himself. Better to be quick than linger. "I'm afraid I have some bad news. Mr. Mosher is dead."

He had never seen a woman faint. She didn't fall so much as she melted into the rug. Her knees hit, then she keeled over gently on her side. He wasn't sure how long he stood over her, staring down at her slightly parted lips, flushed cheeks, and bosom rising and falling tenderly as a sleeping kitten. Should he go for a doctor? Maybe it wasn't wise to leave her. He didn't know. He had become noticeably aroused, which wasn't helping him to think. It seemed like a very long time before he was able to compose himself enough to kneel and pat her hand. He tried not to notice how soft and warm and needful it felt. She responded to his touch and once again he found it difficult to think.

"What happened?" She pushed herself up a little and stared at him as if she had never seen him.

"You had a spell." She stared for another moment then she let out a small cry and clamped a hand over her mouth. He took hold of her other elbow and helped her up. Then he took a step away and folded his arms hoping to look official and concerned, hoping more that this would close the front of his coat. "I am sorry I had to be the one to break the news. I'm a policeman. We're looking into what happened. I take it you're his office girl."

"Yes. Elizabeth Murray."

"Is that Miss or Mrs.?"

"Miss."

"Well, happy to meet you, Miss Murray."

She paused and raised her eyebrows at him, then went back to digging in a small handbag.

"Well, not happy it's…My name is Squire…Kenneth…Kenny." He jammed his hands in his coat pockets and rocked forward on his toes, then settled back on his heels and scratched his head.

"Please excuse me for a moment, Kenny." The digging had produced a hanky. She blew into it with a loud honk. She shrugged at him as she finished wiping, then asked, "Did Victor have a heart attack?"

"Was he under a lot of pressure lately?" Squire looked around the office as he asked the question. He had moved over to the desk. But he had not touched anything, afraid the mess would collapse like a card tower.

"I started working for Mr. Mosher two years ago. His office was always a little messy. Lately is been more of a disaster." Elizabeth had moved around to the other side of the desk and begun poking around. Then she stopped and looked up at Squire. "I was looking for his notes on the tramway proposal. I promised I would have them organized and typed up for tomorrow morning. I guess it doesn't matter now." She took out the hanky again and walked over to the window behind the desk. She stared out past the dewdrops on the glass into the nothingness of the grey sky.

"So Mr. Mosher was acting differently over the past few weeks?"

"He was still very nice to me. He kept working hard, same as always. But he stopped putting things away or cleaning up, as you can see. I tried to pick up. He shooed me away. He was forgetting things, appointments, names. He never forgot things before. Sometimes I would find him here at the window when he was supposed to be in a meeting." She blew her nose again.

"Did you ask him about any of it?"

She looked away from the window for just a moment. Still she did not look at him. She shook her head. Wiping at her eyes, she said, "He never stopped being real busy. I didn't know what to ask, and it wasn't really my place."

"Was anyone new or strange coming to see him?" Squire was still at the desk, he had discovered that the preserves in the shoebox were peach and the cigars in the ashtray were Cuban. But he kept his hands in his pockets.

"Not that I know of."

"Do you know anything about his private business, or his home life? Did you hear anything? Maybe he said something?"

"Not to me." She turned now and did look at him. Coming away from the window, back toward the desk, she asked, "What are you looking for? I thought you said Mr. Mosher had a heart attack."

"No, that was your idea." He stepped back from the desk just a little, though he didn't look away.

"Are you going to tell me what happened?" She crossed her arms and waited, the hanky dangling from one hand.

"We don't know yet, other than he was murdered. I was sent here this morning to search for clues. But to be honest I have no idea what to look for and in this mess...well..." He took one hand out of his coat and waved toward the desk and the general upside-down state of affairs.

"Do you see a red book anywhere, softcover, leather? It will have all sorts of notes and papers stuffed between the pages. You would never know it was his appointment book. He guarded it like a diary. He would never let me write things in it for him." She took the half empty tea cups and set them out of the way on a chair, then began picking more things off the desk, forming them into piles.

"I don't see it anywhere." Squire had begun to help, more confident with an example to follow.

"It wasn't with him when..."

Seeing the look on her face, Squire saved her from having to finish the thought and shook his head. Then he asked, "Did you look in the desk?"

She nodded, then added, "But, I couldn't look in the centre drawer, it's locked."

He drew the ring of keys from his pants pocket. It took a few tries to find that the right key was there. He slid the drawer open. There were two folders and a book on top. "Is that it?"

"Uh-huh."

He withdrew it carefully. It was just as Elizabeth had described, crammed full. He knew he needed to take it. He was equally certain Baxter would want the first look. "Do you know what's in those folders?"

"No. Those are white. All the office file folders are brown with labels…see." She pointed at various piles as she spoke. "I keep them in a cabinet by my desk." She nodded toward the door.

Squire looked around. There was a small attaché leaning against the side of the desk. It was empty. He stuffed in the book and the folders. "What was it you said you came in to work on this morning?"

"Notes on the proposal to expand the city tramway," she said, continuing to sort folders and books and newspapers into piles.

"Expand it how?" Squire asked, holding the attaché in one hand and handing her things to keep piling.

"Don't you read the papers?"

"Not very often."

"More lines north and west. Some people are all for it, say it would be good for the city. Others say it costs too much and we don't need it."

"What side was Councilman Mosher on?"

Elizabeth stopped piling and put her hands on her hips and squared her shoulders. Caught up in the work of straightening out the place and looking for evidence Squire had not been looking at her. Now he had to be careful to look her in the eye. "Well, that's a funny thing. At first he was strongly against the idea. Then a couple of weeks ago he changed his mind, decided to support the proposal. He was drawing up an argument to bring to Council, that's what the notes were for."

"Are they here?"

"No, here." She handed them over and taking them he touched her hand. He couldn't discern if she had any reaction.

"Did anyone else know Victor had changed his mind?"

"I don't think so, he asked me not to discuss it."

"Elizabeth, can you think of anything else that might be important, or anyone who might want to hurt your boss—an angry constituent, someone he had bad business dealings with, anyone at all."

"No, I never met anyone that had a bad word to say about him. He was a saint." She looked like she might cry again. Her eyes were full, but they didn't spill over.

"All right then. I have orders to close up this office and seal it off. Do you have a key?"

"Yes."

"I need you to give it to me. Does anyone else have a key?"

"I don't think so."

Elizabeth dug in her bag for the key while Squire found a pen and paper and made up the sign Baxter wanted on the door. "I don't know what to do with myself. I thought I would be here much of the day." She held out the key as if she had been denied communion and was giving back the sacrament.

"Miss Murray, I had better take your address. Just in case I need to get in touch. The chief inspector is in charge of this case, he may have more questions."

"I live at 104 Grafton Street, room three. Don't you need to write that down too?" she asked, nodding at the sign Squire had tacked to the door.

"No, I won't forget."

———•———

Squire walked Miss Elizabeth Murray downstairs to the building's front door and held it for her. He watched her move across the Grand Parade, then up the steps onto Argyle Street. She walked with her head down, in no particular hurry. Next to the loss of the wife and family which neither of them had ever met, her loss was minor, though Squire could see it didn't feel that way to Elizabeth. He wondered how long the list of affected persons would be. What would the murder of Victor Mosher end up meaning to him?

After his father got sick, he and his mother had run the farm. He had started school late that fall, after the harvest, but he was determined to keep up his studies. He was a long time finishing. The man they took away from his house that day was moved from the hospital to a special ward at the county poorhouse. Kenny visited, hoping his father would return. He only went farther away. Squire shook hands with a stranger before leaving for Halifax on the train. There was no one to blame, that was the worst of it. At times he had looked for excuses, tried to pick fights at school or around town. It never came to much. Everyone felt too sorry for him and his family. Maybe Victor's family would feel better if they had someone to blame.

When Squire pushed open the door to the police station, Mackay was back behind the front counter. Squire assumed Ellen was still downstairs. "What are you doing back here? You're not on duty this morning." Mackay double-checked a roster sheet he had pulled from somewhere under the counter.

"The chief inspector has me checking on some things. Is he in yet?"

"Haven't seen him. What you got there, stuff from Mosher's office?" Squire couldn't hide his mix of surprise and fear. Then he looked over at the door that led downstairs. "That's right, Ellen and I had a little talk, she opened right up to me." Squire stepped closer to the counter, measuring the distance to Mackay. He forced the sergeant to look him in the eye.

Mackay held his ground and then Squire got a whiff. Of course Mackay wouldn't enter Ellen's cell, she was unafraid of the likes of him. And she would tell him nothing unless he did something for her and there could only be one thing. Squire stepped back from the counter.

"The chief inspector will be in a little later," he said through a wry smile. "No doubt he'll want to speak to Ellen one more time. Do you suppose she'll say who's been serving her drinks?" He glanced at the clock on the wall. Five past ten. Baxter would have finished with the doctor, he must still be with Victor's wife. Squire walked backwards to the door, enjoying the look on Mackay's face. He pushed though and headed down the hall. He would go to Victor's business office then come back.

———•———

This time when Baxter stepped out onto Hollis Street, his clothes didn't stink of death, but sorrow had him by the heart and throat. Catherine had eventually called the boys to her side. The three of them had huddled on the small sofa in quiet mourning. The stuffed birds and animals seemed to turn away, giving them room to grieve. Learning it was murder added anger to feelings of shock and loss. Waiting for the daughter was agony. Breaking the news to her, the rest of the family would relive their own horror from the start. Baxter could not bear witness. He mumbled his condolences and slipped out quietly. He knew his reprieve would be short. Once the initial wave of grief had passed through the family, their cries for justice would begin. They would turn to the chief of police, who would look to him. They could mourn quietly at home, he would have to keep right on working through his pain. Maybe he was better off.

As uncomfortable as it was, he had to do it. As he walked, he replayed the scenes while they were fresh and he could see them clearly. He paid particular attention to things not said. No one offered a theory of the crime, a common guilty urge. No one volunteered an alibi, a further sign of guilt he was relieved not to have seen. The inability to breathe between sobs, the tears, the snot, the turning inside-out with no attention paid whatsoever to his reaction. These people were to be pitied, not investigated. But what was it Catherine had said about her husband? "He's down in Windsor visiting with his brother. I expect him back this afternoon." While Catherine didn't know Victor had stayed in the city, his brother surely did. Baxter reached around for his watch. It was going on ten thirty. The North Street Station was twenty minutes away. He picked up his stride.

———•———

By the time Baxter walked into his office it was quarter to one. His morning tea had worn off. He was heavy and slow from lack of sleep and the strain of bearing bad news. And he was famished. Squire was waiting for him, flaked out in the same chair Baxter had found him in less than twelve hours ago. It felt much longer. Squire had taken off his greatcoat and draped it over himself like a blanket. He's getting better at this, Baxter thought to himself and then was even more envious of the other man's rest. There was the shape of something other than his folded arms under Squire's coat. Baxter was curious and hopeful that the young policeman might have found some useful information. He reached down and gave Squire's shoulder a good shake. "Let's see what you've come up with," he said. His voice sounded even more tired than he felt.

Squire opened his eyes slowly. He remained still for a few seconds. Baxter slumped into his chair and switched on the desk lamp. Its light was soft and shaded, but seemed harsh to the both of them and their eyes blinked against it. Squire pushed himself up into a sitting position and his coat slid to the floor. He continued to hug Victor's attaché. He let go with one hand to wipe at his eyes and reach for his coat, and heaved himself up. He let the coat drag behind him as he walked a slow unsteady line over to the coat stand by the door. He continued clutching the attaché to his chest with one hand as he scratched, and tucked and hoisted with the other on his way back to his chair. "Now that you're all spruced up, tell me what you've found." Baxter had picked up a pencil and was tapping his desk blotter. He pointed at the small brown case Squire was guarding like his first-born.

"I got this stuff from Victor's office upstairs. It's his appointment book. Elizabeth, that's his office girl, she said he was very private about it. It's stuffed with all sorts of notes and papers. I'm not sure what's in the folders. They were locked in his desk along with the book so I guessed they were important." Squire leaned out of his chair and handed over the attaché. The chief inspector stood to receive it, then began laying the contents on his desk and poking through them. Squire continued on, described the chaos of Victor's office, that it was out of character apparently and that Victor had recently changed his opinion on whether or not the city needed more streetcars. They had found Victor's latest notes on the topic. Squire had put them in the book. His office girl had said that no one strange or threatening had been to see him. That as far as she was concerned, Victor was a saint. She had no idea who would want to hurt him. Squire decided not to embarrass Elizabeth by mentioning her fainting. And there was certainly no need to mention his ogling of an unconscious young woman.

Baxter remained standing behind his desk carefully turning the pages of Victor Mosher's appointment book as he listened to the junior officer. When Squire finished, he studied in silence for a few more moments, then he said, "This office girl, what was her name again?"

"Elizabeth, Elizabeth Murray."

"She has been very helpful."

"Have you found something important?" Squire leaned forward in his chair.

"Is she young?"

"About my age, I would say." Squire was still leaning forward though he no longer looked as if he were expecting congratulations.

"Pretty?"

"Uh…well, I guess some might say so," he said, sitting back, looking at the floor.

"What would you say?" Baxter continued, between the sounds of dry heavy pages turning.

"Yes."

"What do you suppose her boss thought? This pretty young woman… you had her account for her whereabouts since she left work on Friday… yes? Of course you got names of people who could confirm her story? These details are all recorded in your patrolman's log book…yes?" Baxter looking up briefly, at the crown of Squire's head, then went back to his studies.

"I got her address." Squire cleared his throat and finally managed to pick his eyes up off the floor.

"I see…so you planned to do some checking first, then check with her again in case elements of her story didn't match. Such a quick study." Baxter's tone and tactic were apophatic enough to embarrass but not shame, lest the lesson learned be the wrong one. Squire kept his eyes and the thoughts behind them to himself. "I doubt this young lady is cold-blooded enough to kill her boss and carry on with a straight face. Still, you get my point. You're a policeman, you have to be sure. She didn't have any cuts on her hands, did she?" Baxter glanced down at a page of Victor's notes and the bandage on the hand that was holding it.

It was three thirty when Baxter let himself accept that there was no more to be gained at the moment from turning back and forth through Victor's appointment book or papers or the business ledger that was in one of the folders. The thought of finding something important, maybe identifying a suspect to talk to, had kept him going for a while. Now that rush had faded. He was tired, and more hungry than he could ever remember being. Squire was very clearly in the same boat and needed no persuading when Baxter said it was time to eat and collect their thoughts.

"Where are we going?" Squire asked as they dragged themselves up the steps from the Grand Parade onto Argyle Street, the same steps Squire had watched Elizabeth Murray struggle with that morning. Baxter turned south and Squire followed, too tired to repeat the question when Baxter walked on saying nothing. The day had remained grey and still. The city smelled of fog and ash and coal smoke. All the singing birds had gone south. Occasionally a lone seagull drifting low would let out a short squawking burst that ricocheted off the buildings. There were a few people walking, slowly, their thoughts keeping them aloft in the dull soup like a seagull's wings.

As they turned up Sackville Street, Baxter said, "My wife will fix us something. We can eat in the kitchen and talk." Both men kept silent the rest of the way.

Jane was busy in her sewing room. She was pleased to meet the young policeman, despite the terrible circumstances. There was a ham in the oven. It wouldn't be done to the bone for at least another hour, but the edges would be fit. There were some fresh rolls under a tea towel and butter in the pantry. Mind they didn't spoil their supper. "You are welcome of course, Mr. Squire." Jane's smile was genuine, though she didn't get up from her sewing. Watching his wife chat with the young officer, Baxter was soothed by her calm strength. He seldom brought his work home like this. He wanted to keep her from seeing the tawdry and the ugly, bad enough she had to smell it on his clothes sometimes at the end of the day. On the other hand, maybe he should have brought work home more often, instead of wrestling with it alone in his office, away from her. From the doorway, he could see the needle delicately pinched, the pieces of a new frock she would soon be showing off, cut out on the table behind her. She was not hiding in this room trying to stitch up the past. She needed no protection, she was offering it. There was a delicious meal in the making. If he did as she advised, ate some now and not too much, he would regain the strength he needed to finish up with Squire, and still be able to sit with her at the table later. She was surer and stronger than he found it easy to acknowledge, or take advantage of when he most needed to. Was pride keeping him from showing his vulnerability, from being a better husband? Maybe even a better policeman? He really needed to get something in his stomach. He patted Squire on the shoulder and nodded to his wife and held her gaze for just a moment before heading through to the kitchen. She returned a small smile as she pushed the needle through and drew the line of thread up tight.

"Your wife is a good cook," Squire said, blowing on the piece of ham at the end of his fork. They were seated at the small table in the kitchen. Jane had opened the window. The heat of the oven drifted out along with the smell of the ham. It mingled with the smells of other Sunday dinners and the slow plinking of piano practice and screaking strings of budding violinists. As he ate and listened, Squire's mind wandered. It seemed likely that things had their own peculiar way here in this part of the city between the richest and the poorest. More and more the same sounds and smells drifted overhead. More and more the people here smelled and listened mostly to each other; more and more they smelled and sounded alike. More and more the look on their faces became the same. Was it a smugness they might grow out of? Or was it something worse, some sort of degenerative physical condition, an impotence or loss of vision maybe?

"Yes, she is. Think while you eat," Baxter said around his own mouthful of ham, glancing toward the hall.

"Well, we know that from the time Victor's appointment book begins last April up until the end of January his life seems to have been very routine, the same appointments every week, same times."

"And he wrote freely, using complete names and detailed descriptions," Baxter completed the thought.

"He left some interesting notes and comments. Do you suppose councilman Geldart had any idea Victor thought he was a fool? 'His upper storey is unfurnished.' I never heard that before." Squire smiled and shook his head as he buttered a roll.

"Victor was too wise a politician to say such things. I'm surprised he wrote them down," Baxter replied, reaching for a roll of his own.

"Maybe someone saw something he wrote and took offence. Maybe that's why he started using initials and abbreviations from this past February on."

"But as we've said, that would not account for him becoming messy and erratic and taking meetings he never seemed to have had before. I think he was writing that way in case someone looked, not because someone did. He was being cautious because he had a secret. I want to know who he was meeting with, particularly this M.S." He was eating too fast. Baxter put down his fork and sat back, playing with his napkin.

"Any new ideas on the five letters in the folder?" Squire had cleaned his plate and was finishing a second roll. Ruining his supper didn't seem to be a concern.

"They are formal. They look like business, receipts maybe? If that's what they are, there were no matching entries in his business ledger." Baxter eyed the ham left on his plate, then continued playing with his napkin. "And written in Latin. More disguise, keeping secrets."

"Still no idea what '*Latorem extemplo dare spondes*' means?" Squire had his elbows on the table, looking out at the gazebo surrounded by a small sea of dead grass and fallen branches.

"No, but we can find that out without too much trouble. Finding out whose initials are at the bottom of each page, that is the hard part." Baxter picked up his fork and speared a small piece of ham. He chewed it slowly as he laid the fork back down.

"Why do you suppose Victor changed his mind on the tramway?" Squire had given up his study of the backyard and was looking directly at the chief inspector.

"No idea, but it's all connected, the strange behaviour, the secrecy, those letters, changing his tune on the tramway proposal. I'm sure of that."

"If only someone could tell us how."

"I know one person who can tell us some of it at least." Baxter went on to say how he had gone over what had happened with Catherine, the awkwardness at the door, her good manners and then the huddle of tears on the small sofa that looked as if it might collapse under the sadness. "When I asked her where Victor was, Catherine's exact words were, 'He's down in Windsor visiting with his brother. I expect him back this afternoon.'" Baxter reached into his pocket and took out a small piece of paper and passed it across the table.

Squire unfolded it carefully. After reading it twice, he said, "This was sent today. How does a dead man send a telegram?"

"Victor's wife had no idea her husband never left town. His brother Carmine knew it, though, or at least he knew Victor didn't come to see him. And since Catherine didn't get any telegrams wondering where Victor was, I don't think Carmine was expecting him. So when I left Catherine's I went to the North Street Station and sent a telegram to Victor care of his brother. It said I needed to reach Victor immediately on an urgent matter. I waited an hour and that's what came back. 'I'll be back in the city by 4 P.M., Victor.'"

"So Carmine is covering for his brother. He has no idea Victor is dead." The food had done Squire good, he seemed fresh again, excited. Baxter felt better but he could not match the speed of Squire's recuperation.

"It seems that way. The question is, can Carmine tell us why Victor was lying to his wife? What was he doing Friday night? Who was he with?"

"Do you suppose Carmine sent a second telegram to his brother to warn him?"

Baxter nodded in approval of the thinking behind the question. "I thought of that and waited. A couple of telegrams came in from Windsor. Nothing came in for Victor. I'll take the early train to Windsor in the morning. By then Catherine will likely have sent word breaking the bad news. Hopefully Carmine will not bother lying about what he did or try to pretend he has no idea what was going on with his brother. He knows something."

"If you're going to Windsor, should I go in for my regular shift tomorrow?"

Baxter didn't disappoint him. "No. That Friday meal receipt you found in the suit hanging in Victor's business office, where was it from?"

"The Royal Hotel."

"Go there, see if Victor had lunch with someone or a meeting. After that go to the Union Bank, we know Victor did business there. Ask for Mr. Saunders, he's the manager. Have him examine Victor's ledger for irregularities. Have him look at those letters too, see if he can tell us what they mean. While he's working on that go to City Hall, talk to the other councilmen, office girls, and so on. Go easy, be discreet. If anyone seems suspicious or reluctant, don't push at them, wait for me." Baxter watched Squire nod at each instruction like a boxer between rounds. He wasn't sure the young man was listening, but he was sure of his determination and enthusiasm.

"When will you be back?"

"If the trains are on time, I should be back in my office by two in the afternoon. We'll meet there about that time."

Baxter walked Squire to the door. Moving reminded them both that they were still tired, yet the food had helped, one more than the other. They didn't have an eyewitness or an obvious motive. They did have directions to follow. And that was something. "You did some good work today, Mr. Squire. I trust you secured Victor's offices."

"I posted signs. I collected Miss Murray's key and added it to the ring. I boarded up the office on Albemarle."

"Good."

Squire straightened his coat then paused with his hand on the door latch. "Detective, what do you think happened to Victor? Everybody says he was such a good man."

Baxter shook his head. The question would be popular for days. He hoped there was a good answer. For now all he could say was, "It's hard to fight off the world."

"Do you think he may have taken ill? That can happen."

"We have to face up to whatever we find." He watched the young policeman down the steps. As he closed the door he thought of Victor's family. If there was facing up to do, it would be hardest on them.

Baxter found Jane in the kitchen basting the ham. He leaned against the door jamb and watched her work. "Where's our daughter?" he asked, suddenly realizing he had not seen her.

"Up in her room, back at that medical book. She had better not try bringing it to the table."

"You taught her better than that." And we both know what she really needs to be doing is getting out, letting herself be seen as eligible for marriage. This he didn't say.

"It worries me, she's so headstrong, can't imagine where she gets it." Jane looked at him as she closed the oven door. He thought he saw her read his mind, thought he saw agreement in her expression.

"I have to go see the chief. I won't be long, don't start without me." He almost hugged his wife before he left. He hoped she knew he wanted to.

———•———

The chief lived on Queen Street. Not in the deep south end of the city, just closer to it than any other policeman. The house was new and as square as the bricks it was made of. The short steep roof sat on top of the second storey, neat as a bowler hat. It was much the same as other houses on the street, sturdy and proud of its modesty.

Baxter was not completely surprised that the chief had been expecting him. He was responsible to be on top of things. It was the way the chief came by information and what he chose to do or not do with it that sometimes stuck in Baxter's craw. When the time came he and Jane would remain in the wood frame house they had come up in. The sewing room and workshop would have to go, be made over into spaces more suitable for receiving guests. What Catherine had done for Victor, Jane would do for him. He would learn to make small talk, in Catholic circles at least. Maybe even with a few Protestant guests able to accept him for the good work he would do. They had always imagined a home more filled up with life and purpose, and finally it would be. Outside he would be a firm and forthright chief and the city would be better for it. There was a small weight of guilt and shame trailing behind these thoughts, that the death of a man might lift him up. Victor was not a friend, but there was nonetheless a kinship. He had also wanted more for himself and for the city. All day long Baxter had been weighed down by loss, struggling under the weight of a tired sadness. Being here, being reminded of his larger mission, lifted that away; his thoughts were clear.

Martin Tolliver was a big man, as tall as Baxter, but sloppy. Pressed and polished he still had the look of an unmade bed. He had large, coarse

features and a complexion as open and uneven as melting snow. Despite
all that, he was not unpleasant looking. Most people took him for gentle
and easygoing.

They were standing in the large drawing room of the chief's home.
A spattered canvas drop cloth covered the floor in the far corner. The
watercolour in the easel was nearly done. Baxter recognized Saint Paul's.
There was a subtlety in the work, a deftness of touch. He never would
have taken the chief for an artist. Tolliver followed Baxter's gaze. For a
moment he looked as if he were about to say something about it, talk in
a friendly way. Then he looked back as if the painting wasn't there and
Baxter was a stranger.

"Have you gotten anywhere?" The chief ambled over to the sideboard and poured two fingers of bourbon into a short crystal tumbler.
He turned and leaned his weight, ignoring the glassware and bottles as
they clinked in protest. He looked at Baxter over the rim of his glass. He
didn't bother offering him a drink.

"He was stabbed once, here." Baxter touched his side. "We don't know
where it happened yet, but it looks as if someone put his clothes back on
after he was stabbed."

"Uh-huh. What else."

"Catherine thought Victor was in Windsor with his brother. I think
he can help us. I'm going to Windsor in the morning."

"Any business troubles?"

"I'm having his ledger examined and some letters we found. They're
in Latin. Lato something spondes."

"*Latorem extemplo dare spondes.*" The chief turned, and as he refilled his glass said in a voice that was low and matter of fact, without
shock or sadness, "Pay the bearer on demand." He turned back around
and leaned once more, the glassware performed another soft symphony.
The chief sipped and swallowed. Baxter waited. "How much?" the chief
finally asked without looking up, continuing to study the contents of
his glass.

"Five thousand in total." Baxter waited, a feeling of impatience growing along with an idea he was being cheated or held off. He waited for
the chief to help him, to be on his side. He waited for him to tell him

whatever it was he seemed to know about Victor Mosher or this case or both. At the very least the chief could tell him how he happened to know any Latin. Neither of them had any secondary schooling. Baxter knew the ritual responses of Mass, which didn't say anything about IOUs. So how did Tolliver know? What else did he know? Was the chief mocking him with silence? Baxter felt he had a right to know, it was his job to know and the chief's responsibility to tell him.

The chief raised himself up and took a full breath. He started to raise his glass, then set it on the sideboard. Baxter could feel himself being studied, weighed. He remained still, eye to eye. "Cully, tread carefully on this."

He had come out of a sense of duty and respect for the chain of command. He had been met with suspicion and a lack of confidence. Baxter could feel his fingernails digging into the palms of his hands. He tried to unclench his fists and couldn't. His throat was tighter than his fists, which kept him from speaking, which was surely a good thing. "Let's talk tomorrow." The chief patted him on the shoulder as he moved by on his way to opening the front door. Baxter heard the latch and voices from the street coming in on the evening air. Finally he turned. He didn't stomp or accidentally knock anything over. What he couldn't bring himself to do was look the chief in the face as he passed.

It was a pleasant meal. Grace seemed to be able to repeat every word she'd read. He was grateful not to have to talk, and for the balm of her youthful innocence. He asked questions in passing between mouthfuls of ham and scalloped potatoes, then Boston cream pie. Grace went on in detail about rigor mortis and pulmonary oedema. Baxter didn't bother pretending his questions were not work related. After supper he and Jane did the dishes together, excusing their daughter who still wasn't tired of reading.

Jane left him alone afterward. He wandered into his little repair shop. On one of the work tables he had a rocking chair in pieces. He had pulled it out of a snowbank, where it may have been buried all winter. He had made the new runner it needed. He fixed it in a vice and picked up a pencil and carpenter's ruler. Of course the letters were IOUs. Why write them in Latin and lock them away in a drawer if they were simple receipts or bills as he had originally thought? He told himself it would have come to him as soon as he had had some rest. He measured for the holes and marked the spots.

Squire had known. Of course he read Latin. He had graduated from the Pictou Academy. Why did he hold back? What was he up to? Baxter found the auger. He needed to change the bit. And the chief was hiding something, he didn't need to be a detective to know that. The chief didn't seem surprised about the circumstances of Victor's death or that he owed or recently paid off a large amount of debt, secret debt, debt kept off the books. He locked the proper bit in place and began turning the first hole. Was the chief not surprised because he had known of Victor's troubles for some time? Or had he just found out? Did he find out from Squire? Is that how he knew? Had the chief told Squire to hold back information, slow up the investigation? Baxter withdrew the auger and blew at the curly wood shavings. He changed position to begin the second hole.

His stomach was beginning to churn, souring on the ham. He remembered a case from not long ago, a bank robbery. The thief had made his getaway, but was fool enough to return to the city. Some clever work and a bit of luck and Baxter had his man. Then strings were pulled, a deal was made. Most of the money turned up, no more questions asked. The reward that had been offered was no longer available. It wasn't the money Baxter resented, though it would have been a help. He was more aggravated by the injustice of it, that he had got no credit for his work. He blew at the second hole.

It wasn't the first time. These past few years there seemed to be a wall in front of him just as the chief had stonewalled him this evening. Perhaps it was the will of God. He began to work with a chisel, cleaning up the rough edges left by the auger. He hated the wall most for its silence, its failure to explain itself.

He blew into the first hole again, then checked its smoothness with a finger. He would clean up the second hole then try to get some sleep. As always his anger was followed by guilt. He had no right to be angry, to overstep, to want what was not given. The second hole had struck a knot in the wood and was more difficult to clear. He held the runner firm with one hand to keep it steady and with the other dug harder with the chisel. He was chief inspector. His wife was proud of him and loyal. They had been granted one daughter at least and she was bright and strong and would make the most of the life in front of her. He worked the chisel harder still, unable to cut through the end of the knot fouling the hole. And then he was overcome by a second surge of anger. It was not enough. He spoke his blasphemy aloud and he was aghast and ashamed. His hand slipped on the chisel. The first drops of blood shone like tiny red suns on the clean white flesh of the wood, anointing it. Then more spilled on the floor where it was dried up by the sawdust. His thumb was badly cut. He held it tightly. He took his time moving to the kitchen. Hurried steps might draw attention.

Monday

The first train out was at seven. Only forty miles to Windsor, but at least a dozen stops. The first would be at Rockingham, Bedford next. Then the train would change over to the Dominion Atlantic line at Windsor Junction. Then more stops at Beaverbank, Mount Uniacke, and he couldn't remember where all else. It would be at least half past nine by the time he could speak to Carmine. He took a seat in the dining car. The waiter took his time, eventually Baxter ordered tea.

The first lurch of the train clicked his teeth against the rim of the cup. He brushed at his tunic. He would have been more comfortable travelling in his own clothes. Already he was feeling overheated and the uniform was discouraging the company and conversation that could help pass the time. Ladies smiled, men tipped their hats. Everyone moved past. No one sat down next to him. Much as he would have enjoyed the distraction, it was more important that Carmine be fully aware that he was under investigation and had misled the police. As the train got into its slow drunken lumber, Baxter sipped his tea and stared out the window.

Eventually the train turned away from the coal smoke and factory whistles and the low mechanical thrumming of city people. For a while there was nothing other than track through a tunnel of scrub forest. Then things began to open up, distant farm houses with cows and fences and fields scattered with the remnants of the harvest. The sun came out and farther on the smells of melting morning frost, mud, and the unexpected gift of a warm day began drifting in behind the conductor's calls to board.

These were safe smells, simple smells, the kind that would be good for Grace, he thought. He had spent his life in the city, fighting for its soul, for its redemption, to save it from itself, to save it for his daughter. Had he been wrong? Were concrete and steel inherently evil? Was it impossible for people to be good and decent living on top of one another, in the falling-down tenements of the upper streets? The neighbourhood seemed to be sliding down the hill into the harbour to be sunk and done with once and for all. Maybe it was for the best. The stately mansions along the wide flat avenues of the city's better neighbourhoods were in no danger of sinking. Were the owners holed up in them any better off? He began to wonder if God and the Devil had struck a bargain. Cities with their factory smoke and tavern music and lust for money would be home to Satan, the country with its grass underfoot and trees overhead and living by the season would always belong to God.

The train slowed down on its way into a station. The scene from his window moved in slow time, like a child falling from a tree, an agony and fascination of detail. On a small rise a few hundred feet from the track a picket fence squared itself around a house and barn. The house, with its two sections of roof pitched high and proud over a two-storey L, stood off at an angle from the track, its shoulders square. It greeted the interloping moon faces behind the glass of the temporarily slow-moving future with a nod that was curt, yet not unfriendly or judgemental. The large double doors of the barn stood wide open like the mouth of some giant animal. From a distance looking into the sun, the contents of its belly remained a secret.

The shingles, white for the house, red for the barn, were bright and freshly painted. The crops must have been good this year. In lean times the struggle to maintain land and family and some sense of pride would seem a burden, but not today. Beyond the pickets, corralled by pens and lines of split rail, animals gathered in small groups to feed and reassure themselves, each unto to their own space, all of one family nonetheless, sprung from the same ground, as tight and alike as the kernels on a new ear of corn. Beyond them the fields stretched and yawned. Tired from their summer labours, they made themselves ready for a winter slumber.

By the time Baxter's gaze followed back to where it started, a small party had gathered just inside the picket fence, four children and their mother, no space between them. The head of the household stood a step apart, not as a show of authority or distance. The slight angle toward them in his stance and glances in their direction drew the eye of the onlooker to his family which he seemed to be showing off with pride. The youngest looked to be five or six. There was likely no more than two years between him and his next older brother. The third child was a girl, ten maybe. From Baxter's distance only her pigtails gave her away. Father and children all wore overalls tucked into high rubber boots. The oldest boy was nearly as tall as his mother, but his narrow shoulders and thin face said he was most likely in a growth spurt and still only a lad of twelve or thirteen. All of the children had their mother's sandy hair. They fell off her shoulder tallest to shortest as if in military rank, as orderly and protective as the pickets in front of them.

It was the mother who most caught Baxter's eye and wonder. She would be at least twelve years older than Grace. Four children had not taken her figure. Her long hair was tied up, except for a few loose strands caught in the breeze and sunlight. She wiped at them in a carefree way that matched the smile that came to her face now and then. She looked to Baxter every bit a happy person, glad to be who and where she was, that there could be no better place than this. As if to confirm his thought, she reached out now for her husband with one hand and waved to the train with the other. Maybe she could make out his face and was forming her own thoughts of him and was waving as if to say, we are what you see, the soul of this place and we shall endure, you be careful on your way.

He raised his own hand, just for a moment and gave back a smaller wave. He was not waving at the woman a few hundred feet away, he was waving to a vision he had conjured of his daughter, of a Grace in a possible future. If she was so determined to study medicine she could study animal medicine. If she was determined to be modern let her practice the science of farming, of crop rotation and irrigation and plant breeding and animal husbandry and maximum yield per acre. Here there was no waiting on a man's return. Husband and wife worked side by side and with her share of responsibility she could find the balance of power she seemed to think was right.

Cities were supposedly beacons leading mankind out of the darkness. Most days Halifax was just a racket where a few dollars pooled at the cost of so much waste and filth. People here knew better than to expect more from a place where all you produced with your time was someone else's money. Grace could be well and happy here and he could rest easy knowing that.

As the train pulled into the station, then rolled back up to speed and on ahead, the bright red and white shingles and the picket of smiling faces and sandy hair disappeared from view. He slumped back into his seat, crossed his arms, let his head fall and tried not to worry about his daughter, about what machinations Tolliver and Squire might be up to and whether or not Carmine had any useful information, and where to turn the investigation if he didn't. Sometime later Baxter woke with a start. The conductor had given him a not too gentle nudge. Now the man was bellowing like a town crier, "Windsor! This stop, Windsor!"

In the dream they had all gone to the circus. They walked the midway, he had gotten three rings on a peg. Grace ignored the dolls and picked a magnifying glass. He could not recall what else had happened, only the monsters. He was hot and closed in and finding it hard to breathe. He desperately needed some open space.

The conductor was homely and gruff and too fat for his suit, but he was not a monster, he was real. Baxter stayed on the conductor's heels until he had been led off the train.

———•———

The door of a modest two-storey brick townhouse opened after the third knock. "Good morning, can I help you?"

"Are you Mr. Carmine Mosher?" The post office was next to the train station. Baxter had gotten directions from there. He didn't really have to ask the man in front of him who he was. He was a little taller and heavier than his younger brother, but he had the same big face with heavy jowls and large round nose that Wilfred Mosher had passed on to both his sons.

"Yes."

"My name is Baxter. I'm with the police in Halifax. I need to speak with you, may I come in?" Carmine turned and faded more than walked back into the dimmer light of the entranceway. As he turned back to face his visitor he said in a voice stirred by sadness, "I suppose your being here has something to do with Victor."

"Catherine sent word?" Baxter looked to a small side table, the telegram was hanging off the edge. The envelope it had come in was on the floor. They looked as if they had been dropped.

"So how can I help you?" Carmine kept his eyes on Baxter. He'd seen the telegram once, that was enough.

"I'm trying to find out who killed your brother." Baxter remained as square to Carmine as his words.

"And you think I may have had something to do with it?" A kind of defensiveness had been added to stiffen the batter of sadness. Carmine took a step forward. Baxter kept looking him in the eye, and sensed more than saw Carmine clench his fists. Both men were still for a moment. Then Carmine turned. He bent over slowly and picked the envelope up from the floor. As he placed it on the table, he said, through a long rattling exhale in which Baxter could almost see vaporous images of Victor's childhood and hear trailing echoes of brothers talking across the dark of a shared room and feel the squeezing of his own heart, "Victor and I were not as close as we used to be. We always got along, though. I loved my brother."

Baxter let out the dry empty breath he was holding. "I don't think you killed your brother. I do think you can help me. Can we sit somewhere and talk?"

Carmine wiped at his eyes and shook his head. He began patting himself down as he moved past Baxter to a coat stand by the door. "I'm late for work."

"I'm sure they would understand," Baxter suggested. When Carmine continued his search, Baxter replaced the peaked cap he had taken off as he'd come through the door.

"I need to keep busy. I work at the school, King's Collegiate, it's not far, you can walk with me if you like." Carmine pointed out the front door with the house key he had finally found in one of his pockets.

Baxter glanced at the grandfather clock that had been keeping an undertaker's eye on things from the respectful distance of a small front parlour off the entranceway. It was only twenty after nine. He was better than he had expected for time. "Fine then," he said, checking his hat in a mirror by the parlour door. He waited on the sidewalk as Carmine put the key in his pocket and closed the door without locking it. Baxter pretended he hadn't imagined the clock dressed in a dark suit with sleeves that ended in mortician hands, hands washed colourless with disinfectant soap, hands that still left a whiff of corpse on everything they touched.

They walked together, away from the death notice and the undertaker clock into the confluence of small town life. Baxter was more accustomed to city life. All small towns were alike to him, a bit foreign. The sights and sounds of business seemed confined to a small centre square. Plate glass windows with prices and help wanted signs. No market stalls and screaming hawkers, only the tinkling of bells at the opening of shop doors, the popping of paper bags. The "Come again" of a sale made and the "Try so and so's" of one lost. The lines of streets and houses ran off the centre square. They didn't go far and they didn't know any strangers. He could imagine the taste of factory smoke coming in from the edge of town along with the sound of a train whistle and the screech of brakes. He could not imagine the air here ever feeling close or stifling, or being without the scent of earth and manure that seemed to linger below every other smell. And he was equally sure that the number one sound, particularly at night, would be quiet.

Baxter was bigger than most men. He seemed small next to Carmine. As they walked along, every now and then they had to step aside to let someone pass. "I haven't got a lot of time, so I'll be direct."

They were at a corner, not far from Carmine's house. He turned left and Baxter followed. "You want to know why I pretended to be my brother in that telegram."

"What was your brother up to?"

An elderly man stepped off his yard onto the sidewalk. Carmine and Baxter stopped and gave him a wide path between them. Carmine said hello. The old man tipped his hat. Carmine watched him for a moment then turned to Baxter and said in a voice low but warning, "My brother was a good man." Then he continued walking, a step faster than before.

As Baxter caught up, he said, "I know he was, I didn't mean… Still, there was something going on."

They turned right. Carmine cleared his throat and it seemed to take the steel out of his voice. He explained that a few weeks ago the school principal had asked if Victor might speak to some senior students about city government, public administration, that sort of thing. "He knew of Victor through me and before that our father." Carmine took Baxter through his letter to Victor, and his brother's agreement to pay a visit. When he had arrived two weeks later, Victor had seemed troubled. Then after the school visit he was all smiles. When he left the next morning his usual energy was back. He had walked off to the train station like someone finally rid of a bad tooth.

"So what picked him up?"

A wagon was coming toward them at a slow clop, the horse paying more attention than the driver. Carmine forced a smile and waved. "I have no idea."

Out of reflex or perhaps to look less conspicuous for Carmine's sake, Baxter joined in the wave. "Victor said nothing?"

Carmine dropped his hand and went on with his story. "Victor came down that morning. He spoke to the students. Afterward he sat with the headmaster for a while. We had dinner together in the evening. We talked about family mostly. So far as being at the school, all he said was that it had gone very well."

They were coming onto the grounds. The school stood at the end of a wide driveway, three storeys of stone blocks with four large columns out front. Under different circumstances, Baxter would have taken greater notice of its architecture. Instead he found himself watching the shine fade off his shoes. Halfway to the school, with the dust heavy enough to begin compressing itself into a skin, Baxter asked, "What day was Victor here?"

"Wednesday last."

"All right, Victor leaves. Then what happens?"

Carmine took his time. He led to the left, away from the front entrance, then came to a stop on a walkway that carried on around the side
of the building. The two men stood facing each other, a couple of paces
between them. Carmine continued, "Two days later I get a strange telegram. Victor says if anyone happens to be looking for him this weekend,
I should cover for him. He would explain later."

"Do you think he was afraid, was he hiding from someone?"

Carmine paused for a moment, then shrugged. "You mean violence…
No, I think it was Catherine he was worried about."

Baxter picked up a small stick from the grass at the edge of the walkway. He tried to bang some of the dust off his shoes. Then he put it to
better use digging at a spot high up between his shoulder blades. The itch
relieved, he returned to his train of thought. "So Victor tells Catherine
he's coming here, and tells you to cover for him. Has anyone looked for
him?"

"Just you."

"And you don't know where he really went on Friday, or what he was
doing?"

"He just asked me to cover for him."

Baxter played with the stick for a few moments, going over things in
his head. While Carmine appeared to watch a group of students in cadet
uniforms practising their drill, Baxter was sure Carmine had no idea the
students were there. He looked completely lost. Baxter thought about
asking if there was a wife or grown children, someone Carmine could
lean on. He guessed if there was Carmine would not have come to work.
More questions would just be cruel, not that he could think of any that
would help either of them. The best Baxter could do for Carmine now
was to leave him be. Maybe he could get something from the headmaster.
He was just about to ask Carmine where to find him when Carmine said,
"The headmaster's name is Wigan. Through the front, and to the right…
My office is this way." He pointed. "I suppose I'll see you again at the
service." He didn't wait for an answer, or offer his hand in departure. He
just walked off, slow and a bit unsteady as if he had Victor's body over
one shoulder, refusing to leave his brother on the field of battle. Baxter
tossed the stick back in the grass and headed for the front doors.

———•———

The secretary was used to dealing with contrite students and syco-phantic parents. The sight of a large policeman, who didn't seem interested in whether or not headmaster Wigan was busy, took her by surprise. She may have peed herself just a little. She showed Baxter through. He introduced himself. "Good morning, Headmaster Wigan, I'm Chief Inspector Baxter of the Halifax police. Could we have a word?" The secretary let out a small sigh of relief when the headmaster dismissed her with a nod.

Baxter stepped into the office and closed the door. The room was sparsely furnished, everything neat and straight as a pointer. A large desk sat dead centre of the room, clean except for a few papers, which the headmaster now pushed aside as he stood and extended his hand. He had gone grey except for his moustache, which was still dark and full. His voice was strong and clear, perfect for quieting a rowdy hallway or ripples of chatter across a school assembly. "Good morning, Chief Inspector, how can I help you?" When he explained that Carmine had just lost his brother to violence, the headmaster took it harder than Baxter had expected. He seemed genuinely sorry.

"I was very impressed by Victor. I can't imagine why someone should want to kill him." The headmaster stepped away as he spoke, moving to the window at the back of the room. He followed the flight of a small bird as it flew fast and low over a sports field at the end of the school grounds.

"I understand you spoke with him the day he was here." Baxter re-moved his peaked cap and tucked it under his arm.

Wigan continued to watch the field as he spoke, as if he were wait-ing for the bird to make another pass. "Yes, I met him when he arrived, introduced him to the students. Later he stopped by here."

So far the trip had not turned up anything important, and he had an-other train ride to face. Still, Baxter listened closely, a little over-anxious, sifting the headmaster's story, hoping for a useful fact or better still a lead. Wigan went on in random detail. At one point he said something about photos in a hallway. Baxter was struggling to imagine some pos-sible relevance. No, he was not aware that Maynard Sinclair Wallace had attended King's Collegiate, though it was no great surprise. The school was known for bringing up the rich. Baxter was surprised that this fact should be of interest to Victor Mosher. Victor had done well. He had not done so well Baxter could imagine him being more interested in inheritance than hard work.

Seeming to give up on the bird's return, the headmaster turned slowly away from the window and came back to his desk. He looked at his chair and seemed to decide against it. He remained standing, very still, hands behind his back. "Yes, he was extremely interested. And as I said to Mr. Mosher, we are still very proud." Now leaning forward slightly on his toes, he added, "We know the meaning of honour here at King's." Suddenly the headmaster looked and sounded like a freshman making a pledge.

Baxter's eyes narrowed as he tried to make sense of what he had just heard, and the headmaster's sudden need to justify himself. Finally he gave up. "I'm sorry, Headmaster Wigan, I don't follow."

Wigan glanced at the door, as if someone might be eavesdropping, making ready to break in and attack him before he could divulge what he knew. "Frank McNeally." Now the headmaster looked like a boy caught uttering a profanity in church. At first the name didn't register, it had been nearly three years. Baxter repeated it out loud, joining in the blasphemy that would see both men burst into flames as God unleashed his fury. And then there was a burning, a rekindling of anger and frustration, of justice denied. Of a case he had closed yet never solved. Baxter said the name once more.

"Yes, Frank McNeally. Surely you remember. That business with the bank in Maine, terrible mess. We were so relieved the papers never mentioned the school." Wigan had regained himself. He came round to the side of his desk, directly in front of Baxter.

Now the chief inspector remembered McNeally, all too clearly. He struggled to push his feelings aside, stay in the present. "McNeally was a student here?" he managed to ask.

"Yes, same class as Mr. Wallace. They were quite close. I was a teacher then, just my second year. We were shocked. Frank McNeally was a fine student and he seemed to have grown up to be a perfect gentleman."

"You saw him recently?"

"Yes, well, not recently, but not long before the trouble started. He came alone. Apologized for being unannounced, said he just couldn't resist. We walked the campus, reminisced. He talked about living in Maine, being in banking, all smooth and smiles...the cheek." Wigan looked down and shook his head as he slid his hands into his pants pockets.

"He came from Maine...Was there a class reunion?" Baxter was now marching back and forth in front of the desk, his hat still tucked under one arm, his hands clasped in front.

"No, no, he came up from Halifax. Said he was there on business. He didn't say directly, he did give the impression it was to do with Mr. Wallace."

"What did he say?"

"I can't remember exactly, something about it being pleasant doing business with friends."

"Did he say anything else?"

"No, he was here less than half an hour. Said his goodbyes and dashed off."

Baxter had come back to his spot in front of Wigan. "And back then, Mr. Wigan, you didn't think this was something you should pass on to the police in Halifax?" He had not meant to raise his eyebrows or let the sound of so much disbelief creep into his voice.

Wigan stood his ground. "This is not the city, Mr. Baxter. By the time we saw the Halifax papers the matter had been put to rest. The fact that McNeally was once a student here, or visited years later, has no bearing on what he did and more importantly, it has no bearing on the school."

Baxter took a breath to check himself, then said, "Headmaster Wigan, if you really believed that, you wouldn't have kept quiet or been so pleased that the newspaper stories of Frank McNeally the bank robber never mentioned he was a student here." There was the tinniest twitch of the headmaster's left eye, but otherwise he remained stone-faced. Baxter wondered if he was recalling Shakespeare and the dangers of promising too much. Better not to ask, to reveal that all he knew of Shakespeare ended after a few lines from *Hamlet*. Instead he offered Wigan a rough apology for questioning his actions and the school's good name. "So why let the cat out of the bag with Mr. Mosher?"

The headmaster took a breath and gave a slight shrug of his shoulders. "I don't know really. Victor was so interested. We spoke in confidence. Now you tell me a few days later he's been murdered. I…"

"Don't get ahead of yourself. We are still a long way from knowing what happened, or whether the murder of Victor Mosher had anything to do with your conversation." Baxter said it, and he wanted the headmaster to believe it, although he didn't believe it himself. In the end, of course, it didn't matter what either of them believed. All that mattered was what he could prove as a policeman.

"Is there anything else you can tell me, Mr. Wigan?" Baxter asked, eyeing up Wigan as he straightened his hat. The man's thoughts were all over his face. Had he spoken up back then or kept his mouth shut a week ago, somehow Victor Mosher would still be alive. Maybe he would speak to Carmine through his secretary, at least until he could rationalize away the worst of his feelings. He tried to say the word no. He could only manage to shake his head as he once again extended his hand. Baxter took it and held it long enough for Wigan to find the strength to look him in the eye. "Victor got himself tangled up in something. He's not dead because of anything you did or didn't do. You have been a big help here today. I'll find out who did this." Baxter left the headmaster with his thoughts. The door latch clicked softly beneath the sound of his stacked leather heels moving away at a quick march across the hardwood floor. The secretary kept her knees together and her eyes glued to her desk as Baxter blew past.

———•———

Just outside the reception area he held up. Was it possible that two men with the same name were mixed up in this? He had to see the class picture. A line of large frames began running a divide between floor and ceiling just down the hall. He followed the trail around the corner moving back in time, 1885, 1884…He passed doors on the opposite side of the hall. He could hear bits of questions and answers and the scratch of chalk on boards. No one joined him in the hall. How old was Wallace, late thirties, early forties maybe? 1880, 1879…1870. He stopped in front of a photo labelled "Senior Class – 76." He recognized the entrance and front steps of the school. The faces were thin and clean and looking straight at the camera, into a future that family money had secured. Wallace was standing on one end of the back row. His left hand was inside his coat, as if the camera had caught him going for his watch or playing at an imitation of Napoleon. His right hand was on the shoulder of the classmate seated in front of him.

Baxter leaned in for a closer look at the young man Wallace was holding on to. The face he remembered was heavier and harder, though every bit as smug. There was only one Frank McNeally.

McNeally had stolen $300,000 from the Saco and Biddleford Savings Bank in Maine. He was believed to have taken a train to Halifax. The wanted poster hung in the station for weeks. Then one day Patrick Berrigan had asked to see Baxter. Patrick had been a bit of a drinker in his younger days. He had grown out of it. He was a decent sort. "How can I help you, Patrick?"

Baxter had had to wait for Patrick to finish wringing the life out of his cloth cap. Finally he was able to clear his throat and say, "It's about my brother." Thomas tried. He remained a hopeless drunk. Patrick had found his brother in an alley the night before.

"So in his stupor he told you he and Ellen Reardon are planning to rob some guest at the Aberdeen Hotel?" Baxter wasn't trying to rush Patrick, only help him along. He told Patrick he would look into it and meanwhile not to worry. Even if there was any money, Thomas and Ellen were hopeless as thieves. Baxter had gone back to his desk. It was more than an hour later that he decided he had better do as he had promised.

No sooner did he get up the steps from the Grand Parade onto Argyle Street than the sky had opened up. It was February and the cold rain had stung his face. His eyes were down, watching for puddles and patches of ice.

It was the case that got his attention, black, round at the top, like a doctor's bag. Baxter looked up. The man made a point of looking Baxter in the face as he passed, touching his free hand to the rim of his bowler.

It was the smugness that had given him away, the wanted poster had had the same expression.

McNeally was just back from travelling Europe in style on the bank's money. In the days to come readers of the local papers were surprised to learn McNeally was not off to jail. He had sailed back to Europe, escorted by a banker and two men who looked like they were hoping for an escape attempt.

Chief of Police Tolliver agreed Baxter deserved the reward. Sadly he could not force the bank to honour its word. Baxter seethed then, and he was seething now. McNeally had been caught red-handed. He should have been held and turned over to the authorities in Maine. He should still be in jail. Tolliver could have made that happen.

Baxter's eyes moved away from the face of the young Frank McNeally. He focused now on the hand resting on McNeally's shoulder. His gaze followed up the arm to the face of Maynard Sinclair Wallace. Before his thoughts could take him any further, the doors on the other side of the hallway began opening up one after the other as students poured into the hallway. Some of them gave him a brief once-over. Most just ignored him as they passed, chatting, glad for a few moments of freedom. Baxter checked his watch. Eleven fifteen. He started back toward the front door, moving slowly through the run of spawning salmon and the mystery of the present now thickened by the mystery of the recent past.

He was almost to the end of the grounds when he heard his name called. Baxter turned. Carmine was at the side of the building, waving. Baxter checked his watch again. He still had time to say goodbye to Carmine, do a better job of offering his sympathies. Baxter turned and watched Carmine come up the main drive. He seemed much steadier on his feet.

---·---

Squire had slept later than he wanted to. It was nearly eight when he opened his eyes. Somehow he had slept through the town clock and the morning factory whistles. Nobody in the house had bothered to get him up, they must have assumed he had the day off or were still in bed themselves. He picked up the pitcher on the small dresser in his room and went to the WC at the end of the hall. He came back with an empty bladder and the pitcher filled with water which he poured into a basin. He bathed and dressed and made his way down to the kitchen.

He hadn't heard any signs of life in the house from upstairs. The downstairs was dead as well. He had poked his head into the small front parlour, nothing save dust in the beams of pale sunlight slanting through the open curtains and two empty chairs. At the back of the house the smell of fried eggs hung in the air. The meal had passed. The chairs were all pushed into the table. He turned a tap to stop its dripping then moved over to pick up the tent of notepaper pitched on the sideboard. His name was written across the front. He recognized Betty's handwriting. He pulled a chair and sat to read the short letter written on the inside of the tent.

She had a niece coming to the city for work, her brother-in-law's girl. She hadn't seen much of that side of the family since losing John, more her fault than theirs. They all looked so much alike, their faces made her feel sad. Then she got a letter asking if she would take a room with Anna, or at least board in the same house and she couldn't say no. She found two rooms at a good rate. She and Anna would be upstairs downstairs, close enough for comfort but not in each other's hair. Betty said she wasn't one for long goodbyes. Squire thought maybe it had something to do with not having been able to say goodbye to her husband. It suddenly occurred to him that he had not gotten to say goodbye to his father, not really. The man that smeared manure on his chest and stopped coming into the house, the man who turned their barn into a junk store, was not his father. The person he shook hands with before coming to the city looked even less like the man Squire tried to keep in memory. Betty never got to say goodbye to John, and sometimes she would see a face that looked like his. At least she didn't have to watch some stranger living in his body. Squire rubbed at his eyes, then went on with Betty's letter. She told him to be careful at work and if she had forgotten to say so, he looked dashing in uniform and there was no doubt in her mind that he was a fine policeman. She could see he had a forgiving spirit. "I know blueberry is your favourite," she said in closing. Then at the bottom: "PS, 11 Morris Street." He would stop by at least once to say thank you and wish her well. He went back to the sideboard and lifted the tea towel. Blueberry pie for breakfast. He got a plate.

After two pieces of pie with coffee he arrived at the station to find the place empty. Everyone was upstairs. Squire fell in at the edge of the crowd as the mayor finished, then stepped aside for the chief. "Good morning, everyone. As the mayor said, this is truly a sad morning." For the benefit of the press who he hoped would sell it to family, friends, and the rest of the city, Tolliver made it clear that justice would be done. Chief Inspector Baxter was absent this morning precisely because he was hot on the trail and this case would be wrapped up in due course. "You can expect to see me before you again very soon, giving you the details of how the case was solved and the identity of the person or persons involved." Tolliver went on to ask for citizen cooperation in bringing forth any information that might help the case. He also cautioned against wasting valuable time with rumours and petty grievances. Those persons who knew Alderman Mosher, many who were listening now, could expect to be contacted by the chief inspector or Officer Squire. "Officer Squire, can you please raise your hand and step forward a little so folks can get a look at you."

The people in front of him made room, and Squire took a few small steps. He felt like someone who had just been caught chewing gum in class, not someone people needed to answer to. While he stood there with his face hanging out, the chief reiterated the need for full cooperation, and that being questioned was not the same as an accusation. People should think of this as a chance to do their part in capturing whoever was responsible for this terrible act. The chief said his thank yous, then he and the mayor began making their way downstairs, surrounded by a small group of reporters asking questions and scribbling in notepads. On his way past, Tolliver gave Squire a nod. On reflex, Squire had touched the brim of his uniform custodian helmet in an awkward salute or sign of recognition, as if the chief needed any from him. Of course, it was the other way around. Squire was sure no one missed the look of surprise on his face when he was recognized and called out, including the chief.

In the walk to see the manager of the Union Bank, Victor's ledger tucked under his arm, he stopped in front of some shop windows to read the signs and when he was sure no one was watching, he practised looking like an investigating officer. The chief had used that word, "officer." He could have said "Constable Squire," which was more accurate. There was no rank of officer, the title just seemed to have more air under it. Maybe the chief felt he needed a little inflating. Trouble was, Squire didn't know how to look like an officer. He tried lowering his brows and tightening his lips. On him it came off as constipation or confusion. He tried looking angry, a crooked lip or squinting eyes. All that did was make him more boyish than ever. He gave up, and hurried on to the bank.

The bank manager's look was perfect. He was not too tall, though not noticeably short. Not too fat or too thin. He wore a grey suit that made no impression. His face was instantly forgettable. Even the name Saunders had no staying power. Customers would remember their anger and disappointment when the bank said no to their loan requests. The shame and loss of a foreclosure might linger for years, but recalling the man who delivered the news would likely be impossible for most. The manager of the Union Bank could put in a hard day of taking money from one and selling it to another and then step into the street wearing a face no one could recall, could pass by without fear of acrimony or abuse. As Squire shook hands and explained his call, he wondered if the manager had ever considered a life of crime. Witness descriptions would fit everyone and no one.

Following Baxter's instructions, Squire left the manager with the ledger and the letters and the task of finding out whatever he could about Victor's business dealings. Squire headed back to City Hall to speak with anyone who might be able to offer some clue as to how Victor had ended up murdered and floating in the harbour. If Squire was lucky, someone might seem suspicious. Victor's mother had likely told him he would be known by the company he kept. As far as Squire could tell, Victor had followed that advice. No one he spoke to at City Hall looked or sounded like a killer; just the opposite.

Alderman Maxwell, who was still in his first year in office, talked about how Victor had helped him to get elected. "He introduced me at functions. The man even came knocking on doors with me a couple of times. He treated me like a son." Maxwell was nearly in tears before he finished. Another alderman pinned Squire in a corner for fifteen minutes with stories of Victor's good deeds. "Who would want to kill him?" He kept asking the question as if he were trying to recall where he had left a set of keys, as if the identity of the killer would suddenly pop into his head. The office girls he spoke to were useless; some just blubbered, while others went on about how polite Victor had always been, none of the fresh comments or demeaning treatment they got from some men, whose names they preferred not to mention. Though one had said, "If I should happen to see a certain wife or two, I might not be able to hold my tongue." After making the rounds for more than an hour Squire was exhausted. Not physically but emotionally. He had felt bad over Victor's death, the way you would over a neighbour losing their dog or reading in the paper about a father needing help to support his family after falling off a roof. Standing next to people who had been close to Victor, that was something different. It brought the loss closer to Squire, sank their sadness into him, like the heat of a funeral pyre.

Squire had gone to City Hall hoping to find clues or evidence to solve a murder. All he got for his trouble was a weight he didn't expect, or want to carry. He was glad to get back outside where the sky was blue to the horizon. The air was warm and full of the ocean, the last of the summer leaves and the sounds of doing business. People on the streets were all smiles, their faces, like the day, showing no signs of winter. Being in the midst of all this should have picked him up. But sorrowful laments, deep breaths against tears, and images of Victor's milk-glass face bobbing in dark water filled his head and blotted out the sun. Perhaps when the afternoon papers came out and the news of Victor's death became widely known the city would show its mourning face, share the weight he was carrying. Until then he couldn't help resenting the good cheer around him. How dare they? The walk back to the Union Bank seemed twice as long.

Saunders was still poring over the details and Squire had to wait. He had missed lunch and the oomph of Betty's blueberry pie had petered out. He sat, dizzy from sadness and hunger, listening to his stomach growl. After a while he slipped into the release of a pleasant daydream, to a place where life was desire, where stomachs were always full and the dead could be revived.

"Ahem…" An unpleasant sound. He wished it away and it was gone. "AHEM… Policeman Squire?" Saunders waited, holding Victor's ledger with both hands like a sacred text, his lips dry from reading aloud. Squire's head remained against the back of the chair, legs outstretched, boots crossed. Finally, Saunders stepped forward and pushed at the boots with the toe of an oxford. Squire opened his eyes, then began to blink, trying to bring Saunders into focus and recollection. His mouth was full of cotton. "Shall we go to my office?" Squire nodded. It wasn't necessary, Saunders had already turned. Squire followed. His line wavered a little as he walked off his daze. Saunders' steps were precise and made absolutely no sound.

"I have gone over Mr. Mosher's ledger very carefully. I have also had a look at his recent transactions with the bank." Saunders waited for Squire to make his way into his office, then he closed the door behind him. He motioned to a chair, but Squire shook his head as he stretched his eyes wide open, still trying to come fully awake.

"Can you tell if he was in any trouble, his business, I mean?" The last part of the sentence came through a yawn, though Squire was coming round.

"His accounts seem to be in perfect order." Saunders had moved over behind his desk, but he didn't sit. He remained standing, still holding the ledger with both hands, more cautious than ever as if it had now become Royal Doulton's finest china.

"So his business was making money?"

"Well, yes…" Saunders looked at the ledger as he spoke, the way you look at a fussy aunt who contradicts everything you say.

"But?"

"There is the matter of these notes." Saunders set the ledger down delicately on his desk as he spoke. He withdrew the letters from it and laid them in a line across the front of his desk.

"IOUs." Squire stepped closer, ignoring the letters.

"Yes," Saunders replied as if the facts of the letters were in plain English. Still he continued to lean over them, while making slight adjustments to their alignment across the desk.

"Were you able to determine who Victor owed money to?" Squire was tapping his helmet against his thigh, marking the slow cadence of the bank manager's thoughts.

"No…" Saunders finally looked up from the letters.

"What is it, Mr. Saunders?" Squire spoke slowly, in rhythm with his helmet.

Saunders straightened himself, pulled at his suit coat. "In my business, discretion is paramount."

Squire kept tapping, a little quicker now. "Is that what you want me to take back to Chief Inspector Baxter?"

"Look at the notes." Saunders kept to his pace with the patience of a first grade teacher.

Squire glanced at the letters. "I've seen them, Mr. Saunders."

"And these initials, what do you make of them?" Saunders leaned over once again. Slowly he moved from one page to the next, pointing to the initials at the bottom of each.

Squire gave in. He laid his helmet on the desk and followed along. "Two sets at the bottom of each note. One set is always the same, looks like… DS or PS."

"Or maybe JS?" Was Saunders also guessing or was he leading? Squire couldn't tell.

"Maybe…hard to say…the way the letters are written one on top of the other." Squire moved to the side of the desk, more for a better angle on Saunders than the letters.

"Hmmmm," Saunders mused. "Distinctive would you say?" He bent over a little further as if to get a closer look, but to Squire it seemed as if the bank manager was merely biding his time.

"I need answers, Mr. Saunders." He wanted to sound commanding. He couldn't keep the last hint of desperation from his voice.

Saunders moved to the opposite end of the desk. Again he made a quick check of his jacket. "These debts were unofficial, off the books, so to speak. As far as I can tell, they are not connected to Mr. Mosher's business. None of them are held by this bank, or any other bank in the city. I made some inquiries."

Squire sensed a shift in the conversation, as if they were now engaged in an instructive dialogue Saunders wanted him to follow. "So these are private debts, gentleman's agreements."

"Gentlemen shake hands, they don't write promissory notes in Latin and have them witnessed."

Squire repeated Saunders' statement in his head, trying to discern the approach he was being asked to take. "You think this PS or JS is the witness?"

"Yes, and the other initials likely represent the lenders or holders of the debt."

"And the Latin?" Squire knew the answer, he just needed time to think.

The question was met with pressed lips and raised eyebrows. Squire wasn't sure if Saunders was being cautious or choosing not to belabour the obvious. "There are likely copies of these letters, with the people Mr. Mosher owed money to…perhaps the witness also." The look on Saunders' face changed to one of anticipation.

Cocking his head a little to one side, Squire asked, "Who witnesses loans here at the bank?"

Saunders nodded ever so slightly. "Depends on the size of the loan and the type." Squire waited, he felt he was on the right track. "Sometimes I act as a witness. Other times lawyers are involved."

Squire looked straight across at the bank manager who had remained at the opposite end of the desk. He seemed to be in semi darkness, off stage, directing from the wings. "I see. And of course you know of lawyers in the city who specialize in these kinds of dealings." Squire did his best to seem impartial, as if he wasn't asking Saunders to point someone out.

Again the look on Saunders' face gave Squire the impression he had provided a properly discreet opening. "So you are asking me for a recommendation?" Saunders asked.

"One I can pass along to the chief inspector." It was an obtuse statement, but Squire needed to be sure.

Saunders nodded, more emphatically this time. He reached for a pen. As he wrote, he said, "One last thing. Mr. Mosher's business was turning a profit and there is some money here on deposit. What if all of these loans had been called in on short notice…"

"He would have been ruined." Squire retrieved his helmet.

Saunders put down his pen and passed Squire a small sheet of folded paper. "Unless he had assets I am unaware of, it would have been difficult for him to pay."

———•———

Baxter saw Squire coming and waved him in before he could knock. "Good afternoon, Mr. Squire." Checking his watch, he said, "Close the door, would you please." Squire did as he was told, and took what was becoming a familiar seat in front of the detective's desk. Baxter pushed aside the duty roster he was still trying to finish. Meagher was well enough to be back at work, but was only at half speed. "You're looking a little haggard, Mr. Squire," he said, sounding more accusatory than concerned.

Squire was sagging into the upholstery of the barrel chair. He let out a great breath of air and at the end of it he said, "Is it always like this?"

"Like what, Mr. Squire?" Baxter was leaning forward, his hands folded as if he were concerned. The tone of his voice made it clear he wasn't. Squire flinched, as if he had been stuck with a pin. He looked down at the ledger he was holding and shook his head. Baxter watched on in cool silence while Squire placed the ledger on the desk and took off his helmet. He patted it lightly, the way you might pat a strange cat that had suddenly jumped in your lap, one that might as well scratch you as purr. Baxter ignored the ledger. He half listened to the usual station racket outside his office door. After a moment, Squire put his helmet on the floor and looked up. "Mr. Saunders went over Victor's ledger, and his accounts at the bank."

Baxter was no longer conscious of the noise outside. He was examining his injuries. He had taken the bandage off of his left index finger. The cut was closed even though it remained quite red. There was blood showing through the new bandage on his right thumb. Looking at it he realized it was throbbing and he eased the clasp of his hands. "And?" he said, looking back up at Squire.

"And he didn't find anything out of order. Victor's business wasn't in trouble, it was making a profit." Squire remained sunken into the chair, unable to get behind the words that floated out of him as softly as the string from a child's bubble pipe.

"I see. And the debts, what did Saunders make of those?" Baxter was more interested in Squire's reaction to the question than his answer. Squire looked straight back, his tired expression unchanged.

"Saunders said if they were all called in at once, Victor would have been in trouble, unless he had some money hidden away."

"He had money on deposit at the bank?" Baxter asked. Squire nodded. "But it would not have been enough." Squire nodded again, as he massaged his forehead.

"As we thought, Saunders said the debts were off the books. He checked around. Victor didn't owe money to any of the banks in town."

As Baxter listened he pulled at a thread on the bandage round his thumb, trying to break it without pulling the bandage free. "These debts were personal, not business." It was a statement more than question. Still he looked at Squire with eyebrows raised.

"Yes, however Saunders thinks they were witnessed, by a lawyer." Baxter let go of the thread.

"So they were personal. They just weren't friendly."

Baxter had come out from behind his desk and was standing over Squire. "I suppose you could put it that way." Squire reached into his pocket and passed on the note Saunders had given him. There were three names on it. "I think Saunders felt strongly about the last name."

"Nothing else at the bank?" Baxter stepped back, looking at the note as if it were a hole card.

"No."

Baxter slipped the paper into a pocket. He took a step back toward Squire. His voice was taut again, as distrustful as the pluck of an E string. "And no one upstairs was helpful or suspicious?"

"No." Squire straightened up in his chair.

Baxter leaned in a little, more wary, almost menacing. "You're sure? You're not leaving anything out?"

Squire was gripping the arms now, as if he were in a dentist's chair. "No..." And then Squire's countenance shifted from guardedness to realization. "Oh, I see. This is about the letters...Yes, I know some Latin."

Baxter huffed, as if Squire's admission were pointless, that he had known all along. "I'm more interested in how well you know the chief."

Squire had relaxed his grip and let his body once again sink into the back of the chair. "How well I know the chief? I don't. All I know about him is that I don't know what to think." Squire held up both his hands then let them fall back into his lap where they lay in senseless death. "My first day on the job, I got introduced. We talked for about two minutes. Then at this morning's meeting the chief points me out, says I'm on this case with you. Nods to me as he leaves, like he has faith in me...or...I don't know what. Now you, I do what you tell me, I do it to the letter... and you look at me like you caught me with my hand in your pocket." Squire sat shaking his head. Baxter couldn't tell if it was an expression of denial or frustration.

"So you didn't see the chief last night, tell him Victor was dead, the things we found. He hasn't got you reporting to him on this." He'd gone this far, pushed Squire to the edge, he had to ask the question, just in case he toppled over. By now Baxter didn't think he would, he just had to be sure.

Squire's voice was tired and resigned. "We shook hands once months ago, that's the only time we've ever spoken. Detective, let me go back on regular patrol. This morning, being around all those people who knew Mr. Mosher, I had no idea what to say. Now you think I'm going behind your back. No thanks. I'd rather break up fights and arrest drunks."

Your family was right sending you to school, Baxter thought, looking at Squire, who seemed even smaller than he was, all pulled back in his chair. Better you use your head, you haven't got the brawn for heavy lifting, or too many bar fights.

"So you don't want to hear what Carmine told me?" There was an invitation in Baxter's voice, it was as close as he could come to an apology, to admitting that ambition had nearly cut off his nose to spite his face, taken away what was probably the best help he could get on this case.

"Is he likely to end up like his brother?"

Baxter saw Squire rise a little in his chair and gave the line a tug. "So you do want to know?"

"I'm not ready to look at another body." He said it as if it were a condition, like they were settling a contract.

Baxter nodded in sympathy for the learning of a young policeman. The uniform was not designed to repel grief; it was expected to absorb it. He didn't say anything about the weight of his own uniform. Instead, Baxter gave Squire a summary of how Victor had ended up at King's

Collegiate and what he had learned in the process. He told Squire the details of the bank robbery. He did not mention his anguish over losing the reward or any credit for the arrest.

"So according to his brother, Victor leaves feeling much better than when he arrived. Carmine doesn't know why exactly. However, you think it is because Victor learned that McNeally and Wallace were classmates and friends." Squire was leaning forward now, his weight in his feet more than in the chair.

"Correct." Baxter was playing with a pencil he had picked up off his desk.

"And three years ago McNeally robs a bank in Maine. You capture him here in Halifax. People from the bank arrive. Instead of McNeally being turned over to the police in Maine, he leaves with men from the bank for Europe to recover bonds he says he has stashed there."

"Right again." Baxter tapped the pencil against his temple.

Squire continued working out the themes of his sonata following Baxter's pencil as if it were a conductor's baton. "When all this happened, you had no idea McNeally went to King's or was a friend of Wallace?"

With his baton at rest, Baxter replied, "But I was always sure Tolliver stepped in because someone asked him to. Or he already knew something about the case he wanted kept quiet."

Continuing without direction, Squire asked, "Who is Wallace?"

"Maynard Sinclair Wallace is the son of Hector Wallace who made a fortune in lumber and fish and then went into politics. Hector is long dead. Maynard is settled gentry, the kind you often hear about. The kind you seldom see. He's American rich. Beats me why he doesn't go there."

Baxter had set the pencil back on his desk. He was taking another look at the bandage on his thumb. "Did Wallace have anything to do with Victor?" Squire asked.

Baxter put his hand down as if it were forbidden fruit. He looked Squire in the eye and offered up all he knew on that score. "I don't know." Then he asked, "No one you talked to upstairs mentioned Wallace?"

Squire thought first to be sure. "No," he said, then went on with his thinking out loud. "But when Victor accidentally discovers the connection between Wallace and McNeally it picks him up out of the doldrums.

Then a couple of days later he's dead in the water under a pier…You want to talk to Wallace."

Baxter looked at his bandage again, then put the hand in a pants pocket. "First I want to talk to Charles Clarke."

"Charles Clarke that owns Clarke's Place?"

"You've heard of Mr. Clarke?"

Squire had been in one position too long. He got up and began knocking his feet together, trying to wake them up. He shrugged in response to Baxter's question. "I've heard things. I've never had any trouble there. What's Clarke got to do with this?"

"I'll explain on the way." Baxter collected his hat from the stand by the door which he held open as Squire picked up his helmet. The two men arranged themselves as they walked side by side toward the door leading out of the police station.

——•——

Small dandelion clouds drifted past the late day sun. The two men moved across the Grand Parade in the changing light. The day was still warm, the mood of the city was as high and light as the clouds, refusing to be dispirited by the dour faces of two policemen.

Victor's death had been in the papers. As Baxter had suspected, most readers missed that bit of news amidst reports from the front. War always took centre stage. There had been plenty of interest in the American Revolutionary War and the War of 1812. A few men from the city had seen action. Running supplies and attacks on American shipping had been far more common and profitable, very profitable for a few. But that was all long before Baxter's time.

He stole a glance at the young man walking by his side. Baxter had been only half as old when the American Civil War broke out. He struggled to recall vague memories of headlines and bits of conversations overheard—Shiloh Casualties Top 23,000—51,000 Fall At Gettysburg—they say 5,000 men died in an hour at Cold Harbour.

Once again there was money to be made in supplies and privateering. The city watched a few men make small fortunes. Some of those men and profits were still here. Others had run off to grander places.

And in that war a good many men and some women from British North America wound up on the battlefields fighting on both sides. The fellow who Baxter would eventually replace on the police force had decided to trade in one uniform for another. He died for the Confederacy defending Richmond. Baxter remembered thinking at the time that he and his predecessor might have had much in common, and yet nothing at all.

When Robert E. Lee surrendered at Appomattox, some thought Grant might march north. Such talk had helped unite the provinces into the Dominion of Canada. This Boer War would be the Dominion's first official foreign war. Nova Scotia had been asked for 125 men. The morning papers had listed the 80 men already signed up, many of them from Halifax. Baxter had not yet seen the list. Later he would recognize a couple of names well known in police court. All ranks of Halifax society would bear arms and wave the flag for Queen and country.

Public distraction could be of some help. His own distraction could be a disaster. In an effort to focus and push back his fatigue Baxter began to think out loud. He admitted that progress had been made. The day had started with a handful of facts and the idea that Victor's business dealings might have had something to do with his death, which was nothing more than theory. They had no suspects. Now only a few hours later, the picture had cleared up enough to reveal that Victor had debt problems, unofficial debts he'd tried his best to hide, which meant it was money owed for shady dealings or to crooked people or both. Charles Clarke was beyond shady. Baxter thought of him as a sucking chest wound that pulled a current of bile and effluent through the upper streets. "His place is politely listed in the city directory as a tavern. Everyone knows it's a brothel." Baxter's tone was a weave of disgust and disbelief.

So far as Baxter was concerned, fire was the only cure. Talk of patience and tolerance was part of the problem. Ugliness never cleaned up easy. Clarke's place was raided from time to time. As a young officer, Baxter had burst in more than once to find a few men having a quiet drink in full compliance with the liquor laws. Any women that happened to be there wore innocent smiles and kept their faces turned down politely. Men would claim them as their guests. No one would know anything about the rooms upstairs. The smalls, the frocks, the tangled sheets, and scents lingering in the air? "What about them?" Clarke would say. "I take in boarders." His angry sarcastic imitation of Clarke was thick with venom. The more he talked the more Baxter's pace quickened, and at times Squire had to take a quick hop-skip to catch up.

One expected to find sailors and soldiers at Clarke's. One did not expect to find men of standing in such places. Popular belief said otherwise. The motley crew of degenerates that buzzed around the city's common toilets could all sink into perdition and good riddance as far as Baxter was concerned. The city didn't need them, would be better off without them. What the city needed desperately was leadership. If the rumours were true, and Baxter knew they were, Charles Clarke was being allowed to lead good men to ruination. He was a whore-master, a predator, and purveyor of the worst kind of sin, a destroyer, a cancer. He deserved to be vilified, locked away, or better still hanged from a gibbet as a warning to others. Yet the man walked the upper streets to smiles and hellos. He was welcome in every shop. Clergymen of all denominations refused to cast him out and prayed for mercy upon his soul. Baxter's belligerence and incredulity may have been directed at the complicity of local politicians. Or maybe he was lamenting the want of a crusading army. Or perhaps he was offering a comment on the failings of the Christian faith. Squire decided it was best not to seek clarification.

Baxter had always thought of Victor Mosher as a moderate. His politics looked for the middle ground. That didn't mean his principles were easily shifted or went up for bid during heated debate. Victor was a man of honour and decency. Baxter could imagine Victor shaking Clarke's hand, same as he would shake the hand of every other voter in his ward. Baxter had often read newspaper accounts of Victor's speeches in Council demanding action against the plague being unleashed upon the city by liquor, vice, and debauchery, and men like Clarke who profited from its manufacture and sale. What Baxter could not imagine, what he had no desire to read about in the city's papers, he now told Squire, "is the sad fact that Victor Mosher lied to his wife, then snuck off to Clarke's Place." They had come to a stop at the corner of George and Grafton. As a pair of hacks went past, Baxter shook his head, still not wanting to accept that reality, trying to erase the images it brought to mind. Over the sound of the horses and whistles of their drivers, he said, "But that is what he did."

As they started off again Baxter remained silent. Squire took the opening. "I heard what you said about Clarke's Place. Now can you tell me how you know Victor went there?"

"Carmine told me." As they turned the corner off George Street on to Albemarle Baxter described how Carmine had waved him down as he was leaving the school grounds. "He said maybe Victor had mentioned where he was going to be."

"Clarke's Place?" Squire turned toward the detective as he spoke. No look came back.

Baxter didn't have to answer. His inability to hide his disappointment, to appear to be holding out for the possibility that Victor had been somewhere else said all that needed to be said. "After he pretended to be his brother, Carmine mulled things over for an hour or so. Then, he sent a second wire. He sent it to 117 Albemarle Street…so Victor would know I was looking for him."

Talking through his thoughts about their conversation in Baxter's kitchen the night before, Squire said, "If you had waited longer at the telegraph…" Whatever else he thought was kept to himself.

Baxter shrugged. Squire was right, but if he had found out earlier about Victor being at Clarke's Place, he might not have gone to Windsor and made the same discovery that Victor found so interesting, the connection between McNeally and Wallace. It was all still veiled in the mist of secrets and of time to come. That didn't stop Baxter from feeling sure that Victor's discovery was related to his death. He was equally sure that Charles Clarke could explain how. What Baxter needed to do was get Clarke to a point where he would explain. Waving forward as he spoke, he said, "The next door is Clarke's. Let me do the talking." Baxter let out a sigh that was more of a growl. Then he clenched his teeth and banged as hard as he could.

A latch clicked and the door began to open almost immediately. It seemed to be moving by itself and it was not in any hurry. At the end of its swing, there was a pause, then a man stepped into the light. He was just over six feet tall, carrying at least two hundred pounds, none of them extra. He might have just finished shining his shoes. The dark pants and white shirt showed some wear. They showed no dirt. The features were neither coarse nor fine. And somehow they came together to form a face that was almost handsome. If Clarke had been carrying a Bible, Squire would have pegged him for a church deacon. As it was, Squire stepped back to recheck the number over the door.

Baxter showed no hesitation. "Good afternoon, Mr. Clarke." The voice was as warm and sunny as the weather and Squire looked quickly again to see where it was coming from.

"Well, well, my favourite policeman." The smile was yellowed and chipped in places, but it made the face handsome for sure. Speaking louder and over his shoulder, Clarke said, "Girls, the chief inspector is here, best be lookin' sharp." Then, still smiling, he said to Baxter, "Who's yer sweetheart?"

Squire blushed. Baxter ignored the taunt. "We have reports of a disturbance, we need to come in."

Clarke looked like he was trying to get the smile off his face and just couldn't. "Slow day at the station or the temperance people up your arse again?"

"Have you been drinking, Mr. Clarke?" Both men knew it wasn't against the law if he had been. That wasn't Baxter's point. He hoped Clarke had been drinking and would be more pliable, easier to trip up.

Clarke stepped forward a little into the sunshine. He tilted his face up and closed his eyes. "Just the sacrament at mornin' Mass. You could check if you want with Father Murphy at Saint Mary's."

Baxter's voice remained pleasant while his eyes turned ice cold. "I'd do better to check you for a cloven hoof." He didn't bother adding that if Clarke had any faith at all it would be Protestant, one of the many derivatives of the one true faith. Father Murphy might not cast him out. On the other hand, allowing Clarke to take Holy Communion would be a disgrace.

Clarke lowered his chin and smiled again without a hint of malice or offence. "Now you done cast the first stone, you goin' tell me what you want?"

Baxter stiffened a little. He didn't move forward. "We need to have a look around."

Clarke dropped the smile and let a pall of boredom fall across his face. "Go on then, I'll feed Preacher." He stepped back into the gloom of the front parlour to his right. A small round rug marked the centre of the room, it looked like a patch of garden soil. A tall end table was rooted there as the base for an equally tall bamboo birdcage with a dome top. A quaker parrot flapped from one perch to another as Clarke picked up a rusting slice of apple from a dish beside the cage. They both ignored the two policemen moving past in single file down the narrow hall.

Baxter and Squire searched in silent awkwardness, glancing quickly into the kitchen, the drawing room, and then the back parlour. It had been a few years since Baxter had been part of a raid at Clarke's Place, but the floor plan hadn't changed. The large pine table in the kitchen with its bench seats was familiar. So were the two large leather chesterfields in the drawing room. He almost said what he was thinking. He was glad he didn't. Such familiarity would raise suspicion no matter how he explained it. For similar reasons he hoped Squire wouldn't say anything that suggested previous knowledge. Back at the station when Squire had said he had had no trouble with Clarke's Place, Baxter had taken that to mean Squire had never been here, under any circumstances. Learning that Victor was known here had been disappointing enough. It was too soon for another lesson in human frailty.

They stopped in the landing below the back stairs. Baxter opened the outside door. The small yard had the look of a deserted child. The stockade fence might have been a tattered jacket; its boards weathered grey and streaked with ferric tears from weeping nail heads. There was a tired shed leaning one way, a flimsy door off its hinges hanging the other way; crooked teeth in a sorry smile. A good bath in the form of a coat of whitewash had not taken place in a very long time. An unswept wooden walkway ran from the shed up to the steps below Baxter's feet. It had the soiled look of ground-in dirt at the back of the neck. There was no grass, only clumps of weeds poking up like sprigs of matted hair though holes in a wool cap. And below that a horrible complexion; piles of dog dirt between footprints and wheel ruts growing hard and crusty in the drying mud. Baxter shook his head as if he were saying no to a beggar and closed the door.

As he stood staring at the steps leading to the rooms on the second level Squire finally broke the silence. He glanced back down the hallway, then spoke in a husky whisper. "Detective, what exactly are we looking for?"

Baxter got a foot on the first step, only for a second. Then he pulled back and stepped to one side into the space between the staircase and the back wall of the house. The spandrel under the stairs had been closed in. The small door that led into the cave-like space didn't close all the way. "You check upstairs, I'll finish looking around down here."

Squire looked at the chief inspector, then up the stairs. "Did you hear something?" he said in a whisper that had suddenly gone dry and caught in his throat.

"Don't dillydally," Baxter said, bending down into what seemed to be a close-up study of his shoes. Without looking up he waved again and pointed up the stairs. Squire took a breath and held it, then began taking the stairs, the creak in each step marking his funeral march pace. When he finally remembered to breathe again at the top of the stairs he hyperventilated for a few seconds. The only light came from a small window in the front landing at the opposite end of the hall. He waited for his eyes and nerves to adjust. He listened as hard as he could for any sounds coming through the doors on either side. It was pointless. All he could hear was the racehorse pumping of his heart and lungs. He gave himself a count of three, then behind another deep breath he made a run down the hall. The air he stirred up cooled the thin sheen of sweat on his face. Four times he knocked lightly, then stuck his head in just long enough for a quick look. His breathing was almost back to normal by the time he rejoined Baxter.

"When my daughter, Grace, was small she dropped a jar of pickles. The brine stained the wood floor. My wife covered it up with a rug." Baxter wasn't bent over anymore, he was however still looking down at the narrow strip of floor beside the stairs and the rectangle of rug that covered most of it.

"Pardon." Squire wasn't really listening, he was still working on his breathing.

Baxter stepped away from the stairs, and faced the front of the house, watching the downstairs hallway. "Anybody home upstairs?" He didn't whisper, but he kept his voice low.

"No. Just mirrors, clothes thrown everywhere and dressers covered with little bottles and brushes. Who was Clarke calling to from the door before he let us in?"

Baxter let out a "Humph" and shook his head. So far nothing had surprised him. "Just Mr. Clarke's way of telling us he had arranged to meet us alone," he said in answer to Squire's question. "All right then, let's continue our chat with this *upstanding citizen*, shall we." He started up the hall. Squire toed in behind, looking not at all sure of what was going on or what he was supposed to do, if anything.

Clarke was still in the front parlour. There were chairs along three of the walls, thick and heavy with high backs and short bowed legs, very Catholic, Baxter had to admit. Clarke was sitting by the window, his long legs crossed, one arm hanging across the back of the chair next to him. "Satisfied?"

"Place is spotless. And empty." Baxter's voice was light, almost friendly, as if he were a real estate agent trying to sell the place. He stepped into the parlour, into the space between the birdcage and the doorway. Squire started in, then thought better and remained in the hall.

Clarke gave a slight wave from the hand resting on the chair. "An' it's Monday."

Baxter took it all in, the posture, the casual wave, the tone of voice, a perfect mix of mild disappointment and explanation. "Or you were expecting me."

Clarke ignored the bait. This time the hand pointed, past Baxter to Squire. "So what's your name?"

"Squire."

"You been here before, maybe at night, without that uniform?" He smirked ever so slightly at the young policeman, then looked stone-faced at his superior.

"No." The crack in Squire's voice made him sound guilty. Baxter did Squire the favour of not turning round to see his face turn scarlet, he could almost feel its heat.

"Well, you come by, without yer boss, first drink's on me." Clarke looked straight at Squire as he spoke. A wink would have been too much. Instead there was a slight movement at one corner of his mouth and a twitch in the eye above it.

Baxter thought about telling Clarke to leave the boy alone, mostly to reassure Squire that his reputation remained intact. He didn't, refusing to grant Clarke the satisfaction, despite any advantage that might be gained from letting Clarke feel as if he had the upper hand. "I see you got the afternoon paper, Mr. Clarke."

Clarke looked down at the pages spread across the seat of the chair beside him. "Yes, sir, I take a regular paper. Use it to line Preacher's cage." He pointed again. The parrot brightened at the sound of its name.

"I haven't had the chance. Any surprises in the latest edition?" Baxter asked, knowing that Victor's death would have at least been mentioned. Clarke couldn't be expected to raise that topic, though he might feign ignorance. If he did it would be an obvious lie. Clarke had gotten the paper for no other reason. A lie might be something Baxter could use.

"Men old as you an' me is past surprises." Clarke closed the paper as he spoke, folded it in half, and set it on the table beside the cage. Preacher jumped from one perch to another.

"So you already knew Victor Mosher was dead."

"I get the paper same time as ev'body else." Clarke smiled again, but his eyes were flat and still. Baxter could feel them looking into him.

"What time did he come in on Friday?" Baxter watched closely for a reaction. He thought he saw something in Clarke's face, he just couldn't be sure. Did he start to look away, then catch himself? Was there a slight wince, a moment of fear?

"Who says a man like that comes here at all?" Clarke shifted himself, crossed his arms at his chest, lowered the cross in his legs from the knee to the ankle. The smile was back. Whatever look Baxter saw or thought he saw was gone.

"I know he was here, Mr. Clarke." Baxter knew because Carmine knew his brother and had tried to protect him. He knew because Clarke had been sitting here waiting for him. He knew because he didn't want it to be true. He knew, despite the lack of proof. And that was what Clarke heard in his voice, a search for truth, not the possession of it. Now Baxter glanced behind him. Not because he was interested in anything Squire was doing or whether he was there at all. He was thinking, taking a peek at his cards.

"You got your mind made up, why you askin' me?" Clarke added a shrug to the smile.

"Was he here with Mr. Wallace?" Still Baxter had no proof. If mentioning Wallace got a reaction, he at least had a start. Again he saw something, a tick, a little ripple in the calm. Only visible for half a second, but it had been there, this time Baxter was sure.

"Mr. Wallace who?" Now it was Clarke who was playing for time, settling his game.

"Maynard Sinclair Wallace." Baxter said the full name, slowly and distinctly as if Clarke had a hearing problem. He enjoyed saying it that way, imagining Wallace cringing at the mention of his name in the midst of a homicide investigation, mentioned in a brothel by a policeman, heard by a panderer, a coloured panderer.

"Oh, now you just talkin' foolishness. That man's got more money than God, what he need this place for?" Clarke spoke as if what he said was as simple and true as blue sky. If it was, Clarke wouldn't bother to look so convincing.

"Don't play dumb, Mr. Clarke."

"All right." Clarke shrugged, then his eyes widened. "You know, bit a sin might do you some good. You could use the back door. Ain't no tell-tales here."

The jibe shouldn't have bothered him and yet it did. Worse still, Clarke saw that it did. "Mind your manners." Baxter heard the anger in his voice and that made him madder still. Again Squire took a step into the room, felt lost, and returned to the safety of the doorway.

Clarke's face lit up as if he had won a prize. "Christ, you and yer precious reputation." He shook his head in mock disbelief and obvious satisfaction.

The first shot stung, this one hurt. If they were in a ring Baxter would be sagging against the ropes. Whatever start he'd made it was gone now. He had nothing left and Clarke knew it. Baxter turned and pointed Squire toward the front door. As he made his retreat he lashed out in desperation. "We'll track down your girls, Charlie. One of them will talk. And then we'll be back."

Clarke feinted, then raised his voice for a parting shot over Baxter's head. "Like I said, Mr. Squire, first drink's on me."

Baxter wanted to slam the door, slam it hard enough to rattle every window in the place. The only thing that stopped him was the thought of giving Clarke another chance to smile. He closed the door with a gentle click of the latch. He stepped into the middle of the sidewalk. He stood there digging through his pockets, as if a train was about to leave and he couldn't find his ticket. Finally he pulled out his watch. He held it to an ear and listened. The sun was still strong. He thought about its warm yellow face. Not about the jaundice yellow in Charlie's malicious grin. The sounds of happy children came from somewhere down Albemarle Street. The children were likely Irish, Catholic and poor, with fathers too often idle and easy prey for the devil. When times were bad, their mothers could get credit in some of the neighbourhood shops, at least for a while. Then it would be thin soup given some taste with bits of fat picked off butcher's twine. But not today. Today it was chase games and kick the can and a full supper. Soon they would be young men and women up against the ways of the world. Some might do well. Others would have their hard work, or their faith, or their ambition quietly held against them. But not today. Baxter breathed. He told himself that he was worthy of his ambition. He was not the one who wriggled between the laws then claimed propriety. He was not the one who deserved to be scorned. For a moment he thought of running to warn the children. He didn't. He stayed where he was and listened to the ticking of his watch.

Squire let his attention fall on a hack as it went by. The driver looked over, hopeful for a fare. Squire waved him off. On the opposite side of the street, two women passed, each with a basket of washing. They walked slow and talked fast, often at the same time. They took no notice of the two policemen standing in front of Clarke's Place. Baxter continued to hold the watch as if it were an ear horn. Squire cleared his throat. Finally, he took a step closer and asked, "What time is it?"

Baxter turned his head toward the voice, it was too young. What was it doing in uniform? Had he ever been that age? Baxter looked the other way. The street was empty. Had children been there playing or was it just a cruel fantasia of the past? He turned back to Squire, his eyes strained as if Squire were far away across a shimmering desert. "What?"

Squire lifted a hand and pointed. "The time?"

Baxter took the watch from his ear. "Ah…ten minutes to four."

"What do we do now?"

"We go see the chief."

They fell in step again, heading back the way they had come. The motion unwound Baxter and he breathed more easily. He was ahead of his demons for the moment. He looked over at Squire and was about to ask him for his thoughts on Clarke's reaction and what they had seen there. But Squire spoke first. "I have never…I wouldn't…I just don't want you to think…" He kept his eyes front, his hands were deep in his pockets. Though the afternoon sun could still be felt through his coat, it could not prevent Squire from drawing his shoulders up into his ears.

Baxter sympathized with the young policeman, appreciated his concern for what others thought of him. His answer was flat with certainty. "That was just part of Mr. Clarke's act, diverting attention, trying to make us believe he had nothing to hide."

Squire's shoulders came down a little and he was able to look Baxter in the eye for a moment before he spoke. "I take it you think he does?"

"What do you think?"

"I thought there would be women. Where were they?"

As they turned down George Street they nearly ran into a man coming up the hill, head down, moving at a pace. He nearly stumbled into the street avoiding a collision. He mumbled an apology. Two steps later, Baxter looked back over his shoulder. The man had stopped at the corner. He was facing down Albemarle, as if he were going that way. Just as Baxter suspected, the man seemed to change his mind, turned, and continued on up the hill. Nothing doing at Clarke's today anyway, Baxter thought to himself as he turned back to watch where he was going. "Good question," he replied, drawing his attention back to Squire. "From what you said of the upstairs, it would seem they left in a hurry."

"So they couldn't talk to the police, couldn't tell us that Victor was there."

Baxter nodded. Squire was right, but only by half. "They know more than that, at least one of them does."

"How can you be sure?"

Baxter hesitated for a moment. He was used to working alone. Squire had no experience to speak of. He was a little lost at times, a bit mixed up maybe. That didn't change the fact that he was bright, which was more than Baxter could say for too many officers on the force. He was tired and needed all the help he could get. He turned and looked at Squire, at his pale skin, thin shoulders, his eagerness. He looked every bit a new potato farm boy, the kind that ran off for adventure only to fall overboard or die on a battlefield, a sad story, not a storyteller. Today the papers were a bully pulpit for talk of duty and right and patriotic glory. Soon enough boys like Squire would be coming home from a business that wasn't really theirs, in boxes or minus an arm or leg that had once held a wife or kicked a ball, parts left in a bucket with so many others under a surgeon's table. What would the talk be then? Was Squire a survivor or a casualty? he wondered. Tomorrow would he decide to listen to the drum beats, decide that carrying a rifle in South Africa was a simpler thing than wearing a badge here at home? Baxter shrugged and answered with a question of his own. "Did you notice how clean the place was?"

"All I could smell was soap and vinegar."

"A little too clean, don't you think?"

"I don't know...I suppose."

"The cleaning materials were in that closet under the back stairs. The rags and buckets were still wet. And the floor in front of a closet door, that's no place for a rug."

"A blood stain?"

As they turned off George onto Argyle Street the town clock chimed the hour. Men stopped and checked their watches, then continued on. Baxter raised his hands in an indication of caution, as if he wasn't sure. It was a momentary pause. He was sure and Squire's jumping to the same conclusion only deepened his certainty. "Of course, Clarke will say it's horse liniment or cooking oil or some other nonsense."

"Then why cover it up?"

"In a back stairwell," Baxter added in a voice that was mocking and overconfident. "That was his mistake." Bold talk, Baxter immediately thought, with nothing more than a tangent to follow and without a shred of evidence.

"But is it Victor's blood?" It was an important question that needed to be asked and might never be answered. Nonetheless, for the moment Baxter was encouraged and a little troubled by Squire's seeming ability to read his thoughts. Maybe not such a new potato.

"We need to find the women who were working there on Friday night." They had come down from Argyle Street into the Grand Parade. The wan shadow of City Hall flattered most of the square with a soft light while Saint Paul's remained sharp edged in the last of the afternoon sun.

"Witnesses," Squire added, again finishing Baxter's thought.

The chief inspector had stopped at the foot of the steps leading into City Hall. Squire was three steps up before he noticed. As he came back down, Baxter continued. "They wouldn't be much good in court. They could be very good at giving us men who would be. If Victor was there, it was likely a night of gentlemen only."

"You think Wallace was part of the group?"

"I do."

"You want to talk to him."

"That's why we need to see the chief." Baxter nodded toward the doors at the top of the stairs. "To convince him to approach Wallace."

"With no evidence?" The look on Squire's face was disbelieving, as if he expected Baxter to reveal some damning secret he'd been holding on to.

"None. But Wallace will meet." The dire conviction in Baxter's voice made a meeting itself sound like damning evidence.

Squire made no effort to hide his confusion. "Why?" he asked.

"Because he's involved."

Further assertion gave Squire little help. "What makes you so sure?"

Baxter had been reading along Barrington Street as if his lines were printed across its storefronts. Now he turned to a study of Squire's face. "You can read Latin, yet last night you hid that fact, why?"

"I don't know."

"You see…?" Baxter waited for Squire to look up. "Just now you hesitated, and looked down. Which tells me you do know." This time Squire looked across the square toward Saint Paul's. "Don't worry, it's not important. When I mentioned Wallace, Clarke insulted me, do you remember?" Squire nodded and as Baxter continued he was able to look him in the eye. "Clarke created a distraction for the same reason you looked away. Wallace is in this somehow. And he'll want to meet to find out what we know, which reminds me. Did you find out if Victor met anyone when he had lunch at the Royal Hotel?"

Squire's shoulders slumped with the weight of more frustration. "No, I forgot, I'm sorry. I could go now."

"The day shift has likely gone home. Go in the morning, first thing." Baxter started up the stairs. Squire hesitated, looking off in the general direction of the Royal Hotel and the chance for a little redemption. After a deep breath he went up, two at a time, to catch Baxter at the door.

———

Tolliver's office was across the hall from the sergeant's desk and the open office area of the station. The door was open. Baxter knocked on the casing as he came in. Squire followed two steps behind. The chief's desk was to the left, at the far end of the rectangular office. The chief was reclining behind it, his hands clasped behind his head. "I expected you before this," he said, coming forward in his chair and folding his hands on the desk. "Are you making any progress, Chief Inspector?"

Squire remained close to the door, as if he expected to be excused. Baxter took a position in the centre of the room, and resisted an urge to pace the width of the office. He wanted to keep his full attention on the chief's reactions. The chief pushed back in his chair, this time angled toward the window. Tolliver didn't seem to be looking at anything, just not at Baxter, which raised his suspicions. Baxter reviewed the events of the day and laid out his theory of the case. There were no signs of tension or alarm, no signs of anything at all. Somehow, though, the chief seemed to be following the details. Squire was paying attention to what Baxter didn't say. Tolliver sat still, staring out the window. When Baxter finished, Tolliver waited a few seconds then leaned forward. Now he looked at Baxter and sighed. "So you're saying one of the city's most respected politicians got himself murdered in a brothel?"

"It's unfortunate," Baxter replied. For him, his family, and those of us who have to clean up the mess, he thought to himself.

The chief's eyes widened even more as he glared back at what he obviously took as understatement. "And you think the richest man in the city was a witness?"

Baxter didn't look away. He did, however, refrain from comment, just nodded slightly to confirm that he had not been misheard. Behind him Squire accidentally kicked the door as he shuffled his feet. The chief flashed him a look of annoyance and the young policeman mumbled an apology that was ignored.

"The fact that Wallace and McNeally were schoolboy chums proves nothing," the chief snapped, pointing a finger at Baxter.

"Would you have felt that way three years ago, when we had McNeally in custody?" The question was part retort, part accusation, but Baxter kept his voice calm, a subtlety that he knew would dig further under the chief's skin.

The chief shook his head in a way that indicated he took the question as a low blow. If they had been alone in the room, Baxter knew the chief would have cursed him up and down. Instead he took aim at the holes in Baxter's theory, now pointing his finger through them and Baxter at the same time. "You have no connection between Wallace and Victor or Wallace and Clarke."

He could fill in the holes a bit by telling the chief about Victor's change of heart on the tramway, although the more Baxter thought about it, the more he was convinced it had to do with Wallace. He could let the chief know that Victor's IOUs had been witnessed by a lawyer, likely another connection. He could spell out the details of his visit to Clarke's. But Baxter said none of these things. In the same flat tone he merely stated the obvious. "We are the police investigating a murder."

The chief's eyes narrowed. He said a few words to himself. Then he looked down at his desk and moved his hands apart slowly across its polished surface. With his head still lowered and a tight grip on the edges of his desk, he said in a voice more resolved than angry, "Leave this with me…I'll be in touch." As Baxter was turning to the door, the chief spoke again. "Past two days there's been a rash of burglaries, all in the south end. The mayor's had some calls. See if Meagher has come up with anything. Make sure he's on top of it."

The chief had looked up from his desktop, the features of his face dry and hard, as if drawn by lines of soil erosion, a face pressed out of secrets and back-scratching and trade-offs, the political muck of the city. When this day was over Baxter would take a long hot bath. He promised to speak to Meagher in the morning then turned and motioned for Squire to go first. At the door he called back over his shoulder, "Open or closed?"

"Close it, please." Just before he pulled the door shut, Baxter heard the chief lift the receiver and then the metallic voice of the operator.

Baxter held the door of his own office for Squire, then closed it behind him. He peered around the letters of his name stencilled across the door window. The office staff had all gone home. The night sergeant had not come in yet. Baxter turned to face Squire. "You handled that well," he said, pleased again by Squire's good sense of when to keep quiet.

Squire didn't answer right away. He was taking another survey of his footwear. Baxter stared at the top of Squire's helmet and waited. The eyes stayed downcast. Finally the helmet spoke. "You left some things out."

Baxter nodded as if Squire could also see through the top of his head. "Best not to tip our hand completely. The only person who knows Victor had changed his mind on the tramway is his office girl?"

"No one else I've talked to mentioned it."

"And you told no one."

Now Squire looked up. "Never said a word."

Baxter stepped over to his desk as he spoke. "Good. Take these home." He handed Squire Victor's appointment book along with his notes on the tramway proposal. "Go over them again. Look for any connection to Wallace, no matter how vague. When you're done at the Royal, meet me here."

Squire tucked the notes in the book and slipped it under his arm. He paused on his way out. "You're going to talk to the people on the list Saunders gave us."

"Just one." Squire started to ask, then cut himself off. He looked like he'd had enough policing for one day. Baxter watched him cross the outer office and say good night to O'Brien, who was now behind the front desk. He glanced over at the chief's door. It was still closed. There was no light under the door. But the twilight was still strong. Baxter thought about knocking instead of guessing. Eventually he decided against it. He was hungry and tired and the events of the long day were beginning to run out his ears. If the chief wanted to, he could reach him at home. He closed his own office door.

————•————

Jane had prepared a fine beef stew with dumplings and apple pie for afters. Grace had come to table with a newspaper. It lay folded by her plate. Normally her mother would not tolerate such behaviour. A part of him wondered at the allowance, the rest of him was too tired to inquire. He would not have to wait long for an answer.

"Have you seen the list of volunteers?" Grace seemed to be asking him. Before he could answer, Jane intervened.

"I should have insisted you put that away."

"I'm sorry, Mother. I just had to see for myself."

"And?"

"His name is on the list, look here." She passed paper.

"Whose name?" He was tired. The stew was delicious. He needed a good night's sleep, a week's worth.

"Peter Lenehan."

"Do we know him?" The name seemed vaguely familiar. The vegetables were perfect, firm not mushy, and the rolls were just the right temperature.

"They sit on the other side of the aisle from us at Mass, Emmet and Marie."

"Their boy enlisted?" With a sigh that was almost longing, he put down his fork and reached for the evidence. He read the name and slowly an image began to form: blond, heavy shoulders, and long droopy arms. He had once asked Baxter if he had always wanted to be a policeman. Baxter had answered with a question of his own. What did the boy want to be? Before he could say, Grace had appeared and dragged him off.

"We've been in the same class since grade three. He is the smartest boy in school."

"Have we seen him lately?"

"Not for a while. We used to...Why would he do such a thing?"

"I'm sure he has his reasons." Baxter had put the paper down and gone back to his supper. As he buttered a roll, he wondered what his daughter wasn't saying about young Peter Lenehan, whom she had known since grade three.

"He's lost all reason more like."

"Grace."

"I'm sorry, Mother, it's just such a waste."

"Perhaps he'll change his mind."

"Bit late, I'm afraid," Baxter said, mopping up a bit of gravy with the last of his roll. He had stopped wondering about Mr. Lenehan and was considering more stew.

"Can we change the subject? Grace, may I have that please?"

Grace took the paper from beside her father's plate and handed it over. She had pushed her luck bringing the paper to the table and turning the dinner conversation towards the contentious, which her mother viewed as bad for digestion and bad form. In deference to her mother Grace didn't chance any new questions about the medical aspects of Victor's case. Or perhaps injuries and death were suddenly too personal and frightening a topic. The meal finished with few more words. Baxter made an offer to help with the dishes, then made a poor job of disguising his relief at being released from duty. He was more grateful still when Jane offered to set up his bath once the dishes were dried and put away. Shooed out of the kitchen, he had wandered into his downstairs bedroom workshop with half a notion to tinker at something. He hoisted himself onto a bar stool. The soft soles of his slippers gripped a bottom rung like monkey feet. The workbench in front of him was cluttered with tools and junk from the dust bins and sidewalks of the city, battered soldiers in various stages of convalescence. He picked up a small carpenter's knife. A couple of gentle scrapes along a forearm confirmed its sharpness. He poked the palm of his hand with the point of the knife hard enough to make a dent, but not break the skin. He watched the impression fade as his flesh rebounded. He wondered what had gone through Victor's mind as his killer's knife had pushed in. Baxter poked himself again. He thought of Carmine trying to protect his brother. He made another dent and watched it fill in. Keeping Squire on the case was turning out better than expected. Poke. He regretted his suspicion of the young policeman. Poke. And his moment of insecurity that had caused it. Poke, poke. The dents were taking longer to fill in. At least the case had not gone cold. The smile would be wiped off Clarke's face. Poke. His taunts regretted. Poke, poke. Ugh. It wasn't serious. He pressed the wound with his thumb for a few seconds then surveyed the damage, just a little blood. As he put the knife down and drew his other hand to his mouth Baxter felt a presence behind him. He turned to see Grace standing at the open door.

"Father, may I speak to you?"

"Of course, darling, what is it?" He picked up the knife and a few other hand tools, put them in a tray and pushed it out of reach. He checked his hand again for blood then closed it up and slipped it into the pocket of his cardigan.

"I need your help." Grace had remained by the door. Now she moved as she spoke, not in a hurry as if she were nervous or afraid, just efficiently. She glided across the room without disturbing the air or making a sound.

"What is it?" Grace was on a second bar stool, her slender hands folded in her lap. Her eyes were a faded blue, like the gingham of a washed-out tablecloth.

"I've taken some tests, at the medical school." She had started off looking her father in the eye. She ended with her head down, her hands no longer still.

"Have you now." His back was tired. He had been slouching. Now he arched himself and folded his arms across his chest, sneaking a peak at his palm as he did. Fatigue and distraction delayed his full understanding of what had just been said.

Grace tilted her head slightly as her fingers tied and untied themselves. She seemed resigned to watching, unable to control their movements. "I'm sorry to have kept this from you and Mother. I didn't want to raise the topic until I found out if there was any hope."

"I take it you have done well on these tests." He was suddenly aware of his heartbeat, still there was a hint of pride in his voice.

"I got the results today. The school is willing to consider my application." There was humility and surprise in Grace's voice. And it seemed to Baxter maybe a little pride of her own.

"Consider." Baxter lowered his chin just a little. His eyes kept looking into his daughter's face, watching it as if it were receding, a trail of past faces, faces with toothy six-year-old smiles, lips bitten over grade-four math, the sublime glow of first communion.

"There have been no promises made, of course. Still I am being encouraged." Here was a new face for his memory, more grownup than child.

"So they may still say no." Did he sound hopeful? Was he wrong to feel that way?

"There are other schools." The blue in Grace's eyes no longer seemed washed out, more like sapphires.

"I see." Now it was the father who watched his hands and wondered what they might do next.

"Do you?" The voice was soft. The question no less hard.

"I have always loved you and wanted the best for you." His words were true and heartfelt and rather pointless in defense.

"I can still marry, have children." She would decide, that was what she was asking him to accept.

"You could do that first." He was reduced to pleading.

"You know what I wanted most when I was young? Brothers and sisters."

"We tried Grace...they didn't...the doctors said..." He was grateful that his mind was too full and tried to recall the sadness of those years, the stillness of the empty rooms.

"I will give you grandchildren one day, I promise. I just have to do this first. Medicine is advancing. I want to...I want to advance with it. Little girls shouldn't have to grow up alone...and this war..."

"Alone?" The clothes, the toys, two rooms made into one, the doting and spoiling. More consolation for her parents, so it seemed.

"I could do some good...make the most of all the things you and Mother have done for me." She was standing now, a little unsteadily it seemed. He thought she might reach out. He would take her hand, steady her the way he used to as they crossed the street. Instead she held out papers that materialized from somewhere.

"What have you got there?" He looked at her to avoid looking at what was in her hand.

"It's my application to the medical school. There are places for your signature. Family support means a great deal to the school. It would mean a great deal to me as well." Before he could take them the telephone rang in reprieve from the hall. He would not have to sign over a future he'd long imagined, not right this moment anyway. Grace moved lithely into the hall and said hello. His steps behind her were slow and heavy.

"It's for you, the chief of police," she whispered, handing over the receiver. "I'm going upstairs to read before bed. I'll leave the papers." She kissed him on the cheek and flew away.

He tried to listen closely. Despite the effort, he had to ask the chief to repeat some details. After he hung up he sat in the chair by the telephone in the dim lamplight of the hallway and waited for Jane to call him for his bath. It seemed a very long time.

Tuesday

Even as a boy James Seabrook had gotten up with the sun. It wasn't a habit formed from any particular need or purpose. It was just his nature. He sat very still with his feet together under the kitchen table in their blue velvet slippers. He unfolded the *Morning Chronicle* and laid it out flat. He pulled his chair in close and leaned forward slightly as he scanned the front page. It all had to do with the goings on in South Africa and the mustering of Canadian troops. In a related story on page three, the Americans were already gearing up for the thirty-fifth anniversary of the surrender at Appomattox Court House. It would be the first of the new century. He was relieved to see nothing further on the death of Victor Mosher, until page four. The sooner that event ceased to be news the better.

He had the kettle on for tea along with a saucepan of water to poach two eggs. The pans creaked with the rising heat of the stove as Seabrook read Victor's obituary. He was nearly ten years older so they had missed each other growing up. Even if they had been the same age, money and social standing would have kept them far apart, the Moshers having less of both than the Seabrooks. Still Victor had not let a rough start hold him back. He had done well, didn't deserve to end up the way he did. The death notice said all those things. There was a short story on the investigation, the police were doing everything possible. No arrests had been made. Of course it was only a matter of time. Yesterday Chief Inspector Baxter and his new partner had been seen outside a particular establishment on Albemarle Street. "There was talk" that perhaps someone at that address was somehow involved. Seabrook guessed the opposite was true. No one was saying too much at all, at least not to the papers, otherwise every word would be in print. So far so good.

The kettle spit droplets of boiling water onto the stovetop. They hissed and popped like tiny fireworks. He filled a teapot on the table and put the kettle on the back of the stove. He turned the water in the saucepan with a fork. He tapped an egg and with a surgeon's touch eased its contents into the boiling whirlpool. The albumen gathered round the yolk and formed a perfect little island. Seabrook created a second island then reached into the pocket of his dressing gown for his watch. 7:18. He liked a three-minute egg. He set out a plate, some bread and orange marmalade, and ate in silence, alone in the small kitchen looking out the window at the young maple in his backyard, the last of its red-orange leaves baking in the morning sunshine. It looked as though the city was in for another day of Indian summer.

Good weather or bad, the story would eventually come out, some version of it anyway. There would be scandal and outrage and for a few weeks the city would be shrill with talk of what the world was coming to, all the worse if this fracas with the Boers turned out messy. There would be a rash of new bylaws and cries for more policing to keep everyone safe from the dangerous classes, and themselves. Seabrook chewed slowly through a mouthful of egg. If he was caught up in the mess at least Millie would be spared. He'd hired a woman to come in twice a week, not for himself. He did it out of respect for her. Millicent Seabrook had always prided herself on the state of their home: silverware spotless, rugs beaten, and curtains evenly drawn. She might have lived longer if she had spent less time overseeing the work of her domestic help and rested more. Near the end her clothes hung off her like sails, no matter how much she took them in, which seemed to bother her more than the sickness itself. Still she went about the house inspecting table polish and floor wax. To read of his disgrace in the papers would likely have killed her even if she hadn't been ill.

He glanced at the paper once more, at the story on the upcoming anniversary. He had been a young man during that war. A good many like him had gone off to fight, just as they would soon go once again.

That time they had not been called. They went anyway. Some went for adventure, some for the money. Seabrook remembered a conversation he had had with a fellow by the name of William Archibald from the Musquodoboit area, a series of communities thirty miles east of the city. William said his father had died in 1860, left him the family farm. Somehow it wasn't enough and William found himself in America fighting on the side of the Union come 1863. Seabrook had met him on his way home two years later. William didn't say so, he just looked as if he had seen horrible things. His only injury had been an accident. He caught his rifle in a tree branch. The shot grazed his scalp. As for enemy fire, William said God was watching over him. The Union was right. Secession was wrong. No more to it than that. William had no opinion on slavery. He finished his tea and left. Seabrook never saw him again.

Back then, Archibald was the exception, not the rule. Halifax was not in the war, only close to it. Close enough to gather up a collection of blockade runners, pirates, ex-soldiers, deserters, diplomats, spies, and provocateurs. They schemed and profited, told stories and lies, and traded in rumours. For a time, as Seabrook remembered it, the seamier sides of life were irreproachable if not respected. In that Halifax, no one noticed a few gentlemen in a brothel. Those days were gone, and this little war would not bring them back. The reformers would see to that. One had to appear proper. It was expected now. Of course, food on the table remained the more important consideration. Seabrook rinsed his dishes and set them neatly by the sink as years of marriage had trained him to do, then went off to dress for work.

———•———

As James Seabrook was digesting the morning paper along with his eggs and tea, Culligan Baxter was moving quietly around his own kitchen. He had not slept enough. Still his energy was high, for now at least, and he felt a great anticipation for the coming meeting with Wallace. He had no personal dislike for the man. He had seen him from across a room or two, noticed his carriage in the streets now and then. Nothing more, they had never met or spoken. Even if they had, it wouldn't matter. Wallace was mixed up in a murder and regardless of who he was he needed to explain himself. If charges were warranted, so be it. Then there was the moral aspect. So far as Baxter was concerned, Wallace was wrong the moment he set foot in Clarke's Place. Maybe his associations with McNeally made him wrong before that. Social improvement was dependent upon example, respectable example. As much as Baxter wanted the facts, he wanted Wallace to know how disappointed he was. Maynard Sinclair Wallace had failed his responsibility.

Baxter was too wound up for a leisurely breakfast over the morning paper. He found some soda biscuits. He washed them down with jam and tea as he stood by the kitchen window shifting his weight back and forth, one foot to the other. The sun was still low in the sky, coming in from the front of the house. It had set fire to the top branches of the backyard trees, their bare branches like bright flaming clumps of tumbleweed set to roll off across the sky. In the gloom below the slanting light the gazebo floated in its tiny sea of brown grass, dozing like a child trying not to get up for school. Baxter sipped his tea. The sticks in the yard needed to be gathered up and burned. The gazebo furniture needed to be put away. And it would be best to run a stone across the scythe before it was hung up for the season. Maybe he could get to some of it this evening. He finished his tea and set his cup by the sink. He moved quietly to the front of the house. He listened at the bottom of the stairs. Only the clock in the hall broke the silence. He eased the door closed behind him. A full breath of morning air came in cool, but with a promise of getting warmer. As he stretched his arms out wide to take in more air, he felt the papers tucked into his coat. Baxter headed toward the station. He'd speak to Meagher if he was in, then make his way to the office of Mr. James Seabrook.

—•—

Seabrook's secretary offered Baxter a seat in an anteroom outside the lawyer's office. "Mr. Seabrook is on the telephone, I'm sure he won't be too long. May I get you some tea?" Baxter looked at his watch. He wasn't trying to reflect his impatience. He was considering interrupting Seabrook. Then again it was only eight thirty. Seabrook would dance with him only a little, not for long. Might as well enjoy the hospitality of the office before being waltzed out its front door.

"Yes please, with just a little milk, no sugar."

By the time the secretary came back, Seabrook still had not appeared. The woman's day dress was silk and too well cut. Still she looked like a hotel waitress pushing the mahogany tea cart with its spoked wheels. There was a full pot of steaming tea, with milk, sugar, and a small array of breakfast sweets. The china was more elegant than Baxter was used to. "I hope this is all to your liking, Chief Inspector. Please call me if there is anything else you need." She made no offer to interrupt her boss. She placed the cart between Baxter and the office door. He took it as a warning. She made a final survey then turned neatly and went back to her desk on short quick strides, arms in a tight little swing. Baxter watched her for a moment, admiring her efficiency and concern for protocol, and to make sure she was affording him proper privacy. He fixed himself a cup, then promptly sidestepped the cart and slipped into Seabrook's office.

He was mindful of his tea. The rug looked expensive. Seabrook was by the window watching something or maybe nothing at all, Baxter couldn't tell. Baxter glanced at the desk. The telephone was set well back. It looked cold, not as if it had been just hung up.

"Good morning, Chief Inspector, sorry for the delay. Did Helen take it upon herself to show you through?" He knew full well she wouldn't and didn't. He watched Baxter sip his tea from the middle of the rug twenty-five feet away.

Baxter ignored Seabrook's effort to scold him. He looked around a little more. A large portrait faced the desk from the opposite side wall, likely Seabrook senior, same hawk nose and cleft chin. Floor to ceiling bookcases either side of the portrait, tools of the trade. A pair of large tufted leather chairs faced each other from either end of the window. Two more in front of the desk. A small company of ornate stands with crystal ashtrays stood as sentries at their posts around the room. They were sparkling clean. Nevertheless, the wood and leather of the room gave off the smell of good cigars and pipe tobacco. Despite its elegance, it was a back room, nothing more. Baxter's work sometimes took him to these places. He was never invited. "This is a very nice office you have here, mind if I sit?" Baxter didn't wait for permission; he took a seat in front of the desk. He placed his hat on the floor beside him and nursed his tea. He could feel Seabrook's eyes upon him but couldn't tell if they were more wary or affronted.

"How can I help you, Mr. Baxter?" Seabrook turned his attention back to the window, hands behind his back now. The sound of hammers and labourers' voices came in faintly through the glass. Maybe they were within view.

"Tell me, Mr. Seabrook, did you help mop up the pool of blood by the back stairs? Maybe you helped get Victor's body down to the water? Or did you just get your coat and hat and leave the dirty work to others?" Baxter's voice was calm and sure, no malice or accusation, just simple questions waiting on simple answers. The tea was very good. He must remember to ask the secretary what brand it was.

Seabrook cleared his throat, though he didn't seem uneasy. "I gather the investigation has completely stalled. You're now at the point of making random allegations, hoping someone will confess. People are right to criticize the force."

"I'm not here by chance, Mr. Seabrook. A witness puts you at the scene." Baxter finished his tea and set the cup and saucer in the ashtray by his chair. He took some papers from his coat.

"If you had a witness that was any good you'd have brought company and skipped the small talk. I'd be under arrest." Seabrook's voice betrayed no fear. He took his time moving from the window and easing into the seat behind his desk. He leaned forward over folded hands and faced his accuser. He didn't go so far as to smile, still his face was pleasant.

Baxter looked closely at Seabrook's hands. Then he held up the papers he had taken from his coat. "Let's move away from the scene of the crime for a moment, shall we, and talk about the struggles Victor was having." Baxter pulled himself closer to his side of the desk and with intentional slowness laid out the IOUs in a neat line, the bottom of each page toward Seabrook. "I'm sure you have your own copies, but we can use mine, well, Victor's actually." Seabrook watched in silence, calm as the morning sea. If anything, Seabrook seemed to be admiring the work behind the visit. Perhaps in future conversations he would challenge those who criticized the force.

"And what are these exactly?" Seabrook asked the question, while sitting back in his chair. He brushed at some invisible lint on his trousers.

"Let's not waste too much time pretending, Mr. Seabrook. As you can see, your signature appears at the bottom of each note." Baxter pointed. Seabrook's eyes continued to study the fabric of his suit. "What I want to know is who the other signatures belong to." Baxter stood up and placed his hands on the desk at either end of his evidence and leaned in to be sure not to miss Seabrook's answer.

"Now who's pretending, Mr. Baxter?" Seabrook's posture remained casual, as if he were in a lawn chair at a summer social. Baxter's glowering frame seemed no more threatening than a sun umbrella. "Let us say for the sake of good humour that I did sign those papers, then I signed them for clients, clients whose identities as well as any work I may have done for them shall remain confidential." Seabrook was as neat and thin as his conversation with pale grey eyes that came in from a distance, but not dispassion. He stood up slowly behind his desk and delicately tucked his hands into the slit pockets of his vest. "If it should come out that Victor's death had some ignominy about it, well, that would be a shame. It's true that ranting on about the indiscretions of a certain class of men would entertain the gossips. And it would benefit no one."

Baxter held his pose for a moment or two, then refolded his ammunition and tucked it away inside his uniform. He found his hat and put it back in place. Just before he got to the end of the rug he turned and spoke in a tone that let Seabrook know he had performed exactly as expected. "The only one who wants to talk can't, he's dead. The rest of you think you can stay quiet too, which is wrong. Eventually you'll talk, then at least one of you is going to jail. All of you will be dragged through the mud and you know it will matter, Mr. Seabrook, it will matter a great deal." Baxter saw himself out. He forgot to ask the secretary about the tea.

———•———

Squire was slow to get up after a night of tossing and turning. He had been too hot, then too cold. He awoke in the centre of his small bed, wrapped around a ball of sheets and blankets. He stayed there for a while, staring at Betty's note which he had tacked to the wall beside his bed. He would miss her around the house. He'd eaten the last of the pie. It would be slim pickings for breakfast this morning. He couldn't remember the last time he had been to the shops. Josie wasn't much of a domestic and William got fed at work.

He found some dry bread and revived it with a bit of molasses. As he pulled the front door closed he noticed a room for rent sign in its window. "Enquire at shop, No. 47 Albemarle." Betty's room was bigger and brighter and only a dollar more a week. He couldn't take it. It seemed sacrilegious in a way he couldn't explain. He'd stay put and hope the person who took Betty's room didn't upset things.

The walk to the Royal Hotel at 119 Argyle took fifteen minutes. He went round the back, found an open door in a fence. He looked in. A cart and a number of heaped-over trash barrels took up most of the small enclosure. As he closed the door behind him, a pair of well-fed rats came through a hole in the opposite side of the fence. They looked him off any confusion he might have had about who got first pickings. Then they showed him their long pink tails and fat rear ends as they waddled over to the buffet. Squire shuddered. He went the other way, through another small door, then a narrow passageway that led into a busy kitchen.

As he came into the clatter of pots and china, he cut across the path of a young scullery maid. She was looking down, wiping her hands on her apron. When they nearly collided, she looked up with a flashing eye, set to give some clumsy cook a piece of her mind. Then she saw the cap badge and the uniform. "Oh…excuse me." She looked down, smoothing her apron.

"I'm sorry, miss, are you all right?" Squire held her shoulders for a second then quickly let go.

"Yes, I'm fine." She fumbled with a lock of hair that had fallen out of her mop hat.

"How do I get upstairs?" Squire took a step back, and looked round the kitchen that had gone quiet from everyone not noticing the policeman.

"Past the sinks, to the left, you'll see the stairs." She pointed, still trying to fix her hair with the other hand. "It was very nice to meet you."

Squire reached out again to touch her on the shoulder, then changed his mind and left behind an awkward wave. The door at the top of the stairs opened into the back of the restaurant. There were a couple of guests huddled over coffee waiting on food. Another young girl like the one who pointed him here was setting empty tables. She hopped about like a nervous bird.

"Excuse me, can I…"

The girl spoke without looking up from her arranging of forks and spoons. "Good morning. Please have a seat wherever you like. Can I get you something to drink?" She stepped to a sideboard and reached for a stack of menus. She held one out, finally looking to see who she was speaking to.

"That's ok, I won't be eating." Not that the dry bread and molasses had given him much of a start. The girl from the kitchen came through with plates of hot food. It smelled good and his stomach growled. "I'm Policeman Squire. Can I speak with you a moment?"

"What about?" She backed away, shielding herself with the cardboard menu.

"Were you working here at lunchtime on Friday?"

A wave of relief eased the tension in her shoulders. She let out the breath she'd been holding as she returned the menu to the sideboard. "I was off on Friday. You can ask Simon, he's the head waiter. That's him over by the bar. He was working on Friday." The girl lit out for the kitchen before Squire could say thanks or think of anything else to ask.

Simon Perry looked as if his morning had gotten far ahead and he was struggling to catch up. His upper lip was split and swollen. He moved behind the bar as Squire made his way over. He took away an empty glass and wiped the bar with a rag.

"You here to pick up where your friend left off?" Perry winced. He patted the lip gently then checked the rag for blood. His eyes were hot. Squire stopped short a few feet from the bar.

"My name is Squire, I'm with the police." He wanted to bite his own lip for stating the obvious.

Perry let out a mocking hiss. "I ain't blind. Look, I didn't want any trouble last night and don't want any now."

Squire held up both hands palms out as if to show he was unarmed. "I have no idea what you're talking about."

"This isn't about me getting into it with your partner?" Perry had taken a step back from the bar and folded his arms across his chest.

"Who?" Squire shrugged, his palms now turning upward.

"The other policeman, Mackay." For the next five minutes Squire listened to Perry tell him how he had had a long day. All he wanted to do was have a few drinks and mind his own business. Squire heard about the fiddle players who came in, one tall, one short. Everybody thought they played pretty well, except this one guy. Perry said, "I just wanted him to shut up, I didn't know he was a policeman." Squire listened some more about the words back and forth and then the shoving. "Next thing I know he takes a swing and we're rolling around on the floor." Perry paused to touch his lip once more. Squire took the opportunity to change the subject.

He took off his helmet and was running a hand through his hair. "Mr. Perry, I don't know anything about that. That's not why I'm here. Were you working here last Friday?"

"Why?" If Perry was trying to sound tough, it wasn't working. Between the hangover and the split lip, he sounded like a confused six-year-old waiting on new front teeth.

"Because I need to know and you look as if you'd like to see me on my way." His expression was sympathetic. He wasn't trying to rile Perry up any more than he already was.

Perry didn't seem to be reassured. He answered anyway. "What about last Friday?"

"Victor Mosher, you know who he is?" Squire had come closer. He laid his helmet on the bar and waited.

There was a rack of shelves on the wall behind the bar. Perry had begun removing bottles and lining them up on the bar. He glanced at the helmet and Squire slid it down a ways. "The councilman, the one found in the harbour?" Perry asked.

"Uh huh. He had lunch here on Friday. You see him with anyone?" Squire watched Perry work, trying to see himself in his shoes.

"I don't remember." Perry had found a pad of paper and a ruler somewhere below the bar.

Squire watched a couple move into the restaurant and seat themselves. His voice was patient. "No?"

Perry had taken a pencil from his shirt pocket. He was measuring levels and making notes. He paid attention to his work, but took a moment to survey Squire again before he answered. "Mackay gonna show up later, try to take me in?"

Squire turned his attention from the restaurant back to Perry. "If he doesn't?"

Perry kept measuring twice before writing on the pad. "Then maybe I remember."

"My guess, you're both on the same page, a little hair of the dog then bed straight after work."

"Robert White. Manager of the Aberdeen Hotel. He came in while Mr. Mosher was eating, sat with him a few minutes then left."

"You hear anything?"

"What they said?" Perry was looking from the measurements he'd just taken to some numbers on other pages in his pad.

Squire reached across the bar and covered the pad with his hand. "Uh huh."

Perry gave Squire a look, then relented. He ignored the pad and rested his pencil behind an ear. "Not really. A name, I think. McNeil or McNare maybe?"

"McNeally?"

Perry was replacing the bottles. He stopped and pointed a finger at Squire. "Yeah, that sounds right." He ignored the bottles now. "You don't think White did it?"

Squire reached for his helmet. "He seem like a killer to you?"

"No." Perry put the last of the bottles away and picked up the pad of paper.

"Let's hope for his sake you're right." Squire was backing away toward the front of the hotel and its door to the street.

"If it's all the same to you," Perry called after him, "I won't count on it." He waved the pad and made a face, then winced and touched his lip. Apparently taking inventory, or his encounter with Mackay, or both, had shaken what faith he had in people. Or confirmed it.

Squire's first thought was to head back to the station, see if Baxter was in and report what he'd learned. It was still too early. It was unfortunate that Simon Perry had got tangled up with Mackay. The man was a thug in a uniform. If Squire stayed on this job he would hear plenty of complaints against his fellow officers. Sometimes he would have to give the injured party more time, maybe even try to do something for them, but not today.

Squire was yet to experience his first winter in Halifax. People had described it for him as grey and suicidal. Spring they said was always late and some years just a cruel trick that lured out the desperate with a bit of sunshine, then crushed what was left of their souls with a late winter storm. With all that to look forward to, the warmth and sunshine of the past two days was a welcome calm before the storm. Though they were still wearing winter coats, everyone Squire passed looked as sunny as the sky. He made his way down Barrington, then up Sackville Street to the corner of Argyle.

The Aberdeen was a step up from the Royal. He'd been in the place on the few occasions he had had a drink with William, before he met his evil twin. Squire went in the front door, past the large front desk to the restaurant. William was bussing tables. Squire nodded to a corner then went and waited.

"What you doin' here?" William set a tray of dirty dishes down on an empty table.

Squire leaned in a little and tried to imitate the Tolliver he'd seen Monday morning at City Hall, the tone that said a reckoning was coming. "I'm looking for Sitting Bull, you seen him?"

William was taller than Squire, and wider. He had a face of perfect proportions that looked back at Squire warm as granite. "Asshole."

Squire couldn't help looking pleased with himself. "I need your help."

William pointed toward a small anteroom full of carts and dishes. "Not here." He picked up his tray and Squire followed.

William moved as carefully as if he were handling a newborn. The dishes made almost no sounds as he carefully scraped and stacked. "Do you know Robert White?" Squire asked.

"He's the manager." William gave Squire a look that said nothing more needed to be said and scraped a half-eaten sausage and bits of scrambled egg into a slop bucket.

Squire had picked up a plate. The sausage hadn't been touched. He sniffed, then passed the empty plate. "What's he like?"

William pointed to another stack of dirty plates. "I don't know, he runs things. I don't see him much, never given me any trouble."

With the sausage hanging out of his mouth like a cigar, Squire delivered the plates. With the sausage back in his fingertips he asked, "You ever hear him mention a man by the name of Frank McNeally?"

William paused, a fork in the air over a plate. "No."

Squire pointed with the sausage. "You ever see him with Victor Mosher?"

"The councilman?"

"Right."

William motioned for another stack of plates. "He do something wrong?"

"Got himself killed."

"Oh, yeah? So they got you playing Sherlock Holmes?"

Squire had finished his sausage and was wiping his mouth with a napkin. He went for another stack. "Now who's the asshole?"

William ignored the taunt. "Mosher came here for lunch sometimes. He was friendly with everyone."

Squire brought over the last stack of plates. "Nothing special between him and White, no special meetings, or arguments or anything unusual?"

"Not that I saw."

Squire spied a carafe on a table at the back of the little room. He felt it and looked round for a clean cup. "You notice White doing anything different lately? Or anything around here strange at all?"

William whipped his hands on his apron then handed Squire a cup the way a mother hands over something her child has been tripping over and still can't find. "It's a hotel, there's always something strange going on."

Squire felt the carafe again just to be sure, then filled his cup. "With White?"

William held out his own cup and Squire poured. "I don't know."

Squire tried his coffee, winced, blew, then tried again. "Can you find out?"

William drank his coffee without any fuss. "You're the policeman."

"One who would owe you a favour," Squire offered between delicate sips.

"I'll see what I can find out. I get fired, I'll be bunking in with you." He gestured with his cup.

"Place isn't the same without Betty." Squire dropped his cup a little and shifted his weight.

William nodded as he poured himself a little more coffee. "She left me a cake."

"Blueberry pie." Squire tossed his dregs in the slop and set the cup in with a pile of others on their way to the kitchen.

William peeked around the corner into the dining area. "I better get back to the tables."

———•———

The chief inspector was at his desk. He still hadn't seen Meagher. His daily reports had little to say. Whoever it was that was having a lark breaking into nice houses, they were likely to get away with it awhile longer. As Squire came in, Baxter looked at his watch then tucked it back in a pocket. "It's nearly nine thirty, you get up late?"

For a moment Squire looked as if he were going to say something cordial, then he simply sat down instead. "No, I made a second stop."

Baxter rolled his eyes up from the paperwork. "After the Royal?"

"I went to the Aberdeen to see Bil...to see a man named William Paul."

Baxter leaned back in his desk chair. "Why?" He would listen, then remind Squire that all he need do was follow instructions. Learning that Robert White had met with Victor the day he died and that Squire's initiative had been fruitful was a lift, despite having to eat a bit of crow, silently of course. His own meeting with Seabrook had taken some wind out of Baxter's sails. The lawyer had given him nothing. He was counting on remaining beyond reproach. Seabrook was very much mistaken of course. So why had Baxter's mood so suddenly clouded over? In order to keep up with Squire's report and push his thoughts aside, he asked, "How is it you know this William Paul?"

Squire looked at the floor and rearranged himself in the chair, "He's at the end of the hall. We live in the same boarding house."

Baxter leaned forward, paying more attention now. "Do you trust him?"

Squire looked up from the floor. He seemed to be considering something. Whatever it was Baxter couldn't see it in his face. "I trust it's in his best interest to help us."

Baxter rapped his knuckles on the desk for emphasis. "You tell him to tread lightly. Do you know who owns the Aberdeen?"

"No."

"Wallace."

Trying to hide it only made the pique of excitement and curiosity in Squire's voice more obvious. "Do you think he sent White to Victor, looking for a favour or delivering a message maybe?"

Baxter liked the idea. He knew better. He liked it anyway. So far nothing about this case was what it seemed. "Too fast. Let's wait and see what this Paul character can find. Meanwhile, let's hear what else you've learned." Squire had pulled Victor's notes from inside his jacket.

"We didn't miss anything obvious. No direct mention of Wallace. The argument Victor was building for the tramway talked about progress, horse power the way of the past, electricity the way of the future, less maintenance, more sanitary. No names, but he drops hints about investment money taking the weight off the taxpayers."

"Look at this." Baxter handed a newspaper clipping across his desk. "This was in the *Morning Chronicle* about a month ago." Baxter waited.

Squire read to himself, then some half lines out loud. "Horses are cheaper...There is strong and well-founded resistance to increased assessment...Electricity may be the way of the future, on the other hand there is no lacking in the present arrangement of the city's street car service. Victor said this?"

"More than once. Now look at this." Baxter handed over another clipping. This time he didn't wait on Squire's reading. "It's an editorial in support of expanding the electric tramway…progressive, cleaner, matches the new direction of the city. And just like Victor's notes, it hints at investment money."

"The *Chronicle*?" Squire waved the second clipping then laid both on Baxter's desk.

"Yes."

"Wallace?" Squire had backed off his earlier excitement, Baxter noticed, and he now seemed more measured.

"You're asking does he own the *Chronicle*? No…well, I don't think so. But I'm sure if he offered them an opinion…Maybe wrote an editorial, I suspect the paper would listen."

"Has he agreed to speak to you?"

"Yes, but not until tomorrow. I suspect he wants time to rehearse, time to make sure everyone else has their stories straight." Of course Wallace and Seabrook had already met. As he spoke, Baxter could see Wallace seated in Seabrook's office in the same chair he had been in just an hour before. Baxter wished this vision had come to him earlier. Rather than trying to read Seabrook, he might have done better trying to draw out whatever anxieties or secrets Wallace may have left buried in the wood and leather of the chair. And as soon as the thought entered his head Baxter could hear his rational self scoff at the notion of such mystical claptrap. Still…

"Did you learn anything from Seabrook?"

"James Seabrook." Baxter said the name with obvious disappointment. "He's likely another graduate of King's Collegiate. The only way he'll tell us anything is if he has to, to save his own neck. We need evidence."

"I did get something else from Victor's appointment book." Squire came round the desk. "In the month before he died, Victor had a number of meetings with MS and W. No times or places are mentioned, only these initials."

Baxter looked over the pages Squired had opened to. "MS for Maynard Sinclair?"

"W for Wallace?"

Baxter spoke without looking up. "It's thin, even if we could prove

Victor and Wallace were meeting, we don't know why, or what it might have to do with Victor's murder."

"So what do we do?" Squire had taken off his helmet. It was back on now and he was trying to catch his reflection in the window of the office door to be sure it was on straight.

Baxter closed Victor's diary. As he spoke, he slid the paperwork on his desk into a drawer along with the book. "Wallace is doing his home-work, getting ready. We need to do the same. I'll have another chat with Saunders at the bank. We need everything he can find on Wallace's busi-ness dealings. Then I'll wire the Maine police, see if they have any idea where Frank McNeally is."

"What do I do?"

Baxter stood by the coat stand buttoning his tunic. Wallace and Seabrook were guilty. They were, however, civilized. He could gather evidence against them in a civilized way. Dealing with the witnesses to what they did was a different matter. "You, Mr. Squire, will work with Sergeant Mackay."

Squire stepped away from the door. "He's a gorilla."

Baxter took his place in front of the window to check his own reflec-tion. "I will agree it's often hard to tell which side of the law he's on. It pains me to say this, but that's exactly what we need just now. The women who were at Clarke's Place on Friday night may have managed to get out of town. Or they may be holed up somewhere here. If they are, Mackay is the fastest way to find them."

"So what will I be doing exactly?"

"Your job is to see that Mackay doesn't do any more damage than necessary. Let's go find him, shall we?" Baxter waved Squire though the door then pulled it shut behind them.

———·———

The first place was on the ground floor, behind a thick wooden door with a narrow slot and a sign that said PRIVATE. Mackay banged hard. After a moment, there was a sliding sound, eyes through a slot, then the door opened. Coming in from the morning brightness, the place seemed even darker than it was. Heavy blinds made sure no sunlight got in. There were candles for light, no harsh intrusions of electric bulbs or clocks. Clouds of perfume and smoke hung in the air, pushed about gently by liquor breath and soft lies, bare shoulders and downy laughter. Perhaps the night had been wild, young men in new uniforms not wanting to leave anything undone before going off to fight the Boers. Others trying to drum up enough courage to join the ranks. Yet there were no signs of that. No one in the place looked new. Everyone looked as if they had just woken up. Behind them there was a yeasty pungency that Squire couldn't quite identify.

From the door no one could see his face, only his uniform. Wary looks came his way from the girls. Their customers looked everywhere else. Mackay followed the doorman to a back corner. No one seemed to notice his uniform. Everyone he passed said hello. Mackay sat at a small table. The doorman went behind a curtain. After a minute or so a woman came back through. She was wearing more years and clothes than the others. She sat at Mackay's table. Squire couldn't hear what they said. He didn't have to to know it wasn't their first meeting. The doorman reappeared as a waiter, carrying a small tray with bottles and glasses. He paused, Mackay said something and nodded toward the door. The waiter moved on.

Squire tried to look as if he wasn't paying attention, let his mind wander while he waited. Mackay had been civil when Baxter came to him with Squire in tow like a visiting cousin that needed watching. They were downstairs. Mackay had been helping roust the cells. Police court was about to go into session. He listened to the chief inspector, seeming to know he was getting a selective summary of the case and not wanting any more. He asked a few questions, feeling the way between exact instructions and what might have to be done. "Squire will be along to help." When Mackay was about to protest, Baxter added, "He needs the experience." Mackay eyed Squire as if he were a termite or some vermin popped up from a hole in the ground. Then he turned back to the chief inspector. The look on Mackay's face was one of wonderment. However, he kept his thoughts to himself. When Baxter finished, Mackay merely pulled on his helmet, tucked its strap under his ample double chin, and made for the stairs. "You'll not be gaining any experience standing there," he muttered over his shoulder and Squire had to run to catch up.

They had said very little as they walked. Mackay mentioned an address near the corner of Sackville and Brunswick Street. They'd start there and work down to the waterfront. When Mackay caught Squire looking at him out of the corner of his eye he stopped short and asked, "What?"

The suddenness of the attack and its hostility so quickly sharpened into a single word brought Squire to a halt as if he were at the tip of a spear. "Just wondering if you're feeling ok, you look a little tired." He wondered if he had looked as foolish as he sounded now replaying things in his head.

"You practising your concern for when you're a mommy?" Mackay had sneered back at him. He seemed to want Squire to come at him. Squire remained still, recalling what Baxter had said about Mackay being strong as an ox, and mean. "You're Baxter's new fart catcher, how lovely for you. Out here, I'm in charge and I'm telling you to stand back. It looks like someone needs their hand held, I'll let you know." Squire had let Mackay get a few strides ahead, let his stomach unclench and some of the redness drain from his face before starting after him.

Signs of a struggle. That's what Squire had been looking for out of the corner of his eye. Some redness or swelling that would match Perry's story and his split lip. Mackay didn't have a mark on him and Squire wondered if Perry had been telling the truth, that it had been Mackay in the bar. The not too faint smell of stale liquor on his breath and the match-strike temper said it likely was. And with all that, Squire had to ask himself what chance there was of him keeping Mackay from going too far. Watching him now, in a back corner with this lady abbess, the only place Squire saw Mackay going was through the curtain. If that happened he'd be more at a loss than he had been out on the street.

When Mackay finally stood up and came back toward him, his boulder head looking like it might crash through him and then the door, Squire's stomach tightened up again, though a little of the tension fell out of his shoulders. He stepped out of the track Mackay was on, and the big man lumbered past, then Squire fell in behind. A collective sigh of relief helped push the door closed behind them, and Squire knew he had at least one thing in common with everyone inside—a healthy fear of Police Sergeant Finton Mackay.

The scene behind the second door was much the same, dim and wilted looking. The keeper was a man this time. He could have been Mackay's brother, same barrel chest and rattlesnake charm. Mackay did have a drink this time and paid no attention to Squire in the process. Even if he had, at that point Squire was more interested in getting along than following the police manual.

Once again Squire followed Mackay out the door at a safe distance. After a block or so he dared to get shoulder to shoulder. Looking straight ahead he asked in a voice he tried to make strong enough to draw an answer without being tough enough to pick a fight, "So, you going to tell me what's going on, or you expect me to keep pretending I'm deaf and dumb?"

"You know this case better than me," Mackay said. "What do you think we're doing? We're looking for witnesses."

"So far all you've done is talk to a couple of brothel keepers. What can they tell us?"

"They can tell us what we need to know." Mackay was impatient. Squire held in.

"Which is?"

"Where to find Annie Higgenbottom."

He expected no answer at all. He asked anyway. "Who?"

"A girl who has been working at Clarke's lately. And before you bother asking, it's not a matter of how I know. All that matters to you, or the chief inspector, is that Annie will talk to me, maybe help with the case, if we can find her."

"Maybe she left town."

Mackay shrugged, walked a few steps in silence, suddenly interested in the sidewalk. "That could be. I think she has brothers in the Boston states. That's it, though. Most of her family is here. Mind you they don't see eye to eye, given her...ah...profession."

"You think she went from Clarke's to another..." Squire almost said whorehouse, but thought better of it. He had heard Mackay curse

Ellen Reardon, call her a hedge whore. In spite of that, he sensed the sergeant made distinctions and wouldn't hear a bad word about Miss Higgenbottom. "Place of work?" Now it was Mackay looking him over from the corner of an eye. Squire couldn't tell if Mackay was merely confirming his low opinion or if Squire might be getting some benefit of the doubt. In any case Mackay kept talking.

"Likely all of Charlie's girls went to other keepers or they're hiding out in boarding houses."

"How many girls do you think were at Clarke's that night?" Squire got another sidelong glance but Mackay didn't bother playing dumb.

"If it was the sort of night Baxter thinks is was, likely only three or four."

"And Clarke knows where they are."

"Depends on how scared they are."

"Scared of Charlie?"

"Charlie's no saint, but he's not the kind to hurt his girls."

"A customer then."

Mackay looked direct at him now. "Is that what Baxter thinks?"

Squire shook his head. "I think…We just met really…He seems angry."

Mackay had come to a stop. He pointed at the door at the top of the stairs he was facing. "Tell you what I know. If we don't strike some pay dirt here we're in trouble. You can be sure word is spreading. If one of these girls really did see what happened, soon as she hears we're looking, the race out of town will be on."

They climbed the stairs and Mackay knocked. There was no slot with eyes darting side to side, no hesitation. The door opened wide and a trim middle-aged woman appeared. Her dark hair was pulled back, netted, and pinned into a tight bun. Her black dress began at the tip of her shoes and ended in a tight ruffle high on her neck, its sleeves were tight and came a little past the wrist into the palm of her hand. Her face was pale and plain, no powder or rouge. She looked as though she might be giving lessons in classical piano or temperance lectures. Mackay must have knocked on the wrong door. "Sergeant Mackay, Constable Squire, please come in." She left them at the door and went through an archway into a large drawing room. Mackay waved Squire through, then closed the door.

Mackay did not bother asking why this woman seemed to be expecting them or how she knew Squire's name, questions Squire would have asked. Mackay got straight to the point. "Georgina, I need your help."

"You're looking for Annie."

Mackay flashed Squire a satiric glance before he answered. Word was spreading like a brush fire. "Is she still here?"

"I told her to get on a train, even offered her some travel money."

"She'll be all right, Georgina. I promise." The look he got from Georgina said she trusted Mackay, and she would go on worrying for Annie all the same.

Slowly Georgina moved aside and for the first time Squire realized there was a fourth person in the room.

Most of the time, Annie was a pretty girl. Not today. Lack of sleep and worry had taken the shine out of her eyes. Her hair was in her face. She looked run over.

Mackay took a step forward as Annie spoke. He seemed to move on instinct or as if drawn by a magnetic force. Then he halted too quickly. "You look good," he said.

"You're a lousy liar."

A couple of other girls had crept up behind Annie. Their eyes were sympathetic, but they stood on their toes, ready to run if need be. Squire watched Georgina come across the room toward the nervous covey. Her walk was slow and seductive and it occurred to Squire how far off his first impression had been. Glad to be shooed away, the girls skittered down the hall whence they came. Georgina paused at Annie's shoulder. She spoke in a soft voice. The look she gave Mackay was anything but. "You want them to leave, you come get me." She patted Annie's shoulder, then clapped her hands to scatter the birds a little farther.

"You should sit." Mackay pointed to a divan on the opposite wall. Annie nodded. The house was warm. She wrapped her arms about herself as if she was very cold. The short walk seemed to take a great deal out of her. Maybe it was because her place was on the second floor or that she thought sunlight was a disinfectant. If Squire were forced to guess he would say it was because Georgina had no qualms with the path money took into her pocket. Whatever the reason, the drapes on the large window were drawn back full. The light pouring in lit up the far end of the room. The frizzy ends of Annie's wild blond hair turned orange and waved lightly on tiny currents of air. As she sat small and stiff on the divan all Squire could picture was the unfortunate women of Salem he had once read about in school. He felt a sudden stab of pity. He also didn't want to get too near the blaze.

Mackay showed no such fear. He followed Annie and sat close enough to give her strength and not so close he might scare her any more than she already was. His delicacy was more powerful because he seemed incapable of it. The flames died down a little, or perhaps it was just Mackay's body blocking some of the light.

Squire stood in the pale shadow across the room like a child eavesdropping on an adult conversation. Annie was slow to speak, as if her words were hard to find and fit in place. Yes, she knew who Victor Mosher was and yes, she was sure he was one of the men at Clarke's last Friday night.

"Who else was there?" Mackay asked. His voice was light and buoyant, trying to take some of her weight.

"Martha and Sarah were with me. We're the youngest." She shrugged as if to say this was to be expected.

"Who was with Victor?"

"Oh...ah...I don't know."

"Think, Annie."

She sighed and looked at the ceiling, seeming to get only broken images. "That man with the...He's always...government..."

"An alderman like Victor?" Mackay asked.

"No, the other one."

"The provincial government."

"Yeah. They called him assemblyman...Lovett, that's it...Samuel Lovett."

"That's good, Annie. Who else?" Mackay pushed.

Her eyes came down from the ceiling. She looked at Squire for only a moment then focused on Mackay. "Honest, Finny, I don't know."

"Just tell me what else you remember."

"It was a card game. Me and Martha and Sarah were there just in case. Charlie told us to stay in the front parlour."

"Did you?" Now it was Mackay that took a quick look his way. Squire couldn't tell if he was being warned to pay attention or not to.

"Me and Martha did." Now Annie looked away from Mackay, not out the window, only as far as its glass. "That's where we were when Sarah screamed. We thought one of them had hurt her." When Mackay asked where Sarah was at that moment, Annie went on, in a kind of trance, to tell how she had gone upstairs with Victor, how they had gone upstairs once or twice before. And although Sarah wouldn't say too much, Annie was pretty sure they had met a few times in nicer places.

"So where was Sarah when she screamed?"

Annie blinked and looked down from the window pane and studied her hands. At first Squire thought she had not heard the question. Finally she said, "In the back landing, by the stairs."

Mackey put a hand on the divan between them. "Did you see what happened?"

"No, Martha and I were too afraid to move. There was a commotion, a fight, I think. We stayed put. Then Charlie came and said something bad had happened and we had to get out."

Annie didn't keep a room at Clarke's. She said Charlie was always good to them. "He would never touch our things or overcharge for board." Still Annie preferred to keep her distance.

"You sure you didn't see anything? You need to tell me, Annie." For the first time Mackay sounded like a policeman.

"I was scared for Sarah, but I didn't want to see…I had my coat right there. I ran all the way, all three blocks. I locked the door to my room and hid under the covers."

"Martha?"

Now Annie let a hand slip out of her lap onto the divan, almost touching Mackay's, though not quite. His hand didn't move. "I don't kn…" Her voice caught before she could finish.

This time the glance Mackay gave him was a simple request and Squire did him the courtesy of looking away. Mackay covered Annie's hand with his own. "But…?" he asked gently without losing his insistence.

"Next morning I heard a knock…real quiet. At first I thought it was down the hall."

"It was Sarah?"

"I wouldn't answer at first, she had to tell me it was her through the door."

"Did she…" Mackay checked himself. "Keep going."

"She was trying not to show it, still I could see she was real scared. Someone took her to the Aberdeen Hotel."

"Who?"

Annie looked at the ceiling again then shook her head. "She didn't say…only that the room was nice. The man came back in the morning with breakfast. Told her it was best she stay, he would come back later. She ate a little, then snuck out."

"Came to you."

"Uh huh."

"To tell you what happened."

"To check on me…be with someone she could trust."

Mackay took his hand off hers and cleared his throat. Being patient was an effort for him. "Tell me what Sarah told you, Annie, tell me who killed Victor."

Her eyes got wide and for the first time her voice was almost loud. "I swear to God, Finny, she didn't say. All she told me was that Victor was dead. Stabbed, she said."

"You want me to help you, I need the truth."

"That's all I know. We talked about other things to keep our minds off being scared. Next morning Sarah got up and left."

"To go where?"

"She wouldn't tell me."

"Was she planning to stay in the city? Get on a train? Did she have any money?"

"I don't know for Christ's sake…"

Georgina reappeared. She looked reassuringly at Annie and hard at Mackay. Annie let out a long breath and relaxed her shoulders. "After Sarah left, I felt really alone and then even more afraid. I used to work for Georgina…I couldn't think of anywhere else to go."

"You did the right thing, honey," Georgina added in a manner that made Squire think it would be terrible to have her as an enemy.

"So you've been here since Sunday?" Mackay asked. Annie managed a nod.

"Anybody look for you?"

"Just you two," Georgina answered for her.

"What should I do, Finny?"

It occurred to Squire at this point that he had no idea how old Sergeant Mackay was. Older than himself, certainly. Sometimes as old as dirt it seemed. Mackay patted Annie's hand and then stood up.

"Stay bottled up here with Georgina." They exchanged nods. "Martha may be able to tell us something more. We know Sarah can. We'll find them and get this mess cleared up."

———•———

Culligan Baxter was not a betting man. He guessed even the most reckless gambler wouldn't take a bet on what might happen. If Squire said the wrong thing, which could be just about anything, he could find himself on the seat of his pants rubbing his jaw. On the other hand, the young man was showing himself to be no fool and Baxter thought there was a toughness to him, strength Squire didn't know he had, and if Mackay did get ugly, he might get a surprise. Watching the two men leave, Baxter thought less about them finding a way to get along, and more about what might happen if they couldn't find a witness. He pushed that thought aside. He dug for his watch as he climbed the stairs. Twenty past ten. Saunders would have all afternoon. Baxter just needed to get his hat.

"There you are, Chief Inspector. I've been going in circles." Meagher had the look of a lost toddler who had just been found. Baxter thought his relief might lift him off the ground.

"Then it's a draw."

"Pardon?"

"Earlier it was me who was looking for you."

His whole body rippled like a bed sheet in the wind and Baxter couldn't tell if Meagher had been taken by a chill, or nerves. "Oh, yes. I'm sorry, Sir, I'm still fighting off this bug, I just can't seem to shake it."

"Tolliver wants a stop put to these break-ins. The mayor is getting calls."

Meagher managed to steady himself a little. "Not break-ins really. Seems whoever is doing this just reaches in and makes off with the first thing they find on a coat rack. Or someone's domestic help steps in off the porch for just a moment, and this character is off with a pair of freshly shined shoes."

"I read the reports." They had come to Baxter's office. Meagher waited outside.

As the chief inspector came out adjusting his hat, Meagher continued. "I've set up additional patrols. Some likely culprits have been questioned."

"Let it be known in the upper streets we are very interested in this. The responsible party is one of them, you can be sure. Given a little incentive, a neighbour will point us in the right direction."

"Any progress on the Mosher case?" Baxter knew the question was just honest curiosity, not a rib, still it piqued him just a little.

"We're talking to people."

"But you haven't gotten a confession?"

Baxter stiffened, and Meagher couldn't stop his hand from coming up as if to protect himself. Baxter started to say something, then looked at Meagher as if they had never met. Before Meagher could say anything else, Baxter said, "See to this foolishness before the mayor gets another call, will you please." As he spoke, Baxter patted the sergeant on the shoulder then stepped around him as if he were furniture. Baxter was nearly at a run by the time he reached the door.

———•———

He had been shown in by a teller. Though the man showed no reaction one way or the other, Baxter didn't expect Saunders was glad to see him. "What can I do for you, Chief Inspector?"

"I'd like to thank you for the recommendation you passed on to Constable Squire." Saunders gave a slight nod saying nothing, waited for Baxter to continue. "This time I thought it best we speak in person." Saunders remained silent. By the time Baxter had finished telling him what he wanted the bank manager had become paler than usual.

Saunders remained still, outwardly calm. But his desk seemed to have gotten larger and he began to appear like a small nocturnal animal that had poked its head up too early and was dazed by the light. "Do you have any idea what you're asking me to do?"

"Your civic duty."

"When did professional suicide become a duty?"

"Don't be dramatic."

"Don't be naive." Saunders seemed to have gotten over his initial fright. He had come out from behind his desk.

"Be careful, Mr. Saunders."

Saunders waved a hand as if reeling in his sarcasm. "My apologies, Chief Inspector. You must know, however, if I start poking into Mr. Wallace's affairs, it won't be long before someone else's name is on that door." He pointed, and paused for effect, or perhaps in real fright from a glimpse of his own prophecy. "Meanwhile I'll be blacklisted with every financial institution between here and Montreal. I'm not suited to manual labour, Mr. Baxter."

"Better than prison, don't you think? Obstruction of a Crown investigation is a serious matter." It was heavy handed, it had to be, he was getting short on time. Soon the press would be on Tolliver with hard questions. Tolliver would then turn to him, and not with Meagher's accidental insinuations.

"Be reasonable."

"You are an intelligent man, Mr. Saunders. Don't whisper in secret. Work on Wallace's behalf, as if you're confirming his assets for the government, part of some deal that's in the works." Baxter had no idea of financial matters, he was making it up as he went along. It seemed to work. A tinge of hope and colour eased the pallor of Saunders's face.

"Do you really think a man like Mr. Wallace could be mixed up in a murder?"

"In my job, Mr. Saunders, disappointment is a constant." Baxter pulled his watch from a pocket. "What time do you finish for the day?"

"We close the doors at three, but I'm here until five." Saunders had pulled at the bottom of his suit vest to be sure it was flat and smooth before moving back into position behind his desk, which had come back under his command. He glanced at a small address book taken from a drawer.

"Listen for my knock at four thirty. I expect by then you should have what I need." Saunders nodded. He already had the receiver in his ear, listing to the ring signal.

Outside the bank Baxter regretted that he may have given Saunders the impression he would feel bad for Wallace. Or more than mild surprise at his failings. All the same, the more he followed this case, the more his disappointment and sadness seemed to grow, trailing along behind him like a sidewalk shadow. And despite the warm weather, he was getting chills at the back of his neck; ice water chills that ran down his back and jerked his shoulders. Just thinking about it brought one on strong enough to knock him off stride as he crossed the street. He gathered himself and turned his face up to the sun seeking warmth for his body and spirit. Maybe he was coming down with something. Perhaps Grace could give him a checkup. It was a bitter thought he instantly regretted and moved away from.

"Great men are almost always bad men." Who said that? Wallace was not a great man. He was merely a son left with a great man's money and power. Victor had risen under his own steam into a higher class. His roots stayed firmly planted, a sans-culotte at heart. Who could be surprised or disappointed if such men acted badly? Tolliver, ever ready to pick up a corner of the rug and sweep; Clarke with his lying smile; Mackay as much criminal as copper; all of them were just following the nature of their coarseness. Things were no better at home. Grace was following her own advice, not his. What fatherly advice had Peter Lenehan ignored? Baxter's stakes were not as high, still he felt powerless and despondent. So what if he solved this case? Victor would still be dead. Jane would still be without the comfort of grandchildren. And he would remain where he was, weaving the emperor's new clothes from remnants of the truth. No. NO! He must not think this way. Victor deserved to see his killer brought to justice. Even if he didn't, his family did and so did the rest of the city. And if he could do that perhaps God would give him the strength.

Western Union was on the other side of Hollis Street, next door to the Halifax Club. If godlessness could claim a chapel in Halifax, surely the Halifax Club was it. Only the wealthiest of plunderers were granted membership. They gathered there, surrounded by oak panel, servants, and cigar smoke, to carve up the city's treasure and keep an eye on the masses. For all he knew Wallace was there this very moment, leaning over eggs Benedict and the morning papers, certain in the knowledge that the club's thick walls and the even thicker blood of his family name would continue to insulate him from the unpleasantness of life's details. Lost in his thoughts and with his face still turned toward the sun and its comforting warmth, Baxter was not looking in the direction he was moving. Neither was Thomas Berrigan.

Thomas was a hundred and sixty pounds in the pouring rain. In the midst of an Indian summer morning like this one, a few pounds less. Baxter had at least fifty to his advantage. Thomas went down in a pile, not hard, more like the gentle collapse of a wobbly spring calf. The look on this face was just as cow-like, eyes wet and brown and off in the distance, a distance that wasn't there amidst the squat ghoulish buildings that seemed to shoulder together and crowd in and tower over them.

"Hey, you fuc…Sorry, Chief Inspector, didn't mean to get in your way."

"Thomas."

Baxter held out a large hand, cold as a shovel. His first instinct was to scrape Thomas off the street like a horse dropping. Then as it hung in the air the hand softened, the buildings stepped back a little, Thomas reached up, and Baxter pulled him gently to his feet. The already tattered and grimy coat had collected some fresh dirt in the fall. Baxter moved to brush it away, then felt awkward and turned to check himself. The hand flicked at the tunic. Thomas watched. Baxter looked up for a moment, not expecting to lock eyes with Thomas. And for a moment the face before him was clean and clear, the hair washed and neatly cut and the clothes in perfect order from collar to shoe tops. The face belonged to a boy not a man, a boy who loved his father and whose mother still adored him and hoped he would soon find a way home. Baxter blinked the boy away, and he went back to his tunic. Without looking up again he asked, "Thomas, you getting enough to eat?"

"Most days."

Baxter nodded and drew a heavy breath, one that if he were a priest would have been followed by a Biblical reference and the handing off of Thomas to a Sister of Charity. There was no time for that. Baxter was a policeman, one with troubles of his own buried in a case it might be better not to solve. A puff of wind helped clear his thoughts and as he stepped by Thomas to be on his way he pointed, and Thomas turned to see. With surprising agility he won the race against the breeze and an oncoming hack. As Baxter pulled open the door to the Western Union office, Thomas was disappearing round the corner. His hat looked good as new.

———•———

B ack behind his desk, hands folded, set still as a tree but not faced up to God, Baxter imagined the mind of Montcalm watching the redcoats gather on the Plains of Abraham, or Lee contemplating the Union campfires along Cemetery Ridge. Both men changed history, just not as they would have liked. He closed his eyes then opened them again and whispered to himself, "I must have patience." Once again Baxter began poring over the details of the case, sometimes catching them before his eyes, letting them refract the light of his desk lamp into sundogs, hoping that one of them might confess something while looking in the mirror. He tried making notes. It didn't help. The pieces of the puzzle didn't move about the page as they did in his head, and the sound of the pencil on the paper only gave voice to his anxiety. He was rolling the pencil between his hands and staring at a ball of paper on his desk when Squire knocked at his door window. The hollow rattle gave him a start, but he was glad to see the young policeman.

"Where is Mackay?" Baxter asked, looking past Squire.

"Oh, Finny...I think he went downstairs."

"Become friends have you?"

Squire took a seat in front of the desk. "I don't think he likes policemen."

"Told you to stay out of his way?"

"He really didn't need any help." Squire's eyes went away for a moment as he watched something in his mind.

"Did you have to be his witness?"

Squire knew the word Baxter meant to use was conscience and that he was being asked if Mackay had done anything he should report. "No."

Baxter knew Mackay had likely crossed some lines, that Squire had likely just seen some new sides of the city or at least one side of a fellow officer that he didn't know what to do with. For now he would let Squire hold on to what he'd seen and trust if there was something he should know he would hear it directly from Squire and not third-hand from the newspapers or in the wind whispering through the upper streets.

Squire didn't bother with detailed descriptions of the places he had just come from. He guessed Baxter had seen plenty of them and Squire had no desire to compare notes. He got quickly to the point.

Baxter listened closely, then came back with a single question. "So this Annie Higgenbottom, you believe her?"

"I believe her fear."

"A city councilman, a lawyer, the richest man in the city, now a member of the provincial government. Why not hat makers and bookkeepers and surgeons too, perhaps we'll find out the archbishop himself was there." Baxter slammed his knuckles into the desk, not for emphasis. It was punishment for the blasphemy. In a more contrite voice he asked, "And this Sarah Riley and Victor…?"

Squire saw Mackay and Annie sitting on the sofa. He knew if he had not been there, Mackay would have held her instead of just patting her hand. He looked back at Baxter and shrugged. As if his name had been spoken, Mackay appeared in the office doorway. He didn't ask to come in. Had there been anything in his path he would have walked through it, or them. He seemed possessed or maybe he just needed a little more hair of the dog, Squire couldn't tell. He wasn't fool enough to ask.

Mackay halted his charge at Baxter's desk. "This came for you." He handed over a small envelope.

Baxter took the delivery, glanced at it for a moment, then set it on the desk. Looking straight at Mackay he said, "The police in Maine have no idea where McNeally might be?" Baxter wasn't asking Mackay a question as much as he was letting the sergeant know he preferred to open his own mail.

"You asked me to help, I'm helping."

Mackay seemed more impatient and belligerent than usual. Noticeably enough that Baxter was about to ask why. When Mackay kept talking the thought was lost.

"They said they would make some inquiries. They'll let you know if anything turns up." Mackay pointed at the envelope. Some of the edge had come off his voice.

Baxter knew it was as much as he was going to get, from Mackay and the authorities in Maine. He nodded his head. "Squire was just bringing me up to date."

Squire was still in the chair in the corner of Mackay's eye and the sergeant left him there. Keeping his attention on Baxter, he answered, "Uh-huh."

"You did some fine police work, by the book."

Mackay waved off Baxter's appreciation of restraint. "I'm not worried about the book I'm wor…We need to find Sarah Riley."

"Maybe the other one, what's her name…" Baxter looked from Mackay to Squire.

"Annie," Squire answered, and Mackay turned to let him out of the corner of his eye for just a moment.

"Maybe she knows more than she's telling."

Squire tried to answer but Mackay cut him off. "She gave us all she could. Leave her out of it from here."

"Thank you, Sergeant, but that's my decision not yours." The steel in Baxter's voice did nothing to put Mackay in his place. It only encouraged him to draw his sword.

"Well, how about you decide to go downstairs and ask Martha Green what she knows?" The tone poked Baxter like an insolent finger.

Baxter looked over to Squire who had pulled back in his chair lest the sparks between the sergeant and the chief inspector set him ablaze. "He means the other woman who was at Clarke's?" Squire indicated Baxter was right, at the same time he held himself well back in his chair and said nothing.

"You know any other Martha Green?" Mackay's sarcasm cast a deeper shade of red across Baxter's face.

"Sergeant, are you saying she's in custody?"

"Brought in an hour ago."

"You could have said that when you walked in. Instead you dance me round a circle?" Baxter had stood up. He remained behind his desk. What he wanted to do was rush at Mackay, shake some sense into him, shake out his own frustrations. The best he could do was to deny Mackay the satisfaction. He sighed and pulled at his uniform as if he were about to go on parade. "Well, gentlemen," Baxter looked up from his tidying and caught Mackay's eye to let him know the term applied only to Squire. "I suggest we retire to the basement for a chat with Miss Green."

———•———

Martha Green drank with her customers. Sometimes she drank to calm her fears. She was not a drunk. Occasionally she made the mistake of drinking with one. Ellen had wanted her to keep on drinking. Martha said she had had enough and was going home. They were pushing and shoving when a policeman showed up. Ellen had seen him coming and dummied up. She stopped struggling too and Martha looked to be the troublemaker. When the officer wrapped Martha up in a bear hug, Ellen came back to life with a story of how this crazy woman had attacked her for no good reason. When the two of them were gone, Ellen went back down the alley and found the bottle.

Martha was intoxicated. She was not intoxicated enough to overcome her nature. She was a light sleeper. The sound of the three men coming down the hall was enough to wake her.

"Good morning, Miss Green."

Martha blinked, looked round the cell then back at Baxter. "Have I been asleep that long?"

"Don't pay any attention," Mackay said, shaking his head.

"You want some water?" Squire asked. She nodded. Mackay pointed to the glass on the table beside the cot. Squire took it from her through the bars and moved off to the WC at the end of the hall. Mackay opened the cell and motioned Martha back to the cot.

"Miss Green, I am Chief Inspector Baxter. This is Sergeant Mackay and your waiter here is Constable Squire." Squire, who had returned just at the mention of his name, glanced at Baxter, then at Mackay, who shrugged in acquiescence. Squire was careful handing over the water, then sat down in the lone chair. Baxter stared at him for a moment while he waited. Squire kept his eyes on Martha as she drained the glass.

"Better?" Baxter asked with no real concern at all. "Wonderful," he said out loud and only to himself. "Miss Green, I understand you were at Mr. Clarke's establishment this past Friday night. I want to know who and what you saw. No stories, please, just stick to the facts."

Martha looked back at him over the rim of the glass as she lowered it from her lips. He thought he saw a flicker of sense in her eyes, hopefully enough to know this was serious business.

The glass was empty. Martha tipped it up again anyway, then slowly handed it back to Squire. "Thank you," she said. Then with her eyes still trained on his and an expression of genuine curiosity she asked, "Is he always such a prick?"

Mackay cleared his throat. Squire held on to Martha's gaze and shook his head slightly. Baxter's jaw muscles tightened. A profanity charge would teach her nothing and get him nowhere. "Miss Green, anything you could tell us would be greatly appreciated." He managed to keep his voice almost free of derision.

Martha smiled. Her honour defended, she went on in good judgement to tell what she knew. Her audience listened, looked at each other now and then, saying nothing for the several minutes it took Martha to unwind. When she finished, it was Mackay who spoke first. "Martha, have you seen Sarah? Do you know where she is?"

"Are you going to tell me what happened? Is she all right?" Martha looked from one face to the other.

"Charlie didn't tell you?" Mackay asked.

"No."

Before Mackay got into a conversation there was no time for, Baxter asked, "Miss Green, tell me again what men you saw that night."

Martha widened her eyes at the chief inspector and leaned forward a little as she spoke. "I told you, Victor Mosher, Samuel Lovett, and James Seabrook are the only names I know. The other three I never saw before. Now what about Sarah?"

Baxter nodded to Squire who took his queue. "Victor Mosher was killed." It was a hard fact. And as he had hoped Squire threw it straight with no warning. Baxter watched closely. Martha's surprise seemed genuine. She hadn't known. That's good, he thought to himself.

"That's a shame, I liked him," Martha replied after a moment. Then with more trepidation this time she asked again, "And Sarah?"

This time Squire shook his head in a way that let Martha know she needn't expect the worst. "She was with Annie on Saturday. She left Sunday morning."

"Where did she go?"

"We're not sure," Squire said, which was the straight truth.

"She wasn't hurt?"

"No," Mackay said, which was comforting if not completely true.

Martha folded her arms and rocked herself a little on the edge of the cot.

He reminded himself that she had been drinking. Of course she would never be called to testify. That didn't mean she couldn't be useful. Baxter was looking for cooperation and his tone said so. "Miss Green, if we showed you some pictures, do you think you could identify the other men, did you see their faces well enough?"

Martha continued her gentle motion, looking at the floor. "I came down early, before Annie. I was in the front parlour, they all stopped to say hello."

Baxter motioned Squire and Mackay into the hall as he spoke. He pushed the cell door fully open and left it there. "We'll be back in a few minutes. The WC is at the end of the hall if you require."

Martha stilled herself but didn't look up. "Are you going to charge me with anything?"

"No."

Now she looked up, caught Baxter's eye, and held it. "But I'm in trouble."

"We'll look after you," Baxter replied. Martha looked from Baxter to Mackay, who was holding a bar in each hand looking back at her. When he nodded she began to breathe again and went back to rocking and staring at the floor.

———•———

Mackay waited until they were down the hall. Still he kept his voice low. "Why didn't you just ask her if Wallace was there?"

Baxter had to wait a moment before answering. A large part of him wanted to mock, or prod at Mackay a little more. If he did, it would only make him smaller. He wouldn't go so far as to apologize for suggesting Mackay was no gentleman. He would at least return to civil ground. He turned and looked straight at Mackay as he spoke. "I'm just being careful, Sergeant. I want her to tell me what she knows, not what she thinks I want to hear."

"So where are we going now?"

"To my office."

"I don't recall seeing a picture of Wallace on your desk." There was still some fight left in Mackay. Baxter refused the bait.

"Do you recall seeing a pile of old newspapers in the corner? We'll need some scissors, check at the front desk."

Even if he had looked Mackay in the eye and told him to get the scissors, the sergeant would have left it to Squire. Baxter told himself it wasn't a point worth making as he listened to Squire opening drawers. He continued on ahead to his office, now the department archives. Jane poked fun at him for the way he held on to things long after they were ready for the dust bin. Worse still, he dragged home other people's junk. "Another lost soul, messiah?" she would say as he tried to sneak into his workshop with a stopped clock or an end table in pieces. He was never sure what it was that gave him away. She never had to put her head in the hall to see what he was up to, or gauge his mood. She just knew. Just as she knew the household accounts. Saving pennies for a rainy day. Hoping for one grand sunny day in the backyard. Better Jane had told fortunes. Except her sense of dignity and privacy would never allow it. And despite her jibes, which were really meant as plasters for his wounds, his reclamation projects did well at church bazaars.

The newspapers, the case notes, the stray bits and pieces that might turn into evidence—these things could not be repaired and sent back into service. No more than they could be thrown away. The best he could do was store things neatly, though he was running out of space. The newspapers were stacked against the wall, neatly bound with twine six months at a time. If Mackay had asked, Baxter would have skirted the truth; said there could be two years' worth. It was four and a half and counting. The rest of his compulsion was tucked away in drawers or in the wardrobe in the back corner where Tolliver assumed his chief inspector kept a few shirts and an extra uniform, to wake himself up with after sleeping at his desk. Baxter never made any lists or inventories. He didn't have to. The process of neat storage had committed much to memory.

"I thought you said *a* pile. Jesus Christ, you expect us to thumb through all these?"

"We should only have to look at a few." Baxter had pulled a bundle of papers from the middle of the last pile and sat it on his desk. He took a moment to make things even, finishing his thought in the process. "Summer before last was big for society weddings. The rich often get married on the continent. For some reason, that year getting married in Halifax seemed to be the thing to do." Baxter shrugged. "The weather was good, maybe that's all it was." He paused then nodded to himself. Squire had come in with a heavy pair of black-handled shears. They looked as if they could take off a finger and Squire was holding them out point first. Baxter moved past Squire carefully, as if it were a sword he was pointing. As he hung up his hat and unbuttoned his tunic he motioned Squire to the desk. "See if you can cut that twine without drawing blood." Mackay, who had been about to sit himself down in one of the chairs in front of the desk, took a second thought and moved off to the side as Squire pressed the attack, the scissors still pointed forward.

"You sure you weren't at Clarke's place on Friday night?" Mackay's voice had finally gained some light. He wasn't trying to get Squire's goat.

Squire pulled up the twine. Over the slow chopping scrape of the scissors he said, "I've never lost my temper in a bar. Mind you, if it happens, I hope I can think twice before getting into a fight. I am a policeman after all." Squire set the shears on the desk and dropped the bits of string into a wastebasket. Then he took a paper off the pile and sat down to study it.

Baxter had been paying close attention to the rolling up of his sleeves. He may have missed a flash of surprise or anger on Mackay's face. More

likely it was a sneer at Squire's suggestion that discretion might sometimes be the better part of valour. Mackay hadn't graduated from the
Pictou Academy, and Baxter doubted he spent much time pondering his
actions, before or after. A thought almost formed in Baxter's mind, it was
more of a feeling really, on doing what was right. It was gone before he
could see it clearly and he was finished rolling up his sleeves.

"This isn't history class, Mr. Squire, don't bother with the headlines."
Baxter had gone round behind the desk. He took off the top third of the
pile and set it aside. At the same time he reached a hand toward Squire
and waited for him to give back the paper he'd taken. As Baxter refolded
it and put it back on the pile, he said, "We should only have to go through
June and July." He picked through the main pile a little further then
set aside another wad of papers. Then he passed some to Squire and to
Mackay, whose expression had cleared and who was now sitting in the
chair next to Squire. "There aren't many, but if memory serves, there are
a few pictures of prominent guests. You should find them on page three
or four." The room filled with the rustle and crack of turning newsprint.
Few words were spoken. Most papers were set aside intact. Occasionally
there was a call for the scissors. For a while the office had the aura of a
grade three classroom, Sister Baxter the teacher in charge.

"Why the extra pictures?" Mackay wanted to know. He was picking
up scraps while Baxter hunted for some fresh twine and Squire refolded
papers. Their group project, eight pictures in two groups of four, lay in a
neat arrangement on the desk.

"Well, for one, I want to believe her, Sergeant. If Miss Green can pick
out Wallace, and Seabrook and Lovett from this group as the men she
saw that night, then I'm more inclined to do so."

"Pick them out of a crowd," Mackay said to himself, accepting that
logic without seeing the rest of it. Still looking a little puzzled, he said to
Baxter, "And reason number two?"

"No court will convict these men on the testimony of a Martha Green.
Doesn't matter what she saw, all the jury will see is her reputation."

"Just because…"

Baxter held up his hand. There was no time and he didn't care to
discuss a harlot's virtues, the two were polar opposites as far he was

concerned. "Look, Sergeant, Wallace is coming in tomorrow. If he sees that I believe Miss Green, he'll realize what she might do to public opinion and that can be used against him."

Guessing that Squire had already made sense of things, Baxter looked to him to show agreement, and give Mackay further assurance. Baxter wanted to stay on his good side. He had the feeling he would need more of the sergeant's help. Mackay seemed to mull things over as he played with a sliver of paper. Just when Baxter was sure Squire was going to be no help at all and before Mackay could ask another question or take greater offence at Baxter's opinions of Martha, and by extension Annie, Squire gave the sergeant a quick pat on the shoulder as he said, "And with the extra pictures, maybe we get lucky and Martha sees someone else she knows."

—·—

The sun was low and drowsy in the afternoon sky on the way back to the bank. Long thin shadows ran off the sidewalks out into the streets or up the sides of buildings, ghosts that danced then vanished in the gloom of a passing cloud. Baxter was trying to count the hours of sleep he'd had since finding Victor under Mitchell's Wharf. Being generous didn't clear his mind or fool his body into feeling better. He yawned so hard he felt faint from exertion and lack of oxygen. He reached for a lamp standard, missed it at first, and nearly stumbled into the street. He stood for a few seconds with his back against it looking at the sign above the door of the Union Bank a block away, wondering if he could make it. There were a few deep breaths. The rhythmic clop, clop, clop of a peddler's horse cart provided something to focus on. Shoppers and schoolchildren passing by were unsure what to make of the vacant stare and gave him a wide berth, which he was grateful for. After a minute, perhaps two, Baxter felt steady enough to leave the comfort of the stanchion and carry on to the bank.

The door was locked and he could see no movement, only a few lights. He banged too hard on the glass door and the shockwave ran from his knuckles along the bones of his arm, and rang in his skull like a cymbal. He clenched his teeth against the noise and pain and came back from the door as if it had shoved him. He waited, terrified he might have to step up and bang the glass a second time. He was massaging his temples when he caught a glimpse, something far inside the bank coming into line with the door, halting for a moment then moving again, forward into focus. It was Saunders. Baxter's heart rate slowed and he was able to drop his hands, the skull rattle easing to a hum then melting away like ripples on a lake. His ears had stopped ringing. Saunders fumbled a moment with the door lock. "Good afternoon, Chief Inspector."

"What have you got for me, Mr. Saunders?" Baxter noticed a briefcase by the door as he came in.

Saunders motioned to some chairs. "We're alone. I've closed my office." Baxter removed his hat and played with it in both hands. He remained standing.

Saunders drew a breath then let it out in raspy resignation. "Fine then. Where shall I begin?"

"Spare the drum roll. We're not at a Christmas pageant."

"Businessmen tend to be conservative, they are not quick to divulge. I could…"

"Mr. Saunders, please."

"Very well. Mr. Wallace has a variety of business interests."

Baxter set his hat in a chair then began to move in circles around it. "The Aberdeen Hotel."

"Yes and the market next to it and a carriage factory nearby." Saunders remained in his spot, looking more like a maestro than a bank manager. "These are personal assets held in his own name. There are other city properties that may be owned or controlled by Mr. Wallace."

"Such as?"

"I'm not sure."

"You had all…How can you not be sure?"

"Because matters of business are not as simple as you might think." Baxter ignored the reproach and waited. "Some of Mr. Wallace's affairs are managed by someone within the Eastern Trust Company. You will have to check with them."

Now it was Baxter's turn to be critical. "That's it?"

"No."

Baxter stopped his circling. Saunders remained mute. Was he gathering his thoughts or being huffy? Baxter couldn't be sure. Finally he thrust both hands toward him in exasperation. "Forgive me, Mr. Saunders, please continue." Baxter went back to rounding the chair, now counter-clockwise.

"Wallace also seems to have an interest in, or a first option to purchase various tracts of land including a piece of undeveloped land along Lower Water Street."

In the dim and fading light it remained possible to look one another in the eye. "Are any of these particularly valuable or important in some way? Anything unusual about them?"

"Not that anyone said."

Baxter continued to move while holding Saunders' eye, navigating from it. "Anything they didn't say make you wonder?"

"No."

Satisfied, Baxter turned and let his eyes follow his footsteps. "Ok, what else?"

"There are stocks or part ownership in several companies. I couldn't gain exact figures. Certainly the total value would be significant. I made a list."

Saunders came forward, reaching into a vest pocket. Baxter unfolded the paper. Angling for light he read slowly and aloud.

CURRENTLY HELD
Merchant's Bank of Halifax
Bank of British North America
I.C.R
Canadian Pacific
Standard Oil
Richmond Union Passenger Railway
Halifax Street Car Co. (large interest)

RECENTLY SOLD
Redpath Sugar Refinery (low)

"Just the one sale," Baxter said to himself. Then to Saunders, "How long had Wallace owned shares in Redpath?"

Saunders had gone back to the comfort of his distance. "That stock was part of what his father left him, I believe, about twenty years."

"Company sinking?'

"On the contrary."

Baxter wasn't sure if he had made himself dizzy from going round the chair or if it was just fatigue. He thought about sitting, and knew he didn't dare. Waving the note, at least willing to lean against the chair, he said, "But Wallace suddenly sells, and cheap."

"I wouldn't say cheap. He sold for less than what he might have gotten. A few months ago."

"Who was the buyer?"

"Redpath."

The idea that all this might actually be getting somewhere gave him a boost. "I see. And Redpath, did they happen to recently sell a large interest in the Halifax Street Car Company?"

"As a matter of fact they did."

Baxter had let go of the chair and was back squarely on both feet. "And none of this strikes you as odd?'

"Mr. Wallace is a shrewd businessman."

"So you're not sure what he's up to?"

"I can't say that he's up to anything, Chief Inspector. Two companies traded stock. It happens every day."

"Is there anything else you can tell me?"

Saunders hesitated, pulled at the points on the bottom of his suit vest. "Make of this what you will," he said still looking down. Then he raised his eyes to Baxter's. "Some of the people I spoke with mentioned that Mr. Mosher had also made some inquiries regarding Mr. Wallace."

"I see, and when was that?"

"Very recently, a few days before he…" Saunders looked away.

"Before he was murdered, Mr. Saunders."

"Yes a few days before that." Saunders nodded. He managed to draw his gaze closer to the chief inspector. He did not manage to look directly at him.

"So Victor knew the things you just told me?"

"Perhaps."

"I'm far too tired for games, Mr. Saunders. What do you mean perhaps?" Baxter moved a little closer and squarely into Saunders' line of sight.

"From what I understand, the nature of Mr. Mosher's inquiry was a little different. He was interested in the past, specifically any dealings Mr. Wallace had in late '96 or early in 1897."

"And what came of this inquiry?"

"Nothing earth-shattering. All that Mr. Mosher learned from the gentlemen I spoke with this afternoon was that Mr. Wallace sent some money to Europe around that time, London or Paris, they were not certain, perhaps a thousand dollars. And before you ask, no."

"No, what?"

"I don't know to whom or why the money was sent."

Baxter stepped forward a little farther. "Hazard a guess."

"No thank you."

Baxter made a sweeping gesture and gave Saunders a moment's rest from his interrogating vision "We're alone, Mr. Saunders, you said so yourself."

"That's not the point."

"Then please, Mr. Saunders, tell me what is the point."

"The Napoleon Fish."

"Excuse me?"

Saunders' eyes narrowed a little. "When I was a little boy, my mother told me a story about fish, what small fish do to get away from big hungry fish. The small fish swim as fast as they can. The big fish comes straight behind. When the school turns, one small fish goes the other way, the Napoleon Fish. A few of his friends follow. And when Napoleon stops, they stop."

"And the big fish has lunch."

"Yes, Mr. Baxter, but the school gets away."

"And the Napoleon Fish?"

Saunders sighed against the hard truth. "He lives, of course. I was a grown man before I learned that the Humphead Wrasse or Napoleon

Fish is really a big fish. What my mother told me was a fiction, her way of telling me my father was a tyrant whose followers would be sacrificed. Things tuned out well for her though. She's been a much happier widow than a wife."

"Mr. Saunders, it's my job to see that justice is done."

"And I appreciate that, Mr. Baxter. I would also appreciate not being served up in the process. Now please don't come back here again unless it's to open an account." Saunders stepped aside, giving the chief inspector a wide path to the door.

———•———

Kenny Squire rounded the corner at Prince onto Albemarle Street. Clarke's Place was in a row of houses behind him two blocks north. Up to now he had lived in this neighbourhood without giving it much thought. Then three nights ago, he saw the corpse of Victor Mosher, with its one eye and yellowy-white bloated flesh that reminded him of river water and the belly of a trout. Now in the tranquil windless clarity of this warm October afternoon, that corpse came back to him along with older feelings of loss. He turned now and looked back toward the scene of the crime. He saw people and horses made ripe and golden by the low angle of the sun, moving slow and sanguine. Voices spoke, hooves clopped, heels clicked, and doors creaked open and slammed shut, all with a softness, a gentle reassuring pleasantness that was a sickening lie. Past the bright sunlight, the fresh air, the warm ground, on the other side of thick concealing walls the world could be very dark. Squire sniffed the air like a hound in search of scent. His gaze drifted up to second- and third-storey windows and he wondered what horrors might right now be taking place behind their sightless eyes as he stood only a few yards distant in a universe far, far away. He saw the knife go into Victor's side. He felt the insanity of his father's barn turned upside down, and Kenny Squire thought for a moment he might never go indoors again.

He turned and kept walking, in a hurry now, not to get to his own door, just away from Clarke's. The warmth of the day had not yet faded, and he prayed it would quickly melt the icy shiver at his back. As the images of his father and Victor Mosher began to fade, new ones took their place. The grinning rats behind the Royal Hotel, the cherry pie in Simon Perry's split lip, and William Paul, a friend bent into a spy. He was done with the rats and Perry's lip. He wasn't finished with William. He had left Baxter's office with instructions to return first thing next morning with whatever intelligence had been gathered. He would speak to William at the hotel. He would not bring this into the house. He didn't want to lose William. And he was tired of being between Baxter and Mackay. The chief inspector's ambitions were tolerable from a distance. Unfortunately Mackay's penchants kept pushing him up against them. Each of them was a self-appointed saviour. Each of them was trying to hide it. Both of them were failing miserably and making those about them miserable in the process, most of all Kenny Squire.

The sound of his name seemed so real. He braced himself against some new horror.

"Mr. Squire, is that you?" All his demons knew him very well; pretending not to know him must be part of some new game. He was standing in front of his door. How long had he been there, afraid to go inside?

"Mr. Squire." The voice knew him now, the demons were done playing. He felt a tug at his sleeve and he nearly jumped across the street.

"I'm so very sorry, are you all right?" Her voice was caught between apology and bursting into laughter.

Squire turned. Just seconds before he had felt as though he would be crushed into the mud by the weight of sadness. Suddenly there was hope, a sun rising before his eyes as the western sky faded behind him. Was this a trick or was she really there? If he could just speak, maybe she would answer and he would know he was among the sane and not following in his father's footsteps.

"Miss Murray. What are you…I mean, how nice…Forgive me, it's been a very long day."

She hid her smile behind a hand to save him as best she could. That was as far as it went. Her eyes sparkled and her shoulders shook. Squire had to force himself to prevent his eyes from falling to her bosom. "Well, it's over now," she said lightly and patted him on the arm. "Do you know this building?" She nodded toward the door. "I hear there's a room for rent." He stepped back so she could see the sign. "Ah, so it's true."

"It's a tough spot," he said, looking to get even. "I'm here all the time."

"Raids, you mean?" She looked the building over as she spoke, as if it might suddenly reveal its true colours.

He waited for a moment, let her imagination run on a bit further. Then he held up a key. "Would you care to be introduced?"

He got the look of mild pique mixed with excitement that he'd hoped for. "You live here?"

"No," he said as he turned the key and pushed the door. "I'm studying to be a thief. I'm hoping you'll help me look for valuables."

"I'll not let this go," she said with a curt nod, and a look that was all play. "And yes, thank you very much, I will have a look." He followed her inside, the heartbeat in his ears silencing the demons, at least for now.

———•———

The walk away from the Union Bank came in the fading light of a day long enough to have started a week ago. He wanted to feel tired again, go home, let Jane take care of him. He couldn't. He was too angry now. Napoleon Fish. He wasn't leading anyone to destruction, he was trying to lead them away from it. He squeezed his fists in anger and he felt a sting in his palm from where he had broken the skin the night before. He looked at it now, a dot of redness, a bloodless pilot hole. If he had the knife now he could score the other hand and then his feet, markers for the nailers, the likes of Saunders. His legs had started towards home on instinct. He was at the corner of Sackville Street. He watched a lamplighter in the block ahead angle the ladder and make his next climb. He could follow the lanterns home to his wife and daughter. He turned and went the other way.

He sat for some time, staring from inertia into the small pool of desk light. He watched reports and other papers drift like dry leaves on a lake. In the background he could hear the building creak and crack as the heat of the day was lost to the cool of night. Now and then he thought he heard the steps or voices of other hangers-on, overwhelmed with work or hiding within it. Now he was sitting in a chair by the shore. Watching the sun dance on the water and smelling the warm salt air. He looked down and found a book in his hands and he began to read. It was a story of adventure, familiar, though he did not recognize any of the characters. The more he read the more the pages faded until all the words were gone. Still he turned the pages and it seemed the book would never end its silence. Now he could hear a voice calling to him. He came to the edge of a forest. There was a flash of skin or the blink of an eye through the leaves and branches. The voice was young, then older, then sad, then far away. He paced along the edge of the trees where the grass was high and scratched his legs. The forest threw him back when he tried to enter. He went off in search of fire. When he returned there was only desert and he was alone in the torch light.

As Baxter passed from one fitful dream to the next the building settled into silence. The rest of the hangers-on from offices above slipped out one by one. The night sergeant dozed behind his own desk unaware that he was not alone. And in the wastebasket beside her father's desk lay Grace's application to medical school, crumpled in a ball.

Wednesday

He crept downstairs in a nightshirt and slippers, navigating by cracks of dull grey light. The house was damp and cold. He knew before he pulled back the first curtain that the string of sunny days had broken. He opened Jane's sewing room, then his repair shop. He stubbed a toe trying to step around the stools in front of the workbench. Hopping on one foot, he noticed an old housecoat hanging behind the door. He tied the belt and limped into the kitchen.

The curtains were already drawn. There was a low fire in the stove. Smells of food hung in the air. He knew a plate waited for him in the warmer and the thought of having it made him feel like a thief. Jane could have never done anything so wrong that she deserved him.

He built up the fire a little and put water on for tea. It looked like an all-day rain, quiet even on a tin roof, a rain you wouldn't mind walking through. The backyard was doused. He'd missed his chance to do any work. It might be a while before he got another. An all-day rain could go on for a week in Halifax. Rain would soon be snow.

He made tea and said grace and vowed quietly that he would be gracious at the home of his mother-in-law on Saturday. He could do that much. He uncovered his plate and laid the tea towel in his lap. He hadn't seen yesterday's papers. The *Evening Chronicle* was laid out flat on the table. It looked fresh. Jane may not have read it. Grace most likely had, this one or a copy she had taken to her room.

The front page was all war news. The list of volunteers had grown, more families proud and anxious. Pages two and three were more of business and politics at home and far away. Amidst the local gossip on page five there was an announcement regarding services for the city's fallen alderman, Thursday 10 A.M. at Saint Matthews. A little farther down there was a short piece on crime in the city. "Are decent people safe?" the author wanted to know. "What is to become of us, a city of shut-ins? Venturing out for work and provisions, then early nights broken by nervous peeks under the bed?"

Baxter blew on his tea. He could feel the waters rising. The funeral service would be packed, the latecomers forced to gather round the open doors and down the steps into the street. When all was ready, the pastor would take his place before the throng and official mourning for Victor Mosher would commence. There would be scriptures read, moments recalled, and the air made so thick with the weight of loss it would become almost impossible to breathe. Heads would bow and eyes would close and everyone would see Catherine all in black and stoic, the children neat in line beside her, chins up, and Carmine looking so much like his brother the eyes would snap back open expecting to find things right after all, it was only a bad dream. Then there would be the slow filing out and the shuffling parade of agony. Thankfully it would be short, just down a ways and across the street. Latecomers would now be early, responsible to make room at graveside for the family. With the frost now in the ground, if the air was just warm enough it would appear as though smoke were rising up from flames below and everyone would try to find some other place to look, or fumble with the marbles of small talk. Finally all places would be taken, the last words said, and the box lowered on its ropes away. The shuffle would go back through the cemetery gates, out in all directions back into regular clothes. The shovels would be taken from their hiding place and the ground made even once again.

The papers would see the troops off to war. Then they would be out for blood. If there was no killer to be sacrificed, the mayor and the chief would be quick to make an offering of their chief inspector. The eggs had turned to rubber. His tea had gone tepid. He moved off in a parade of one upstairs to get dressed, his dishes laid out carefully on the tea towel by the sink.

Before getting back into bed Jane had hung a fresh uniform on the valet. He dressed as quietly as he could, feeling for buttons and arm holes in the half light. He kept himself turned away like a paramour on the skate or as if perhaps the hurricane gathering in his head might travel with his gaze, cloud in the air over the bed and storm away its peace.

At the bottom landing, he stood fumbling with his tunic, his shoes still in the other hand. The house had remained quiet on his way back down the stairs. Her voice took him by surprise and a shoe landed on a sock foot.

"Oh…Good morning, Father," she said, looking at him only briefly. "I can't remember the last time you were the first one up making breakfast." He managed a faint smile. She came a little farther down the hallway. "Remember how you used to make me scrambled eggs and sweet milk tea, then hold my hand to school."

He nodded and stole a glance up the stairs. It was dark beneath their bedroom door, and Baxter remembered why he had been the one to walk Grace to school. "You used to think lying in was the same as sleeping in," he said. Then neither of them said anything as people often do in momentary thoughts of the departed. He sat focusing on the tying of a shoe as if it were complex math. "It wasn't me really," he said without looking up.

"Pardon?"

"In the kitchen…It wasn't me. Mother was up, then went back to bed."

"Oh…Has there been a break in the case?"

"I'm working with a new man. He's been more help than I expected. We're meeting this morning with a person who may shed some light on things."

"You've managed to find some evidence?"

He had drawn the laces up too tightly. He untied his shoes and wiggled his toes, then started over. "We know Victor had some money problems. We know where he was the night he died…And we…we're confident this won't take much longer." He spoke with trepidation and she followed his words with furtive glances. The house creaked and groaned from the dampness in the air. Finished with his shoes, he reached for the newel post and stood.

"Have you discovered a motive?" she asked. She stood near the door to the sewing room, close enough to speak quietly, not close enough to make him feel cornered. She had dressed before coming down.

He wondered where she might be going. "We don't have all the details, though I suspect it has to do with money." He was saying more than he normally would about such things.

"It wasn't a crime of passion." It was a statement, not a question, very forward and not about his case at all.

"Are you suggesting I should take passion into account?"

"Perhaps ambition would be more accurate…or service."

"I would rather not be forced to consider the matter at all."

"I'm sorry, Father, I didn't mean to keep you." Grace turned away. The ticking of a clock exaggerated the silence. For the next few minutes it seemed to Baxter that time ceased to flow. Moments were lost or thrown away. Only random images remained as if turned from a deck of cards. They landed in silence, though not without the jolt of a nightmare's waking scene. He saw Grace silhouetted against the light from the kitchen, in mid-stride halfway down the hall, her arms stiff at her sides. He saw his large limestone hands carved into the dim light, reaching for his hat and coat. Outside, looking back at the house from the shelter of his umbrella, he could see that the rain had darkened the spaces between the shingles, making them stand out like the bright shiny teeth in the smile of a killer.

He walked slowly in step with the rain that seemed torn between giving up all together and becoming something stronger. There were other umbrellas and morning papers over hats moving along the sidewalks, on their way to offices and shops that would not open until their owners arrived and had time to settle in. He thought of waiting in his own office and then dismissed the idea. Keeping still behind a desk would take more energy than he could afford. He needed to pace himself.

———•———

It was just before eight when an irresistible urge opened Ellen's eyes. It took her a few seconds to realize where she was. The hay poking her in the face and the smell of horse said she was most likely in some livery stable. An empty bottle lay beside her. Had she shared it with someone?

She couldn't think past the weight of her head and the pressure on her bladder. Her left eye was twitching. She struggled to her feet and groped along the half wall. In the twilight far below the grimy windows near the roof she was all but blind. The eye that wasn't twitching was swollen half shut. She must have had company at some point. She fumbled with the latch on the stall then pushed through a side door. In the better light she recognized the alley between O'Brien's and the vacant shop next door. She flapped her arms out of the heavy coat and draped it over a shoulder. She worked her petticoat down and her dress up into a bunch at her waist. She felt for the barn wall behind her then lowered herself down.

Baxter had made the turn around Saint Mary's and was now coming up Albemarle Street. The rain had stopped. Most everyone who needed to be at work early had arrived. It wasn't time yet for school or shoppers or peddlers' carts. The city was quiet in between. Ellen's water drilled into the mud. The alley rolled itself into a trumpet and its mouth became the shore of a raging river. Baxter heard and then he saw. If Ellen heard or saw she paid no mind.

Part of him wanted to ignore her, only a small part. He spoke looking down the street, as if he were keeping watch rather than trying not to see any more than he already had. "Must you be so vulgar? Could you not find a proper place to do that?"

Ellen didn't startle at the bark of his voice, or stop. Speaking to the ground in front of her boots she said in a voice flat with abject certainty, "The horses don't mind."

Baxter huffed at the logic. Typical, he thought, of such a woman, if she could be called that. Of course she would be first concerned with the sensibility of beasts. "I'm sure they don't, but decent people do. Put yourself together and go home, before I throw you in a cell."

Ellen had finished her business but stayed as she was. She seemed to be thinking or perhaps her mind had just gone blank and her body would remain frozen until she remembered she could move. Slowly she turned her head. Though he was still looking away he could see. She knew this and so she waited until finally Baxter looked down the alley and met her eye. She smiled her yellow broken smile and through it said, "Well then, before we go could I borrow your handkerchief?"

She enjoyed watching his face go dull white and hard like bacon fat cooling in the pan. Had she been closer she might have picked up a scent, not the hickory of a smoke house. This was a more acrid and bitter smell, a smouldering conceit. As much as he was certain she deserved it, he would not curse her, would not give her that satisfaction. He went on down the street, quickly now. A husky, choking, coughing laughter grew as it tumbled down the alley megaphone and rolled around in the street behind him, without a place to call its own and not one bit lost or at all ashamed.

Baxter checked his watch. The Eastern Trust Company was half a dozen blocks down towards the water. After the second block his pace slowed again. Ellen's unsightliness had at least cleared his thoughts of Grace and raised his blood. He began to focus on the task at hand.

The Eastern Trust Company was in a line of stone buildings that began at the corner of Bedford Row and Cheapside, across from the post office and customs house. The main entrance to number sixty was open. Inside the main lobby was a sombre horseshoe of frosted glass doors, shiny metal name plates with bold black letters and high wainscoting in a stately dark wood. Baxter sensed movement behind the glass. The people here would be gently wrapped in silk and linen and ultra-fine merino wool. They would be battling against the evils of equality and benevolence. They would be following the divine wisdom of the ledger. The sanctuary of the Eastern Trust Company was two doors down on the left. For a moment he was halted by the fears of an outsider, then in the bottom of his vision he caught a glimpse of the brass buttons on his tunic and he moved forward.

The door opened into a smaller lobby with a desk and curate in the form of a secretary in a plain but handsome dress. The dark hair pulled back into a tight knot, the voice equally efficient and controlled. "Good morning. May I help you?"

"Good morning. I'm Chief Inspector Baxter. I need to speak with your office manager or whoever is in charge, please."

She stood without a word. As she disappeared through a narrow archway behind her desk it occurred to Baxter that he had no idea of her age. In the dim light and smell of furniture polish everything seemed eternal.

In a moment she was back. "This way, please." She disappeared again and Baxter had to step lively to stay close.

"Mr. Woodside, Chief Inspector Baxter." The secretary waited for a nod, and when she got it she closed the door behind him. She had made no sound coming or going and Baxter wondered if she might be wearing slippers. He hadn't looked at her feet. Woodside was standing behind his desk. He motioned to a leather armchair in front of it. Baxter remained standing, momentarily distracted by the question of whether or not Woodside was wearing shoes.

The office had a high white ceiling and small chandelier. No windows. The walls were thick and papered with a subtle pattern. Words spoken here had the confidence of a confessional with a touch of ballroom elegance. Woodside was a man of middle age, just heavy enough to cast assurance. His moustache was full, though very neatly trimmed. He might have stepped out of some gilded frame. He spoke with an accent that was vaguely European. "Chief Inspector, how may I be of service?"

"Maynard Sinclair Wallace. You look after things for him, yes? I need you to tell me about that."

"Perhaps that's true, but in any case I'm not at liberty to say."

"Rest assured, sir, you will not remain at liberty if you don't."

Despite the aura of great resolve that hung about him in the rarefied air, Woodside put up no more resistance than the backbiting hooligans of the upper streets who bore witness against one another just for spite or for the small share the court would give them should any fines be paid. "Well, since you put it that way, Chief Inspector, are you familiar with what a holding company does?"

Baxter reconsidered the chair and the office became an elementary class in business. For the next several minutes Woodside's moustache moved in a gentle, steady rhythm. His hands went into motion now and then to emphasize a point or signal a pause for questions. There were none until the end. "So, this holding company...what was it...?

"Harbour City Limited."

"This Harbour City owns several properties?" Baxter had followed the details. He just couldn't see the angle of them.

"Correct."

"And as the head of Harbour City, you oversee all of its affairs?"

"Correct again." Baxter wasn't sure if he was being praised or patronized. He pushed on.

"And Harbour City Limited is owned by Chebucto Enterprises Company."

"That's right." Now Baxter recognized the tone. Woodside had spent time teaching his children.

"And you say that while Maynard Sinclair Wallace does not sit on the board of Chebucto, he owns a controlling interest in this company."

Woodside stiffened a little. The metal swivel at the base of his desk chair let out a small squeak, it needed oil. "That is what I have heard."

"From men who are on the board.'

"Yes."

Baxter leaned forward. His leather armchair had no metal bits. It announced his movement with the creak of something stuck being pulled free. The heel of his left foot lifted and his thigh began to bounce. The movement was unintentional, an involuntary reflex, a habit, but not without effect. It acted on his memory, in the way of a particular scent on a pillow or melody in the distance or spice in a soup you don't have often enough, and he could almost feel the weight of a little girl and hear Grace squealing giddy up. He spoke quickly now and with great intent, trying to get away from the thought. "What you're saying is you have no records, no proof of that."

"Only Chebucto would have such records."

"What can you tell me from the records of Harbour City Limited?"

"Not very much, really. As I said, it is a holding company. Its only function is to manage assets purchased or held in the company name. In this case the assets are small and overseen by me, the sole officer of the firm."

"And what are those assets exactly?"

"Buildings rented out for various purposes, shops, living quarters, that sort of thing."

"And you do what…find tenants, collect rents…see to repairs…?"

There was a sliding sound as Woodside opened a drawer and took out a folder of papers. He went through it as he answered. "Well, not directly. As I said, my role, the role of Harbour City Limited, is management. I see that such things are done." He handed a single sheet across the desk.

"These are the properties currently held by Harbour City. A real estate firm finds tenants, collects rents, et cetera. That firm files quarterly reports with revenues. I look things over and when I'm satisfied that all is correct, I attach my own report and turn the lot over to Chebucto."

Baxter took the paper. It contained a list of six addresses. It was typed without corrections or accidental spaces and with all necessary punctuation. It ran down from the top right corner aligned at a one-inch margin, in alphabetical order. He went down the list once, then again. Without looking up, he asked, "How long has all this been in place?"

"That is more than I can say. I was appointed to Harbour City only for a two-year term. It ends next month."

"The assets, the real estate firm, they came with the appointment?"

"Along with a set of instructions."

"And a salary." Baxter had gotten back to his feet. He folded the paper neatly. He watched its edges, admiring their certainty and truth, unspoiled by lies or disappointments. He slipped it inside his tunic and checked his hat.

"Chief Inspector, I've done nothing wrong here and to the best of my knowledge, neither has anyone else."

Baxter sighed, not for Woodside or his protest. He sighed for Jesus in the temple and the sadness and the anger that he suffered at the hands of the moneychangers. "What's the name of the real estate firm?"

———•———

Kenny Squire woke up Wednesday morning bright and energetic. It had nothing to do with the weather. As he stood, in no hurry to button his shirt, the damp and cold came through the thin glass of the window and then through his flimsy undershirt. Over the roof next door he could see the greyness hanging over the city. Between the houses, the eaves and windowsills dripped in slow time. At least the sky wasn't falling hard. He watched the drops fall out of sight, listening to their soft padding rhythm in the mud below. Yesterday or a week ago, such a day would have been hard to bear. If he were pushed to honesty, he had been vaguely unhappy and ambivalent for weeks. But not today.

He looked down at the buttons of his open shirt and his arms hanging at his sides happy in their stillness. It was early and he was up and washed. Of course, that had more to do with putting body in line with spirit than any other purpose. He glanced over at the rest of his uniform strewn across the only chair. Its intentions were good, protection of the innocent, not letting the guilty get away. In order to do any good he had to endure the hell between men like Baxter and Mackay. Had he known, he never would have joined the force. There were other things worth doing. He had enough saved for a few tools or a ticket west. His father would have no opinion on the matter. If his father should come back from wherever he was, that would be the most important chapter in the family history, more memorable than anything his son was likely to accomplish in a policeman's uniform. His mother had never seen him in it. Her letters were filled with pride of what she could imagine.

Despite the sorry sight of the city shivering beneath a grey blanket of sop. Despite the air and the mud and the wood and stone of every building being infused with the burnt sulfuric stench of coal fires. Despite being caught between Baxter's Catholic Puritanism and Mackay's frontier justice. Despite being powerless to rescue his father or ease the suffering of his mother. Despite all of these things Kenny Squire had a shy smile on his face. There had been all manner of fault found with the room. She had hoped it would be bigger. There was only the one dresser. Such a small kitchen, how could they all manage? She went on in her protestations for more than half an hour and two trips up the stairs, then lingered at the door with talk of all the things she would miss. She left saying she would need some time to make up her mind. It was all theatre, her trying to get even and succeeding not at all. Elizabeth Murray would move in and the thought pleased him and unnerved him all at once and the feeling was as good as any he could recall from recent memory. He looked once more at the chair. As he buttoned his shirt he felt less daunted by its call. He would remain a policeman for a while longer. The envelopes it sent home were thin. At least they were steady. He was no crusader. Still his notion of right wanted to see some measure of justice for Victor's family, even though he had never met them. And the thought of leaving the city just now seemed more loss than gain. The front door key turned the bolt then slipped into a pocket, a final look overhead before stepping off. The sky glowered but was holding for now. The Aberdeen Hotel wasn't far. Halfway across the street in the midst of a full breath of morning air heavy with an exhilarating mist, the devil whispered in his ear. What if he was wrong and Elizabeth Murray was having her revenge after all? He took a second deeper breath and shifted his thoughts to what William Paul might have to say. A heavy drop landed on his shoulder. Two more made dark staring eyes on the sidewalk. Squire looked away and quickened his pace.

Normally his office closed out the world to let him think or work, sometimes until he fell asleep. He seldom turned on the overhead lights, the small island created by his desk lamp made the room even smaller and the walls thicker. The tightness and order of the place reflected and restored his sense of control. It gave him sanctuary. However, at this moment the room was bright and as taut as catgut.

Both men had discarded their ties and tunics and rolled their sleeves to the elbow. Half-empty tea cups had been pushed aside and steam drifted off fresh ones just got in. Every remnant and piece of evidence of the case lay strewn about the surface of the desk, held down in places by cups and pads of paper and pencils that were taken up now and then and tapped against the arm of a chair or a rim with the rhythm of a thought, the back and forth of tribal drums. Neither man had yet found sufficient patience or enough of a vision of the coming battle to make any useful notes.

Baxter seldom made notes. Years on the force had taught him how to write detailed final reports. His natural ambition saw that they included his key insights and decisions. Until then Baxter carried an investigation in his head. He had brought out the pencils and writing pads perhaps in some subconscious deference to Squire's education or the increasing demand for a show of some sort of scientific method in all matters claiming to be serious. He was somewhat surprised to find Squire inimical to their use. Of course, Squire must be more of a reader. Baxter read the papers, not much else. When he was promoted to sergeant he forced himself to read some military history, Roman conquests, European battles, and an account of the American Civil War. He found few parallels between the fight against an enemy army and the struggle to make his city better, though it might be easier with the power of a general. At the moment he was far from any notions of command. Instead it seemed to him that he and Squire were in the terrifying deafness of the hypogeum below the floor of the Coliseum waiting in an elevator to be hauled up before the screaming mob, then torn to pieces for its amusement. Or they could just as easily be hunkered down in a trench counting the minutes before the final charge that would be ordered once the cannons stopped or started.

Baxter blew on his tea then put it down without taking a sip. As he rummaged through the papers on the desk he said, "We only have half an hour more."

Squire had gotten up. His arms were stretched over his head and he was fighting off a yawn brought on more by anxiety than fatigue. "If he has any decent council, he's being advised to stay away."

Baxter waved off the idea. "Wallace will be here." Looking at a newspaper photo he had picked up, he added, "Just late enough to remind us."

"Of what?"

"That he needn't be afraid, that he is beyond our reach."

Squire bent to touch his toes. "But he can't stay there."

Baxter waited until Squire came back up, then dangled the photo at him. "So long as he does not become distasteful to the public or the upper crust that rests upon it, maybe he can."

Squire sat back down and reached for his tea. Between careful sips, he said, "So we prove his involvement. Make him distasteful."

Baxter had let go of the photo and gone back to his own tea. The cup was halfway to his lips. He put it back in the saucer with a sharp clink. His voice grew even sharper. "After five days of investigation, what can we prove?" Holding things up as if Squire had never seen them before, he went on in his frustration. "The medical report proves Victor was murdered. It does not prove who killed him." Baxter tossed it back into the pile. "His clothes show he was at least partly undressed when he was killed, but we still can't prove where it happened. His appointment book shows he was meeting with a 'W' and an 'MS.' We think that was Wallace. Can we prove that? No. We know he owed money, perhaps for gambling, and that he was about to reverse his politics and come out in support of expanding the electric tramway. So far we can't prove those things are connected to his death or to Wallace or anyone else."

Squire had held on to his tea, mostly to protect it from Baxter's rearrangement of the desk. He sipped again and it seemed to give him his reply. "We know Victor was last seen alive at Clarke's Place and that Wallace was there, we have a witness."

Baxter wasn't hollering. He hadn't spoken softly ether. Heads turned in the outer office, and then quickly went back to minding their own business. His voice shifted from frustration to something more contemplative. "Martha Green tells us we're on the right track. Even if she agreed to testify, who'd believe her?

"Mackay could testi…" The incredulous look on Baxter's face finished the thought. Squire tried again. "We'll find Sarah Riley."

"Wallace is on his way."

"We can use what William told me this morning about Robert White."

Baxter had moved away from the desk as if it were a bad smell. "The bartender at the Royal Hotel…what was his name?"

"Simon Perry."

"He claimed it was White who met Victor at lunch on Friday. Now your William says some bellhop is sure Frank McNeally met with Wallace at the Aberdeen before he robbed the bank in Maine three years ago."

Looking hopeful, Squire pulled at the thread a little more. "And that in the wee hours of last Saturday morning, White brought a woman into the Aberdeen, a woman who disappeared a few hours later. That had to have been Sarah Riley."

"Likely. Sadly we don't have time to talk to White and even if we did…" Baxter shrugged. He had taken up a pace across the short distance between the desk and the door, his long legs taking only half strides as if he were in complete darkness. "White, Perry, Carmine Mosher…most of what they gave us has to do with a bank robbery that happened in Maine, not here."

"But that has something to do with Victor's murder."

"Something we have yet to figure out. We'll never find McNeally."

Squire changed tack, determined to move forward. "Then we use what Saunders told you. Wallace buys a large share of the Halifax Tramway Company. Victor opposes tramway expansion. Victor noses around in Wallace's business. Victor is murdered. If I was Wallace and you threw that in my face it would make me nervous."

Baxter nodded as he made a tight about-face. Squire was right in his approach. They had to shake Wallace's confidence. This, however, would have the opposite effect. "We do that and Wallace knows our case is merely circumstantial."

"What about his dealings with the Eastern Trust Company, that holding company he controls without owning?"

"Harbour City."

Squire turned his head and waited until Baxter came directly in front of him. Shaking his head against all possibility he could be wrong, he said, "That's too much trouble for nothing, Wallace is using it to hide something or do some dirt."

Baxter stood still. He looked directly at Squire, at his cowlicks and clear eyes, at what he had done over the past few days. He wanted to trust him. Baxter started to speak and as he did Squire's expression showed his anticipation of a confidence. Then suddenly Baxter saw Wallace reading Squire like a book and he started again. "As it stands, it's just more suspicion."

Squire blinked as if Baxter had gone out of focus. "We have good reason to be suspicious…"

"So does Wallace." Baxter was still looking at Squire, but he was seeing something else. "Do you know what Sergeant Meagher asked me yesterday?"

Baxter's question was rhetorical. Squire answered out of reflex. "No."

Baxter kept talking, not realizing Squire had spoken. "He asked me if anyone had confessed…I had forgotten." Baxter had picked up his tunic. He had one arm in and was circling in search of the other sleeve.

Squire held up his hands signalling his confusion. He followed the chief inspector's lead all the same and reached for his own tunic. "No one confessed to me."

Baxter brushed at some lint, then looked Squire over as if he were much younger and they were visiting the in-laws. "We had better go see if our guest has arrived."

Baxter leaned his weight against one of the heavy oak doors at the entrance of City Hall and pushed his way outside. He held it for Squire, then let it go. The door eased itself back into place behind them. Baxter stood on the granite threshold at the top of the stairs and took a few deep breaths of cool wet air and looked over the Grand Parade. The square was often host to some celebration or another, particularly in the summer months. But on this particular Wednesday morning it was the making ready for war that had things going on. There was more than the usual traffic of workers from the various shops and docks along the waterfront. At the beginning and end of every workday, the square served as a shortcut to homes in the upper streets and those on the north side of Citadel Hill. Baxter watched groups of men file past in cloth caps and heavy work shirts, shoulders damp from the weather, sleeves rolled back from hands carrying lunch pails and tool bags. He removed his hat and dug for a hankie to wipe his brow. It was always warm in his office, he ruled out the possibility of nerves. Between dabs he looked to the opposite side of the square at Saint Paul's. On Sunday its double doors would open wide to the Anglican faithful. They would file past as they hoped to one day file past Saint Peter at the Pearly Gates. Today the doors were drawn, no worshippers, no weddings, no funerals. Anglicans were on their own, some at least were being faithful. Hopefully those that weren't would not get in his way. There was still no sign of Wallace.

Squire mopped his own brow with the back of his hand. Drops continued to fall from branches, clotheslines, and window ledges. He glanced upward. The grey wool blanket had grown lighter and fluffy like cotton balls. The sky was holding. He kept his hat in his hand. Still looking about the square and down Barrington Street, he asked, "Why are we waiting out here?"

Baxter didn't have a reason, no conscious one anyway. It wasn't as if a brother or favourite aunt was coming home and he wanted to spot them as they got off the train. The meeting was set for Tolliver's office. It made no difference if Tolliver and Wallace spoke in private beforehand. Even if he had a mind to, the chief could be of no help to Wallace. Baxter looked over at Squire with an expression that said he had given the matter much thought. "Our guest deserves an escort into the building, don't you think." Then he added as he turned away, "Besides, the weather's picking up a little."

Baxter rocked from heel to toe, and his thoughts wandered to Victor Mosher. The man had been an alderman for seven years. Had he been worn down by the long meetings, the petty politics, the vote trading, and the constant dirty dealing? Maybe it was the desperate futility of it all. At one time Britain's North American colonies were vital to the Empire. King George III helped drive the most productive ones into revolt. A few decades later the rest had become an administrative burden. So they were set free in 1867 to become the Dominion of Canada. For a time thereafter, Halifax was known in London, and was a sister to Boston and New York. Now she was hardly anything more than Ottawa's red-headed stepchild. A great deal of wind had billowed out of her sails, along with droves of young talent off to larger cities and greater opportunities. Men like Wallace, able to start from money, were bound to do well. Others who were able to pull themselves up far enough to become less desperate and more proud appointed themselves as guardians. Most just made do.

Maybe he was being too harsh, or perhaps naïve. The city had plenty of men weak for liquor, gambling, and women. Perhaps Victor was one of them, no more, no less.

He let out a long sigh. He checked his watch. Two minutes past ten. Not late enough. Wallace would be at least a few minutes more. Baxter moved out to the end of the landing and began making his way down the steps leading into the Grand Parade. He took each stair slowly as if it might suddenly give way. By the third step, he could see Grace. She was ten years old. The square was filled with people milling about the tables and booths and small stages. As he kept going, the clouds cleared away. The ground dried up. He could see the festivities. He couldn't remember their purpose, only that Grace had been excited for days. Her face was golden in the afternoon sun. He could see himself looking down into it. He couldn't remember what he thought or felt, only how perfect she looked.

"Father, can we go now?"

"Are you sure…you didn't miss anything?"

She answered with a pirouette. Her long braid swung out straight. Its shadow turned the clock round full. "I think I've had enough." Pointing at a booth with a line of children screaming and jumping up and down, she added, "And I don't care to throw three balls at the head of a coloured man for a nickel."

Had he said something? If he did he couldn't remember what. Then he heard Grace's voice again, breathless with enthusiasm.

"Can we stop at Sanford's Market and get some oranges? I saw them on the way." She didn't wait for his confirmation. She skipped off toward the steps up to Argyle Street. He watched as he hurried to catch up.

"The air smells so good, they must be cutting the grass on the Commons." She took deep breaths through her nose and looked at him so he could see how grand a thing it was and he took his own deep breath. "Oooh, look, Father, here comes a dog. This guy seems real friendly, look at his tail go, here, boy!"

"Be careful, Grace, let him sniff your hand."

"His fur is real soft. Pet him, Father. His nose is cold, that means he's healthy right? What kind of dog is he?"

"Some sort of beagle, I suppose. Smells like a beagle." He sniffed his hand and made a face.

"You're a good boy, aren't ya, yes you are. And you never mind my father, you don't stink, you just smell like a dog is supposed to. Father, can we get him a bone at the market?"

"I don't know. We'll see, Grace, come on, let's get going."

"Come on, boy, come on. Look, Father, he's walking right beside me."

"Be careful, watch where you're going. Grace, don't cross Prince Street by yourself, wait for me."

"Maybe his owner doesn't really want him."

"Maybe his owner doesn't know he's out."

"Hey, boy, stop chasing that hack, come here, boy, come here... Look out!"

"Grace, don't look. Come here."

He watched the driver get down. Watched him look, then shake his head. "Was it your dog, young lady? He just ran out in front of my team from behind that hack, I couldn't stop the horses."

"It wasn't your fault." She had been able to hold on in silence. Speaking broke the dam. The tears ran down her cheeks. She tried holding her breath and pressing her lips together. It worked for a second, then they quivered and her breath came in sobs.

A few people had stopped. He showed his badge and gave instructions. Then he picked up Grace and hurried off.

"Oh, Father, did you hear the sound he made?"

"Here, let's have a look at the oranges." He had stopped at the entrance to the market. He felt her head shake against his shoulder. He waited. It shook again and he walked on.

"I never heard anything like that. He didn't see the horses coming 'til it was too late."

"The driver was very sorry."

"It's not fair."

"What's not fair?" Squire had come down and was standing beside him at the foot of the stairs.

Baxter tuned to look, for a moment still seeing the face of a ten-year-old. "Excuse me?"

"You said something wasn't fair."

"Did I?" He had thought of saying more, of asking Squire what he thought, or perhaps giving him some advice should he get married and have children of his own, or maybe warning him against the dangers of having faith in people. It was too late now. Wallace had arrived.

An elegant black coach was being pulled through the gate into the square by a well-dressed driver, complete with fine leather gloves and top hat. He guided the rig to a stop at the foot of the stairs as if the two great animals and the weight they pulled were all part of his own body. The horses stood absolutely motionless as their driver knotted the reins and climbed down from his finely upholstered seat. As Baxter watched, a bit mesmerized by the perfectly choreographed ballet, he caught the scent of the shampoo used on the horses. A medicinal flowery smell masked their natural pungency. The driver opened the door of the coach, then stood back, his arms behind his back as if he were a soldier on parade ordered to stand at ease.

The man who emerged from the coach was decked out in a fine riding habit from Edward Minister and Son in London. Baxter knew Maynard Sinclair Wallace to be short and a bit portly. That was not apparent in his perfectly tailored jacket of soft brown wool and loosely fitting britches tucked into his riding boots. He looked taller and slimmer. He stood still for just a moment as if to give his audience a chance to take him in, maybe think of what to say. Then he gracefully removed his black bowler, stepped forward, and extended his hand. Behind him, his driver moved as if on command to shut the coach door, and then stepped back into place. "Very good to see you, Chief Inspector, hope we didn't startle you."

The greeting broke Baxter's trance and he moved forward to take Wallace's hand. His own was larger and thicker and police work hadn't made it any smoother or weaker. Wallace wore fine gloves that had a satin sheen and left behind a hint of eau de cologne. Still the grip had surprising firmness. Baxter guessed it was practiced, like the removal of the hat, a movement within the routine of manners Wallace used when he chose to gently communicate his superiority. "Good morning, Mr. Wallace." Baxter heard a reverence in his voice despite himself and he could see that Wallace heard it too. Then Wallace looked away briefly to take Squire's hand. He said nothing, merely nodded, letting Squire know he was expected to be seen but not heard.

In fact Wallace was at least a foot shorter than Baxter. It didn't feel that way to Baxter as Wallace turned from Squire to look him in the eye. "Mr. Tolliver tells me you would like to have a word…Terrible what happed to Victor. I'll help, of course, in any way I can." As Wallace spoke, his driver went into motion, moving to stand in front of the team, far enough away to at least feign ignorance of whatever else his employer might say.

"I expect the chief is waiting on us." Baxter started up the steps and Squire followed.

"Actually, he's not." Wallace had let them get halfway up the stairs. When Baxter turned, the face staring up at him wore a taunting smirk, masterfully hidden by an expressionless façade with dull eyes and a flat line mouth. Baxter struggled to see past the reflection, as if he were trying to see out of a window at night. When he sensed Wallace's enjoyment he became still.

"I see," Baxter replied. Either the chief was trying to protect himself or Wallace didn't trust him. "My office then." Baxter waited this time, and shot Squire a glance to hold him in place. He was done seeing Wallace make sport of the Halifax Police.

"I thought we might be more discreet…" Wallace nodded toward the carriage. Without being told, or seen to move, the driver had opened the door and was now waiting patiently for master and guests to board so he could gently close it up again. Wallace turned, and nodded again, this time toward Squire. "…and private."

Baxter came down the steps in a jaunty rush. Waving first to Squire then toward the coach he said, "There is room for three." He gave the driver a quick pat on the shoulder then dropped his weight heavily into a seat and enjoyed the feeling of the coach swaying on its springs. At that moment, if Wallace had ordered him out and called the meeting off, or reproached him for a lack of respect, Baxter would have only been all the more pleased for a clear sign he had struck a nerve. He would feel no shame for refusing to show deference to a man who felt he deserved it just because he had more money than everyone else. Wallace was guilty; Baxter believed it now more than ever. Unfortunately he also had a growing sense that Wallace would admit nothing and that what was about to happen was merely an exercise in power.

Baxter sat up straight with his long arms and legs stretched out straight, feet crossed at the ankles, hands in his lap, fingers loosely interlocked. The weather outside was still dank and grey, yet Baxter was all sunny day. Squire humbly took a place beside him, feet under him, hands gripping the seat either side of his body which leaned slightly forward as if he were on a tram that was coming to his stop. Wallace sat in the middle of the opposite seat, unnerved by Baxter's feet which rested just in front of him. As the coach rolled out of the Grand Parade and south on Barrington Street,

Wallace casually crossed his own legs at the knee, turned his body on a slight angle, and let one arm rest along the back of his seat. Then he took on a look of great sadness, of a man about to see a son leave home, perhaps never to return. Baxter was sure he had learned it on the way, staring out the window of his coach into the faces of so many common people who were wearing it for real. Through his pain Wallace finally spoke. "Victor's family must be devastated." He paused, sucked in a long slow breath that acted as a sea change upon his face now lost of all sentimentality. "Chief Tolliver tells me you have questions regarding my relationship with Mr. Mosher."

Wallace was safe and comfortable with a business tone. Baxter wanted to keep things closer to the personal. "You seem to be holding up. I understand you and Victor were quite close."

"Only in passing really. He did his best for the city." The face remained placid, detached and all lie as far as Baxter was concerned.

"Seems he decided the city needs more electric streetcars. I wonder what changed his mind?" Baxter had tucked Victor's appointment book into his tunic. He withdrew it now, and from it, the letters of debt found in Victor's desk. He began leafing through them absently as if he were passing a slow Sunday afternoon reminiscing with old photos. Yet all the while Baxter stayed finely attuned to Wallace's reaction. There was none, just as there had been none in Seabrook's office. And in that Baxter was sure Wallace too recognized the letters, they were no surprise, and so a show of indifference came with ease.

The lips came only to the edge of a smile and only for a second. It was enough. If Wallace had thought he would be easy to manage, perhaps he was feeling differently now. Baxter worried he may have shown too much too soon.

"I like to think I'm as progressive as the next man, but as you can see I've always been fond of horses," Wallace answered glibly with a wave of his hand toward his attire and the coach they were riding in.

With the letters still in his hand and a look as smooth as Wallace's tone, Baxter countered. "More fond of good investments it seems. I hear the Richmond Union Passenger Railway is a good investment. That's an electric street car system, isn't it?" There was no point in caution now, he had decided.

The coach had turned up Spring Garden Road, and Wallace spoke without taking his eyes off the traffic of people and horses. There was, however, a new flint to his voice. "Investing is risky. A person needs to be very careful."

Squire heard the warning and passed his concerns along in a quick glance. Baxter ignored him. "Being good with numbers, that would help. I never was. You did well in school. Oxford, very impressive. King's Collegiate before that."

Wallace turned from the window. "You seem to be good with history." His eyes followed for a moment, the book and letters Baxter was once again locking away in his tunic. "I never cared for it." With a look of genuine curiosity he opened a second front. "What about you, Mr. Squire? Was it numbers or letters for you at the Pictou Academy?"

Squire could not help show his surprise at being addressed. But he answered without hesitation as if the query was of a friendly nature. "My mother encouraged me in both."

"And your father…how is he?"

The blow landed flush on Squire's chin, and though his own face never lost its pretence of congeniality, Wallace enjoyed the look of hurt and confusion that came over the chief inspector. Squire blinked, then answered in a voice that was cool steel. "How is Frank McNeally? You keep in touch from your days at Kings?"

"And from their more recent dealings," Baxter added, looking squarely at Squire as he spoke, not bothering to follow Wallace from the corner of his eye. He knew Wallace was retreating. He had not been able to divide and conquer. Instead it was very clearly two against one.

"Poor Frank. I never would have thought." Wallace had turned his attention back to the window, which was now featuring the movement along Brunswick Street. The citadel would soon come into view. Baxter could feel Wallace waiting, a bit surprised perhaps, very far from nervous. Baxter could end it here, thank Wallace for his time, and ask to be let out. Wallace would go on waiting in the comfort of knowing Baxter was unlikely to find any damning evidence. And then he would forget altogether. Baxter had to push a little harder. "And who would have thought that Victor Mosher would be murdered in Clarke's Place?

I wouldn't be caught dead…That's what many will say. You've said so yourself, I'm sure."

Wallace stayed at the window, but answered calmly. "My mother taught me to be careful with my words."

Baxter continued to push. "Someone else we spoke to confessed that very same thing."

"Well, good for both of us then."

"Seems you know each other too…Miss Sarah Riley."

Now it was Wallace who was stung, and some innate reflex got ahead of his self-control and his head snapped away from the window. "I'm sorry…I don't recall that name."

Seeing Wallace flinch gave Baxter a needle jab of satisfaction. In the second it took to pass he realized this might be as close as he and the people of the city would ever get to knowing what had really happened that night at Clarke's Place. Wallace had come to find out how much danger he was in and now he knew. No doubt he already had people scouring the city for Sarah Riley. Now he would pay them double if he had to. Once he found her, he would see to it that Sarah Riley had nothing else to say about that night. And he was done talking to the police. "Well, a man as busy and important as you can't remember every acquaintance."

"I am very busy. In fact, I'm on my way to a meeting at the medical school. I'm on the board. The city needs physicians. You will let me know if you should run into any good applicants." And now it was Baxter's turn. It wasn't like being punched or kicked. At first it felt shaming and humiliating, like the slap Jane might give him if she were someone else and she knew what he had done. Then came the fear and vulnerability. How could Wallace know? And what was he suggesting?

"It was good of you to take this time." Baxter spoke to the floor as Wallace tapped the roof and the coach moved to the curb. He reached across Squire for the door and was on the ground before the driver could pull the horses completely in. He wanted to stare back at Wallace like an empty plate, give him nothing other than his worst imaginings to chew on.

"Not at all. Sorry to be of so little help. If you should need anything else…"

"I'll let you know tomorrow." It was said without thinking, not an intentional threat. And for that it was better than any parting shot he might have managed if he had been able to try. Wallace had regained that look of banality on troubles that were not his, yet this assertion seemed to rattle him. Baxter's shoulders squared and he checked the angle of his hat in the shine of Wallace's coach.

"Excuse me?"

"Victor's funeral."

"Yes, of course." The door slammed shut and Baxter watched the coach turn the corner onto Duke Street. The driver had to pull the horses back against the steep downhill slope. Wallace would not risk a stop on Albemarle Street in broad daylight, having left the police only a block away. That didn't change the fact that Baxter didn't have much time. Before he could say what he was thinking, Squire began muttering. Then he bent down and came up with a rock the size of an apple. He took a couple of quick steps then let fly. The coach was never in any danger. The rock found mud, then a puddle, which caused a seagull to flap a few feet into the air before resettling over its breakfast. Squire grunted, and turned to Baxter as he pointed down the street.

"That bastard is guilty of something and I want to be the one who escorts him to jail."

"Fortunately we no longer sentence people to stoning. Pull yourself together, Mr. Squire, we have work to do." Baxter didn't wait for any reply, he was already headed down George Street. Squire simmered for a few seconds longer, and then ran to catch up.

—·—

"Well, well, look who's back, but you brought yer daddy again." It was going on eleven, but Clarke was still in pyjamas and a robe that Baxter had to look twice at to be sure wasn't his. Were bathrobes like Christmas fruitcake and children's mittens, finite in number, indestructible, re-gifting themselves through time? Baxter couldn't tell what bothered him more, the idea that he and Clarke had the same robe or that Clarke looked as formal and well dressed in his as a palace footman.

"Don't try me, Mr. Clarke." Baxter barged forward as he spoke, drawing Squire in his wake through the door behind him.

"Well, come on in." Clarke stepped aside and bowed slightly, as if playing up to Baxter's thoughts and annoying his guest all the more.

"We know Victor was here Friday night. It's time you told us the truth about what happened."

Clarke took on a look of worried sadness and spoke to Squire as if they were commiserating about a misbehaving child. "When he's like this, yer boss, he reminds me of my father."

"That's Victor's blood by your back stairs, Mr. Clarke."

Continuing to ignore Baxter as if he were a petulant toddler, Clarke said to no one in particular, "You know, I been askin' about that forever. Course you know what landlords is like."

They were standing in the front parlour. In the dreary light, through sheer curtains, the heavy chairs on three walls looked in on Baxter, pouting, blaming him for their emptiness. Preacher was lying still in his nest box, a tiny patch of moss in the forest breathing gently. The floorboards creaked. Baxter inhaled the melancholy, let it assuage his anger, and Clarke reappeared as the dark pieces from the corner of a puzzle waiting desperately to complete the picture. "Do you think that's what Martha and Annie and Sarah Riley will say?"

It wouldn't be that easy. Clarke had remained in the hall, his look even farther away. "I guess I'll make some tea." He turned and moved slowly out of Baxter's view.

"This is not a social call." Baxter stayed where he was, but raised his voice and sent it in pursuit down the hall. Preacher stared up at him.

The voice that came back up the hall didn't care if it was heard or not. "I don't recall offerin' you any tea."

"I could arrest you and hold you in a cell until you're willing to talk."

"I'll be in the kitchen, you know where 'tis."

Baxter stared back at the bird, its tiny pearl eye unblinking. He wondered if it could talk. Finally he looked to Squire who broke the silence with the only possible response. "After you," he said, nodding toward the door. The sound of their heavy shoes began to roll like thunder. Farther down the hall Clarke moved along softly in his slippers. Otherwise the house was silent. It was a small victory. Baxter would enjoy it nonetheless.

The kitchen was larger than the parlour, kept wide awake and sharp by bare windows either side of the sink. Clarke was in the far corner, back to, filling the kettle and placing it on the stove. His words were strong now, searching Baxter out, and looking straight at him. "How long you and the rest of the do-gooders in this town been trying to close me down, ten…fifteen years?"

A kitchen table with bench seating stood ready in the corner near the door. Squire sat. Baxter stayed on his feet, weight even, shoulders at an angle. "We'll die trying, is that it?"

Clarke quietly scuffed along the length of the kitchen to the large ice box opposite the table. He bent over and spoke into it as he reached for milk and a plate draped in a tea towel. His words came back as cold as they were matter of fact. "Sin sells, Mr. Baxter, always has."

Baxter followed Clarke to the table with a scathing look. "Don't make excuses for what you do."

Still matter of fact, though perhaps with a hint of invitation, Clarke replied, "You don't know nothin' about what I do or why I'm in this business."

Baxter waved him off. "That is not my concern. Victor Mosher was murdered here, that's what matters to me."

Clarke was halfway back to the stove. He stopped and stood square, taking a full measure of Baxter from a few feet away. "So his life's important and mine ain't?" The face that danced in smile and played at the door had now frozen into an opera mask of hate.

"Places like this destroy the lives of good people, they're a cancer." Baxter's eyes burned on Clarke, glowing embers scorching holes through his clothes and his flesh.

The mask spit back through the smoke. "And yer the worst sorta hard-on."

"I'm a devout Catholic."

"Like I said."

Squire had gotten up from the table and made it to the space between Baxter and Clarke just before it closed. He kept his eyes front toward the shelves near the stove. He spoke out of both ears to the men at his sides. "I think the water is ready. I'll get the cups." He paused for a three count, and then stepped off the middle ground. Another pause followed, and in that time the deafening whirl of pent-up rage unleashing that had filled the room disappeared like a funnel cloud, leaving behind an eerie, edgy silence. Each man now focused on staying out of the way of the other in the course of making a cup of tea, and coming to rest at the table.

Clarke was the first to regain his voice. He spoke through a mouthful of biscuit while nodding toward the plate. "It's ok to like 'em. I learned to cook in my mother's kitchen." With his free hand he gently herded a few crumbs into a pile. He drew the flakey white flesh towards his mouth again then stopped to look at it instead. "I opened a restaurant. Coloured folks came...when they could. I needed white customers to make any money. Not many come to a coloured place for food. Plenty come for liquor, though. So that's what I did. Then women started coming to meet the soldiers. One night when I was lockin' up I hear something round back. So I go see. He paid her two dollars. She give him what he paid her for. Then he want his money back. She was a awful mess." Clarke washed down the bitter memory and the last of his biscuit with some tea.

Baxter stared at the plate but kept his hands round his cup. The worst of his anger had passed and taken his appetite with it. His tea was bitter. Its heat was still soothing. He wondered how long it would take Clarke to finish his plea for sympathy. He might have some to give him if he would just stop with this nonsense and get to the truth. Maybe he would start carrying a small mirror. He could hold it up to men like Clarke so they could see how ridiculous they looked; offer them a chance to preserve some dignity. For now he would have to rely on patience. He would concede the point in order to move on. "So this place isn't a brothel, it's a rescue mission. And you're a saint, not a common bawd."

The smile returned for a moment, incredulous this time and directed inward not outward, a reflection of genuine bewilderment. "Jesus Christ, what d'you care? Why you so bothered with folks, and with this case, what's Victor Mosher to you anyhow?"

Sometimes Baxter wondered if he spoke Greek. Of course he didn't. People hear what they want to hear. "Victor Mosher is a victim who deserves justice. And what you see in me, Mr. Clarke, is commitment, someone trying to pull this city out of the muck, make things better. Of course a man like you would be confused by the sight of decency."

Clarke turned to Squire, clearly unconvinced. "That's a real nice speech," he said blithely as he reached for a second biscuit.

Baxter took one hand off his teacup and drummed the table in a slow, firm rhythm that matched his voice. "I'm not here to convince you of anything. It's you that needs to do the convincing and very soon. I'm running out of time and patience."

Clarke seemed more concerned with the quality of his baking. "So you say." He took more tea, then continued, as if the chief inspector had left the room. "He really does remind me a my father."

Squire looked across the table. Baxter couldn't tell if he was seeking direction or wondering what he would do if his boss committed an assault. Before Baxter could decide, Squire answered, "Is that relevant?"

"Yer father relevant to you?"

"Go on."

Clarke reached for the teapot and refilled Squire's cup then his own before setting it back on the table. Baxter ignored the slight. Clarke began. "My father's name was Marcus. He was born a slave in Georgia. He had an older brother name a Henry. One day the master just up and shot Henry. My father said he never knew why. They buried Henry behind the family cabin. Next day my grandmother, she looked my father in the eye and told him to run before he ended up in the ground next to his brother. His Uncle Benjamin run with 'im. Took a whole year to make it to Boston. They was ok there for a year. Then they run into a couple a bounty hunters. There was a fight in an alley. Benjamin was kilt but my father got away. He landed here in 1853."

"Is he still alive?"

"Dead five years."

"You still miss him." Baxter wanted to yell across the table at Squire or better still reach across and shake him. Don't let him draw you in! We have no time for pointless stories! he screamed to himself in silence.

"Course I miss 'im. I'm happy for 'im too, though. He lived here a free man for more than thirty years. But deep down he still a slave, always looking over his shoulder, afraid to look a white man in the eye. Now he finally restin' easy knowing ain't nobody gonna up and drag his black ass back to Georgia."

Now he had had enough. Baxter simultaneously pushed away his cup and himself up from the table. "Mr. Clarke, you're just wasting time."

Clarke looked up, undeterred. "No, Mr. Baxter, I'm tryin' to help you. You see, my father talked every day 'bout how good it was to be free. He could say free, he just couldn't live free, never really knew what it felt like. Finally that contro-diction grew bigger 'an he was and crushed his heart. I look at you and I see the same thing. There's some kinda contro-diction in you. Something eatin' at you and 'til you..."

It was all a ploy. Clarke had no insight, merely a strong and cunning survival instinct. But Baxter felt his face flush. He heard a defensive tone creep into his voice. "That's enough about your father, Charlie, and the only contradiction I see is the one between what comes out of your mouth and the truth. I came here for the truth and I will have it. Do you understand?"

Squire set his cup down, clinking it against the saucer. Clarke's attention turned toward the sound. "Mr. Clarke, do you know what projection is?" Squire asked.

"What?"

"Projection. It's a new idea from a man named Sigmund Freud."

"Let me guess, man's a preacher." Baxter took a step away. Not because he was rebuffed by the judgmental look Clarke threw at him. He moved because he feared Clarke's latest imprecation might finally bring on that long overdue lightning bolt of almighty judgement.

Squire waited until he had regained Clarke's attention. "No, he's... What he says is that people often deny their own troubles by finding fault with others. Sometimes people do it without realizing. I think maybe you are your father's son and all this is just your way of denying the truth, trying to hide something."

The young man hadn't been taken in; he was working on taking Clarke in. There might be a detective in that uniform after all. Now he would take it from here. "What are you hiding, Mr. Clarke?" Baxter saw his man fumble for words. He stepped forward.

"I ain't my father's son, not the way you say. I'm not denyin' anythin'. I'm free and I intend to stay that way. My conscience is clear, 'spite what you think. What about you, Mr. Baxter...?" Clarke pointed a self-righteous finger. Baxter was having none of it.

"Victor owed money for gambling, did he refuse to pay? Is that what happened?"

"Looks to me like you the one gamblin'."

Baxter had both hands on the table now, leaning in on Clarke. "Or did Wallace and Victor get into it over something to do with the city tramway?"

Clarke didn't cower. If he had lost any composure, it had now been found. "I should take the tram more oftin. Most days, though, I'd rather walk."

"We know Victor didn't just come here to play cards and have a drink. He was paying for...he was coming here to see Sarah Riley. Did something happen between them? Was she blackmailing him?"

Clarke had been looking straight at Baxter. Now he turned back to Squire. "What's that thing you said?"

"Projection?"

"Yeah, pro-jection." Now Clarke's dark eyes despised the chief inspector. "You should learn to pro-ject a little good on people, stop actin' like yer the only one capable of doin' any."

Baxter tightened his grip on the edge of the table. He lifted it slightly then slammed it back to the floor. The high treble of teacups hopping and jittering in their saucers was underscored by the bass of Baxter's raised voice. "You need to give us some answers."

Clarke drew himself up slowly. He raised his arms and leaned back in a great stretch. Then he untied and retied his robe. Blinking slowly, as if he had just come awake and all that had just gone on was a bad dream, he said, "I need some more tea, maybe with a little somethin' in it this time. You two stayin'?" He looked from Squire to Baxter as if they were two cousins who always wore their welcome thin and were never turned away.

Baxter released the table and levered himself back upright. He checked his uniform then pulled his coat back on, seeming to find his words in the process. They came without anger or huff but with no less warning. "I can't tell if you're just pretending or if you are fool enough to believe this game can work. We just spoke to Wallace. He knows that we know about the gambling debts, that this is the place where Victor died. He knows we are aware that he and Victor were mixed up in some business to do with the city's tramway company. Wallace knows we can prove he was here on Friday night and that we are going to keep on investigating. He knows it is only a matter of time, and not too long, before Robert White or James Seabrook or Samuel Lovett lose their nerve and start singing like canaries. And when that happens everything that Sarah Riley has to say will become spun gold. Now do you really think that Mr. Maynard Sinclair Wallace is just going to stand idly by? No, sir. Before any of that can happen, he is going to be the one projecting, projecting blame. And you know where it will land. He is likely with the chief of police right now."

Clarke pushed his lips together, tilting his head one way then the other. He picked up the teapot and made his way to the sink. As he rinsed away the dregs, he said, "I can't speak for Mr. Wallace, don't know the man. And so long as I ain't under arrest, I think I'll keep my peace. Time comes you take me in, anythin' I got to say, I say to a lawyer."

"Well then, you enjoy your tea. Meanwhile I'll wait…and watch the jackals circle. Then when I come back to arrest you, Charlie, anything you might have to say won't matter anymore." Baxter's prophecy hung in the air like flypaper, waiting to still the tiny wings of any secrets that might escape through a pressure crack in Clarke's remorseless outer shell. What he got instead was the crack of a sardonic, "not today" smile. It sent Baxter off in a stomp. Squire had gotten up from the table and was at the kitchen door. As Baxter blew past, Squire started to bid their host good afternoon, then checked himself and gave the door casing a curt rap of his knuckles instead, gavelling the meeting to a close.

A moment later Clarke called after him with an addendum. "You keep watching out for them pro-jections, Mr. Squire."

Baxter let Squire out ahead of him, then followed, slamming the front door for all he was worth. A few heads turned. They would have quickly turned away except for the sight of a big policeman stomping back and forth, talking to himself in one voice and then another, held their attention until he glared at them. After a handful had taken in the show, Squire finally spoke. "That's a shame about his father."

Baxter stopped in mid-rant and stared incredulously. "The shame, Mr. Squire, is what happened to Victor, what happens in places like this every day." Baxter pointed back at the door they had just come out of, while continuing to hold Squire by both eyes. Then he slowly let go, to look up and down the street, then back at his subordinate who was now moving off toward the corner.

Squire spoke over his shoulder without looking back. "So who do you think did it? Was it Wallace or Clarke or somebody else?"

Baxter turned skyward. The grey was low and full, but still, the air too heavy to move. Baxter set after Squire in long slow strides. "Right now it's not what we know that matters. It's what happens next. Patience will be our virtue."

"And what exactly are we waiting for?"

"I wasn't bluffing in there. Someone will crack or make a mistake." He was telling the truth, the truth of years of experience. Few crimes would ever be solved if people didn't give themselves away. Speaking the truth should have been more reassuring.

"And if nobody cracks?

They were moving downhill and Baxter let that be the reason for quickening his steps. "We need to find Mackay and the chief." They walked on through the wet, murky air to the sound of their heels crushing into the ground, to the voices of passersby, and the screech of trolley wheels and foghorns in the distance. Down in the Grand Parade, an army sergeant barked at a mix of soldiers too old for this fight, members of the garrison and the Salvation Army bands and a smattering of others. The order had been given. Company H would leave that afternoon. The city was in a patriotic mood. Of course a rousing send-off would not happen by itself. Baxter hoped Clarke did not get distracted by the fuss. Baxter knew what comfort that could be. He was glad not to be alone with his own thoughts on this particular day.

As they approached the steps of City Hall, Baxter was relieved to look up and see Mackay at the front doors. He waited at the bottom, trying to read the language of the burly frame. He'd known Mackay for twenty years. He'd never grown to like him, but he had come to admire the man's immunity. He was as hard and permanent as the granite of the coastline. He needed that strength now, not the deep lines, creaky knees, and stooping posture lumbering toward him. He had never noticed the weight Mackay carried and suddenly his own seemed heavier. He glanced at Squire, thin, still growing. His stride slowed a step by the pace of the past few days. His was a tiredness from which he would quickly recover, not one caused by the drag of years and the frustration of giving oneself to a cause only half led. Baxter tried to remember what it felt like to be young. He had to force himself to look away. "Have you had any luck, Sergeant?"

Mackay let out an indignant puff. "I was born here."

Baxter corrected himself. "Any luck finding Sarah Riley."

"You'd have heard if I had."

"We were out."

Mackay gave Squire a quick nod, then put his hands in his pockets and studied his shoes. "Let me guess, Wallace didn't scare easy."

Baxter mirrored Mackay's stance and tightened his lips at the metallic grey muck smearing the soles and welts of his new Madisons. "He knows to be careful."

"So you went to Clarke's before he could."

"Yes."

Now Mackay looked up and waited for Baxter to follow. "And?"

"And we still need to find Sarah Riley." He desperately wanted not to sound so desperate, to not be dependent on Mackay and his familiarity with the notorious. He just could not see any other way.

"I tried to get Martha to go home, hoping Sarah might come back. She's terrified to leave that cell and I didn't have the heart to force her. I checked in with Annie." Mackay shook his head, and then in consolation added, "Every man on the force knows to bring Sarah in if they see her."

Without realizing he was about to do it, Baxter reached out and placed a hand on Mackay's shoulder. The spot of new pink flesh in the centre of his palm scraped against the rough wool of the tunic. His tone was not commanding. It was a mix of urgency and gratitude, un-begrudged, that sounded almost apologetic. "The minute anything happens."

Mackay's eyebrows went up for a split second, then he cleared his throat and renewed his interest in his shoes. His voice was filled with solemn promise and fingers crossed for luck. "You'll be the first to know."

Baxter took back his hand. Mackay moved off toward the stairs leading up from the Grand Parade to Argyle Street. The army sergeant and his mob were already halfway to the top. Baxter shook his head, imagining Mackay taking the musicians and soldiers to Georgina's to guard Annie and play some music to cheer her up. He turned to Squire before the thought could go any further. "Best you wait in my office. If Wallace is with the chief, no point in both of us suffering more of his abuse." Squire squinted, then opened his mouth seemingly about to question or protest, then thought better of it and went through the front doors ahead of Baxter.

———•———

The telephone was hung up just as Baxter arrived. The chief was massaging his ear and cursing under his breath. Baxter could see that Wallace was not there in the flesh. That the man had just been there in spirit was every bit as obvious. Baxter wished he had taken a minute to visit the WC or clean his shoes, anything to have allowed some of the steam to vent. Now he would have to take the brunt of the rage. "That was council for Mr. Wallace. He is recommending his client pursue charges against you for harassment and defamation of character." The chief was shouting now. "I've also been told to expect a reprimand from the mayor for not keeping you properly leashed." The chief stood and pointed at Baxter as if his screaming wasn't emphasis enough. "And of course you are to be removed from the case immediately. I thought I told you to go easy on this."

A part of him wanted to give what he was getting. The rest of him knew his place and that that would be a mistake. Better to let this ill wind blow itself out than to lean hard against it. He held his voice low but steady. "I didn't accuse Wallace of anything. I asked him a few questions. It was all very gentlemanly."

Tolliver stabbed a finger at the telephone. "His lawyer says you accused Wallace of being mixed up with Frank McNeally and that business with the Saco Bank."

Baxter wouldn't lie. What he would do in this case was permit a little dancing round the straight truth. "McNeally came up in conversation. No one said anything about the Saco Bank."

Even that much of a concession eased some of the gust. Tolliver had come round his desk. The two were now just a few feet apart in the centre of the room. "Uh-huh. And I'll tell you so you can stop wondering. Not being there wasn't my decision."

Coward, Baxter said to himself. You were happy to let the mayor or Wallace decide for you. Then to the chief he said, "Wallace is making threats because he is worried, and he is worried because he is guilty."

Tolliver's voice was back to conversational level. It was no less biting. He had turned away from Baxter to pace across the bow of his desk. "Ooooh…Well then, by all means, let's lock him up." He threw his hands into the air in mock surrender.

"I was just…"

The release of sarcasm brought Tolliver down a little further. "For God's sake, Cully, do you really think Maynard Wallace stabbed Victor Mosher to death in an upper street brothel?"

Here Baxter could walk a straight line. "Maybe. Or he saw what happened. At the very least we know he was there."

Tolliver's temperature spiked again. "Because she says so?" He poked his chin toward the window and the upper streets beyond it. "Wallace's lawyer will paint a picture of a tart. Mackay will leap over the rail in chivalrous defence and the trial will be over. You'll need more than the likes of Annie Higgenbottom."

Tolliver was right about Mackay. And he would need more. The chief was a collector. He acquired debts through favours. A good many people were beholden to him. Baxter disliked going to this well in the same way he was bothered by relying on Mackay's associations with the upper streets. But come tomorrow, he would not find himself looking at Victor's family thinking there was more he might have done. "Can you give me anything?" he asked.

The chief stopped his pacing. He seemed to be taking inventory or weighing what to say or whether to say anything at all. Finally he spoke. "A little more time, that's it. I'll duck the Mayor for the rest of the day. I can't avoid standing with him at the funeral tomorrow. You stay clear."

Ensuring the thorough investigation of a crime, the murder of a popular politician, was his job, nothing more. Of course, Tolliver would see it differently, believe he now owned a small piece of his chief detective. Let him think as he chooses, Baxter told himself. He would compromise nothing. And then a new thought came to him. A question that might have been more dangerous than the first, depending on where the man before him really stood in all of this. "I'll maintain a respectful distance…Oh, by the way, sir, have you been face to face with Wallace at some point these past few days?"

This time the chief looked away from Baxter, back toward the window as he spoke. There was no hesitation, no answer either. "Why?"

"He was wearing gloves when he met with me."

"So?"

"So I'm wondering if you have seen his hands." Baxter knew no jury would convict Wallace on a cut, even though it was physical evidence, better than the word of a harlot.

"That's as close as I've been." Tolliver nodded toward the telephone. Baxter waited. The chief remained a statue at the window, as still and mournful-looking as the dull grey sky and the bare corn broom trees he was looking at.

A full breath of the room's dead air gave him no hope at all. He would try once more regardless. "This can't be swept under the rug."

The chief turned from the window, no longer distant and opaque, now close and as see-through as the glass. "And no one's going to jail for not living up to your standards."

"*I* enforce the law," Baxter shot back.

"Yes, you do, to the very letter…I'll let the mayor know you're sorry for offending one of our finest citizens." The chief looked toward the door, and then turned back to his window.

Baxter told himself there was never any point in arguing with someone who couldn't tell black from white. He didn't slam the chief's door. He left it against the wall where he found it. He marched across the hall past the front desk, ignoring the man on duty behind it. He closed his office door slowly against the low hubbub of conversation and the slow peck of typewriter keys on the other side. He stood leaning on the handle as if he expected someone to try and force their way in.

"Was Wallace with the chief?" Squire was in one of the chairs in front of the desk. He'd been there often enough now Baxter knew the room would seem empty when this ended and Squire went back to his regular patrol.

Baxter let go of the door. Instead of moving behind his desk, he sat next to Squire. "No, Wallace just sicced his dog on him."

Taking Baxter's reference, and showing no signs of regret, Squire replied, "I thought about reading law."

In the future, if anyone were to ever ask him about it, Baxter would admit it wasn't planned. They weren't really new anymore, but he still didn't automatically think to use one. He had certainly never spent any time pondering the unique qualities of a telephone conversation, until now. Leaning in with the gentle curiosity of a child doctor, Baxter asked, "Did you ever think about being a newspaper reporter?"

"No...?"

He patted Squire's knee then stood and began digging in a drawer. "Time to start. You sit here. I'll find the number."

———•———

They sat shoulder to shoulder, each of them huddled around a paper cup of steaming tea. They blew and sipped and watched through the gloom of a late fall afternoon. A bit of wind was picking up. Now and then a tram would shunt, and spark, and ding its way by. Baxter studied them for clues. All he saw were the tired sullen faces of stevedores and factory workers dragging north to their crowded tenements, early suppers and short sleeps. The war supply effort had them all on double shifts. For the first time in days there were no soldiers on the streets. About the same time that Baxter was leaving the chief's office, the 125 volunteer troops, including Peter Lenehan, had emptied out of Brunswick Street barracks and the armouries building. They formed a confident procession through the streets to the waiting cars at the North Street Station. The sidewalks had caught the tears of family and friends. The buildings had reverberated with patriotic shouts. The whistle blew. The great pistons, assisted by the collective will of city, nation, and empire, had overcome the force of inertia and the engine wheels made that first skidding turn. The train moved, first by inches then a few car lengths, then miles per hour. When the caboose had trailed round the arc of the basin out of sight, heading north then west, the throngs finally turned to saunter arm in arm away from thoughts of battles far away, and back to matters close at hand. It would be recalled suddenly, as if it had happened long ago, that Victor Mosher had been murdered. No, they would remind one another, his body had been found only days before. Baxter lifted one hand off his tea then put it back. Looking at his watch would only make him more anxious. Squire followed Baxter's movement then rolled his eyes round their little cabin, at the low canopy roof overhead, stuck out like the brim of a hat. The walls were mostly window. The half-doors across the front, closed up tight against their knees. He took another sip of tea then asked, "Why does the police department have a hansom cab?"

Baxter knew the story. If Squire hadn't asked, he would have offered it up to pass the time. "Years ago a commander of the garrison sent a letter off to England, to the officer about to replace him. He reported on the troops, daily routines, and the absence of any military threat. He went on to say he had grown weary of the lax discipline that went with a port city, all the worse, he complained, because his bed was hard and he could never get a cab. The new man arrived from London with a feather mattress and this. When it came his turn to leave, somehow the cab ended up in our stables."

"And the mattress?"

"One story says he gave it to a mistress he kept on Brunswick Street."

"Are you sure it wasn't Albemarle? Maybe that mattress was a witness to the murder we are in this cab trying to solve."

Baxter couldn't tell if Squire was trying to be flip or ironic, or if it mattered in any way at all if what he said turned out to be true. "Now you're sounding like a story, Mr. Squire."

The young man wasn't finished. "You don't think God has a sense of humour?"

Baxter stomped his feet to wake them up and move some blood against the weather. "Better you ponder almighty wrath and try not to incur it."

"What do we do if we get a fare?"

Baxter answered the question with a sidelong glance. But he didn't want to kill the conversation altogether, it guarded against the chill and other discomforts. "Tell me, Mr. Squire, what happened to your father?"

Squire was looking through his window, following a stray cat. It gingerly climbed a set of stairs to sniff at the smells from beneath someone's front door. "I thought we were here on police work."

"We are." Baxter waited.

"Seems Wallace is doing some police work of his own, bastard... pardon the language." Squire tapped his window. The cat ignored him.

"You're new to him, he's looking for things he might use against you if he needs to."

"What are you asking me?"

He had lost all interest in the cat. Squire was now turned toward the chief inspector. The look that came over his cup was hotter than the tea. The reaction caught Baxter by surprise. He held up a hand to ward it off. "No need to get your dander up. You're new to me too. I saw he struck a nerve is all. Mind you, it backfired when you came back at him with McNeally."

"Reflex." Squire shrugged, and then looked again for the cat. It had moved on. He took another sip of tea. "You think it was a mistake."

"On the contrary." He was about to offer stronger praise, point out that it wasn't just any man who could put Maynard Sinclair Wallace on his heels. He missed the chance when Squire went on too quickly.

"My father got sick."

Baxter accepted the invitation. "The doctors couldn't help?"

"Not that kind of sick."

"I see." Baxter blinked against images of his bedroom door closed in the middle of the day, his young wife unable to get out of bed. He saw himself telling Grace not to worry, things would soon be back to normal. He saw them both hoping it was true.

"I was ten when it started. By the time I was twelve, he was living in the barn like an animal. When they came, my mother sent me into the house. He fought. They tried not to hurt him putting on the jacket. My mother stood in the yard and cried. I stayed inside with my little sisters. We waved through the screen door without thinking. He couldn't move his arms." Squire put his cup to his lips, then made a face and tossed it into the street.

Baxter tried then couldn't keep from asking. "You had been close?"

Squire rubbed his face with both hands. "My father was a strong man, he could do anything including never making me feel weak. He told me I could be whatever I imagined."

"So he encouraged you in school?"

They were eye to eye now. Squire slowed his voice and watched for signs of understanding as he spoke. "He never hired a hand. He did the work I might have done on the farm. He was determined I would not be him."

His head tilting back, his eyes narrowing, Baxter asked, "What if he had kept you on the farm…?"

"I would have become Jethro Tull, out of respect." Squire had a mollifying look on his face but his voice was sincere.

"Who?"

Squire shook his head, seeming to admonish himself, then said quickly, "British farmer, invented the seed drill in the seventeenth century. I read about him in school."

Baxter raised his eyebrows and searched his memory, then gave up. His tea had lost its warmth, he finished it anyway out of habit. "What do you suppose your father would think of you being a policeman?"

A group of boys crossed the street in the next block, wearing after-school faces. Though their jibes and jokes were lost in the wind and distance, their fraternity was unmistakeable. Squire watched them for a moment or two, then came back to Baxter with a question of his own.

"Wallace didn't just know about my father. He was after you too. What was that bit about the medical school just before he threw us out?"

"I haven't the faintest idea. Just noise, muddying the waters. Wallace isn't a sinister mastermind. He's just a rich degenerate with his hand in the wringer."

Baxter leaned forward, the mud on his shoes suddenly important. Squire drew himself in, trying to create a little more room. "It's not his hand in the wringer." Squire decided after he had forced himself as far over as he could.

Without looking up, still fiddling at his feet, Baxter replied, "Appears the Pictou Academy didn't polish all the edges off the stone."

As Baxter sat back up and brushed his hands, Squire, wearing a half smile and a cocked eyebrow, said, "It didn't teach me to ignore the obvious either."

Having regained himself and glad for the young man's good sense, he offered him a chance to put it to further use. "So what does your worldly wisdom expect to happen next?"

Squire looked out at the now empty street. "You put me on the telephone to Seabrook pretending I'm a reporter whose been talking to Sarah Riley. Now here we are like a pair of peeping toms waiting on Godiva. You expect Seabrook to run to Wallace or one of the others or them to come here. But how does that help us?"

In truth he wasn't sure. "We could sit in my office and wait for the chief to give in to Wallace and the mayor."

"So we're desperate." There was a tone in the voice. Was it resignation or realization? Baxter wasn't sure. Either way he was not about to concede.

"I prefer cunning."

The afternoon light remained low but hung on. Their pauses grew longer. Squire mentioned that a room had come vacant in his boarding house. Elizabeth Murray might take it. No matter how this case turned out, he would be glad for meeting her. Baxter remembered he had promised to visit his mother-in-law on Sunday. He had also pledged to go with a smile on his face. Of course, if matters forced him to put their visit off, well, he wouldn't be disappointed. "No matter what I say she won't believe her daughter and granddaughter are safe from murderers. She won't come right out and say it's my fault." Baxter sulked, and they said nothing for what seemed a long while. Squire flagged down a peddler's cart and got a couple of apples for their horse. As Squire was climbing back into the cab, Baxter was about to ask him what he might know about medical school. The thought was lost.

"There's our man."

Squire watched Seabrook take a great gulp of air and check the sky before moving slowly down the block. "He looks calm."

"Half the city is seeing off the troops. What's he doing here?" Baxter wanted to know. "Too late for lunch, too early for home."

"Court?"

"No briefcase," Baxter pointed out.

"Client?"

"Lawyers with an office like his have clients come to them." Squire reached for the reins and was about to prod the horse when Baxter touched his arm. "Don't move yet, wait until he gets to the corner."

"He went straight," Squire said with obvious urgency.

"Yes, Mr. Squire. Pull up to the end of the block."

Squire did as he was told. That didn't change the look on his face which said the end of the block wasn't far enough. "He's gone past Province House, we need to be closer. Look, he's gone down Prince."

"I see that." Baxter pointed left. "Go down here and park in front of the Union Bank on Hollis Street, quickly, Mr. Squire."

"We need to see where he's going," Squire complained as he worked the reins. The metal shoes scraped and shuddered on the cobblestones as the horse fought to pull them tightly round the corner.

Baxter was leaning back, his arms crossed. "I know where he's going."

The afternoon finally gave way to twilight, then to darkness. Lights came on behind curtains here and there. Overhead, stars came out, one by one. They took turns walking down the block to stay warm and not too much in one another's thoughts. At all times there was at least one set of eyes on the thick oak doors of the Halifax Club. And as they waited and walked and watched, the parties gathered.

Just as Baxter knew he would, Seabrook turned off Prince onto Hollis, and made his way to the Club. Young men fight wars. If they are lucky they survive to profit from the next one. Seabrook's marching days, if there had been any, were long behind him. He flowed casually as if he were on his way to a drink and a cigar before dinner. Taking time perhaps to ponder how this fight with the Boers might bring new business to his law firm. Had he bothered to look behind him he might have noticed that the same hansom cab parked across the street from his office when he left had come along with him. Had his curiosity been piqued, he would have recognized the passengers as policemen, and the larger one as the city's chief inspector. And had that happened Baxter would have smiled and waved. If Seabrook did realize he was being watched, he never let on. He gave no indication of noticing anything at all and Baxter knew why. Seabrook was too busy being afraid.

Not long after Seabrook arrived, Samuel Lovett walked past the cab. He came from behind, walking on the west side of Hollis. The government was in session at Province House and Baxter assumed Lovett had just come from there. No doubt just having had the floor to thunder away on matters vital and important to the war effort. Being busy, and likely having only just received notice to be here, Lovett had had less time to worry. He was of medium build and height. There was nothing remarkable about him that Baxter could make out as he strode past, other than an elegant stovepipe hat that could have belonged to Lincoln. Lovett was no statesman, Baxter was sure of that, but his quickening pace gave Baxter reason to think perhaps Lovett was in a worried state of mind after all.

More men came and went through the great heavy doors. Some faces he recognized, others he couldn't make out. He was sure one of the faces belonged to George Youngston. Baxter didn't know where his money came from, only that Youngston had enough of it to belong to the colony's elite. His was the only other face Martha thought she recognized from the pictures. She couldn't be sure. Nor was it sure the killer was there at all. Before that thought could grow into crushing despair, a message in a bottle turned off Sackville into Hollis Street. The air had much dried out and the temperature fallen just a little further. All sound was perfect. The great spoked wheels came over the cobblestones softly, like dice rolling in the hand, background, along with the distant sounds of the waterfront, to the clop, clop, clop of the hooves, louder and louder until the driver's baritone called them to whooooa.

Baxter watched as the driver climbed down and opened the door. Wallace popped out as if by spring. He had traded in his riding kit for an evening suit. The driver held up the greatcoat Wallace handed to him. Once he'd slipped his arms in, Wallace stood for a few minutes delivering further instructions that Baxter couldn't hear. The driver nodded. Wallace remained on the sidewalk until the carriage departed. Then he cleared his throat and pulled the door handle.

A block away, the two policemen waited. It did not take long for Squire's increased impatience to begin to show. "What do you think is happening?"

"Wallace is calming the waters, assuring them he has us under control."

"Arrogant f—"

"Mr. Squire, I was thinking more about what happened to your father. Yesterday after I left here," he nodded out the window towards the Union Bank, "I bumped into Thomas Berrigan right there." He pointed to the place in the street where the carriage had been moments before.

"Berrigan...?"

"One of our most hapless drunks. He's been a mess in the street so long, I forget he has family." Baxter's voice trailed off as he tried to recall how old Thomas might be. Thirty-four or thirty-five? He looked fifty.

"Here in the city?"

"Who is in the city...?"

Squire glanced over, holding a hand in the air. "Oh yes," Baxter continued. "Here in the city. Catherine Mosher was Catherine Berrigan. Victor was Thomas's brother-in-law." Baxter paused again, sifting his memory. "For years his older brother Patrick looked after Thomas. Catherine felt worse for Patrick than she did for Thomas. She had Victor arrange a job for Patrick with the railroad. I guess she thought that if Patrick were away, Thomas would have to look after himself. They would both be saved. A man from the railroad went to see Patrick, told him he could start the next day. He didn't know it wasn't Patrick who answered the door. Thomas lasted about a week."

"Victor couldn't patch things up?" Squire asked, now caught up in the saga.

"I guess not. I doubt Catherine ever forgave Thomas. He was already a degenerate, now a Judas." Baxter was surprised that Grace should come to mind. Perhaps there were untold advantages to being an only child.

"And Patrick?"

"I've often wondered if Catherine told him." The door to the Halifax Club opened and the conversation in the cab disappeared in a sudden inhale. A man tucked in his scarf and pulled on his gloves, then blurred into the darkness beyond the light over the door. "Did you see who that was?" Baxter whispered. The farther the man got, the more they leaned forward.

"No, but none of our men was wearing a red scarf, were they?" His question seemed rhetorical. Baxter hoped the young man was as confident as he sounded because he hadn't taken note of the colour of anyone's scarf.

"Right you are," he replied, feeling a bit sheepish. Getting to the point of his story suddenly seemed more important. "As I was saying, part of me hopes Catherine never let on."

"I don't see you wanting to protect Thomas."

"You're right. On the other hand, if Patrick did know, then maybe he tried to use me to get even."

If Squire had had any suspicions about Baxter's eye for colour they seemed forgotten. He turned his shoulders to look and listen more directly. "Go on."

"When I told you about arresting McNeally I left out some of the details. Two days before his arrest, Ellen Reardon was in the man's hotel room." Baxter refrained from comment on that point, beyond a look of disgust. "She saw the money he was carrying and told Thomas. Their plan to rob McNeally went awry, when Thomas showed up to the caper with a bottle. As usual Patrick found Thomas in a ditch. In his stupor Thomas spilled the beans. Before the would-be bandits could regroup, Patrick came to me."

"You think he wanted revenge for Thomas ruining his chances with the railroad, maybe to see his brother go to jail?"

"He said he was trying to protect Thomas, and some innocent traveller. He still keeps an eye out. When I saw Thomas yesterday he was wearing a new hat, no doubt it came from Patrick." Baxter straightened his back against the seat and folded his arms on his chest. At the time, as things turned out, Patrick's motivation was unimportant. He wasn't sure why it should suddenly matter now, why he had brought the whole thing up.

"They both seem like pitiful characters. What I don't see is what they have got to do with me and my father." The question came as a relief. Baxter had lost his train of thought and become mired in the sinking moral quicksand of upper street family dynamics. Who could tell what was in the hearts and minds of any of them. "Ah yes. Thomas could have made better of himself. You were about the same age when your father… My point, Mr. Squire, was to support your earlier attack on arrogance. Wallace and the rest of them are resting in luxury, being waited on hand and foot while they attempt to cover up a murder. Are they concerned at all with Victor's children, who must grow up without a father? I think not."

They fell into a silence. Baxter sulked and chastised himself for having made the simple complicated. Victor's family deserved justice. His killer deserved prison. Children become adults. Drunkenness is immoral. Human pity is worthless. On the other side of the cab, Squire's suffering was physical, fatigue brought on by a dwindling resistance to the cold. Finally he took a walk in search of some body heat.

The cab rocked on its springs, and the horse snorted and flapped its tail as Squire climbed back into his seat. He blew on his hands then cupped his ears. "They have been in there nearly two hours now."

"Wallace will have insisted on a meal. Food calms. I'm sure it's very good here."

"They eat and grow fatter while we sit out here solving nothing and getting colder by the minute." Squire blew on his hands again.

While Squire was gone, Baxter had removed the heavy candle from the cab's lantern. There were some matches in the pocket on his door. The candle burned between his feet. He nudged it over and Squire hovered above the flame. "Haven't you been paying attention? Youngston hasn't come out, so it looks as though we have another confirmed suspect or witness. We know there is enough fear in the group to call a meeting. We can't find Sarah Riley. What we know now at least is that they haven't found her either."

"How can you be so sure?" Squire had opened his coat. The candle was now burning in a tent. Baxter expected Squire to catch fire any second.

"If they knew where she was before you called, Seabrook would have hung up and gone back to work. If she had been located in the time since, Wallace would be there, not here."

Squire lowered a tent flap so Baxter could see his face. "Unless one of his henchmen found Sarah three days ago when she left Martha's and he's just playing with all of us."

Baxter reached round the tent to warm one hand then the other. "Wallace was mixed up in that bank robbery three years ago. This time, it's murder. McNeally, Sarah Riley, Charles Clarke, a crowd of nervous gentlemen. Wallace doesn't dare play at anything."

"Then why not drop in on them, stir things up even more?"

"Here with the king in their castle, the knights are brave. We need them alone with their doubts."

"That takes time." Squire sat back, hugging himself, holding in what heat he had managed to collect.

Baxter drew the candle back a little closer. "The funeral will raise emotions."

"Confidence is an emotion. So is patience."

Baxter let out a long breath, which he would likely soon be able to see. The young man's cynicism was not unwarranted but it wasn't helping. The colder he got, the less help he would be. Baxter hoped his thicker frame could fend off the chill a little longer. There might be a horse blanket in the cab's trunk. His mind made up, he said, "I will stay here until this meeting ends, just in case anything should happen. You go back to the station, check with Mackay. If there is any news on Miss Riley, come get me. Otherwise go home. Maybe someone needs help moving in."

Squire remained still. Baxter knew he wasn't staying, just drawing up the energy to go. He looked arthritic pulling himself out of the cab. Baxter couldn't deny that his work had taken a toll over the years. So far he could honestly say it hadn't weakened him physically. Long johns had been a great help. Squire's steps faded quickly. Baxter waited a little longer then got out to stretch his legs and look in the trunk. He was in luck.

The blanket was musty but thick enough to keep out the night air. The carriage returned without a sound. If voices had stayed low, it could have left unnoticed. Brandy was to blame. Lovett was congratulating Wallace on a fine coach and an even finer meal. He was listing hard to port. Seabrook was standing close, to see Lovett didn't overturn. Baxter lowered the hood of his blanket poncho, the cold air helping to wake him. In his dream someone had been speaking without a tongue. Was it a woman? He couldn't tell what was being said, only that the message was urgent. He rubbed his face, closed his eyes tight, then opened them. The coach, its driver, and the four men in the street were still there. This was real. He leaned forward, struggling to see and hear.

Wallace was speaking now, in low tones. The hens bobbed in silent rhythm. Then Lovett squawked again, "We need more than calm, what we need..." Wallace held up a hand to call for order and Seabrook put his arm around Lovett, patting him on the back and pulling him and his great top hat up straight. There were a few more murmurings, then nods in agreement, and parting gestures. Seabrook guided Lovett round the corner up Prince. He would likely be left to sleep it off in the lawyer's office. Youngston took Wallace's hand. He didn't accept his offer of a ride. The last thread pulled loose and walked south on Hollis. The coach driver remained stone-faced, ready with the door. Just before stepping in Wallace looked north, drawn perhaps by a flickering gas light or the groan of a hull slipping against a wharf. The sky was high and clear, the street still and empty for the next three blocks, except for a cab in front of the Union Bank, which was as closed up and dark as the buildings leaning against it. The horse seemed to be asleep. There was no steam rising from the heap of dung behind it. The cab had been parked for some time. Wallace turned his shoulders, square to the cab now, searching its interior.

Baxter finished throwing off the blanket. He reached for his hat and shifted himself to the centre of the bench seat. The cab lurched on its springs. The horse came to life with a backward glance. Baxter snapped the reins and clicked his tongue. The cab rolled forward toward the circle of light from the streetlamp on the corner. In mid-turn the cab's interior went bright. When Baxter was sure he had been recognized, he nodded to Wallace then showed him the back of the cab as he rode away.

———•———

Late as it was, supper waited. The table was pulled closer, the fire stoked. From the end chair back to the stove, there was the nourishment of heat and food. Baxter took both slowly. "What time do you think we should leave in the morning?" Jane had always wound the household clock. She knew pace and timing far better than her husband. There had to be some other reason for the caution in her voice.

She knew full well. He answered anyway, as it seemed to be required. "There will be seats reserved for city officials."

"We should walk, the carriages will be lined up for a mile."

"The weather has cleared, pray it stays that way."

The wait had dried the meat. Jane refilled her water. "I sent Catherine a card. Have you spoken to her again?"

"No." He imagined Catherine on the sofa fumbling with the letter opener. The floor a litter of torn envelopes and discarded notes, none of them the one she was looking for, the one from her husband telling her not to worry, this was all some outrageous mistake.

Grace had been quiet at the table, which was not like her at all. Nor was she one to pick at her food. She dug trench lines in her mashed potatoes. She spoke now as she laid her fork beside her plate. "Doctor David Drummond is giving a lecture tomorrow morning. It's open to the public."

"It may be cancelled." Jane was looking toward the end of the table, not across it.

Lack of appetite hadn't taken any strength from Grace's voice and she looked in both directions as she spoke. "He's visiting from Newcastle, England. He will be speaking on his work there at the Sick Children's Hospital. He is an important man, it's a rare opportunity."

Her father's response was equally strong and immediate. "You have a more important obligation."

"It's terrible what happened to Mr. Mosher. But he wasn't a friend of our family."

"He worked hard for this city. He deserves our respect, your respect."

Jane could see the flush. It wasn't heat from the stove. Grace's eyes gave off sparks as her shoulders raised and her chest filled. Her lips pressed tight then opened. Jane spoke before her daughter could. "The lecture starts at nine. Perhaps you could come to the church afterward."

They were words of peace, of compromise. Baxter winced as if struck by a poison dart. "You knew about this?"

Grace answered her mother to draw him off. "There will be questions and discussion and I'll need to complete my notes while it's all still fresh."

Baxter stared at his daughter. At first she appeared as a picture of his wife in a larger frame, then small and far away at the wrong end of the looking glass. He could feel the arms of a ten-year-old round his neck. He glanced at the window, through its curtains out into a sunny backyard, and he could feel ten, now turned twenty, on his arm, dressed to give away. "Grace, you need to stop all this. You know it can't possibly lead anywhere."

"Why? Because I don't wear pants?"

"Grace."

"No, Mother. I want to hear him say it. I want to hear him say I can't be what I choose, only what he chooses."

Baxter struggled with the looking glass trying to find the image of the future he had always been able to see so clearly. "I want what is best for you."

Grace hurled herself at her father like a rock toward a pane of glass. "You want me to walk down the aisle, then fill a house with babies. Stop feeling sorry for me because I was an only child."

"Stop it, Grace. You're being mean."

To her mother she said, "The world is a mean place these days."

Then she turned to father. "What did you do with it?"

Baxter stared at his plate. He rearranged the napkin in his lap. He picked up his fork, then laid it down. "What is she talking about?"

"Tell her." There was such certainty in her voice Baxter wondered if his daughter was clairvoyant as well as unmanageable.

Jane watched her husband try to be invisible. Then her shoulders drooped and she shook her head at Grace. "I thought we agreed it was best that come through me."

Baxter stepped out of his hiding place and looked defiantly and disbelievingly from one to the other. "So it's a conspiracy."

Jane was standing now, straight and square, arms pressed at her sides. The first order was given to her husband "Don't you dare give me that look. She is my daughter too."

Now Grace got up on the other side of the table, moving as if pulled by wires. As she spoke, her hands and arms flapped and flopped and pointed off in all directions. "He's just trying to dodge the question. It's ok, Father, you don't have to answer. I'm going to that lecture tomorrow and I'm going to medical school, one way or another. I'll sell myself if I have to."

"Grace Baxter." Jane's second order would have sent Grace to her room. It wasn't necessary. The wires had already launched her daughter into a wild waving stomp down the hall and up the stairs.

Baxter watched his daughter disappear. "This is your fault."

The words demeaned them both. Neither could look at the other. A door slammed overhead. The wood Jane had brought in before supper had been wet from rain. The fire hissed and popped. The meal went on drying up and going to waste. Finally Jane broke the spell. "I admire her gumption...Guilty as charged...Shall I put up my hands, Chief Inspector?" She let the silence back in for a moment, daring him to answer. Her voice was flat. "This isn't some case, Cully, this is your family. I know this case is important and...But so..." Jane drew a deep breath, and shook her head as if she were silently dismissing options on what to say next. After a moment she continued. "Grace went to see Peter... well, all the troops off this morning. She hasn't said, she didn't have to. I just thought you should know." Jane turned away slowly, her heels were quiet and exact down the hall.

Baxter sat for some time, listening to the stove and the ticking of a clock. Eventually he pushed the table back in place. He salvaged what he could, and gave the rest to the slop bucket. He made it seem important to avoid thoughts of tomorrow's service, or the look Wallace had given him an hour before. It was the same superiority and smugness he'd seen on the wall at King's Collegiate. A gentle reminder not to waste his time. There was water on the stove. Doing the dishes brought back the comfort of distraction until it came time to dry his hands. As he worked the dishtowel he began to see the hands of midwives glistening with blood and mucus. He saw Dr. Trenaman's hands as cold and white as his lab coat. All Grace had seen was pictures in a book.

Jane pulled herself farther to her side of the bed as he lifted the covers. In the darkness he couldn't tell if she was awake or if her body took it upon itself to continue his punishment while her mind rested. He lay there in exile until rescued by exhaustion.

He may have been in reprieve minutes or hours. There was no way to tell. He knew only that the house was cold and the draft on his feet from under the front door made it worse. He had managed to stop the horrible ringing. He had also dropped the receiver. He could hear it speaking to him as he groped blindly. "Chief Inspector...are you there?"

"Yes...Just a minute...Yes?"

There was a long pause. Maybe he had drifted off or this was just a bad joke. Then the thing in his hand spoke again. "It's Mackay. I found Sarah Riley."

Thursday

His steps were quick. Not because he was in any hurry to see what waited. The images from the little room in Dr. Trenaman's basement were still vivid and raw in his memory. Standing over Victor's naked corpse with its missing eye and small mouth carved into its side, Baxter had felt his insides chill. Normally such feelings could be overcome with thoughts of grandchildren or a swing in the backyard. Now such thoughts left him colder still. He pulled his shoulders closer to his ears as he turned the corner onto Brunswick Street. The morgue was at the end of the next block. The street was quiet and empty. The whirl and fuss of amassing troops and sending them off had died down. Unlike his own, the shoulders of the city sagged in a great exhale. The empire had been serviced once again and another long winter was on its way. In days to come he would have time to ponder the grander scale of things. In this moment his mind was on the conduct of genteel young women. They should be concerned with the designs of a proper courtship and home-making and motherhood. Grace had no business in rooms decorated with specimen jars and smelling of iodine. These facts were indisputable. Yet here he was, alone on the tundra, rejected and unpardoned. His quick pace was an effort to get warm. Truth always has a temperature. In the city of Halifax, during the wee hours of this particular Thursday morning, it was cold.

Trenaman had left the front door to the city morgue unlocked behind him. It did nothing to make the place more welcoming. The coat was crisp and white. It moved about the slab in a slow circle. Now and then there was a pause and a deep bend to peer over his small glasses. On the way back up, a pencil played a short concerto against a clipboard, its notes echoing off the drab green walls. It was all familiar, much as it had been a few nights before, and not the same at all. It was the difference that left Baxter not just cold but weak.

Baxter tried to keep his eye on the doctor and avoid looking at his "patient." Much as he tried, he couldn't help see her, couldn't help imagining a young woman who walked and talked and who had colour in her cheeks. Even now, lying breathless on a cold metal table with a stained sheet pulled up to her bare shoulders, Sarah Riley was angelic.

"If this continues, tongues will wag." The voice came from afar.

"Excuse me?"

Trenaman checked him with a glance then went back to his notes. "These late night meetings."

As much as he was glad to be pulled away from his thoughts, the doctor's attempt at humour, if that's what it was, struck him as annoying. "Let's do without the theatre, shall we, Doctor?"

Equally unamused by the chief inspector's air, Trenaman replied, "That would be nice." He looked up from the clipboard. "Sergeant Mackay tells me her name is...was, Sarah Riley."

"Where is the sergeant?"

The doctor's eyes squinted in an effort to remember. "He mentioned some names, Martha, I think, and..."

"Annie."

"Yes, I think that's right." With an expression that seemed relieved, or perhaps impressed with his recall of the unimportant, the doctor looked back to his clipboard, following his last note with the tip of his pencil.

Baxter moved nearer to the foot of the slab where the doctor was now standing, glad no longer to be caught in the vacant stare. "Did she drown?"

"No stab wounds this time."

"Any other signs of foul play?"

Trenaman slipped his pencil into the breast pocket of the lab coat. He drew a breath as he folded his arms, the clipboard now against his chest. "Nothing obvious, no bruising or broken bones. She may have been poisoned, I suppose. I could do some tests."

Baxter wasn't sure if the doctor was being thorough or was again practicing his humour. "And if she wasn't poisoned?"

"Preliminary?"

"Your professional opinion."

Trenaman pursed his lips and drew another deep breath that he let out slowly. When he was ready, he spoke with certainty. "She went into the water sometime in the last thirty-six hours."

The doctor had already said there were no signs of foul play. Baxter asked the question anyway, just to be sure. "With or without help?"

This time the doctor's answer came behind a doubtful look over the rim of his spectacles. "You'll need a witness for that."

"Or a confession." Baxter wasn't expecting one and his face said so.

"There is one other thing." The doctor had pushed his glasses back up and was following the lines on the floor.

"Well."

"She did not go in alone…" The clinical manner had given way to something more personal and sad. The doctor's eyes moved quickly. Baxter did not miss were they went.

He heard a sadness come into his own voice as he spoke the words Trenaman had avoided. "She was with child."

"Two, maybe three months. I'll have a report by the end of the day."

Again the doctor's voice came from far away. The recovery he had managed relapsed into a greater weakness. Suddenly Baxter was acutely aware of his surroundings, the metal trays and odd shaped bowls that didn't stain and the long sharp blades with heavy handles that didn't need to be delicate. This was not a place of healing. And that smell of a swamp in the heat admixing with dark blood and bile and disinfectant. What had kept him from gagging, from seeing this chamber of horrors? He closed his eyes in search of an escape. He saw rooms in his house that went from being empty to being filled with consolation. He saw the upstairs rooms at Clarke's place with their revolving doors. He saw more rooms in country houses where things were just as they had been left and would remain that way until those who remembered were all gone. Baxter's eyes snapped open, now searching for the way out. He managed a hasty instruction in his rush to fresh air. "This needs to be kept quiet, Doctor, not a word about this to anyone."

The doctor had gone back to his pencil. "The people I see are not very chatty," he replied with a matter-of-factness that was lost in the heavy steps fleeing down the hall toward the front door.

———•———

The room seemed smaller than it was in the dim light of daybreak. Baxter fumbled with the curtains while shapes in the room remained vague, with no edges, like a mossy forest floor. What he took for a narrow bed was in the darkest corner. There appeared to be a lump in its centre. He listened but could hear nothing past his own breathing. He must have run all the way from the morgue, he couldn't remember. He bent over slowly, reaching out. His hand came to something that felt round and woolly, a shoulder maybe. "Mr. Squire…MR. SQUIRE…"

The lump did not move but two specks appeared and began to flicker like bits of quartz in a piece of granite. Then the rock spoke. "Chief Inspector? Is that you? What are you doing here?"

Baxter spoke quickly in between deep breaths. "Get up, you have a train to catch."

There was some movement now from the corner. "How did you get in here?"

"The hostess let me in." He was not trying to be sarcastic. It was all he could think to say. Who had let him in? He looked back through the open door. He remembered being in the hallway. A man, no, a woman. Did he get her name? She had gone back to her room. Baxter stared at the wall over the bed. Johanna? Josephine?

Squire had managed to get his feet on the floor. He sat hunched over, rubbing his face. "Did you say train?"

"Sarah Riley's been found."

"Where is she?"

There was a pause. Had there been enough light, Squire would not have had to wait. He could have seen the horror Baxter was still wearing like a sickness. "In the morgue. A watchman spotted her bobbing on the tide. Looks like she drowned."

There was a second pause then simply, "Oh."

Baxter had felt his way back to the door jamb. He turned and spoke to the silhouette on the edge of the bed, the chin still resting on one hand. "Make yourself presentable. Is there someplace downstairs I can wait?"

"There's a kitchen."

Baxter laid his hat and coat on one chair and sat in another, one elbow leaning on the small table. As the light outside grew and pushed in through the window the room slowly came awake. The white enamel of the oven door took on a good-morning smile. The ice box looked anxious to be opened. A small pantry promised to lend a hand with any effort. The pots were round and made of iron. There was nothing to remind him of the dead. Traces of food, and shoe polish and cigarette smoke lingered in the air. Simple signs of life that in this moment were remarkable and restorative. For the first time since Mackay's telephone call had pulled him out of bed he did not feel a chill. Over his head Baxter heard footsteps back and forth, water moving though pipes in walls, doors opening and closing, and whispered conversations. After a while there was a creaking of stairs and then a fresh-faced uniformed Squire with boots in hand stood at the kitchen doorway.

"I never met her." Squire had set his boots in the hall and was getting some water on to boil.

Once again Baxter was grateful for the young man's intuition, that he would not have to explain the mission. "You're not writing her obituary, you're just letting the family know she's gone."

"Sure, that's all." Squire gave a dismissive wave as he set the kettle on the stove.

"This is the job," Baxter replied, ignoring the wave and its incriminations. It was the job and Baxter had been doing it a long time, too long to be as bothered as he was by this case and its players. He had no connection to Sarah Riley either. In general he believed that brothel inmates were deserving of no sympathy. Bad apples fallen from poisonous trees so far as he was concerned. So why all this care for her or the family? Perhaps he was mourning the loss of something different? So long as Miss Riley was alive there was some hope, hope she might be believed and a killer brought to justice. His feelings for the unborn who would never grow into the futures imagined for them was an old and familiar sadness. That it should extend even to this poor bastard was of some surprise. He could hear Mackay barking in his ear, "Telegrams are a goddamn crime." It was true. They were not foreigners. They were not ministers out of some war office in Ottawa or London. They were policemen in Halifax not a hundred miles away. There was no excuse. Of course sending Mackay would be no comfort. The family's worst imaginings were carved into his face. In Squire they might see the daughter they remembered. Baxter could say none of this. He would have to rely on his own face, for Squire to see it there.

Squire had lit the stove. He came back to the table with a single cup, knowing the chief inspector would not be staying. "And when they ask questions?"

"Perhaps she fell."

"The newspapers will…"

"Newspapers are often wrong."

"You are telling me to lie?"

"I'm telling you things are already bad enough. Ask them about her. Listen, then leave them to their grief." Baxter looked to the window, feigning concern for the weather. If Squire knew too much there would be no point in sending him. He would not be able to conceal the fact that the family had lost more than a daughter.

"Where am I going?" It was the right question and Baxter was relieved.

"Antigonish." Baxter stood and Squire handed him his hat and coat. "The desk sergeant will have funds for a ticket and a room. There is no return train until tomorrow."

"I remember." Baxter paused for a moment then went on with his buttons. He had forgotten that Squire would pass by his hometown on the way to Miss Riley's. Perhaps seeing his own family would help him get over seeing hers, or perhaps it would be a second hardship.

"Send a telegram if you are going to be longer." Squire gave no answer. He was busy looking out the window. The kettle began to whistle. He took no notice. Baxter nodded and showed himself out.

———•———

The station lay at rest, regaining its strength. The men on night patrol were still out. The day shift and the office staff were yet to arrive. When news of a woman's body had come in, Mackay had Meagher take over for him. He was propped up on a stool behind the front counter, the back of his head against the wall, mouth open, eyes shut. Meagher's snoring was loud enough to mask his chief inspector's approach and passing.

Baxter made an entry in the ledger then returned it with the lockbox to a desk drawer. He sealed the money in an envelope then returned to the front counter. Meagher's hands were folded in his lap. His respirations remained steady and peaceful as the envelope got wedged in place.

Baxter sighed then stepped quietly back to his office. He closed the door and stripped to his skivvies and socks. A reflection would have shown vulnerability, drawn comparisons with Victor and Miss Riley on the slab. The uniform was hung neatly, a blanket taken from a shelf and the wardrobe door that had no mirror got gently closed. The chairs in front of the desk became a sit bed. An arm reached out and the desk lamp switched off. Soon Squire would arrive, then leave.

Meagher would reprimand himself. He didn't expect to sleep. He hoped only that his mind would let him rest for an hour or so. Then he had a real estate agent to visit and funeral to attend.

Eventually enough noise filtered in from the outer office to wake him. There were a few moments of befuddlement, then a frantic digging to find his watch, nearly nine o'clock. He got on his pants and shoes then stopped. He sat at his desk trying to find the number in his head. Then he began pulling drawers looking for the list of the few he used. Then it came to him and he reached for the telephone.

"Baxter residence." He could hear the hurry and anxiety in her voice and he kicked himself again for falling asleep.

"How are you?"

"Tired."

"You didn't get back to sleep." Of course she hadn't but he could think of nothing else to say.

"Where are you? The service starts in an hour."

"You go when you're ready. I'll meet you there." There was no time to explain or apologize or reassure, to wait for her voice to soften as he tried to dig his way out. "Is…"

"No…Grace has left already. She didn't mention where she was going, which she didn't have to. I think we both know." Her voice stopped short and Baxter knew his wife was considering, and being considerate, her tongue held firmly against the roof of her mouth until she added, "She certainly does."

"Grace is eighteen. She…"

"Cully, I have to get a move on or I'll be late."

"I'll meet you outside the church." As he was placing the receiver back on its hook it occurred to him that Jane could have called to look for him. Of course if he had had that thought a moment sooner he would be in more trouble. He would have been told that a lady did not go hollering after her husband all over town. Grace would have been quick to make the call, if she had wanted to. Baxter rushed out of the station no better for the rest.

———•———

The two men had never actually met. Baxter knew of Edgar Nevers by reputation only. His real estate ads were a constant in all the papers. His placards were glued to fences and walls all over town. You could think the place belonged to him.

In 1869 the city had opened its new post office and customs house; Renaissance-style stonework, complete with grand columns and an ornate cupola. Nevers was next door in an old wooden building with stooped shoulders and rough grey skin. A clean window with fresh stenciling did what it could to ward off the worst impressions, "Edgar Nevers, Real Estate Agt." Baxter couldn't see anyone moving about behind the letters. He could see a light on. He pushed the bell. A male voice called him in. Baxter closed the door and waited. Across the room, the top of a small desk was completely covered with stacks of papers. Several "For Sale" and "For Rent" signs bearing the company name leaned against the far wall. The handles of shovels, rakes, a scythe, and who knew what all else made a teepee in the corner to the left of the door. The only picture on the wall was a young Victoria in profile. The place was full to overflowing, but there seemed to be an order to it all. Baxter expected the place to smell like a basement. He was wrong and surprised. There was a hint of lilac in the air. The place was almost cozy.

"Edger Nevers, how can I help you?" He had come down a hallway that ran back from the right side of the desk. Edger Nevers was not a large man but he had a full round face. A fresh corona-size cigar bounced in the corner of his mouth as he spoke. Nevers followed his hand across the room. Baxter brought forth his own. If he hadn't, he suspected Nevers would have done it for him.

"I'm Chief Inspector Baxter."

"Yes, I know. You have a lovely place on Dresden Row, blue, two storeys, fenced backyard with a small gazebo. The house could go another year maybe two. You should paint the gazebo this summer I think. I can make arrangements for that if you should like." Seems that won't be necessary, Baxter thought to himself.

Two, maybe three times in his life, he had been laid low by a flu. Still he managed to get out of bed long enough to shave. Nevers didn't look sick, but he had not been near a razor in at least three days. The band of grey hair below the bald plateau was wild enough there could be anything nesting in it. Yet the shirt was crisp and radiant white, the dark pants sharply pressed and the shoes polished bright, not even a hint of dust in the welts. "You seem to know a great deal about me, Mr. Nevers."

"Only what I see in the papers now and then, Mr. Baxter…May I call you Mr. Baxter? What I know is real estate. I know every property in this city and whether or not it's worth having. Are you in the market?"

Baxter unfolded the sheet of paper he'd taken from Woodside yesterday morning and handed it to Nevers. "I'm told you manage these places. I need you to tell me about that."

"Why…is something wrong?"

"Just answer the question, Mr. Nevers, and quickly please, I'm pressed for time."

Nevers held the paper at arm's length. The cigar in his other hand now a pointer, he followed its end down the list of addresses. "All right, well, they are all in good shape." He tapped the paper then nodded to himself. "This one will soon need a new roof. They are all fully rented. What do…"

He needed to give Nevers some time. He could not give him too much. "How long have you been looking after these places?"

"Coming up on eight years."

"All of them."

Nevers looked up then turned the paper so Baxter could see the address identified by his thumb. "Just this one at first."

Baxter took a breath and let it out slowly, still impatient though he was getting where he needed to go. "Tell me how it started."

Nevers handed back the list then moved both hands through his bird's nest. To Baxter he seemed to be looking for the truth not a lie. "A well-dressed man came in one day. Said he was a lawyer representing certain interests. When he gave me the address, I suggested it might be easier to sell if it were vacated. He said he was looking for someone to manage the property, not sell it. I told him I wasn't interested."

"Until he mentioned your fee."

"All I had to do was collect rent and see to repairs." The indignation in his voice was mild but clear. The cigar was back in his teeth.

Baxter raised an eyebrow. It was a weak excuse. For a man who did so well selling for a living, Baxter had expected a better pitch. "And later there were more buildings and more fees and it was all just good business."

Nevers bristled at the further attack on his character. His indignation turned to defiance. "I've done nothing wrong," he shot back, taking the cigar from his mouth and pointing it at the chest of the chief inspector.

Baxter thought otherwise. Sin once or twice removed was sin nonetheless. Pretensions were proof enough of that. The city had started off with too many shiftless sods from London's lower orders. What few industrious souls there were took the paths of least resistance and the greatest profit. Brewers and distillers, smugglers and privateers, brothel keepers, victuallers who overcharged the army and the navy and government men from home and far away who paid high prices only so they could use the place now and then to defend greater interests elsewhere—this was Halifax. The mob that had grown up within the upper streets over the past century and a half, what chance had they to learn better habits with minions like Nevers and their masters living off their baser instincts? Baxter kept all this to himself. He had no time to argue. "I'm not your priest, Mr. Nevers, I'm only interested in the owner."

His hackles relaxed in the momentary ease of seeing he was not the target of Baxter's investigation, whatever it was all about. Then the eyes widened and the fists clenched as Nevers realized he had been cornered. "I never met the owner. I reported to the lawyer at first. Then a new man every other year."

Baxter smiled, not in mockery or meanness, nor in sympathy or triumph. It was a wry smile at how often desperation tried to pass for loyalty. "You knew which house was mine, the colour of my gazebo, and that it needs paint."

Small beads of perspiration had sprouted on Nevers' upper lip. His palms were in the air. "I don't want to make trouble for anyone."

The smile disappeared. "The trouble will be yours if you keep me standing here any longer."

Nevers' eyes went round the room, to the loud signs, the shiny window, and finally to the Queen Mother on the wall. Was he looking for salvation or waving goodbye? Baxter couldn't tell. It didn't matter so long as the man spoke, and finally he did. "In this business it helps to know who to approach, who owns what, that's all." Baxter stepped forward. Nevers stepped away, hands now waving in surrender. "Yes, yes, all right. I have a friend in the assessment office. All the buildings are currently assessed to Chebucto Enterprises."

Baxter took another step forward and reached out as if to take Nevers into custody. He scampered away behind the desk. Baxter pointed and he froze, eyes abulge, nose twitching. "But it wasn't always that way was it, Mr. Nevers?"

"No." The head shook just in case the voice that had gone faint was not heard.

Baxter did not come any closer. What he did do was make sure the look on his face told Nevers he would if he had to. "I need to hear you say it, Mr. Nevers."

The wall seemed to reach out and take Nevers more than he leaned against it. He looked around again, this time as if he expected a cigarette and blindfold. "When I started with the first building it was assessed to Mr. Wallace."

Baxter followed Nevers' gaze, until he was forced to look him in the eye. Then Baxter spoke his question in three clear drum beats. "Maynard Sinclair Wallace?"

Nevers closed his eyes. "Yes, him…Maynard Sinclair Wallace."

"He was the owner?"

"Correct."

"Very good, Mr. Nevers. We are nearly done. Now tell me, when you started, who occupied the building?"

Nevers opened his eyes. His cigar had slipped from his grasp. He stared at it for a moment then stooped to pick it up. "It was the same business then as it is now, if that's what you mean."

"Run by the same man?"

"Yes." There was a small wastebasket at the side of the desk. Nevers tossed his cigar then pulled out the chair and slumped down.

"Thank you, Mr. Nevers." Baxter pointed a shoulder toward the door then held up. "One last thing. What was the lawyer's name?"

Nevers was massaging his face. He looked out between his fingers then laid his hands on the desk and pushed himself up. It seemed a great effort. "Seabrook…Mr. James Seabrook." As Baxter retreated slowly down the little hallway he added, "Could you lock the door on your way out?"

———•———

The air was still and dry and cold. There were no signs of yesterday's rain or the warmth of the days before. Mourners gathered on the sidewalk in threes and fours, buttoned to the neck, hands deep in the pockets of their coats. Only now and then did clouds of condensation appear. No one seemed to have much to say before making their way inside.

Baxter knew these people. They were used to saying goodbye. Fishing boats, merchant ships, and passenger liners or trains headed west and south in search of work and better times. For them it was more a matter of routine than sadness. They had faith in the sojourner's return and letters in the meantime. Yesterday had been different. A goodbye to a soldier might be a farewell. And in the meantime the postman would be met with trepidation.

There would be no trepidation along the home front, however, when the boys came marching home, or were carried by their mates. The dead would be laid to rest with honours and the brave sacrifice of their families would be mentioned in sermons and memorials and whenever the city needed a shot in the arm for years to come. For the rest of their lives the wounded would be stared at by those with no idea of combat and a gulf of awe and horror and vicarious thrill and a desire to forget would forever keep them at a distance, but not apart.

The city kept a place for those who went off in uniform to fight. Baxter knew this, just as he had known many who left in civilian clothes. They hadn't gone to march or pull a trigger. They went to hammer nails or work their way up some office ladder. "Go on," they were told, or told themselves. "There is more for you there than here." When they did as they were told they never meant to say this place was less worth having. He could have left, and Baxter felt more could have stayed just as he had done. How could the city become a better place if it could not count on the people it needed most?

Of course no one coming through the doors of Saint Matthew's church had to think twice about forgiving Victor Mosher, not today. He had come up rough and poor. He was bright enough and determined enough not to let that hold him back. He had done well, more importantly, he had done well in Halifax, and helped others along the way. Still and all he was a middling toad in a small puddle, not deserving of a state funeral. True perhaps. Just as it was true that looking back the city might regret not having said a grander farewell.

The church eventually filled to half. Catherine, the children, and Carmine and the rest of the immediate family filled the first two rows. Military matters kept the premier of the province from attending. The mayor, the chief of police, and a good many other men in office and their wives were able to attend and filled the next three rows. Even if he had arrived earlier, Baxter would have heeded Tolliver's warning to stay clear of the mayor. He and Jane sat near the back.

The service opened with the usual platitudes of loss and shock. Nothing insightful or specific, that was the essential magic of all warm comforts. Carmine stood and took the hand of the bereaved and walked with them in the footsteps of his brother's life. Not a word was missed. No one could look away though most eyes had spilled over by the time Carmine stepped down from the altar. The choir led three simple hymns sung back to them in strong voice without the need of hymnals. The small procession to the graveside was almost martial in precision. The minister led a final prayer. Just before it was lowered away, Catherine came forward and placed a hand on the casket and spoke in private to her husband. The crowd pulled back to the cemetery gates then lingered, the course of bearing witness not quite at its end.

Catherine wore a dark hooded cape that flared from her waist to the ground in a perfect cone. She seemed to float down the narrow path by magic, or perhaps on a rip current of grief. She was accompanied by the music of gravel crumbling softly as eggshells. Her face showed the strain of the past few days. Jane was the first to come forward. Catherine took the hand extended to her with genuine gratitude, saying, "I got your card, Jane, very kind."

"It was a lovely service."

Catherine nodded. Not letting go, she waved apathetically with her other hand, saying, "A week from now it will all be forgotten, maybe sooner with our men gone off to this latest war." There was perhaps a hint of bitterness from the corner of one eye that was overcome by a look of acceptance that spread slowly across her face.

Baxter was still in the doghouse. Jane would let none of that show in public. As Catherine finally released her hand, Jane took her husband's arm and in the process drew him to her side. He had been warned not to say anything upsetting, particularly if Catherine, in morbid curiosity, asked questions she should never hear the answers to. Knowing he had to at least say something and feeling that he was being signalled that this was the time, Baxter now dared to speak. "Your husband will be remembered. We will remember him. And you will see his…justice will be done."

Jane stared at her shoes. Baxter knew she was holding her breath. He prayed Catherine's attention would be drawn away by others wanting to show their respects. But her eyes were locked on his. "My oldest son talks of justice and what he would do if he could get his hands on someone. He looks grown up. Says he never believed in Santa Claus. Will you do something for me, Mr. Baxter?"

"If I can." Jane's grip tightened.

"Whatever it is you and Carmine are not telling me, I expect you to do everything you can to keep it from my children."

Baxter was grateful for Catherine's wisdom, for not putting him in a place where he could only hurt them both, yet leaving him free to tell the truth. "Your husband was a good man," he said while nodding yes.

"I will hold you to that." Catherine's face was pallid and the great cape exaggerated her smallness and frailty. Her voice remained iron strong.

Jane's voice softened the air as she patted her husband's arm and began to ease them away. "Catherine, I believe Chief Tolliver and the mayor want to pay their respects. Please excuse us."

"Yes of course."

At the last moment Jane went a little further. "Catherine, may I call on you?" It would be difficult with his work between them, Baxter thought, and then admired his wife's sense of propriety all the more.

The widow Mosher managed a wan smile as she replied, "I'd like that very much."

While Jane had been extending her goodwill, Baxter had been watching the mayor and the chief approach. From Tolliver's face it was clear Baxter had best avoid speaking to the mayor or so much as look in his direction. Apparently Tolliver was still expected to remove his chief inspector from the case. If he wanted any more time he had best stay out of range. Baxter shifted his gaze. He noticed a man looking in through the north fence of the cemetery. Something about him seemed familiar and Baxter took a closer look. Now as he and Jane were moving through the gate onto the sidewalk away from his superiors and closer to his intuition, Baxter pulled up. "There is something I have to do. Will you be all right getting home?"

"I thought we might take a walk." It was an olive branch he desperately wanted to reach for.

He looked again for the man. He was no longer at the fence. He was moving up Spring Garden Road. "This can't wait."

Inside the graveyard, closer to the solitude of death, away from the bustle and concerns of life, there seemed to be no sound. As they had come back into the world Baxter was suddenly aware of all sound, a hammer pounding nails not far away, the wheels of a passing cart, his own heartbeat. The urgency in Jane's voice was clearest of all. Things at home could not wait either. "She still believes, you know…Grace…She still believes in Santa…she still believes in a lot of thing. She has dreams, Cully."

He did not mean to be glib or flippant. He was simply caught off guard. "Children dream, adults do what's right."

"It would hurt her very much to hear you say that. She is trying very hard to do what's right." Baxter heard the sorrow mixed with anger in Jane's voice. He heard the foreboding and insistent ticking of the clock and he heard his footsteps moving round the corner up Spring Garden Road. Jane started to say something else then held her tongue. He would hear her thoughts once he got home.

———•———

Baxter fell in beside Clarke walking north along Grafton Street behind the basilica. Clarke glanced over at the chief inspector as if he were expected. "Which gates you s'pose he's at?"

"If you read your Bible, Mr. Clarke, you would know that for whosoever shall call upon the name of the Lord shall be saved."

Clarke smiled and in his best preacher's voice reminded Baxter he was familiar with the good book. "But the fearful, and unbelievin', and the abominable, and murderers, and whoremongers, and sorcerers, and idolaters, and all liars, shall have their part in the lake which burneth with fire and brimstone."

"So you are planning a deathbed confession."

"Confessin's for you Catholics. Us Protestants makes our own peace with God." They crossed Blowers Street, pausing for a passing hack.

"Then you know there will be no peace until you tell me what happened."

They had come to a stop. "You ain't my God and it's chilly and I'm hungry, best be gettin' home," Clarke said, breathing into his hands and looking up Blowers to the corner at Albemarle.

"The Aberdeen is closer, my treat," Baxter replied looking through the buildings toward the corner of Sackville and Argyle.

"Have the roast beef. Victor always liked it."

"Have it with me and I'll tell you about my meeting with Sarah Riley."

Clarke had begun to pull away. Now he stopped. "You found her?"

"This morning."

"How is she?"

Baxter began walking, quickly, not wanting to betray doubt or give either of them room to change their mind. "You'll join me then, good." Clarke pushed at him. Baxter held mute, refusing to say a word until they were inside and at a table. He was hoping Clarke truly was cold and hungry and that the atmosphere of the Aberdeen would hold him still.

A waiter came with menus and Baxter spoke as he studied, suddenly aware that he might be hungry too. "Now that we are past pretending, Mr. Clarke, best you start from the beginning."

Clarke ignored his menu. "If you talked to Sarah, don't know what more I can tell you. And you still ain't said how she is."

Baxter continued reading as he answered, though he had already decided what to have. "With child, Victor's child, which you knew all along. But Victor didn't know until last Friday night, did he?"

"No need of it, 'specially with Victor and the like."

Baxter preened a little like a schoolteacher hearing correct sums. Both points had been conceded without resistance, welcome progress. Now what to make of the new topic Clarke had raised. He set his menu down. "No need of what?"

"Of gettin' in the family way."

"The regular wages of sin."

Clarke pushed back in his chair and folded his arms across his chest. "Don't you ever take a break from bein' an asshole?" There was no playfulness in his voice.

Baxter leaned forward gripping both sides of the small table. "You run a brothel, Mr. Clarke, not a chapel or a rescue mission."

Clarke smiled that handsome yellow smile and cocked his head to one side. "How many times we gonna have this conversation? If you could close my place an' every other place like it and the taverns and the gambling joints, what then? We all wake up in the Garden of Eden? They finally make you chief a police?"

He was not ashamed. It was just too much to have his vision and ambition treated crassly...and by the likes of this man. "Immorality must be stamped out."

Now Clarke moved his head from side to side. The smile became a mocking twist. "Stamp, stamp, stamp, here come the Salvation Army band. And some a them fellas sneakin' round my place too, by the way. Long with some of yer policemen and Victor Mosher and even Maynard Sinclair Wallace."

"Hypocrisy is just another sin," Baxter shot back. Their voices had become louder than they realized. It was nearly noon. More people had come in. At the moment most of them were more interested in the back corner of the room than on deciding what to eat. Their waiter approached slowly, ready to flee if necessary. Baxter called for steaks well done and coffee, which the young man poured with a shaky hand.

As Clarke spooned sugar he went on, in a voice that let others mind their business. "You taken a good look round this town lately? Enlisted men still can't marry. You see any women on our fishin' boats or mer-chan' marines? You see men strikin' it rich every other day? No. What ya see is men with plenty of frustration and wives gettin' sick a their husbands..."

"That's all just..."

"I ain't finished," Clarke interrupted, now pointing with his spoon. "You 'spect men to die for some queen they ain't never seen and a country don't know them from Adam. Or, work like dogs ten hours a day. But if you catch 'em spending a little of their hard-earned wages on a bottle or some female comp'ny you cast 'em out, curse the women even worse. And who are they? Doe-mestic help knocked up and sent packing 'fore the lady a the house gets wind. Young girls looking for another soldier to take up with fer a time. How many 're-spectable' women in this town once had a room in a bawdyhouse? More'n a few and you know it."

Baxter took a sip of his black coffee, then looked over his cup with wide eyes. "Oh, well then, I'll expect to see Ellen Reardon in the society pages any day now."

Clarke continued stirring. "She ain't the sort I'm talkin' about and you know that too. Ellen's the worst sort a hedge whore, do anything for a drink. She just can't help it. Lotsa folks tried ta fix her. She nearly burnt my place to the ground one time, upset a oil lamp." Clarke finally lifted his cup, and then set it down carefully. He stared into his brew as if it had conjured up the past before his eyes. "It was middle a the night. She was blind drunk. Still had enough good sense ta douse the flames with her chamber pot. I still had to put her out, mind you, room stank a burnt piss for a week."

"You mourn the tragedy of young women while you depend upon it," Baxter replied, seething with indignation. Still he managed to keep his volume in check.

"It's a scant livin' hounded by the likes a you. Meanwhile, the men who own this town are doin' worse things for money 'an I ever done. Who you think yer talkin' to? You gone coloured blind?" He had a point. And debating the morality of Charlie's "profession" was counterproductive. Better to try this new opening before it closed.

"If I suffered from that sort of blindness, Mr. Clarke, you would already be in jail. I don't think you killed Victor Mosher. You want me to see you differently, tell me who did."

"What Sarah say?"

Baxter took another sip of his unsweetened coffee. There was no concealing this truth any longer. "Nothing, she's in the morgue."

"You lyin' bastard." Clarke slapped the table. Dots of coffee stained the linen on both sides of the table. Behind them a few menus lowered then raised again. "Why ain't I surprised. Jesus Christ…What happened? And no more a yer bullshit." Baxter looked straight across the table. The sorrow Clarke was wearing was real and familiar. He'd seen it earlier this morning on the face of Catherine Mosher.

He was never much good at being gentle. He fiddled with his cutlery. "She was found in the harbour early this morning. Medical examiner says she may have been in the water a day and a half." He thought of Victor's face and the closed casket. Her family at least would see their daughter one last time.

"And?"

"Most likely she drowned, but so far that's as much as I know."

Clarke reached for his coffee then put it down. Around the small dining room china clinked and more casual conversation murmured. Finally Clarke asked, "Her people?"

"Officer Squire is on his way. Would she…"

"Do 'way with herself an' her child?" Clarke shook his head, emphatically, then looked unsure. "No…I don't think so…maybe…Jesus. She was a lot tougher'n you might think." He looked down once more, the past again playing out on the shimmering surface of his coffee. "I didn't want anythin' to do with her at first. I told her I got no room for any more girls and I got no use for some hayseed thinks she can do somethin' she can't."

Baxter needed the conversation to continue. He desperately wanted to ask just the right questions. The only one he could think of came as a surprise and made him a little afraid. "Whatever possessed her to come to you in the first place?"

Clarke looked up at the ceiling for a moment then straight across the table. Baxter couldn't tell if the process of recall was reducing Clarke's pain or making it worse. "Martha found her. Usual story, country girl run outta work and money, embarrassed and not much ta go home to or nothin' there she wanted." He cleared his throat, took a moment to find his place. "Three of us was standin' in the front parlour just starin' at one another. All the sudden Preacher decides to show off his voice. Laced mutton, ca-caw, three-penny upright, ca-caw, he says…crazy fuckin' bird. Listen to him, I said, he's tellin' your fortune. You're pretty enough, go back to wherever you come from and find some dirt farmer. You can watch him work himself to death buyin' you whatever you want and you'll never have to wash yer quim three times a night or see the unholy side a Christian husbands."

The image knocked any sympathy from Baxter's thoughts. "That's disgusting."

Clarke shrugged, unapologetic. "It was the truth. Thought it might scare her off. I 'spected she'd blush and slap my face. She just smiled. My name is Miss Sarah Riley, she says. And rather than worryin' about my delicate sensibilities, Mr. Clarke, you should be worryin' 'bout whether or not I can keep the customers buyin' me watered-down drinks and whether or not I can get 'em to pay top dollar for taking me upstairs."

"How very industrial and all the more disgusting."

"Tougher than she looked." The waiter arrived and mutely set the plates and refilled the coffee, more interested in getting away than plying for a tip.

Baxter got as far as picking up a fork. He did nothing with it. He just needed to do something physical to trigger his next question. His appetite had vanished as suddenly as it appeared. "So how did she get involved with Victor?"

Perhaps Clarke had a genuine appetite. Maybe he had decided to eat for spite or to try and feel better. So long as he kept talking, he could eat his meal and Baxter's too. "Accident. Sarah knew how to keep men buyin' drinks all right. By the time they got her upstairs they was never much good. Whatever happened she'd send 'em away with a big kiss and a smile and of course she collected up front."

"Clearly things went differently with Victor."

Clarke took a second cut of meat, chewed, then went on. "Victor was a politician. He come in once in a while to socialize, have a drink or two. Mostly he come ta play poker. Sometimes when his cards went cold, he'd sit out for a bit. Guess that's how it started. Lotsa men can't talk to their wives. Others like to talk themselves up. Sometimes a woman's ear can do more for a man's pride than her touch." Baxter thought of Jane and the olive branch he had so wanted to accept. The thought stuck him like a pin. That a brothel keeper could have any sense of what decent people felt was a double stick.

Clarke had pulled himself closer to the table as if the waiter might reach for his plate. For a moment Baxter admired the gusto, then he thought of Catherine. "Let's not bother with the false sentiment. We're not here to protect Victor's reputation."

Clarke spoke through a mouthful and pointed with his steak knife. "We ain't here protectin' yer simple sense of right and wrong neither. Sarah wasn't taking any a Victor's money. He trusted her."

"With what?"

"Who knows…gossip…true stories no one would believe…his weaknesses? If I made it my business to ask, I wouldn't have no business."

"You're hiding something."

"You just crazy."

Baxter pointed back with his clean fork. "I'm doing my job."

"No, you doin' more than that, you punishin' yourself." Clarke took no notice of the fork. He was staring at Baxter's hands, the bandaged thumb, the freshly healed index finger. Perhaps he had seen the knife point in the palm. Certainly there were older scars to see. "Them could be the hands of a butcher or a wood carver. They don't look like no policeman's hands. And don't say paper cuts." Clarke looked up and caught Baxter's eyes before he could look away. "You think if you pass harsh judgment on yourself, God won't? Christ, you got stranger ideas than the people I have to throw outta my place."

Baxter hid his hands in his lap under the table. No one had ever said anything of the kind to his face. Was there talk behind his back? Was he just another story of the city told to newcomers? No, Clarke was scrambling, trying to find a way to put him off. "I'll thank you, Mr. Clarke, not to confuse me with anyone you might know. Move on to what happened Friday night."

Clarke chewed another mouthful and stared for a few moments before continuing. Under the table Baxter pulled at the bandage on his thumb.

"It wasn't a regular night, invitation only, just a few gentlemen for cards. Victor'd been losing lately, more'n he could afford, I think. That night his luck turned. I don't know if Sarah asked him to sit out or maybe he was just tryin' to protect his winnings. Don't matter. They sat in the back parlour for a while, then all the sudden they was gone, upstairs, I figured."

"And the card game?"

"Kept goin'. I went out front, shooed away a couple sailors, reminded the girls ta keep the door locked and not let in any more friends to help them pass the time. I talked to Martha and Annie for a bit. I was comin' back to check on drinks and then I heard Sarah and I went straight for my bat."

Baxter was not sure of the image, only that it was horrible. "She screamed."

Clarke waved the piece of meat on the end of his fork. "Whistled. Most men know enough to behave themselves in my place. I tell all my girls, first hint a trouble, keep playin' nice but start whistlin' a tune loud as you can."

"You said she was with Victor."

"Didn't make sense to me neither. I got my bat all the same."

Baxter had gotten over his shame, his hands were on the table and he was leaning forward. "And then…?"

"I find Sarah by the back door. Victor's on the stairs with a knife Nothin' on but the look of a man lost his mind."

"Sarah had broken the news?"

Clarke had put down his fork. He gave his plate a push. "Afterward, when she was tryin' to tell us what happened, Sarah said Victor was calm at first, told her not to worry, things would work themselves out. She said he asked her if she would fix him a drink. She put on a dressing gown and came downstairs."

Baxter rapped his knuckles on the table as if he were signalling a pass in 45s. "You're lying. Victor wouldn't carry a knife."

Clarke laid a trump. "I didn't say it was his. Girls eat in their rooms, always leavin' dirty dishes lyin' round. Doesn't matter where he got the knife."

"Well, if Victor had the knife, how does he wind up dead?"

"'Cause he wasn't being careful."

Clarke looked at him as if the answer was obvious and he couldn't understand why Baxter was lost. "Careful…What are you talking about?"

"Safes."

"What?"

"Safes, you know, what a man puts on if he don't want no babies…or anything else." Baxter looked around the room expecting to see all eyes on them. "No, Mr. Clarke, I don't know," he whispered, another look of disgust on his face.

"Well, Wallace did. They was his idea. He wouldn't go near otherwise. He saw to it there was always plenty round. But Sarah let Victor think with his dick, now they both dead. Not Wallace. He was careful."

The testimony would be scandalous. The courtroom would ripple with oohs and ahs and squirms of discomfort. Be that as it may. Wallace was going to stand trial. He could see him sweating in the witness box.

He could see Tolliver and the mayor watching in hair shirts. "He was protecting his investment."

"What da ya mean?"

Baxter scowled as you would at a child's foolish ploy. "Don't play dumb. You and Wallace are business partners."

Clarke rolled his eyes. "You bump yer head? Me and Wallace partners…talk sense."

Baxter continued to push. "He owns the building."

"Owns what buildin'?"

"Your place."

"No he don't. I pay rent to that real estate prig…Nevers."

Baxter withdrew, took a measure. Clarke did not look away. His forehead was creased, his shoulders a little hunched. "You ever hear of a holding company?"

"A what?"

Baxter let out a small sigh of impatience. Clarke was supposed to be the one doing the telling. "A business front for the well-to-do, so I've learned. Nevers is a beard. Wallace is your landlord."

Clarke's eyes narrowed. He leaned back a little. "Since when?"

Baxter thought for moment to be sure. "Seven, eight years."

Clarke pushed back from the table with an angry scrape of wood on tile. His voice grew loud. "That son of a bitch…I gotta go."

Now all eyes were upon them. Baxter tried to look them off while getting to his feet. "You have to finish. Victor didn't stab himself." He spoke in a whisper. No doubt a few of the closer tables heard anyway.

Clarke was back in his coat and three steps from the table. "I gave you all the help I can," he said, not looking back from his beeline for the door.

Baxter sat back down and replaced the napkin in his lap, waiting for the room to look away. He had hardly touched his food. He took a cut of steak. It was cold and tasted like sawdust and took forever to get down. He gave up and waved to the waiter for the cheque.

Outside the hotel, he stood for a few moments looking down Argyle toward City Hall, trying to summon up the will to go back to work. There were things to be done. Routine things, things that would not solve this case. Finally he turned the other way, rounded the corner onto Sackville and began walking home. His legs felt weak and he moved awkwardly as if he had been running hard or struggling under some great weight. He would lie down once he got home. Maybe he would be able to fall asleep.

———•———

C larke had not gone home. The Carleton Hotel was at the end of the block, on the other side of the street from the Aberdeen. Clarke was hidden from view, standing in the recessed entranceway. Now and then a patron came or went. He played doorman to ward off suspicion. He watched Baxter on the sidewalk. He looked to be waiting on a hack. One soon pulled up. Baxter ignored it until the driver gave his horse a touch of the whip and moved on. Baxter stood with his hands in his greatcoat, his shoulders rising and falling as if he were struggling for air or trying to take in enough of it to lift himself off the ground and into the breeze. Finally he resigned himself to walking and went round the corner out of sight. Clarke waited another minute in case Baxter had a change of heart, then he came out form his cubbyhole and made his way back down to the Aberdeen.

Clarke stood just inside the door. When he saw who he was looking for he waved.

William Paul approached, balancing a tray of dirty dishes on one shoulder. "You're the one they call Billy right?"

"Some do." William's eyes narrowed.

Clarke waved one hand slightly as an indication he was no threat. "Billy, is the boss in?"

"Mr. White, you mean?" He peeked back over his shoulder.

"Yeah."

"No, he's out, said he'd be back around four I think."

"You still be here then?" The door opened behind them. Charlie and William both turned, wearing guilty faces. The woman clutched her bag and hurried past, looking back twice.

"Yeah, I'll be here 'til ten or so."

"I need you ta give him a message for me."

William balanced his tray on an empty umbrella stand and began patting the pockets of his apron. When he came up empty, he said, "You want me to get you a pen and paper?"

"Naw. You know who I am?"

"Charles Clarke, right?"

Behind them the woman was speaking to a man across the front desk. They were taking turns glancing toward the door. "That's right, you tell White his boss needs to come see me. Tell him I ain't waitin' long."

"Who is it you want to come see you?"

The man had come around the desk and was walking slowly toward them. The woman stood watching, arms folded, nose in the air. Clarke looked back at William, leaning the hotel front door open as he spoke. "You just tell White what I said, he knows."

"All right, Mr. Clarke, I'll tell him."

———•———

There was just the one telephone. It was in the library. Wallace used it for business, mostly to make calls, not take them. Wallace looked after his business affairs in the morning. Afternoons were for other things. The telephone rang for some time before someone picked it up. "Ah, hello…"

"Yes."

"This is Mr. Edger Nevers calling. I wish to speak with Mr. Wallace."

"Is he expecting your call?"

"…No, I…"

"How did you get this number?"

"I have urgent business."

"What was the name again?"

"Nevers, M…"

"Just one moment."

The receiver lay on the desk for several minutes. "Mr. Nevers."

"Yes."

"What can I do for you?"

"Mr. Wallace?"

"Yes."

"Mr. Wallace, my name is Edgar Nevers, of Edgar Nevers Real Estate."

"I think we've established that." The sarcasm in the voice was most intentional.

"Yes, I'm sorry, I'm sure you are very busy. You may not remember, sir, but I work for you, well, not directly. You are discreet, of course. You have...A man..."

"Mr. Nevers, did someone call you or did you speak in person?"

"We spoke in person."

"And did you speak with a newspaper reporter or someone else?"

"Someone else."

"A policeman?"

"Yes, sir." Now it was fear that was evident on the line.

"It was Chief Inspector Baxter, was it not?"

"He threatened me, Mr. Wallace. I had no choice. I would never..."

"Thank you very much for calling, Mr. Nevers. Good afternoon."

———•———

R obert White had gotten the message. Not long after he passed it on, the telephone in his small office rang in response. White had picked it up before the second ring. He followed the instructions it gave him to the letter. A little after midnight, he heard the roar of the mob under the wheels of the great black coach as it crushed the gravel of the courtyard. He stood by for ten minutes as directed, then made himself scarce.

Wallace stepped out of the carriage looking as if he might have stolen it, dressed in a worn wool jacket, heavy leather boots, the peak of a newsboy cap pulled low. He swung the coach door very slowly, then leaned against it gently, bringing it to latch. He looked up at the driver and nodded. A quiet double click of the tongue and the carriage began rolling back whence it came, its opaque windows and lacquer sheen more sinister in the night light than a black cat. Wallace moved at the same time, his tracks in the gravel lost in the greater thunder of the horde as it again rose up beneath the wheels.

A tall stockade fence closed the courtyard on three sides and separated the hotel from the rooming house next door. Usually the door in the fence was padlocked. Just now that padlock was tucked away in a small drawer of the Aberdeen's front desk. A slip of paper bookmarking the hotel ledger would remind Mr. White to put it back in the morning.

Wallace shut the fence door behind him. The gaslights that lit the back of the hotel were of almost no use now. He waited a moment. Thinking his eyes well enough adjusted he stepped off with confidence across the yard. After only two steps he banged his shin on a broken axle from a hawker's cart. He cursed and limped on. Watching the ground, he was nearly decapitated by a low-hanging clothesline. He cursed again and made his way around a few more hostile shapes in the tall dead grass. The minefield galled him all the more because he owned it. Later he would see to it that Mr. Woodside lit a fire under that piss-ant Nevers. Why was it so hard to find good help? Across the gauntlet with no further damage, he made his way down the alley between the rooming house and Sanford's Market and came out on Argyle Street at a point two streets down and two blocks over from Clarke's.

"I'm not used to being summoned." The look from under the peaked cap was as indignant as the words.

Most of the knocks on his door came late at night. When things were hopping he was often slow to answer. No matter, his customers would wait. This time Clarke was not slow to the door because he was busy. He was slow because he knew who was there. The thought of facing Wallace's snobbery did nothing to raise any sympathy or hurry. "Might remember that next time yer givin' orders," Clarke suggested, not looking very hopeful.

"Thank you for that valuable advice on etiquette and manners, but what is it that you really want to discuss?" Wallace took a step forward. Clarke remained in his path, one hand planted firmly on the door casing.

He waited for Wallace to step back. "Thought we might talk about the future."

Wallace pulled off his cap, indignance boiling into rage. "So you mean to threaten me."

Restraint only at the last minute kept the play out of his voice and prevented him from smiling. Outwardly, Clarke remained all calm and matter of fact. "I mean to collect a debt."

"What is it you think I owe you, Charlie?" Wallace demanded. He said the name as if it belonged to one of his lowest minions who needed to be reminded of their place.

Now a slow smile did cross Clarke's face. It was a show of force, not humour. "Well, Maynard, how 'bout a bit a truth to start." Now Clarke stepped aside, allowing Wallace to cross the threshold. Clarke locked the door then stepped round Wallace and moved on into the front parlour. Clarke took his time sitting down. He didn't invite Wallace to a chair.

Wallace watched while Clarke crossed his legs and set his back just right. The wait took none of the sauce from his voice. "It seems to me you have your truth already."

"I wanta hear it from you."

Wallace looked down at the chair closest to the door. After he had crossed his own legs and set the cloth cap on the seat next to him as carefully as he would a fine top hat, he looked at Clarke with a bald expression and said, "What do you want to hear, Charlie, that I own this place? I once owned it, yes, now I merely have control over it, which to you is the same thing, I suppose." He finished with a dismissive wave of his hand before letting it fall back on his knee.

Clarke leaned forward just a little and blinked once or twice as if it were a problem of Euclidean geometry he was trying to solve. "So I work for you, an' it's been that way for years."

"You pay rent to a company I have interest in, hardly the same thing. Have I ever told you what to do or asked you for anything other than discretion? You have any paystubs signed by me?"

Clarke sat back. His chin and eyes followed the top of the opposite wall along the thin line where it joined the ceiling. He spoke to himself as much as to Wallace. "Don't know why I didn't figure it out long ago. You send word you's comin'. You and yer guests take over, play cards, fuck the girls, all like you in yer own house. You less bold about it, but you ain't much different than the man owned my father."

Wallace joined in the study of the wall for a moment, then came back to Clarke. "We're a long way from…Georgia, was it, where your father came from." He waited to be corrected, then continued when he wasn't.

"I desired certain entertainments. I arranged for them in a way that would not draw attention to myself or my associates." His expression remained as flat and even as a balance sheet.

Now Clarke shook his head and the smile that came to his face this time was a mix of humour and sadness and resignation. "Daytime you a re-spectable gentleman. Sneakin' round here at night in yer handyman costume you is somethin' else."

"I protected…"

The smile snapped, the legs uncrossed, and the voice fired in a warning shot. "No! I done the protectin'. You ever feel a knife in yer ribs? Yer wife ever get a note in the mail?"

Wallace avoided Clarke's exigent glare and brushed at his pants. "Everything was well taken care of."

Clarke let out a great "HAH" and a similar mocking squawk erupted from the hidden interior of Preacher's cage. "Payin' yourself it turns out. But that ain't it. Nobody in this place cared who you was, or Victor or the rest of yer highfalutin friends. Sure we pretended at romance, that's the job. But we wasn't deceitful. We was honest and you played us for fools."

Wallace seemed unperturbed by the volume or its protest. He rolled his eyes up slowly from his pants and spoke with an instructor's patience. "So the blackmail you are leading up to now is not tawdry and predictable, because you are going about it honestly, is that it? And the reason we are playing out this little whorehouse drama in the middle of the night isn't because a man is dead. This is all because I didn't tell you my business?"

Clarke found both knees with his hands and pushed himself up. As he spoke he uncovered the cage and from a nearby dish fed the bird some fruit. "Last couple of days I been thinkin' a lot about my father. He come here, managed to scratch out a living. Give you the shirt off his back, didn't dare hold his head up though. I ain't ashamed. I'm just done lookin' at my shoes."

"And of course you need money to turn over a new leaf." The first three words were delivered in the rising tone of an unsurprised eureka.

Clarke turned from the cage and stood over Wallace, giving back his doubtless tone. "Takes more'n money for a man to hold his head up. Way

I see it, time you found me a legitimate job, somethin' I can work at and get someplace. Time goes by people be sayin' there goes Charles Clarke, you know he came up from nothin'."

Wallace pursed his lips as if in serious thought, then asked, "What then, you get elected to city council? And what do you do with those bloody floorboards, have them made into a desk?"

"Fuck off."

Wallace shot up a hand as if he were starting a race or as if he truly had discovered something new and wonderful. "That's more like it, Charlie. You had me worried for a minute."

Charlie's face rolled over to something as hard, rolled precise and deadly like a revolver. "You think I won't talk to Baxter? I've already told him most of it."

Wallace stared back as you would at a toy gun. "So you finish, and you wait. And you know what happens…nothing. There is no evidence. The only witness has flown the coop. And should she reappear, I'm sure she can be managed. Meanwhile, this city isn't about to side with a pimp against some of its most reputable citizens."

Clarke resumed his seat and watched the bird pick its feathers. "Must be nice"

"Excuse me?"

"Havin' things all figured out."

Wallace shrugged and glanced toward his cap, almost reaching for it then holding off. "It's just the way things are, Charlie. You know what else is true?"

"Shit stinks."

"There would be no thank yous. People don't like handling dirty laundry. No one would say you were brave and good after all, you coming forward and all. And when you eventually die in the poorhouse, bent and toothless and reeking of urine, even your own kind will say good riddance." He looked expectantly at Clarke as he finished, anticipating sparks from having poked the fire.

A spark did come to Charlie's eye, not from provocation. It came from his own reckoning. "You right, lotsa folks will want to shoot the messenger. Lots of 'em, not all of 'em. And you may not get off the hook so easy."

"And why might that be, Charlie?" Wallace was amused, not concerned.

"Lotsa folks here poor and strugglin'. They ain't goin' feel sorry for the likes a you. They goin' be on the side of Victor's widow and her children. And Miss Sarah too."

Wallace nodded at the mention of the bereaved then set them off in the margin. To the matter of Miss Riley, he replied, "Just a harlot bearing more bad news. She'll wish she stayed in hiding."

"She was here, but not for long. Not long 'nough for people overlook the fact she was a preacher's daughter. The papers will show her picture, young and innocent and pretty. And right 'longside that will be the sad sad faces of her momma and her daddy." Clarke was back to a study of the wall as if it were an enlarged copy of the news.

Wallace read the wall differently. "It would all be lost amidst dispatches from the war."

Clarke turned to look at Wallace. "You sure? Casualty reports hit folks hard, churns up their emotions. Maybe they feel all the more for the loss of a young momma ta be."

Wallace looked back at the wall, then at Clarke again. "What are you talking about?"

"That's right. Sarah's come out of hiding. She's at the morgue. Wait for the morning papers." His face was confident, urging Wallace to leave immediately to wait at the newsstand.

"But I…"

"Had nothin' ta do with it? Won't look that way. Victor owed you money, didn't he? And there was other things 'tween you two I think. So you killed him, and then Sarah too to keep her quiet. And that poor baby." By the time he was done speculating Clarke's face was honest in its sadness, not for Wallace.

"That's not true and you know it." It was difficult to tell if Wallace was afraid or more annoyed.

"You know what else is bound to happen. Some father lost a son will scream rich man's war, poor man's fight. And then all the sudden Sarah and Martha and me and Annie we ain't horrible no more. We casualties just like that dead soldier boy. And there you is a rich man. Still think folks'll be on your side?"

Wallace listened and solidified himself as best he could, then took aim at Clarke's motives. "Tell me, Charlie, will your father rest easier?"

The counterattack came quick and easy. "He never had much sympathy for rich white men. Ask me it's more likely yer father rollin' in his grave."

The hardness remained intact but the torpor of egotism or patience or whatever it was that had held him in place was overcome. Wallace reached for his cap. "So what now."

"So now you know how things really is, you go home start figurin' out how you goin' take care a me, and Martha and Annie too."

Wallace looked back from the door. Clarke had not bothered to get up to see him out. "And what do you do?"

"What do *we* do…? We all practice being blind, deaf, an' dumb."

———•———

At least one more telephone rang in the city before morning. This particular telephone was a long time being answered. "Is that you, Martin?"

"Who is this?" The voice was still half asleep, able nonetheless to communicate its anger.

"It's Maynard."

"Jesus Christ, Maynard, it's the middle of the night."

"Sorry about the hour." The statement seemed more reflex than felt.

"Is something the matter?" The anger had not vanished completely behind a policeman's sense of duty.

"Do you think they might forgive us?"

"Who?" Curious and a bit leery.

"The dead."

"Have you been drinking?" There was a sigh of understanding.

"Just a dram or two. Did you know my father?"

"Not well." Some conversation seemed unavoidable.

"He believed in charity. He was not big on forgiveness. Do you think maybe he's changed?"

"I don't believe in ghosts." His humouring would only go so far.

"Nobody does until they see one."

"You saw a ghost?" Of course he hadn't. He didn't sound as if he could see much of anything.

"Heard."

"You heard a ghost?" Likely someone banging on the ceiling saying you'd had enough.

"I heard a certain young woman turned up dead." Now there was some logic, very serious indeed.

"And you're afraid she won't rest easy."

"I'm worried about suspicion."

"And perhaps my chief inspector was right all along." This was not meant to be said out loud. That did not prevent the receiver from catching it and sending it along.

"Now you see why I called."

"All right, Maynard, I'll hear you out. Not tonight, tomorrow at my office…with the chief inspector."

"Shall we say ten?"

"Fine."

"Martin?"

"Yes."

"You're wrong you know." He genuinely hoped so.

"To be suspicious?"

"Not to believe in ghosts."

"Stop drinking, Maynard, and go to bed."

Friday

He had lumbered home Thursday night from the Aberdeen Hotel under a great tiredness. His body seemed to have doubled in weight and lost all hope. The moment he had seen Victor's one-eyed monster face floating just under the water, he was genuinely sad. Sad for Victor, his family, and the city. He had had another thought and at the time it didn't seem ghoulish or self-serving. It was already up to him to bring the family justice. If doing so took him finally from chief inspector to chief of police, that was a separate justice. Sparing the rod was spoiling the city and some of its better men. Where others bent he would be firm and all would be better off. That night under the wharf he had seen it all so clearly.

Now all he could see was disaster. Wallace had killed Victor. He was sure of that. Unfortunately the best witness was dead. There was no physical evidence, save a cut maybe, and that would heal. There were some letters and records that suggested motive, nothing more. Even if McNeally could be found and made to testify, the bank was a separate matter. A thief was not necessarily a murderer, though Baxter knew this one was. His proof that Wallace was at least there that night was backed up by a pair of trollops who would impugn themselves. Wallace would not need a lawyer for that. And Clarke was refusing to say any more and even if he did, would he be any more credible to a jury? Meanwhile, Seabrook and the rest were not in any hurry to incriminate themselves.

There had been other cases he could not solve. The difference was that in those cases there had been no witnesses, no evidence, no way to know what had happened. This time the guilty party was right in front of him. Yet it was the city's chief inspector who was in bad odour, so much so he was practically in hiding, home in the middle of the day, moving down not up. So much for ambition, which had not only been thwarted, it had been forced to suffer scrutiny from the likes of Charles Clarke. Not satisfied with insult, the man had thrown wild accusations. Baxter worked with tools sometimes when he was tired and distracted. Clarke knew a few lines from the Bible, he had no sense of faith. He had not been tested.

Neither had Grace. For that he may have had himself to blame. Had they spoiled her? Her lack of faith was now added to his test. Now when he needed her most, Jane was at a distance. He was not sure if either of them were home when he dragged in, only that he was not greeted at the door. He hung his hat and greatcoat and sat on the stairs to deal with his shoes and the buttons of his tunic and shirt. At times he thought he heard footsteps or sounds not being made, that mice were listening closely in case they should want to flee. He looked toward the kitchen and tasted the sawdust steak from the Aberdeen. A bath would be more work than he could manage.

He should not have been surprised that he slept straight through. Still, the morning light confused him. Had Jane held him in the night or held the ticking on her side of the mattress? He could sense the remnants of dreams, no details, just a vague feeling of loss. There was breakfast with a note, Jane was at the market. If she did not return before he left, he could expect dinner at the usual time. She had not deserted him entirely. Grace on the other hand was either hiding in her room or gone out. For her, he remained beyond the pale. They would all be together for the evening meal, which he expected to be as sombre as yesterday's service. If there was a eulogy this time it would be for the future not the past. He left for work not feeling good, despite being rested for the first time in a week.

He found Squire in his office, dozing. He stirred as Baxter entered. A good night's sleep had not yet come his way. Baxter had already imagined the worst. He had to ask anyway. "How did they take it?"

Squire pulled himself more upright as he spoke. His voice was thick. "How would you take it?"

There was no point in going any further on that topic. He tried another tack. "You came straight back."

Squire rubbed at this face and stood to stretch. "I'd had enough of seeing people at their worst."

Baxter thought of saying more. He didn't. He fiddled with things at his desk. "No one needs a policeman or a doctor or a priest when they're at their best."

"Maybe I should be a cook, food makes people happy."

Baxter waved him off. "There will always be plenty of cooks." At the same time he thought of the quiet house he had come home to yesterday. The wife he had missed so much time with over the years. The daughter he had hoped so much for who was becoming someone he didn't know.

Squire had gone from rubbing his face to a routine of calisthenics. Baxter thought back to Wednesday night in the hansom cab. He would stick to his long underwear. "The funeral was hard on the family?" Squire asked between jumping jacks.

"The church only came to half full. People are preoccupied with South Africa I suppose. The granite monument is impressive."

"And the family?" Squire had moved on to knee bends.

"We'll have to wait and see, maybe years." The question brought Thomas Berrigan to mind and what losing his father had done to him. Had he made it to his brother-in-law's funeral? Baxter tried to recall his face from the crowd.

"What about the mayor?"

Unlike Thomas, that face was all too vivid in his mind. "He was there, we looked past one another."

"Wallace?" Squire was finished waking up. Baxter noticed the young man's breathing had remained even, his undershirt bone dry. He had put his uniform shirt back on and was now tucking it in. There was no need to undo the belt and pants that were loose about the thin waist. Baxter reminded himself of the value of experience.

"We also had a look at one another."

"Has he had anything more to say?"

As Squire finished putting himself back together Baxter told him about Wallace's late-night call and the one he had received from Tolliver just as he was leaving home.

"So you think he is going to confess?"

"Or point the finger at someone else."

"Clarke."

"You think Wallace and the chief are in cahoots, this meeting is all for show?" Baxter took a second survey of the young policeman sitting across his desk where he had been so often this past week. He was still new. He was no longer innocent of politics and power and Baxter wished he could take him to the meeting.

"It's something we have to consider."

———•———

When the time came for him to leave, Baxter left Squire with instructions to wait in his office or find something to do around the station. He must not, however, leave. He was not sure what was about to happen. Regardless, he thought Squire deserved first-hand news. He did not say so, though the look on his face likely did. In case things came out badly for him or the case or both, Squire's presence would be some comfort.

He knocked. Chief Tolliver came to the door. "Come in, Chief Inspector."

"You haven't started without me I hope." He was not looking for a fight, just a casual entrance. He didn't find it.

"Mistrustful as always. Tell me, Mr. Baxter, do you think your wife may be poisoning you slowly?" Wallace looked the worse for wear. There would be no lacquer-smooth social graces on display this morning.

His daughter maybe, Baxter thought, but not his wife. "I think yours would have more call than mine," he replied.

"If you two are done exchanging pleasantries, perhaps we could get to the point?" Tolliver seemed well aware he sounded like a grade two teacher, and by that knowledge, annoyed all the more.

Wallace cleared his throat and took on the airs of a magistrate, looking at Tolliver and Baxter as if it were they who were being called to answer and not him. "As you can see, I am here without the benefit of council. It's my preference to resolve this with a gentlemen's agreement."

"You are asking us to trust you." Baxter pulled his eyebrows down but not too quickly.

"I killed a man, Mr. Baxter, and I will answer to God for that, not you."

"Just tell us what happened." Tolliver threw Baxter a look that said he was tired of playing schoolmarm.

Wallace settled himself. "I liked Victor. We were true friends, no class between us. Ten years ago a seat opened up at our regular card game. Sam Lovett nominated Victor, that's how we met. Back then we played at my house."

"And then you acquired a certain establishment." Baxter got a vision of Wallace before a grand fireplace with a pipe and a thick volume from Dickens, reminding himself of his higher culture before tramping through the muck of the upper streets.

Two plush wing chairs sat near the window, angled towards each other and the end of the room. Wallace was reclined in one. The chief had gotten equally comfortable behind his enormous oak partner's desk. Wallace had been looking toward the chief as he spoke. He now turned languidly to Baxter who had remained standing. "You don't gamble, do you, Mr. Baxter."

Of course I don't, nor should I, he thought. Still, he felt a twinge of defensiveness. "I live within my means."

Wallace made a face as if his food were bad. "How dull. Of course as a policeman you know people seldom have a single vice. A win must be celebrated and losses consoled. Moving our game to Charlie's made things more practical and exciting at the same time."

Tolliver saved the look this time. Through a resigned release of breath he asked, "So what went wrong?"

"For a long time, years in fact, nothing at all. Then Victor had some bad luck. Some law of averages I suppose. Instead of paying up and staying away for a while, he tried to win his way out of trouble."

"You didn't have to invite him back," Baxter pointed out in the dead man's defense.

Wallace sidestepped neatly, perhaps he was feeling a little better. "Victor got where he was in life because he was hard to refuse."

"But he refused to pay."

"No. He owed all of us. And he was paying a little at a time through his business. Unfortunately he kept losing." Wallace shifted in his chair, then cleared his throat. "I consolidated his debt."

Baxter had taken his arms from behind his back and crossed them on his chest. He leaned forward now from the waist and said, "What you mean to say is you bought his markers."

"Correct."

"Why?" Tolliver wanted to know.

"Some of the players were tired of carrying Victor. Mostly I wanted the leverage."

"To do with the tramway."

"Yes and the Electric Light and Power Company, a merger and then expansion. It would be good for the city." Tolliver said nothing, but remained eye to eye with Wallace as he spoke. There was a sudden whiff of politics in the air. Baxter got an image of a dog kicking dirt over its mess. He should have insisted on having Squire as a witness. He needed someone on his side.

"And good for you, too," Baxter pointed out, though he had not managed to raise the proper amount of cynicism in his voice to make Wallace seem as rotten as he was.

"There are a number of investors," Wallace replied blithely. Baxter gritted his teeth and for a second wished for Mackay, then quickly rebuked himself. He would restrict himself to questioning the witness.

"What did you need from Victor?"

"Council needed to approve the deal, and commit some public funds. Victor could sway the vote."

"But he was opposed." Tell us the truth, you killed Victor over politics and money, he wanted to say. He was tired of letting Wallace set the pace.

"He saw the future need. He wanted the investors to carry more of the initial short-term costs. Victor was overly cautious with the public purse. If he had only been as tight-fisted with his own money…"

No you don't, Baxter thought, then said in an accusing voice, more effective this time, "So you were blackmailing him."

"I was making a bet."

Baxter came closer now, shaking his head, refusing to let Wallace whitewash the scene. "You were threatening him and it was working, until Victor dug up a little dirt of his own."

"How do you mean, Inspector?"

Baxter turned to the chief hoping to see some supportive scepticism in his face. All he got was a stare as beige and vacant and infuriating as the Sphinx. He went back at Wallace. "Victor learned you and Frank McNeally were chums at school. That sent him looking into your business dealings around the time McNeally robbed that bank in Maine. He found proof you were involved, isn't that what happened?"

"That is interesting news."

"You didn't know?" asked Tolliver. Was there honest disbelief in the chief's question? Baxter wondered. Or was he siding with Wallace, pointing him toward an appearance of some innocence and away from greater suspicion?

"No, I should have guessed, I suppose. Victor was in high spirits that night. His confidence had returned," Wallace answered looking at himself in the window. Was he checking to see if his face had remained straight? Baxter couldn't tell. From where he stood there was no reflection. Outside the sky was low. Horses pulled hacks and slovens up and down Barrington Street as they did every other day, the people of the city as reconciled to the harness as the beasts that carried them. Would the truth of this case, if it ever came out, matter to them? Those who had just gone off to fight, was it because they cared or because they didn't? A rich degenerate, a fallen politician, and the life of another young girl lost. It would have been nothing new to the plebeians of Rome. Fifteen centuries later, a job, a roof, and enough good health to hold on to them mattered more than high ideals of justice, or so it seemed in the dull and weathered faces beyond this particular pane of spotted glass. Too much rest was allowing Baxter's mind to wander.

"Victor started winning." Baxter wished he'd phrased it as a question. He waited expectantly, but neither the chief nor Wallace asked how he might know. Maybe they were keeping it quiet to protect secrets of their own.

"That night the rest of us were as bad as he was good. In a couple of hours Victor had won back much of what he owed."

"Then he sat out."

"A little celebration."

"That becomes a nightmare." Baxter reminded himself of how angry Clarke had been leaving the Aberdeen. Of course he and Wallace had had it out. And now, Baxter thought, Wallace is going to hang Clarke before Clarke can point a finger at him. Was the chief in on a play to neatly close the case? Baxter looked at the floor half expecting it to turn to quicksand.

Wallace had retreated into his own thoughts or maybe he had been trying to read Baxter's. Now he was talking again. "The game went on for a while, but without Victor there wasn't much interest. Seabrook had been the biggest loser. He was just getting up to go talk to one of the girls when someone ran down the hall. I thought it was a raid. I think we all did. I don't remember anyone saying anything. We just kept still. After a bit, I pulled the sliding door just a crack. There were no voices, only grunts and thuds. I couldn't see what was going on. I didn't want to. All I wanted to do at that point was run for the front door."

"But you didn't." Baxter tried to sound encouraging without seeming sympathetic. Wallace seemed to finally be near the moment of truth. The chief looked stunned or disinterested. It was always hard to gauge his capacity, a castle built from guile and leavings.

"No…"

"What did you do?"

"I remember sliding the door shut, then watching from the end of the hallway.

Wallace stalled. Baxter gave him a nudge. "And?"

"And they were on the floor of the landing, in front of the back stairs. Victor had gone up with Sarah. He hadn't bothered to get redressed. He was stark naked. Victor never tanned. He was as huge and white as a polar bear. Charlie isn't small, but pinned under Victor he looked like a little brown harbour seal.

"Who had the knife?" Baxter had never been sure that Charlie had told the truth. He claimed Victor had sent Sarah to fetch him a drink, supposedly to help him take the news of her condition. She had put on a nightdress and gone downstairs. She was in the landing on her way back up when she saw Victor on the stairs. No clothes, just a steak knife from an un-cleared plate and a face she didn't know, a face that told her to call for help. She had managed to whistle before she froze. And if he was to be believed, Charlie had come running with his bait.

"Neither of them," Wallace said, his voice thin as if coming from far away. "They were wrestling, trying to prevent each other from getting a bat that lay on the floor a few feet away against the bottom stair. All of the sudden Victor let go and stood up. He rolled away then slowly got to his feet. I was relieved. I really thought he had come to his senses, that whatever was going on was some sort of misunderstanding that could be explained. So did Charlie."

"Where was Miss Riley?"

"She was crouched in the corner by the back door, knees under her chin, toes curled up. A tumbler with two fingers of whiskey sat on the floor beside her. Neither of them could move." The memory of Sarah's paralysis put Wallace in a trance of his own. This time it was the chief who gave him a push.

"And Victor?"

Wallace twitched and took a sharp breath. "Victor had his back to me. He was struggling for air. He smelled like a wet animal. You know what else I remember?"

Wallace was looking straight at him. He had a queer look on his face as if he had a bad stomach. "What?" Baxter asked, unsure what to expect.

"Victor's feet. I'd never seen him in bare feet. His toenails were a rotten yellow and he had huge bunions. They were the ugliest feet I've ever seen. Her feet were shapely and light. How does that happen?" Wallace turned from Baxter to the chief, as if he had asked an ordinary question to which there was a simple answer.

"What brings people together you mean?" the chief asked. You sit mute and half asleep and then this is what you ask? Baxter thought to himself.

"Yes."

"They met in a brothel, not at a coming-out party," Baxter snapped. "This was not some fairy-tale romance. He was a married man with a family. She had her virtue up for sale."

"She wasn't the villain," Wallace said calmly, the look on his face now more composed.

The chief gave Baxter a look of incredulity. Then, looking at Wallace with a face of apology, even a little sympathy, he asked, "So Victor got up?"

"Yes. It was a trap, though. He hadn't given up. Charlie was still down on one knee, he took his eyes off Victor just for a second. Victor lunged forward. I knew the force of his personality. I never realized how strong he was. His fist struck Charlie on the jaw just below his ear. There was this sound like an egg hitting the floor. I thought Charlie was dead. Victor picked up the bat."

"So this was self-defence." The chief spoke before he could and Baxter felt cheated and a little nauseous. There it was, they were in this together. And even Clarke would be spared. Victor would be made the devil. He thought of Catherine trying to keep her children from the news. He felt his stomach lurch.

"No."

The answer took Baxter into a state of mild shock, unable to respond. The chief stepped into the silence, uncertainly it seemed. "Do you think he could see you through his rage?" he asked.

"That's what I thought too, at first, rage. I couldn't imagine what, but I assumed someone must have said something or done something and Victor had lost his temper. But Victor was beyond anger. He actually looked calm, almost serene. That's what made him so terrifying. And to answer your question, Chief Tolliver, no, I don't think Victor could see me from where he was, mentally I mean. I don't think he had any sense I was there until I yelled, and by then it was too late."

Wallace had started by saying he had killed a man. Now he had just claimed it was not self-defence. There didn't seem to be a plot to get Wallace off the hook. Baxter struggled to regain himself and think. Charlie was unconscious when it happened. Sarah was dead. Regardless of what Victor did or didn't do, for which they only had Wallace's word, he still believed the real motive was somehow money and politics. Would Wallace ever tell the truth? Likely not, Baxter guessed, but he may have to. "You found the knife?" Baxter asked, imagining a jury.

"As you can see." Wallace eased the glove off of his right hand. The bandage was fresh, a spot of blood in the centre. The cut was deep and slow in healing. "Charlie had knocked the knife out of Victor's hand. It was at my feet, I hadn't seen it."

"Victor didn't try to get it back?" Baxter asked, expecting that Victor must have and that from there the end had come.

"No, Mr. Baxter. Remember, Victor had picked up the bat after knocking Charlie out. Victor went for Miss Riley, not the knife. The outside light was on, shining through the backdoor window. I remember thinking how clearly I could see her, see her face. I saw a tear roll down her cheek. It was the only part of her that moved."

"That's when you yelled?" Baxter asked, thinking back to what Annie Higgenbottom remembered hearing.

"More like a high-pitched scream. If anyone has told you they heard Sarah scream, they are wrong. She never made a sound. They heard me. Lucky really. I'm not sure Victor would have reacted to the normal sound of my voice."

"What did he do?" the chief asked. He and Baxter exchanged a glance, both men together for once, bracing themselves for the answer.

Wallace began slowly rubbing his hands along the arms of his chair. "Victor raised the bat over his head. He was going to open Miss Riley's skull like a piñata. Then he turned toward the sound. I know this is going to sound silly but at that moment I felt like a child lost in the forest, one that's been found by the big bad wolf not some friendly woodsman." Now Wallace's hands were still, no longer able to find any manner of control or comfort in the motion.

"You mean Victor turned on you with the bat?" the chief asked, his confusion obvious. Baxter wondered if Wallace was going to claim self-defence after all.

"No…not exactly. When Victor turned toward me I could see…he was very aroused. It was his erection that was pointed at me, not the bat…and those feet." Wallace shook as if taken by a fever chill. "As I told you, his face was placid. I knew he wasn't himself. But it was only at that moment I knew Victor had truly lost his mind. Who else but a crazy man could knock another man unconscious, then casually pick up a bat and prepare to use it on a woman too petrified to move, a woman I know he cared for? Who else but a crazy man does all that wearing nothing but the expression of a dull child and in the process gets a raging erection? I should have fled instead of just stepping back." Wallace paused again, looking from Baxter to the chief and back again. Baxter wasn't sure what Wallace expected him to say. Neither did the chief, it seemed. Both men held off from saying anything, merely waited for Wallace to continue. "That's when I noticed the knife, I'd stepped on the handle. Lucky again…I suppose."

"Victor didn't notice the knife?" Baxter wanted to ask what kind of knife it was or if Wallace knew where it had come from. He let it go. Clarke was right. It didn't matter.

"I thought he did. His eyes went down. But he wasn't looking at the knife. Perhaps the look was a warning. Then he turned back to Miss Riley."

"You picked up the knife."

"I can't say I remember doing it. I remember feeling some pain and the sight of blood, first mine and then Victor's. Apparently I had the knife by the blade as much as the handle. It must not have gone in very far. Victor didn't seem to notice. He had gotten to Sarah, pulled her up and pinned her against the wall with a hand on her throat. He was about to swing the bat when I pushed with the palm of my hand as hard as I could. The knife went into the handle."

Baxter wasn't pinned. He was leaning against the wall, the hours of sleep suddenly unable to hold him steady. As much as he did not want to look at it, the picture had been slowly emerging over the past few days. For months, perhaps years, there had been two Victors, not one. The man Victor was supposed to be, the man Baxter knew, and someone Baxter had no desire to meet. In the end it seemed these two men had to confront one another, reconcile themselves and their deeds face to face. Now Baxter was forced to face them and their struggle and to come to a reconciliation of his own. Had a better man lost or had he only existed in disguise? The person most able to say had reconciled herself to eternity. Had she done so in self-pity or from some notion of a greater good? That question would go unanswered, another ghost of a city all too familiar with misery and sacrifice. Meanwhile, if what Baxter had just heard were true, in the worst of moments, only Wallace had somehow managed to keep his head. Exact truth or not, better he had kept his head sooner rather than later so far as Baxter was concerned. When he was finally able to speak, it was his memory of Victor as the better man and his lament for the best parts of the city that came out of Baxter's mouth. "And then you threw the man you had jus stabbed in the harbour and let him die trying to breathe water in the dark alone."

Wallace flinched as if Baxter had struck him. "I was bloody terrified. You know what he said to me? 'Good to see you, Maynard.' As if we were meeting at the Aberdeen for lunch. Then he pulled out the knife and collapsed."

Baxter still could not let go. "And you don't suppose Victor was terrified? He needed help," he protested. "He wasn't dead."

Wallace's face had gone purple red. "Weren't you listening!" he screamed. "Or are you one of those deaf saints?"

"Say what you mean, Mr. Wallace, deaf Catholic, and no, I'll be the one escorting you to jail." He wanted to say more, holler "Bigot!" and remind Wallace that England and its church had once been Catholic. That he and his high Anglican superiority were mere contrivances that would do him little good in prison. He would have had the chief not cut him off.

"Tell us what happened next," the chief broke in. He looked sorry for both of them and for himself.

"Mr. Baxter seems to know this part already. It was chaos really, everyone screaming and crying. Charlie came around. Someone got down to the Aberdeen and came back with Robert White and my driver. They took care of Sarah. Charlie and I took care of Victor."

"You dumped him in the harbour."

"Are we going to pick scabs or…"

"Send you home with our apologies, sorry to have bothered you?"

This time the chief came from behind his desk and stood between them. "Wallace, you came in looking for a gentlemen's agreement, what did you have in mind?"

———•———

quire was able to keep still for the first half hour. He was not able go back to sleep. The calisthenics prevented that. He had to find something to do. The station was quiet. The office girls filed and gossiped in low voices. He wandered over to the front counter. The door to the chief's office was still closed. "Officer Squire, long time no see. When you coming back to regular patrol? I've been short bodies all week." Sergeant Meagher had a stack of papers in front of him and looked overwhelmed.

"Soon, maybe tomorrow. You back on your feet?" Squire asked, keeping an extra step away in any case.

"Mostly," Meagher sniffed. "It true Maynard Wallace is in with Baxter and the chief?"

"No secrets in a police station." Squire quickly steered to a different topic. "Any more on who's pilfering a wardrobe from the south end?"

Meagher shook his head while trying to sound confident. "Sooner or later his buddies will turn stag and our work will be done. Meanwhile, it's been the usual nonsense."

"You see Mackay?" The man was frightening company, but he would likely want to hear about his visit with Sarah's parents. He needed to tell someone. Much as he was gaining respect for the chief inspector, this would be easier with Mackay.

Meagher made a face and waved in the direction of the upper streets. "He's on patrol. Finally got that Green woman off my hands, God bless him. No sooner I get rid of her, though, and Tommy Berrigan gets dragged in, drunk as a lord."

"I'm yet to have the pleasure," Squire replied, bored already with Meagher and wanting to get away before some inane task came his way.

"You will. Least this time he had some excuse. Victor Mosher was his brother-in-law. Doesn't look such a mess in a suit." Meagher was staring off, a form of some sort in one hand. He was either pondering its meaning or studying an image of Thomas he had conjured up. His trance was broken by the telephone at his elbow.

Squire had a thought. "Was Mr. Berrigan wearing a hat?" he asked.

"A what…?" Meagher picked up the earpiece. "Police station, Sergeant Meagher speaking…Ma'am…Ma'am…"

Squire tried again. "A hat, Thomas Berrigan was wearing a new hat, wasn't he?"

Meagher held the earpiece away from his head. The voice on the other end continued on without him. He looked at Squire from beneath a furrowed brow as he felt the papers spread about the counter. "Yeah…Ah, I don't know…Was he wearing a hat?" Meagher found his pencil and took the notepad Squire handed him with a nod and tried to catch up with the telephone. "How would I know whose pig it is in your backyard, ma'am?" Squire left for the stairway to the basement, glad to escape Meagher.

Thomas Berrigan was asleep in the cell Martha had just left. If either of them were half of what they were made out to be, a cell was the best accommodation they knew. A greatcoat and suit jacket were draped neatly over the end of the bed. Thomas lay on his back, fingers laced across his vest, snoring gently. Meagher was right. Even half out of it, Thomas didn't look such a mess in a suit. On the other hand, the smell gave him away. What was left of the spicy aftershave could not compete with the sour whiskey breath. "Mr. Berrigan?"

"Mr. Berrigan?" Squire kicked the end of the bed.

Thomas's eyes remained closed. His mouth opened to let out an irritated reply. "What?"

"Mr. Berrigan, can we talk for a moment?" Squire had entered the cell and pulled a chair up at the end of the bed. He was admiring the coat and jacket.

Thomas opened one eye and took stock of his guest. "Name's Tommy. You got a fag?"

"No," Squire answered, leaning back in the chair.

Thomas closed the eye back up and adjusted his pillow. "Then how 'bout you let me sleep?"

Squire kicked the bed again. Thomas groaned, perhaps with vague memories of childhood and being called for Mass or school, or more rude awakenings in the alleys of the city.

"Nice clothes. You want to hang them up…least the jacket?"

The other eye opened this time. "You a policeman or a valet?"

"Just curious." Squire looked into the eye. It was too bloodshot to be sure of colour, blue maybe.

"Oh I see. So you're a cat." The more he spoke the more it became clear Thomas would need a few more hours sleep.

"You plan on stealing any more clothes?" Squire gestured toward the end of the bed and then toward what Thomas had on.

Thomas had both eyes open now and had managed to get to his elbows. "I ain't stole nothin', these are mine."

"Where you working, Tommy?" Snide comments in these circumstances came easily from Baxter and Mackay. Maybe if he knew Thomas better it would seem less awkward. He hoped not.

"Get me a fag, maybe I'll tell ya.'

"Tell me the truth, you can be on your way."

Thomas rubbed his face and looked hard at Squire. He was sitting up now, swaying a little. No doubt he had a catalogue of convenient truths. On the other hand telling what really happened could sometimes work. He drained the glass of water someone had left on the table by the bed. He opened his mouth then reconsidered at least twice before he finally spoke. "I just wanted to look good…for Victor. Catherine…she and I… So I took some things, and stashed them."

Squire accepted the statement with no reaction other than to add some detail. "Except the hat."

"Yeah, except the hat. I started with that. Thought I could get away with wearing it around a few days at least."

"Where did it come from?" Squire asked not because he thought it was important.

Thomas seemed to need to say a little more to get his conscience completely clear.

"A man passed me on Barrington Street. I thought to myself, I would look good in that hat, so I followed him. He didn't lock his front door. I opened it a crack. The hat was on a hook less than an arm away." It was tucked out of sight under the bed. Thomas nearly fell over reaching for it. He handed it to Squire, his confession now complete.

Squire rolled the fedora round in his hands. He had solved his first case. If things went badly in the chief's office, a small victory might ease the bitterness. It was made of fine felt, dark brown with an elegant black leather band. Meagher had likely heard from the owner. The band seemed to have something tucked beneath it, perhaps a forgotten smoke.

As Thomas eased himself back down onto the bed Squire unfolded a note. It was on good paper and the handwriting rather stylish.

Squire was now up from the chair, bent over the bed, shaking Thomas by the shoulder and holding the hat under his nose. "Do you remember where the house was?"

Thomas blinked and turned tortoise, withdrawing into the pillow. "A nice place, on Inglis Street," he spluttered.

Squire let him go. "Do I have your word you are done with this?"

Thomas's eyes had fallen shut again. "I got no more reason to be worrin' 'bout how I look."

Squire straightened and moved to the door. "Come on, Thomas, I'll walk you out."

Once again a single eye opened, this time looking for something. "Maybe you should wait a day or two, make sure nothin' else goes missin'."

"Maybe you're right. I'll let Sergeant Meagher know, and I'll see if I can rustle up a few fags."

———•———

"Do either of you remember much about the history of the city's schools?" Wallace was on his feet, moving around, gearing himself up.

"I know we used to have public hangings." To him, Wallace was beginning to wriggle and Baxter was determined to keep him on the hook.

Wallace stopped and looked straight at Baxter for a moment. "Bear with me, Mr. Baxter, in this story the Catholics triumphed." He moved over, his back to the window. Outside, clouds drifted away from the sun. As the backlight hid his face in shadow, Wallace continued. "Just about the time all of us were ready to start school, there were no public schools like we have now. The only schools we had were run privately, by one or the other of the local churches, mostly. Nobody wanted to pay. Finally a school tax was voted in. The city needed a public system. Of course they needed schoolhouses. They could build. If they did it would take a great deal of time and money."

"What does any of this matter?

"Be patient." Baxter was glad Wallace's face remained hidden. He could hear the scheming and the condescension. He didn't have to see it too. "Connolly, the Catholic Archbishop at the time, stepped into the breach. The Church would lease its buildings to the city as public schools if the city would allow some time for Catholic instruction. Council agreed. The city got a public school system, thanks to the Catholic Church." Wallace nodded in Baxter's direction. His face emerged from the darkness wearing a thin unfriendly smile.

Baxter smiled just as warmly, then replied, "Of course in no time more schools were built so innocent Protestant schoolchildren would not be exposed to popish godforsaken Catholics."

"Precisely." Wallace was moving about again, his face in full view. Baxter could see the expression matched the tone of voice, affirming and unapologetic. Baxter tried not to feel a twinge of hot shame. Wallace seemed not to notice, closely following his own thoughts as he went on. "And this is why it matters here. The schoolboard's finances are in a shambles, no one wants more taxes. Ratepayers are in arears as it is. Council is short and slow in turning over funds to the board. Sinking funds to pay off leases and building loans are…" He waved his hand and came to a stop in front of Tolliver. "The point here is that the board needs help…I could move away from the tramway proposal and…"

This time Baxter cut him off. "So the city gets a new school if you stay out of the public eye, and jail, is that it?"

Wallace's voice dropped a bit as he looked at Baxter out of the corner of his eye. "Not quite…"

Baxter was far from finished. The twinge he was feeling now was rage, which he made no attempt to hide. "I can see it now. Red brick and white pillars and green lawns. Somewhere south of Quinpool Road of course. You wouldn't want to encourage the north end public. The Wallace School, where students learn debauchery, deceit, and dirty dealing, the three D's with the three R's. Martin, please tell me you are not considering any of this."

Tolliver, who had been leaning on the edge of his desk arms crossed, took a step toward his chief inspector. He kept his arms in place. His made a polite request with a firm command. "Cully, will you let him finish."

"I have no interest in seeing my name anywhere, that's entirely the point." Wallace managed to sound more pleading than snide.

"You can't just give money to the city without notice, stories in the paper." Baxter tried to focus on the logic, not the man.

"I'm sure I can. Anonymously through lawyers to the managers of the building fund. There will be stories of City Council's prudent management and the results. The mayor and his aldermen will be too busy taking credit to bother about particulars." Baxter could not dispute Wallace's grasp of city politics. He would have to find another point of attack.

"Even if you could do all that, we are not the only ones who know. Others will talk eventually and when they do, the papers will get hold of it and you'll be done." Wallace knew the willful blindness of power. Baxter knew better the momentum of talk in the streets.

"The only ones who can say anything convincingly are Mr. Clarke, Miss Higgenbottom, and Miss Green."

The look on his face told Baxter he had not taken Wallace by surprise or given him any pause. "You have already bought their silence."

Wallace cleared his throat. He glanced at Tolliver then moved back toward the window. The sun had gone behind a cloud. Wallace's face was plain and hard at work. "Try seeing it this way. The place you describe as the most notorious of its kind in the city and its keeper will cease to operate. Two young women will no longer be doing something you deplore. And three more taxpayers will be added to the rolls."

"What I deplore is money replacing justice."

"No real justice comes out of this unless the damage is repaired...or minimized at least."

You only look respectable, Baxter thought. Your fancy words only sound true. "No amount of money brings Victor back. You do wrong, you get punished, people want that, they need to see it happen."

"Or what? Chaos?" Tolliver had gone back to his desk. He seemed to be expecting Baxter to reply. Instead he looked back at Wallace, invited him to continue. "People look out to see what might happen to them. Would they rather see a man in jail for saving lives, or good schools and fewer people before the courts?"

Baxter remained calm and sure of himself and unswayed. "They don't want to see families of murdered men trying to survive."

Wallace moved forward a step. Then one more. The chief stopped leaning back on his desk. "Victor had no legal debts of any consequence. Catherine will be able to hold on to the business until the sons can take it over. On top of that, Victor had some insurance, which I can add to."

Instead of coming toward Wallace, Baxter moved away toward the door. "You'll just stop by with a bag of money. No one would question that."

The chief spoke quietly, yet his voice sailed across the office to his chief inspector like a heaving line. "If money can be added quietly to the public coffers, I'm sure..."

"The chief is quite correct. Catherine will simply get more than she expected. The company will be very sorry for any incorrect information she may have received. Then remind her that her husband knew the value of insurance, et cetera, et cetera."

Baxter came back. He spoke square and hard against the charm of Wallace and his words. "Minions will do the dirty work. The money is not important. You'll forget." Then, looking at the chief with no less challenge, Baxter added, "And you tell yourself the good outweighed the bad. The public never finds out. And life goes on. Convenient, how very convenient."

Wallace returned to his chair. He crossed his legs slowly then straightened himself against the back of the chair and looked Baxter in the eye. "I can't make up my mind if you're more conceited or selfish or paranoid. You act as if there is a plot against you. Only in your dreams are you that important. Try thinking about the real victims. And as for forgetting, you needn't worry. I'll never stop seeing what happened. I may not even be able to forget you." He looked away when he finished, and then after a moment back at the chief inspector.

Tolliver began moving about in front of his desk, hands in his pants pockets, fiddling with change. "Most likely you're both only half right. Let's suppose there is no trial, no scandal or subsequent events. Time goes by, years. And then one day we realize that somehow everybody knows. It's all come undone and floated to the surface. Then what?"

Baxter couldn't tell if Wallace's pause was real consideration, or more theatrics. "In that case people would have heard something they wanted to believe. How did Oscar Wilde put it, if a rich man makes an ass of himself he is poaching on the preserves of the masses? Something like that…In the end, there would be some indignation, nothing more."

"And if you're wrong?"

"Then to anyone who should ask, I say, where is your proof?"

The chief moved his hands behind his back and watched the floor. Baxter stared out the window. Wallace gathered up his coat and stood with it draped over one arm. Finally Tolliver broke the spell. "Gentlemen, I don't think there is anything more to be said. Maynard, thank you for coming in."

Wallace nodded curtly. "Martin." He kept his eye on the door as he passed in front of Baxter. Just before he closed it he spoke with a voice that was either the dispassion of business or personal regret. "Chief Inspector."

———•——

Baxter and Tolliver watched from the window as Wallace's coach pulled slowly off the Grand Parade and headed south on Barrington Street, the oncoming traffic giving it a wide birth. Heads turned along the sidewalk to follow it for a moment before carrying on. Baxter kept his own eyes on the coach as he spoke. "You can't let it end like this."

Tolliver let out a long sigh. "Please don't try and tell me Victor deserves better, not after what we just heard."

The chief knew the basic principles of the law as well as he did. The lowest victim is still a victim and equal under the law. "Wallace confessed to a murder."

Tolliver loosened the collar of his shirt and began working on his cuffs. "He saved lives."

Baxter watched the chief begin to roll the first sleeve. He moved into the wing chair Wallace had not been sitting in. "If you believe him," he pointed out as he undid the top buttons of his tunic.

"I do, and so do you, Cully," the chief said flatly, looking up briefly from the second sleeve.

Baxter's eyes followed as his palms ran back and forth along the arms of his chair. "It's not up to us, Martin, it's for a judge and jury to decide."

The chief moved closer and rested a hand on the back of Wallace's chair. "You know as well as I do no court could convict him. A jury would see it from a utilitarian point of view, the lesser evil, or as a matter of self-defence. And they would be right."

"Wallace was in cahoots with Frank McNeally. He was blackmailing Victor. He…"

"No one said Maynard Wallace was a saint."

Baxter's hands stopped. He looked up to find Tolliver's eyes ready and waiting for him. "A trial would make that clear."

As Tolliver folded his arms across his chest, more of his shirttail came untucked. He widened his stance a little. "To ruin Wallace you would ruin Victor, do more harm to his wife and children, drag the entire city through the mud?"

Baxter looked at Tolliver's hard-set face, at the heavy forearms and the wrinkled shirttail.

A pair of work boots would have been more appropriate than the Oxfords he was wearing. His eyes came back up. "Instead of rolling up your sleeves to do what needs to be done, you think it's better we bury this in the dirt?"

Tolliver tucked his chin into his chest for a moment, then spoke to the floor, thoughtfully, as if the strips of hardwood were learned and keenly listening. "I think words like 'better' and 'justice' and 'right' and 'wrong' are written in grey not black or white."

Baxter did not think the response he was about to give was trite or hollow. He was as determined to hold firm as Tolliver was willing to bend. He stood as he spoke, redoing the buttons of his tunic. "They are written in the things we do."

"Nothing we do can bring back the dead." Tolliver was not pleading or negotiating with his chief inspector, he was stating cold fact.

"And when people find out we did nothing in this case, then what?" Baxter did not go so far as to point a finger or a chin. The look on his face was allegation and warning enough. He would not be taking the blame.

Tolliver was now leaning back against the front of his desk, heavy and moored for weather. Suddenly he came free and banged the desktop hard enough to shake a few things loose. "For the love of Christ, Cully, we *are* doing something. We are exercising the greatest power we have, discretion. Wallace puts his tramway deal on hold. The city gets some money for schools, which it desperately needs, and Victor's children will want for nothing."

"If Wallace keeps his word and if no one gets suspicious." Baxter's voice had become mealy sounding. If he had ever had it, he was slipping from the high ground, whether he realized it or not.

"I think Mr. Clarke will see to that, along with Annie and Martha. Even if they didn't, Wallace truly wants to make amends."

"It's dishonest." Now his chin was out.

Tolliver got a step closer to Baxter. His entire body had become a cannon, not just the barrel finger he pointed. "You want plain truth? All right, Cully, I'll give some plain truth. People don't come to this place anymore, they are born here. At one end of the province we've got what's left of the sad-eyed Acadians who keep praying over the few seeds they put in the ground every spring. Throwing them out of the place only made them want it more. And who's right beside them? Ancestors of the Loyalists who replaced them. And how are they doing with their grander visions and Protestant work ethic? Not all that much better. Mind you at least they tried. At the other end we've got the remnants of some starving Irish and chased-off Huguenots who are sure there is something wonderful and especially noble about an island full of sooty faces and ceilidhs. Of course there isn't. If there was, people wouldn't be running away en masse. We know these things. We don't say them. It hurts too much. And where is Halifax? It's in between, halfway. Everything here is halfway. Nothing here will ever go too far and that's what makes it worth staying, we don't go to extremes. People who want more leave. Some say that holds us back. I think it keeps us safe. And the ones that do stay, they have it tough enough. I'm sure your righteous indignation keeps you warm at night. I'm just as sure it's cold comfort for the rest of us. It is not our job to preach and woe betide us if we should try. You have never learned these things, Chief Inspector, and that's what's held you back.

It was never me or anyone else, only your crippling inability to forgive."

Baxter's chin eased back. He checked his tunic as if it might have holes from the shots just fired. He cleared his throat and spoke as evenly as he could. "I know that a firm hand has made things better here than they used to be." He would continue to take his direction from a higher authority. Real strength was expected to endure the weakness of men like Martin Tolliver.

Tolliver put his hands in his pockets but his voice was still hot and full of lead. "And change has been peaceful because our leaders have not been heavy-handed, they've coaxed people along. That's all I'm asking you to do here, be reasonable, do what's best for the city."

Baxter slammed the door on his way out.

———•———

He stood in the hallway outside the chief's office, every face in the station staring back at him. It would have been that way even if he had not slammed the door. Now that he had, the worst was expected. He felt called to answer for a decision that was not his. What exactly had just happened? He was not sure he knew. He looked across the main office, past the front counter where Meagher and two other officers were pretending to be busy, past desks where he was the only thing going on, to the doorway of his own office where Squire was standing. He turned and looked down the hall toward the front door that led into the Grand Parade and an entire city full of eyes. How did men like Wallace and Tolliver and Victor Mosher look with straight faces into those mirrors? If he went out there now which reflection would he see, his own or theirs? He moved toward his office, afraid to look at the image that was about to appear.

From the first step he became invisible. Suddenly there was the sound of typewriters and telephones, of the clock on the wall and the scraping of chairs and voices back and forth. And he moved with the tide.

Squire had let him pass without a word, then followed, closing the door behind him. Baxter sat at his desk and Squire waited. When Baxter was finally able to look, he was relieved to see nothing more horrible than curiosity in the young man's face. Squire broke the silence. "We all saw

Wallace leave a few minutes ago. You could have heard a pin drop in this place. Did he do it?"

Baxter worked slowly, removing his tunic and handing it to Squire. It got hung too quickly. Baxter motioned for Squire to sit, holding on a few moments longer as if it were Squire's comfort he was waiting on and not his own. When he finally spoke it felt like the lancing of a boil. "It appears that Victor was the victim of a robbery, most likely at the hands of a sailor who has now left the city. That's what the police investigation, our investigation, will show. Or something along those lines."

Squire's chair caught fire. He stood over the desk, his hands in the air. "That's completely untrue and you know it. Look what I found. We can use this on Wallace."

Baxter took the paper Squire handed him and read it. "Please find enclosed payment for your assistance in arranging council for Mr. McNeally. I will accept an additional invoice for your services in arranging a donation to the city's benevolent fund. Signed M.S. Wallace."

Baxter pushed a slow stream of air through his lips. If the first wave of settlers hadn't found a few friends among the Indians. If the French had done better against the British at Louisbourg or Quebec. If Victor had been luckier at cards. If this, if that, he thought. History was nothing more than random chance and timing. "Where did you get this?" he finally asked.

"Thomas Berrigan. Turns out he's the one been swiping clothes. That hat, it didn't come from his brother Patrick, it came from James Seabrook. That was tucked under the sweatband." Squire had picked up the hat that had been sitting on the chair beside him. He offered it like an hors d'oeuvre. Baxter waved it off.

"That's good police work, Mr. Squire. However, Mr. Wallace has confessed."

Squire pointed, his face red hot. "Then what's he doing walking out the front door?"

Baxter sat straight up in this chair, looked straight ahead, more in Squire's direction than at him. "Now that depends on who you ask."

"I asked you."

Now his gaze was more direct. "Here in the privacy of my office, I think he is walking out the front door having presided over his own trial, condemned himself to freedom, and has gone home to begin serving his sentence."

Squire shrugged his shoulders in obvious frustration. "Is that some kind of riddle?"

"Absolutely not." Baxter was as flat as Squire was up in the air. "Maynard Sinclair Wallace murdered Victor Mosher. He confessed to that very fact. Told us he stabbed Victor, showed us a cut on his hand he got in the process."

Still flabbergasted and now curious, Squire asked, "So was it over the tramway or the gambling or both?"

"Neither one. Wallace killed Victor to save Sarah Riley." Baxter could see his answers were not helping.

"To save her from Victor? How does that make any sense?"

"How do you think?" Baxter waited, knowing this wouldn't help either, unless moving Squire from anger and frustration to another point of sadness could be helpful.

"Was she…?"

"She told him that night. According to Clarke, Victor showed no reaction at first, sent Miss Riley to get him a drink, then came looking for her with a knife."

Baxter watched Squire's eyes narrow. He watched himself be judged and waited for the verdict. "You knew all this before you sent me to her family and you kept it from me."

"No, Mr. Squire, I kept it from them."

If the nod meant what he thought it did, Squire recognized the need for silence until now. "Wallace killed a man to save a woman who killed herself…she did kill herself?"

Baxter was glad not to have to deliver any worse news. "The medical examiner found no evidence to the contrary."

"It's not possible…"

"Wallace had anything to do with it? I don't think so. And I don't think Victor Mosher or Miss Riley would be dead or have even met each other if it were not for Maynard Sinclair Wallace." Baxter said what he felt, because he couldn't keep from saying anything else.

Squire's hands went into the air. "Then surely he goes to jail for something?"

Baxter looked toward the chief's office as a way of indicating that his sarcasm and disappointment was not directed at the young policeman in front of him. "If you are concerned with justice or public opinion, then yes."

"But?"

"If you are Chief Tolliver, you are likely whispering in the mayor's ear as we speak, words like compromise and reasonable and greater good."

"And what does that really mean?"

Baxter sank back in his chair. As much as he didn't want to, he knew he had to answer. And he knew each word of explanation would deepen his feelings of complicity and guilt. "It means that Wallace has already made some sort of deal with Clarke. It means that once the chief is finished with the mayor, there will be a short telephone call. Then sometime soon money that would have been invested in a tramway will find its way into city schools and a certain widow and her children will discover an estate much larger than expected."

Squire picked up the note Baxter had let fall on the desk. He waved it in desperate defiance of the greater facts. "What about this, with everything else we have?"

Baxter looked at Squire and saw himself in front of Tolliver. He wanted desperately to be on his side, to have something encouraging to say. "I'm afraid not, Mr. Squire. Our reports can wait. I'm taking the rest of the day. I recommend you do the same."

Squire looked at the note, at the hat, at Victor's attaché and ledger, at the newspaper clippings and reports and the other bits and pieces of the case still lying about the office, things it took a week without sleep to find, things that mattered until a moment ago. Then his face sagged. He dropped the note into the hat and tossed it on the desk. "Meagher would pitch a fit. He wants me back on patrol yesterday."

"You don't belong to him anymore, you belong to me, Detective Squire, and I'm telling you to take the rest of the day."

"I don't know what to say, Chief Inspector…I don't know if I…"

"It's not always like this. Go home, rest up over the weekend. Monday we start fresh."

———•———

The air was cool and very still. The grey sky, the flat steel sea, the colourless trees and dull boulders ran past both sides of his vision in a blur to a pinpoint on the horizon. Baxter stood staring at it from the beach at Point Pleasant under a tree. Behind him the noon gun fired its noise from the fortress on the hill. The reverberations passed through him and died and the scene before him remained unchanged.

He spoke his mind uninterrupted to Victor and Wallace and Martin Tolliver. He put all of them in their place. There are higher immutable truths. Every compromise is proof of that. He would not aspire to mediocrity. He spoke an apology to Mr. and Mrs. Riley and took some responsibility for what their daughter had become and for not being able to save her. Later he would write a letter. In the sorrow and the anger of his solitude he cursed Charles Clarke and Ellen Reardon. He took some solace in the fact that Detective Squire would now be dealing with the likes of them. Better him than Mackay. At least that much good had come of this.

An abrupt gust of wind came off the water. His shoulders hunched against it and his eyes teared up. As if driven by the wind, his thoughts came back upon him. Where was he within his faith? He was a regular at Mass. He was generous to the collection plate. He made time for charity events. Bigotry hurt him, particularly from High Anglicans like Wallace. The question remained. Was he really the good Catholic he claimed to be? He was beginning to tremble. He took a deep breath, trying to calm himself, and was instead struck by thoughts of death and an image of his body with the medical examiner. And then came thoughts of nothingness, of not being, of not knowing anything that ever was or was to come. He crouched down on the shoreline, huddling against a fear that was much colder than the wind.

Why thoughts of death, why now? Like any man his age he knew he had more past than future. He could look back with joy. He had earned the respect he carried. His wife had remained at his side and been all the things a good wife should. His child was grown, intelligent and kind. He had much to be thankful for. There was no more wind yet his chill grew worse, his trembling more violent. The damp salt air had gone inside his clothes, inside of him. There was no movement on the water or in the sky. Up and down the beach and in the trees behind there were no signs of life. He was alone.

He tried to look ahead, find some company and some comfort there. He saw Grace waving, waving in goodbye. He looked to Jane for help and found her on their daughter's side not his. They seemed doomed to grow apart. Where were Squire and the chief and his great reputation? They were there, just as he had left them. The harder he looked at them, the more he saw himself. And what did he see? He saw a man running out of time.

The cold and the trembling were now joined by a pain in his stomach. Not a sick feeling, more as if he had been kicked or maybe even stabbed. He tried to force his arms against his body to subdue the pain or stop the bleeding. They were too weak. He leaned more forward in his crouch and toppled over, the beach rocks driving into his knees. He lay there cold and trembling in a ball and he began to pray. He prayed for time to win his wife and daughter back. He prayed for time to find a way of bringing Wallace in. He prayed for time to teach Squire the things he needed him to know. And he prayed for his time to be the chief, for the city on the hill. He prayed, he prayed aloud, he prayed with his heart and with his life, he talked to God, he beseeched him. He prayed and listened and still he was alone.

He wept in his forsakenness. His pain and cold turned into a numbness of the body and the mind. He listened to his breathing, and for what seemed like a very long time he thought of nothing else. It was the incoming tide that eventually stirred him with a splash in the face. He watched a second small wave come in and crash and creep towards him. He made it to one knee then fell over, his legs still too stiff to straighten. He breathed and waited a moment for more blood to circulate then tried again.

He stumbled but managed to get off the rocks without falling again. By the time he had followed the pathway out of the park, his stride was almost normal. Children were getting out of school. The sounds of work drifted up from the harbourfront. The sun was poking through the clouds. Now and then a flash of golden light came off a window. Baxter moved along unnoticed.

Near Spring Garden Road a tram stopped just ahead of him, people got on and off. Two workmen waved and parted.

"See ya tomorrow, Jimmy."

"God willing."

Baxter stopped. A wave of realization and shame and clarity came over him. "God willing," Baxter repeated as the man moved past.

"God willing," the man said again, nodding at Baxter then looking up into the sunlight and walking on.

He walked slowly the rest of the way home, not because he was still cold and sore. He walked in sober thought. It was not God's will he had been following, it had been his own. Clarke, Wallace, and Tolliver seemed to have recognized his vanity, perhaps his wife and daughter had as well. Everyone except him. Pride had been his fall. It was not up to him to judge, to be the arbiter of sin. It was not God's will that Wallace escape trial. That was not it. It was that Baxter had lost sight of himself, lost sight of grace. That was what he had to accept. Better still if he could also learn to accept the city without giving it up.

———•———

The evening meal was more balm than salt. He let it be known the case was closed and said little more than that. Jane complained that the pickings had been slim at the shops and blamed it on the war. Grace shared the highlights of the Drummond lecture. Everyone trod lightly. He tried to help with the dishes, a gesture that was disallowed by a majority decision that his day had been the hardest.

He was sitting at the bench in his workshop, the pieces of the rocking chair exactly where he had left them on Sunday night. The tools were there as well, untouched. "I didn't want to say anything in front of Mother. Did you remember to pick something up for tomorrow?" Grace kept her voice low, but still glanced back over her shoulder as she spoke.

He covered his face with his hands then muttered between his fingers. "I promised myself…I must have thought of it a dozen times."

Grace pulled one hand away to show him what she had in hers. A sardonyx shell cameo of Flora, goddess of spring, trimmed in gold. "I found this in a shop on Granville Street. What do you think?"

"It's lovely."

"I'll wrap it up then and put your name on the card."

"Better it come from you."

"I'll write both our names."

"Promise me something."

"Father?"

He had put it between the folds of a towel and ironed it as smooth as he could. The envelope was new. As he passed the signed application to his daughter he asked, "Promise me that as soon as you graduate you won't be in a hurry to leave this place. We'll always be dying here. We need nurses more than doctors. But stay anyway, stay for as long as you can."

There was a release of excitement and tears and hugs that brought Jane from the kitchen. In the time that followed there were apologies and promises and plans and visions that were at the same time dependent and inevitable. Jane was the first to leave. While she prepared a bath, Grace and her father found paper and made a pretty present. Then Grace hugged him one last time and ran off to read.

Tired as he was, he did not want to go upstairs. Baxter reached for the pieces of the rocking chair. As he worked his mind drifted. Had the girl Elizabeth taken the room in Squire's boarding house? He had forgotten to ask. He would have to tell Meagher that his making due without Squire was permanent. Tolliver would not resist the promotion. The back of the chair was held together with a number of screws and dowels. He had put them in a small paper bag. Nevers was probably right, the gazebo would need painting in the spring. One of the screws was bent. He looked for a new one. Maybe the gazebo could wait. It would not be needed for anything special. None of the new screws were the right size. He would not wake up to find himself in the Garden of Eden this spring either. Acceptance would not come easy. He would have to straighten the bent screw. He held it firmly against the bench with his thumb and reached for the hammer.

He could hear Clarke laughing.

Acknowledgements

Writers work alone. They succeed with the help of many others. Sue Goyette and Shandi Mitchell encouraged me to write and led by example. Lynda Millar and James Collier read the first draft. Lynda's comments helped give me the confidence to finish what I'd started. James had a great feel for the story. He pushed me to work harder, and this book is better than it ever would have been without him. Shelley Hudson also read for me and patiently corrected my spelling. Patrick Murphy had faith enough to go to publication. He also connected me to Kate Kennedy, who did a fabulous job of editing.